'James is a compelling storyteller and he ratchets up the tension in increments, so that his readers will be suitably terrified. By the time you want to scream 'Look behind you!', it's already too late'
'Halloween Chillers', *Daily Mail*

'This novel from the brilliant Peter James had the hairs standing up on our arms from the first page'
Book of the Week, *Heat Magazine*

'Impeccable'
Sunday Times

'Superbly creepy modern horror story'
Book of the Week, *Sunday Mirror*

'James plays with your expectations – creating a convincing and genuinely terrifying tale that, in the best old-fashioned tradition, will frighten the wits out of you in a most enjoyable way'
Irish Sunday Mirror

'A great piece of escapism that will have you looking over your shoulder'
Scotsman

THE SECRET OF COLD HILL

Peter James is a UK number one bestselling author, best known for writing crime and thriller novels, and the creator of the much-loved Detective Superintendent Roy Grace. Globally, his books have been translated into thirty-seven languages.

Synonymous with plot-twisting page-turners, Peter has garnered an army of loyal fans throughout his storytelling career – which also included stints writing for TV and producing films. He has won over forty awards for his work, including the WHSmith Best Crime Author of All Time Award, Crime Writers' Association Diamond Dagger and a BAFTA nomination for *The Merchant of Venice* starring Al Pacino and Jeremy Irons for which he was an executive producer. Many of Peter's novels have been adapted for film, TV and stage.

Visit his website at www.peterjames.com
Twitter 🐦 @peterjamesuk
Facebook 🅕 facebook.com/peterjames.roygrace
Instagram 📷 Instagram.com/peterjamesuk
YouTube ▶️ Peter James TV

THE SECRET OF COLD HILL

PETER JAMES

PAN BOOKS

First published 2019 by Macmillan

First published in paperback 2019 by Macmillan

This edition published 2020 by Pan Books
an imprint of Pan Macmillan
The Smithson, 6 Briset Street, London EC1M 5NR
Associated companies throughout the world
www.panmacmillan.com

ISBN 978-1-5098-1625-5

Copyright © Really Scary Books/Peter James, 2019

Roy Grace®, Grace®, DS Grace®, DI Grace® and Detective Superintendent Grace®
are registered trademarks of Really Scary Books Limited.

The right of Peter James to be identified as the
author of this work has been asserted by him in accordance
with the Copyright, Designs and Patents Act 1988.

3 5 7 9 8 6 4 2

A CIP catalogue record for this book is available from the British Library.

Typeset by Palimpsest Book Production Ltd, Falkirk, Stirlingshire
Printed and bound by CPI Group (UK) Ltd, Croydon, CR0 4YY

MIX
Paper from
responsible sources
FSC® C116313

Visit **www.panmacmillan.com** to read more about all our books
and to buy them. You will also find features, author interviews and
news of any author events, and you can sign up for e-newsletters
so that you're always first to hear about our new releases.

FOR ISOBEL DIXON,
MY WONDERFUL AGENT

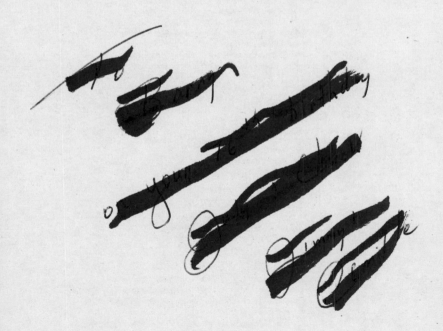

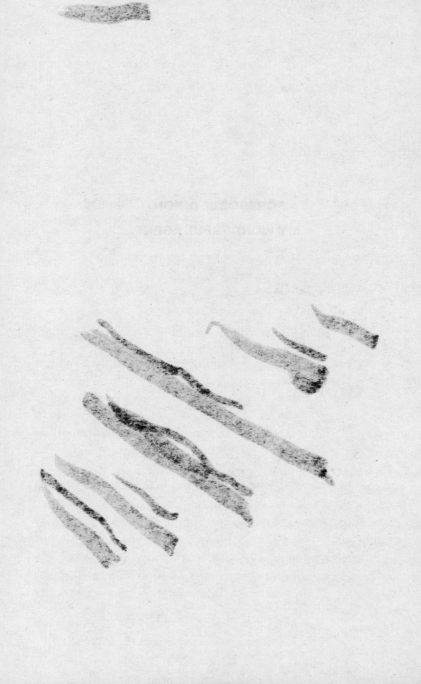

1

Saturday 20 October

'There are, of course, no skeletons in this attic!' the estate agent said with a wink, as she threw open the door with a flourish and ushered her clients into the loft space.

'Wow!' said Mike Diamond.

'Wow!' his wife Julie echoed.

'It sure has the *wow* factor, wouldn't you say, Mr and Mrs Diamond?'

'It sure has,' Mike replied.

And it sure did.

The young couple stared around in wonder as they entered the high-ceilinged room. Painted all in white, it covered almost the entire top-floor area of the brand-new house, and was flooded with light from gable windows at each end. The view to the north was across the long, newly turfed garden ending at the lake, the fields and the hill that rose beyond, and to the south across the partially completed housing estate and down to the village of Cold Hill, half a mile below them. There was a rich smell of fresh paint and timber.

'I can tell you, this is a far superior property to the show house, which was sold in the first hour it was on sale. Far superior.' The agent pointed out the four Sonos speakers and the voice-activated electric blinds, then showed them the equally teched-up en suite bathroom. 'This would make a great master

1

bedroom, or an office,' she enthused. 'It's rare to find a room so well equipped, even in a modern home, you'd have to agree.'

Mike and Julie looked at each other. He pulled a face and his wife grinned at the signal. This estate agent was already irritating them, and they'd only been in the house for a few minutes. An elegant woman in her thirties, with short, dark hair, power-dressed in a black suit, white blouse and court shoes, she marched in front of them, brandishing the particulars as if she was about to present them with a certificate. *Future Owners Extraordinaire of Lake House, No. 47 Lakeview Drive!*

They followed her back down the spiral staircase to the first floor and along a short landing, where she opened another door with an equal flourish, onto a small bedroom. 'This will make a great room for your baby,' she said.

Again, the couple shot another secret glance at each other. Mike frowning and Julie frowning back a *What?* Her pregnancy had only been confirmed yesterday by their doctor, and there was no possible way it could be showing yet.

They followed the agent into two further small bedrooms – perfect spare rooms for guests, she enthused, or maybe one of them a den? Then into the master bedroom. 'You'd have to admit, this is pretty much a *wow* room, too!' She strode confidently across it, unlocked French windows and opened them onto a wide Juliet balcony.

'Can you imagine, on a fine day like today, Mrs Diamond? The two of you sitting out here, having an early morning coffee, looking across the lake?'

'It's north-facing,' Mike said. 'So, no morning sunlight.'

'Who wants morning sunlight in a bedroom?' the agent said. 'Not me! But of course, if that's a concern, then you could make the upstairs space your bedroom.' She gave them a conspiratorial look. 'I tell you, if it was me – and I could afford a house this beautiful – I'd make that loft space my master bedroom. It would make anyone feel they were masters of the universe, just like you two truly are – I can tell!' She glanced at her watch. 'I'm so sorry, we'll have to hurry, I have viewings of this place every twenty minutes today. It won't be staying on the market for long, that's for sure. Not with the shortage of quality new-build stock there is today, believe you me.'

She hurried them through the downstairs: the open-plan kitchen and family room, stacked with smart-gadgets, including the memory fridge; the dining room; the small office; the spacious hall; and then the pièce de résistance – the large, luxuriously carpeted living room with a photochromic-glass conservatory at the rear, overlooking the wide lawn running down to the lake. 'Of course, it would be easy to fence off the lawn part way down, to make it safe for your baby.'

The Diamonds looked at each other. *How does she know about the baby?*

Then, profusely apologetic, she ushered them to the front door. Her next clients were due any moment. If they wished to make an offer, she most strongly advised them to do it sooner rather than later. This was the first day of viewings and this property, priced to sell, would not be hanging around on the market for long.

As she opened the door she said, 'Mr and Mrs Diamond, I can *so* see you living here – in your forever home! And your baby son – what a wonderful environment for him to grow up in. But please, I urge you, don't think about it for too long.'

As they stepped out into the bright, mid-morning sunlight, and the front door closed behind them, Mike and Julie Diamond stood on the path, with the newly turfed lawn on either side, as a car came along the road. They looked at each other. The same look.

What the fuck?
Our 'son'?

A Mini emblazoned with the logo of RICHWARDS ESTATE AGENTS pulled up behind their parked Mercedes. A tubby, smiling man in his forties, in a flamboyant suit, clambered out and hurried across to them, holding a bunch of keys like a gaoler.

'Mr and Mrs Diamond?'

'Yes,' Mike said, hesitantly.

'Paul Jordan, I do apologize for being late – I had a viewing of another property that ran over.' He shook hands with each of them, once again apologizing profusely. 'You are going to love this house, I promise you. It is really quite special. On the whole of the Cold Hill Park development, this is my very favourite, by a country mile.'

As he rummaged through his keys, Julie Diamond said, 'Yes, it is very lovely.'

'Wait until you view the inside! And let me show you the technology – wow!'

'We've actually just seen it,' Mike Diamond said.

Jordan looked at both of them, puzzled. 'Seen it?'

'Your colleague just showed us around.'

'Colleague?'

'Yes.'

The agent frowned. 'I'm sorry – we are the sole agents for this development, and none of my associates are here today.' He looked hesitant. 'Someone showed you around?'

'Yes,' Julie replied. 'A lady, she said she had viewings back to back all day and could only allocate twenty minutes to us.'

'It isn't possible,' Jordan said. 'I – I don't understand. What was her name?'

The couple looked at each other, then Mike shrugged. 'Well, she didn't give us her name. To be honest, she was a bit odd.'

'Can you excuse me?' Jordan asked. 'Please, just a couple of minutes?'

Reluctantly, the couple nodded.

He let himself into the house, walked through the hallway and called out, 'Hello! Hello! It's Paul Jordan – hello!'

He went into each of the downstairs rooms, then up to the first floor, checking each of the rooms there. Then up to the loft, being sure to check the bathroom.

There was no one.

Frowning, he hurried back downstairs and out the front door. And caught a glimpse of the Diamonds' Mercedes, already several hundred yards away.

2

Saturday 27 October

'I love it!'

'You do?'

'Don't you?'

'No!' he said, beaming. 'I don't *love* it – I FUCKING love it!'

Standing in the huge loft, with autumn sunlight streaming in through the south-facing window, Jason put his arm around his wife and hugged her. 'I abso-fucking-lutely love it!'

'You'll have to excuse my husband's language!' Emily said to the estate agent.

'Oh, please, Mrs Danes,' Paul Jordan beamed. 'Artistic licence with language is permitted, for such a famous *artist* as your husband!'

'I'm hardly famous, but thank you,' Jason Danes replied.

'Oh, I would question your modesty, Mr Danes. I took the liberty of looking you up on Wikipedia, and imagine my excitement when I realized I have one of your oil paintings hanging in our living room – a wonderful picture of an old man in an armchair with a spaniel at his feet. So full of charm. My wife bought it for me for Christmas a couple of years ago, from a gallery in Lewes. In the Jordan household, you are indeed famous! And I'm quite certain that should you decide to buy this beautiful, unique home, one day there will be a blue plaque with your name on the wall outside.'

'Not too soon, I hope,' Jason Danes replied. 'You have to be dead for that to happen.'

Jordan smiled. 'Well, don't they say that death is always a good career move for an artist?'

As if given a cue, the sunlight faded behind a cloud. The room darkened, and the expressions on the faces of Jordan's two clients darkened with it. Their enthusiasm for the property suddenly seemed to be draining away.

'Only joking!' Jordan said quickly, trying to recover the situation.

'Of course,' the painter replied. 'I'm only thirty-nine – I hope to have a few more years yet.'

His wife, five years his junior, gave the agent an awkward smile.

Neither of them, looking out at the views in turn, noticed the nervous glance the agent suddenly shot at the doorway.

Jason stared out through the rear gable at the huge lake, and the sloping field beyond, and the soft round contour of the hill rising up steeply beyond that. He watched the ducks – mallards and Indian runners – on the lake. It was so tranquil. 'I could work here, I know I could – it's just, wow, so inspiring! Well, this view to the north is, anyway. It is north I'm looking at?'

'Yes indeed, Mr Danes, and that is part of the South Downs National Park, so it can never be built on.'

'Unlike the other directions?'

The view to the south looked down at the brand-new houses directly opposite, and the rows of houses beyond, most of which were just shells still under construction. To the west was a vast, muddy site, on which there were bulldozers, diggers, men in yellow hard hats with theodolites, and marked-out plots. To the east was a huge empty and overgrown field.

'I'll show you the shape of the whole plan,' the estate agent said, kneeling and unrolling a large map on the bare oak floor.

It was headed, COLD HILL PARK DEVELOPMENT – PHASE 1, PHASE 2, PHASE 3.

'The whole site comprises just over twenty-five acres, Mr and Mrs Danes. Now this, where we are, is part of phase one, which is, frankly, the most exclusive area, with the largest homes, the very best of which – and of which this house is the *very* best – have the lake and rural views. The position is, frankly, superlative – you see, phase one is built on the curtilage of the original mansion that was here: Cold Hill House. Whatever your views on aristocracy and gentry, you have to admit they all knew a thing or two about position and views. And all the infrastructure is already in place – the roads, drains, utilities and, of course, the all-important super-fast fibre broadband. The area to the west, which you can see, is phase two, which will be smaller buildings: townhouses, a few two-storey apartment buildings and some affordable housing.'

'You mean council houses?' Emily quizzed.

Jordan looked a little awkward. 'Well, in all but name, yes. But you'll never even know they're there, with their separate road network. And then to the east, that field, that will also be detached homes, very classy ones.'

'How many residences in total will there be here?' Jason Danes asked.

'When phase three is completed, there will be one hundred and thirty altogether.'

'So, this place will be a building site for the next two years?'

'Yes, Mr and Mrs Danes, but honestly you'll scarcely be affected. There's very little phase one left, and of course the price of this house reflects the temporary inconvenience.'

Jordan noticed the flicker of doubt between the couple and went on, hastily. 'Let me show you a feature that is very rare in modern houses.' He strode over to one window, unlocked it and pulled it up. 'Genuine sash windows, in every room! A true

Georgian feature. You see, this house has been designed almost as a miniature model of Cold Hill House, which once stood here. Sash windows, I tell you – no expense was spared by the builders on this beautiful home.' He smiled. 'For your catering business, Mrs Danes, I don't think you'll find a more magnificent kitchen on the market anywhere in Sussex.'

'Let's take another look at it,' she said.

'Please follow me,' Jordan said, checking his watch, mindful that the Danes had already overrun their allotted thirty minutes and another couple would be arriving for a viewing shortly. But hell, they could wait. He had a good feeling about Mr and Mrs Danes. He could get them over the line.

He rolled up the plan, tucked it under his arm, and led the way down the staircase to the first-floor landing. 'Note how wonderfully light the house feels everywhere, from the clever use of mirrors.'

Jason and Emily looked around, and he was right. Mirrors along the landing walls, and down in the hall, created both light and the illusion of even greater space. Entering the expansive kitchen, Jordan said, 'It's almost as if the architect designed this house with you two in mind. The kitchen perfect for your catering business; the attic a truly divine artist's studio!'

'It is perfect,' Emily said, regaining her former enthusiasm as she strode around. 'So much storage, and how rare to have a walk-in pantry!'

'Not to mention the technology,' Paul Jordan added. 'All the houses on this development have this feature.' He pointed at a small cylindrical device with a glowing green light, sitting on the kitchen unit. 'All the switches and controls and taps throughout the house are voice-activated from that one command box – and its satellite units around the house. You each have to get it to learn your voices. Then anything you want – heating turning up or down, appliances switched on or off, curtains and blinds opened or closed – can be done by simply saying, for instance, "Command! Kitchen blinds down!"'

There was a whirr. The kitchen darkened as blinds lowered over each window.

Again, unnoticed by the couple, Jordan shot another wary glance around, before saying, 'Command! Kitchen blinds up!'

Immediately they rose, and light returned.

'You can even open the fridge and freezer doors by voice command! So hygienic, never needing germ-infected hands to touch any switch or control.'

'Presumably there's a manual override?' Emily asked.

'Absolutely.' He walked over and pressed a button. The command box light turned red. 'Now everything is operated manually, or by remote controls.'

'No one realizes quite how many germs are spread by hands,' Jason Danes said, solemnly. 'The average bowl of peanuts sitting on a pub bar counter contains twelve different traces of urine and five of human faeces.'

Jordan blanched slightly. 'I think I've just developed a peanut allergy!' He rapidly changed the subject. 'And of course you can set up your phones to operate anything in this house remotely – just a simple app – from wherever you are in the country, or indeed the world! You can even be lying on a beach in Greece and check the contents of your fridge if you like!'

Emily opened the integral door to the double garage and utility room and went in, followed by her husband and the agent. The lights flickered on automatically. 'I could make this into my catering kitchen. It would work, don't you think, darling?'

Jason nodded. 'It could.'

'It *really* could!' she insisted. 'I could get all the fridges, freezers and ovens I need into here.'

'Of course,' Jordan said, 'some people – especially an artist of your calibre, Mr Danes – might prefer something old, quaint, historic. Rustic, perhaps? If you would rather view an Edwardian property, or Victorian or even Georgian – I do have some very attractive houses within your price range I could show you. But of course, along with their beauty, old and historic properties come with a raft of maintenance issues. Here, with a totally new build, you get the builder's ten-year guarantee. Ten years maintenance-free! You don't have to worry about draughts or leaks or doors sticking. When you buy new, you are buying worry-free.'

'And germ-free,' Jason Danes added.

'Absolutely, quite right! Germ-free. Ah, yes, indeed, germs are of course not included in the purchase price – they are extra!' Jordan chuckled, but his clients stared blankly at him.

'It's an important consideration,' Emily Danes said. 'Germs.'

'Ah, of course, indeed. In the catering business, you cannot be too careful, I'm sure. Old buildings can be full of bugs and all kind of things. *Yechh!* All of them lying beneath the floorboards and in crevices for years, decades, centuries even, waiting to pounce! Here, in addition to hygienic switch activation, we have the very latest in state-of-the-art insulation. I tell you what, if I found a cockroach in here, I'd name it Houdini.' Behind him, he heard the sound of running water.

'It's actually more for my husband,' she said. 'He doesn't do germs, bugs, dirt.'

'Quite right, who does, eh?' Jordan turned to see his client running his hands under a tap in one of the twin sinks and washing them with liquid soap from an electronic dispenser. 'Germs, eh, Mr Danes – nasty little buggers.'

Absorbed in the ritual of cleaning his hands, Jason did not appear to notice the comment.

Jordan frowned. There was something different about the man, something that was pushing him, just a little, out of his comfort zone. But at the same time, he genuinely did love that painting of the old man with the dog. Every time he looked at it, he wondered what the man was thinking, what his life was – and had been. Clearly Mr Danes was a genius, and weren't all geniuses just a bit eccentric? But would an artistic genius really want to live in a sterile, new-build house?

'The houses on either side of this, Mr Jordan – are they sold?' Emily asked.

'No, not yet, although I believe a couple – a very nice couple, with two children – are going to buy number forty-five – that's the house to the east – if the sale of their house goes through.' He crossed his fingers.

'Children?' Jason said, dubiously. 'What age?'

The agent smiled. 'I know what you're thinking; what a nightmare when you're trying to paint, having screaming children next door. I don't think you need to worry – they are twelve and fourteen. We've not had any couples with young, screaming children looking at any of the properties so far. And there's quite an elderly couple, retired, who are very interested in number forty-nine. They're moving down from Yorkshire to be closer to their daughter, who lives just outside Lewes.'

'How many other people are living on the estate at present?' Emily asked.

'Well . . .' he hesitated, smiling uncomfortably. 'At this moment, there's just the very nice couple diagonally opposite – they've been here a month or so now – and there's a family due to move in opposite you, in number thirty-four, soon. Elsewhere, no one at the moment. But the properties are selling like hot cakes – it's just such a fine development; so near to Brighton and to Lewes, close to rail links to London – just fifty minutes on the Brighton line. And surrounded by beautiful countryside. This is a very special position – quite unique.'

Jordan glanced at his watch again. 'Look, I'm very sorry,

but I have another couple arriving for a viewing. If you'd like to have a think about it and come back to me, we can always book a further appointment. But I do have to warn you, we have so much interest in this property – indeed in the whole estate. We've already sold over half the properties off-plan, and this one, which is the real jewel in the crown, is not going to be on the market for long, I can tell you. And of course, I can help you with a mortgage, should you require. But I really would advise you, if you are interested, to move quickly. The couple I'm waiting for now are coming for their second viewing, and I'm told they don't have any property to sell – they are cash buyers.'

'We'll take it,' Jason said decisively, rinsing his hands then soaping them once again. 'We'll pay the full asking price.' He looked at his wife, who nodded.

Jordan beamed. 'Well! What can I say? I don't think it is a decision you could ever possibly regret. This is the finest house in the best property development I've ever been privileged to handle – and I've handled many, I can tell you. The location, the sheer build quality. The views. You could not have a better investment!'

'So, what do you need from us to take it off the market, immediately, this minute?' Jason Danes asked. 'We're cash buyers, too. We sold our previous home and we're currently renting, and we don't need a mortgage.'

'Good, excellent.' The agent was pensive for a moment. 'It's Saturday, nothing can happen until Monday when solicitors are back at work. If you would like to go to my office and put down a ten thousand-pound deposit – entirely refundable – as a show of good faith, I'll tell the couple who are coming that the house is under offer. I'd be prepared to give you a four- to six-week window to exchange contracts. How does that sound?'

The Danes looked at each other. 'We might be able to move in before Christmas!' Emily said.

Rinsing then soaping his hands again, Jason Danes nodded enthusiastically and said, 'Very fair.'

'I'll even throw in some containers of soap!'

Neither of them smiled.

After an awkward moment, Jordan beamed again. 'In which case, Mr and Mrs Danes, I look forward to handing you the keys and to formally welcoming you to your new home. You won't regret this, I can assure you. This is a very special house. You are going to find it very creative, very creative indeed.'

3

Maurice and Claudette Penze-Weedell peered out through the slats of the blinds of Arden Lodge, 36 Lakeview Drive, watching the activity going on across the street at number forty-seven. They were happy that, after two months, they would no longer be the only people living in the Cold Hill Park development. They were also very curious to catch a glimpse of their new neighbours.

'Not too wide, dear,' Maurice said. 'They'll notice, and we don't want to seem nosey.' Maurice had originally suggested changing to net curtains, like the ones they'd had in their previous home, which prevented passers-by from seeing in while still enabling them to see out. But Mrs P-W – as he referred to his wife – had put her foot down, saying net curtains were far too common. As owners of the grand show house – and the first residents of Cold Hill Park – she insisted they had to set standards. Blinds it had to be, and vertical ones, in her view, were so much more elegant than horizontal ones.

Maurice agreed with Mrs P-W, or 'High Command', as he called her when with his friends. He always agreed with her. It was, he had learned over their years together – the very *many* years – the route to a happy marriage. 'Happy wife, happy life,' he had already told all the regulars, several times, at his new local the Crown, down in the village. Well perhaps more accurately, he reflected, a *tolerable* life. Although his joke at their housewarming party – which, coincidentally and economically, had doubled as their thirtieth wedding anniversary celebration – that he would have got less than thirty years for murder, had fallen somewhat flat.

'It's a rather *grand* design for a not very grand-sized house, don't you think, Maurice?'

'I think it's quite attractive.'

'Quite attractive? It's like a sort of bonsai stately home. Gables in the attic and that ludicrous chimney, like the house is wearing a top hat – it's just *sooooo* pretentious. And with the lake behind it and all. Honestly!'

Unlike its rather uninspired neighbours on both sides, which were rather squat, red-brick houses with pantiled roofs, like a million others on new-build estates, number forty-seven stood proud and aloof. It was a Georgian-style house on three storeys, with large, gabled dormers. The exterior walls were fawn-coloured and the door, framed by a handsome porch, navy blue. The front garden was a compact lawn behind black railings, with a wide drive and parking area and attached double garage to one side.

'I think the estate agent said the house was a nod to the original ruined mansion that was here – that the architect had taken his inspiration from it.'

'So, which grand house did the architect take his inspiration from for ours?'

'I don't know, my love.'

A removals van the size of an ocean liner had pulled up outside the house some ten minutes earlier and the removals men were milling around, two of them smoking, one on his phone. But it was when a silver BMW drove onto the driveway and pulled up in front of the garage that both the Penze-Weedells had taken up position by the window. The driver remained in it, seemingly talking on his phone.

'That car's just like ours!' Claudette Penze-Weedell said with relief in her voice. 'Identical!'

'I'm afraid not,' her husband said, gloomily. 'Ours is a 520; that one is a 540i.'

'Is that more expensive?'

'Much.'

Claudette stared at the car across the street venomously. 'It's probably time to upgrade, isn't it, Maurice?'

Only weeks after moving in, Maurice Penze-Weedell had been made redundant by the insurance company in Brighton which had employed him for twenty-eight years. He had risen from the post-room to become its Chief Operating Officer. Although given a substantial pay-off, a new car for either of them at this moment was out of the question.

He hadn't yet told his wife just how serious their financial situation was and that – heaven forbid – she might actually have to get up off her backside, which seemed to widen every day like the flow of volcanic lava, and get a job. They only had sufficient reserve funds to cover the mortgage for another twelve months, and he had been finding out to his dismay that the jobs market for a fifty-five-year-old in twenty-first century Britain was pretty shitty. 'My dearest, our BMW is only eleven months old. It's fine, we don't need to upgrade it for a few years.'

'In that case we should upgrade my car. I think the Lady of the Manor should have a dignified motor car and not a child's toy. Really, I feel like Noddy every time I get in it.' She was referring to her little Japanese runaround, currently in the garage, plugged into the charger. It was a regular bone of contention between them.

'I hardly think we're the Lord and Lady of the Manor, dear. We've bought the very nice show house on a very nice estate, but I don't think the other residents are going to be queuing at our front door to pay their annual tithe of chickens, bushels of corn and God knows what else.' He hesitated and smiled. 'Although I suppose, of course, *droit du seigneur* might be rather nice.'

'Droit de what?'

He smiled again. 'The ancient right of the Lord of the Manor to deflower any local virgin.'

'Dream on, you wouldn't know what to do with a virgin.' She tried to stop herself in mid-sentence, but it was too late, it came out.

'Quite right – I never had that experience, my dear.' He delivered the trump card she could not defend against. She'd lost her virginity to his original best man three weeks before their wedding. Maurice had caught them himself, in flagrante. It was a hold over her that had served him well for three decades.

'Anyhow,' he added, defensively. 'You hate parking and your car has self-park. You said you liked that feature.'

'Only because I can do it when I'm outside the car, so no one can see me in it.'

Across the road, a tall, gangly man in his late-thirties climbed out of the BMW and tossed his head, shaking his mop of fair hair from his eyes. Dressed in a leather jacket over a black polo-neck jumper, skinny jeans and boots, and arty glasses, he stood looking approvingly up at the front of his house, which was bathed in winter sunlight, then around and across the street. He clocked the twitch of the blinds in the large, rather ugly house over the road, with the flashing blue and green Christmas lights adorning the porch and the hideous Santa's grotto that covered most of the garden.

'That must be him,' Mrs P-W said. 'The painter!'

'Could come in handy when we need to redecorate.'

'Ha ha,' she said. 'Jason Danes is famous. He's the talk of the village shop.' She smiled, coquettishly, at her husband. 'Just a thought – why don't you commission him to do a portrait of me for my birthday?'

'Why would I want that? I've got plenty of photographs of you.'

'That's not the same. God, you used to be so romantic, Maurice! Don't you think a portrait would be a romantic gesture?'

He looked at her. She wasn't quite the svelte beauty he'd first dated, although if he was honest, neither was he still the dashing cavalier of his youth. Both of them now sported double chins that were visual testament to the laws of gravity.

'Hmmm,' he grunted. 'I imagine he charges a fortune.'

'And I'm not worth it?' She peered through the blinds again, very cautiously this time. Then she gasped. 'Please tell me that belongs to the removals company and not to these . . . these people?'

A small, bright-pink refrigerated van, emblazoned with the legend TASTE SENSATIONS – EMILY'S PANTRY, the words separated by a floral logo, pulled up alongside the BMW. An attractive, red-headed woman in her early thirties got out, wearing a baggy crimson parka over black tights and calf-length boots.

'What does she have in there, then, Danish pastries?' Maurice said.

'Huh?' his wife said blankly.

'The Danes. Danish pastries. Geddit?'

'You're full of humour today – you been on the sauce or something?'

The Penze-Weedells watched as the couple kissed, then hugged, then kissed again before heading towards the front door. Then Claudette turned to her husband.

'Maurice,' she said, sternly. 'You are not going to permit them to leave that van parked on their driveway, are you?'

'What do you mean?'

'You know *exactly* what I mean. We're not going to sit here and allow the value of our house to be diminished by a hideous van parked outside a neighbour's property.'

'I really don't see what business it is of ours. It's advertising her business, surely?'

'Yes, well, there's an awful lot you don't seem to see these days. Perhaps you should go to Specsavers and check you don't have cataracts.'

'Don't be absurd, my love. My vision is perfectly good – 6/6 at my recent check-up.'

Releasing the blinds again, she said, 'Don't you remember when we bought this house, the restrictive covenants? One of them said that no commercial vehicles were permitted to be parked on the estate overnight.' She pointed across the road. 'That is a commercial vehicle.'

'It's only a small van.'

'*Small?* It's hideous.'

'I'm getting a little bit confused.' He stroked his threadbare dome with his right hand. 'Do you want me to ask him to paint you, or to put his wife's van inside their garage?'

'Both!' she said emphatically.

'I think we need to be a little diplomatic. I'm not even sure that covenant applies to vehicles owned by residents.'

'Don't be ridiculous. Of course it does. Let me tell you, I do not intend to spend the rest of my life staring out of my drawing room window at a pink van. If you're not man enough to tell them, I certainly will. I'll go over tomorrow and tell them, very politely of course.'

'Perhaps give them a few days,' he suggested.

'A few days?'

He turned and pointed at their Christmas tree. Gaily wrapped presents lay around the base, and fairy lights twinkled in the branches of plastic pine needles. 'Isn't this meant to be the season of goodwill?'

She again parted the blinds, peering at the removals men, who were starting to carry furniture towards the front door of the Danes' house. 'Yes, Maurice, *goodwill*. Which means respecting what this estate is all about. *Aspirational homes*. There are people with a tatty camper van moving in at the end of our road soon – probably travellers – and now we have a pink van opposite. This is all just ghastly. I don't care if he is bloody Rembrandt reincarnated, they are not leaving a pink van on their driveway.' She paused. 'Oh look, a piano, well that's something, I suppose.'

'The people at the end of the road are not *travellers*,' he said.

'No?' she rounded on him. 'They came in a Volkswagen camper with a yellow roundel in the rear window saying, *Nuclear Power – Nein Danke!* They're not *travellers*?'

'No, they're *New Age* people. Probably lovely and very gentle. You have to remember, my love, that this whole estate will have a mix of people, which is no bad thing.'

'Yes, well, I'm beginning to think we've made a terrible mistake moving here.'

All the warmth drained from the room. Maurice and Mrs P-W shivered, suddenly. Inexplicably.

A woman stood right behind them, watching them. She was wearing a long blue dress with yellow shoes, and had an angry, shrivelled face.

Parvenus.

She did not like them, or their ridiculous name.

Penze-Weedell.

Both of them, as if drawn by a magnet, turned their heads.

All they saw was the flashing Christmas tree, and the cards on the mantelpiece above the electric dancing flames of the simulated coal fire in the fake grate.

'Has the heating gone off?' she said, giving her husband a sharp look. 'Are you economizing again?'

He shivered again. 'No, it's set for all day.' He hurried through into the kitchen and then into the utility room. The boiler was blazing away.

4

'Oh my God!' Emily Danes said. 'I hadn't realized just how hideous it is – daylight sort of masked it!' She stared out from the front window of the living room, through the falling darkness, at number thirty-six. At the illuminated Santa's grotto in the front garden, complete with Santa rocking from side to side and with flashing lights for eyes, and a string of elves frozen in mid-dance. 'Can you imagine, we're going to have to look at this until – the sixth of January, isn't it, the date when you have to take decorations down or it's unlucky? God!'

'The curtains shouldn't be too long.'

Emily leaned against a packing case and looked at her checklist. 'Right. I've rung the window cleaner we were recommended and he's going to try to fit us in before Christmas. He asked if we'd mind him coming at the weekend, this once – what do you think?'

'Be good to get them done, they're quite grimy.'

'Probably dust from the construction going on all around us.' She peered at the list again. 'I've called Sky and that's sorted. I've also gone on the council's website and found what day the bins go out – recycling is every other Monday, but it's all going to change after the New Year, so I'll have to check again then.

Oh, and there's a post office counter in the village shop that's open to eight p.m.!'

'That's better than in town.'

'I know, brilliant!'

'And I've finally found the stopcock,' Jason said.

'You'd better show me.'

'Tomorrow, when it's daylight. It's out down the side of the house behind the bin store.'

'OK.'

'Right, time for a celebration, methinks!'

'You said the curtains shouldn't be too long – how long did she say?'

'I spoke to the woman a few days ago – she thought about a month,' he said, coming back in with two champagne flutes. He set them down on the glass coffee table in front of the two huge sofas they had splashed out on, and which were put together in an L-shape.

'God, we're going to have to stare at that awful stuff across the road right through Christmas until they take them down.'

He went back to the kitchen and returned with a cold bottle of champagne that the estate agent had left them in the fridge. 'That's a bit snobby, darling – I think we should at least give them a chance!'

'With Christmas decorations like that? Hmmm. Perhaps we could hang a blackout sheet up in the meantime,' she said with a grin. 'Although I guess that wouldn't exactly be very neighbourly – they might think we were doing it to stop them spying on us.'

'They are spying on us,' he replied.

'What?'

'They are, darling. I saw their blinds move when I got out of the car this morning, and every time I look across, I keep seeing the blinds in the same downstairs window twitching.'

'Perhaps they're curious, like we are, to see who their new neighbours are. They must be happy to have another couple on the estate. The agent said we're only the second owners to move in. It must have felt like living in a ghost town.'

Jason frowned. 'I think – what's his name – Paul Jordan must be mistaken; there are people in the house directly opposite us – the one that looks like a small child's drawing. I saw a couple and two children through one of the windows this morning.'

'Oh, so my husband is a peeping Tom, is he?' she said, peering across at it. 'It's a funny-looking house – two windows upstairs, two down, either side of the front door, and a pointy roof. You're right, like something a child would draw.' She hesitated. 'Are you sure you saw people there?'

'Yes, in one of the upstairs rooms.'

'But there are no lights on, and no car outside.'

'Perhaps they're out.'

'More likely they haven't moved in yet, and were just there measuring up, or whatever,' she said.

'There! Number thirty-six, they're looking at us again, I saw the blinds move!'

'Shall I flash at them?'

'Might be a lechy old perv living there who'd get off on that.'

'Doesn't look much like a lechy old perv's house to me.'

He peered out. 'No, too naff. It's actually horrible – I mean, how did the same architect who designed this place ever think that house was a good idea? Or the one opposite. I mean, ours is a really pretty house – it's like he designed this, got drunk, and came back to his drawing board and did that one and the Grotties.'

'The Grotties! I like that. I think one of us should go over tomorrow and say hi, put them out of their misery so they can see we're actually human. And tell them how much we like their Christmas lights.'

'I'd like to see you do that with a straight face.' He raised the bottle in the air. 'Grrrrrrrrrr, we're your new neighbours, we're the cousins of the Munsters and we are very, very, very weird!'

Emily giggled.

He set the bottle on top of an unopened packing case the removals men had plonked there and began working on the foil.

'Maybe he was just having a laugh,' Emily said, flopping down on one of the sofas. 'Like food critics every now and then describing something utterly disgusting as the most wonderful thing they've ever put in their mouth. Like, what is the most horrible house he could design that someone would buy. Or that portrait you painted of that politician whom you didn't like, deliberately making him look about two hundred years old.'

'I was just trying to show the wisdom of his years etched into his face.' He held the bottle facing safely away from her as he untwisted the wire.

'Of course you were.' She lay back and kicked her legs in the air. 'Woweeee, this sofa is sooooo comfy!'

There was a massive pop and the cork flew out, ricocheting off the ceiling, the champagne squirting and foaming out as if the bottle had been vigorously shaken. He stared at it, startled. Over half the contents had gone by the time it settled.

'Bloody hell!' he said. 'This is a lively one.'

Looking up, she said, 'It's made a mark on the ceiling!'

'We should leave it there – our house-christening mark! Our *forever* home.'

'I like that!'

He filled their glasses and handed her one. Then he picked

up his and, staring her in the eye said, 'Cheers, to our *forever* home.'

'It's going to be a very happy home.'

'It is, my darling.'

'No it isn't,' said a sharp female voice.

5

Both of them froze.

The voice sounded like it had come from the kitchen.

Emily stared at her husband, wide-eyed.

Jason strode through into the kitchen, where the command box he had set up earlier sat on the refectory table, the green light glowing, showing it was operative. The wall-mounted television was on, with some soap playing. A middle-aged man and a woman were arguing furiously.

He stared at the screen. Quietly attempting to pacify the woman, the man insisted, 'I'm telling you, it is!'

'No, it isn't!' she yelled back, at full volume.

'Command!' Jason said. 'Mute television!'

Instantly, the couple continued their argument in silence.

'Command! Television off!'

The screen went dark.

He went back to the living room, smiling with relief. Emily was standing near the front window, peering up at the command box speaker grille set into the wall, high up.

'The wonders of technology,' he said, looking up, too. 'Our home command box with a mind of its own – it must have switched the television on. I'll have a proper fiddle with it tomorrow – I think I tried to set it up too quickly.' He picked up his glass and nodded at the ceiling. 'That christening mark – right?'

28

'Right?' she said, quizzically.

He poured some champagne into his mouth, set his glass down on the glass coffee table, put his arms around her and pressed his lips to hers, gently releasing the bubbly into her mouth. Then he murmured, 'Talking of christening the house, we've been here for ten hours now and we haven't yet bonked.' He ran his hands down her midriff, levered his fingers inside her jeans and popped the buttons.

'Mr Danes,' she murmured back, pleasurably. 'Are you trying to seduce me?'

'No, I'm not trying,' he said as his fingers explored deeper. 'I *am* seducing you.'

'Let's go upstairs.'

'No, here!'

She jerked her head at the window. 'They can see us!'

'Great – let's give them a real show then!'

'No.'

'Yes.'

'No!'

'Yes!' He tugged her jeans down over her buttocks.

'Jason, no, upstairs! You're wicked! Our neighbours can bloody see!'

'So what?' He pulled her, gently, down onto the large, white sofa, kissing her and probing away her objections with his fingers. She tugged hard at his T-shirt, pulling it over his head, then began to work on his flies.

6

'Maurice, I just cannot believe it. They're behaving like animals.'

Her husband was beaming. 'Just like you and I used to.'

'Hmmph.'

He looked at her with a gleam in his eyes. 'Why don't we
– you know – pop upstairs?'

'What? It's only six o'clock in the evening.'

'So, my love? The time of day never bothered you, once.' He
put his arms, clumsily, around her and tried to nuzzle her ear,
but all he got was a faceful of stiff, lacquered hair, before she
shoved him away.

'Stop it! I have to watch *Strictly Come Dancing* on catch-up.
What's got into you?'

'You can watch it later, or another time.'

'Why would I want to do that? Just so you can have your
wicked way?'

'I . . .'

'Yes?'

'I thought it might be nice,' he said, meekly.

'Did you? Well, I think *Strictly* would be a lot nicer.' She
waddled into the kitchen in her pink pom-pom slippers,
opened a cupboard and removed an extra-large Christmas-
special tub of Quality Street chocolates. She carried it into the
lounge, settled into the massive sofa, put her feet up on a

pouffe, and called out, 'Television, BBC iPlayer!' then she added, 'Please.'

Even after weeks of living here, she hadn't fully got her head around giving voice commands to operate just about everything in the house, from the bedroom curtains to all the kitchen appliances.

The wall-mounted television was disguised as a mirror in a gilded frame, either side of which were two marble columns topped with busts of gold angels. She repeated the instruction, starting with the word 'command'. As the show appeared, she popped off the lid of the tub and rustled through the contents until, with a happy smile, she found a red and black Strawberry Delight. Her favourite! She unwrapped it, popped it in her mouth and chewed happily as the show started. So happily, that a minute later she was foraging for another. A shadow passed the door to the hall.

'Maurice!' she called out, sharply.

'Yes, dear?' he peered in, dressed in an overcoat and woolly hat.

'Where are you going?'

'Just popping out for my constitutional.'

'I hope you're not going to have a sneaky cigarette?'

'Of course not. Just some fresh air.' His voice rose a few octaves and he avoided eye contact. She had learned many years ago these were both signs that he was fibbing.

'I won't kiss you if you've got smoky breath,' she said sternly, through a chocolatey mouthful.

'I'll be back in a while.'

'That's what Scott said.'

'Scott?'

'Scott of the Antarctic, who do you think I meant?'

There was a burst of applause and music from the television as a couple in tight sequined clothes pirouetted across the dance floor. The dark background was dazzlingly illuminated by darting blue laser searchlights.

'My dear, that wasn't Scott – it was one of his team, Oates, and I think what he actually said was, "I am just going outside and may be some time."'

'Yes, well, don't be as long as him.'

'Ha ha.'

'Have you wrapped up warm enough?'

'It's not that cold.'

'Have you got your gloves?'

'In my pocket.'

'Make sure Elizabeth doesn't follow you out.'

Checking the cat wasn't behind him, Maurice let himself out of the front door, closing it with a sense of relief that he had a few minutes of escape and freedom. He walked a short distance in the dry, early evening air, careful to keep well out of sight of the lounge window, and lurked in the shadows of Santa's grotto as he pulled out his cigarettes. Then he lit one, inhaling deeply and gratefully. One of his few little pleasures these days, he rued.

As he smoked, he stared at the lights behind the curtain-less windows of the house of the new arrivals. And in particular at the window below which the couple, frantically undressing each other, had sunk. He was feeling both intensely curious and a stirring in his trousers.

And finally, reluctant but unable to stop himself, as if propelled by an unseen hand, he stepped forward, across the lawn, towards number forty-seven, just getting a little closer. Then a little closer still.

7

Friday 14 December

Elizabeth jumped onto the sofa beside Claudette Penze-Weedell. She steadied the Quality Street tub before stroking the cat, absently, staring at the television. Elizabeth purred. On the screen, a man in a red sequined waistcoat, open at the front revealing his toned pecs, danced wildly with a woman with big hair, in a matching dress. Claudette lowered her eyes for a second to peer in the plastic tub, searching for another Strawberry Delight. As her pudgy fingers closed around her prize she realized, disappointed, it was the last one. She eyed several shiny purple wrappers. Her second favourites – she would work her way through those next, she decided.

Glancing back at the screen, a movement in the doorway caught her eye.

A shadowy figure crossed it.

'Maurice!' she called out, crossly. 'Are you back already? You know what the doctor said about walking for thirty minutes every day.'

There was no response.

'Maurice!' she called out, louder.

At that moment on the screen the two dancers tumbled, catastrophically, onto the floor.

'No!' she gasped, as they struggled to their feet and tried to recover the situation, as if nothing had happened. Filled with anxiety for the couple, she plucked a purple chocolate from the tub, unwrapped it, and crammed it into her mouth, her eyes on stalks, riveted by the disaster as she chewed the hazelnut in soft caramel.

Outside, Maurice, reeled in by his urges, continued across the road, keeping clear of the glow from the ersatz Victorian street light directly opposite. He took a final drag of his cigarette, dropped it on the ground and took out a mint from the tin he always carried in his pocket to mask the smell of smoke from his wife.

Sucking on it, and with erotic butterflies fluttering in his stomach, unseen strings pulled him closer to number forty-seven, eyes glued to that window. He was feeling increasingly aroused. Mrs P-W had better be in the mood tonight.

He reached the railings and the open front gate, then stopped and looked over his shoulder at his house, at Santa's grotto and the closed blinds behind which his wife would be absorbed with the show and her chocolates.

He wanted so much to turn back. But his feet seemed disconnected from his mind and he kept going forward. Tiptoeing now. Forward. Invisible in the darkness, inching his reluctant way towards that window.

Definitely invisible.

He was panting. His heart drumming. His face burning with embarrassment.

Must stop. Turn away. Go. Go!

Closer.

Closer.

Something moved behind that window. Pale, naked buttocks rising. Falling. Rising. Falling.

Enough, he must leave right away.

Instead, helplessly, he continued tiptoeing forward.

Could see more of the buttocks.

Just yards away now.

Another step.

Then a face pressed against the window, staring at him venomously.

The thin, wrinkled face of an old woman, her flesh a hideous grey, her eyes filled with hatred.

Almost simultaneously, security lights flooded down on him, spotlighting him like an actor on stage.

Maurice took a startled step back and stumbled, almost falling. Then, shaking in shock and terror, he turned and fled. He did not dare run over to his house in case she was still looking out of the window and would see him. The shame of it. Maurice Penze-Weedell – a pervy voyeur.

He ran along the pavement, curving past two completed but empty houses that were still for sale. Then a dinky one with white clapboarding, with a 'SOLD' sign and a spindly sapling in the front garden. Where the road curved left, there were two partially completed houses on the right, the gardens just mounds of earthworks secured behind steel fencing. A sign outside on a blue square board read, FOREST MILLS DEVELOPMENTS – PLOTS 28 & 29.

He reached a junction, perspiring heavily now, and stopped, panting, badly in need of another cigarette to calm his nerves, hardly daring to look over his shoulder. Finally, he plucked up courage and turned, looking back at number forty-seven. To his relief the security lights had gone off and Lakeview Drive was dark and silent again. The downstairs light in the house where he had seen the couple having sex was still on.

God, who was that hideous-looking woman? That hag?

Directly opposite him was a row of silent, dark, finished houses, all with blue signs on their walls. All as yet unsold. With shaking hands, he fumbled out a cigarette and was about to light it when he smelled a strong whiff of cigar smoke. Where was it coming from? There wasn't a soul around this end of the estate.

Then, with a start, he saw him.

A man standing right across the road, beneath a street light, with a fat cigar glowing in his mouth, giving him a knowing smile. He was in his thirties and looked like he was dressed for a 1970s-themed fancy-dress party – he wore a busy high-collared shirt opened halfway to his navel, flared jeans, Chelsea boots and a leather jacket. A gold medallion glinted on his chest.

'Hi, good evening!' Maurice hailed him. 'Good to see a fellow smoker!'

The man drew on his cigar, the red glow brightening, removed it from his mouth, and blew smoke out.

Holding his own unlit cigarette, Maurice crossed the road towards him. 'How do you do? I'm Maurice Penze-Weedell – we've recently moved into number thirty-six, the house down at the other end.'

As Maurice reached him, holding out an extended hand in greeting, the man vanished.

8

'Probably a fox or a cat,' Jason said, glancing out at the darkness after the alert ended and the security lights had gone out. 'I bet those people in number thirty-six have a cat. They look like cat people. They've probably got a great fat thing called Tiddles or some stupid name.'

Emily said, mischievously, 'Or it could have been the neighbourhood weirdo?'

They lay on the wide, soft sofa, their arms around each other, their bodies pressed tightly together for warmth against the cold draught that blew on them. 'Well, if it was, we sure gave him a good show!' Jason said. 'I think Cold Hill village would have felt a small earth tremor.'

'A small one? I'd say ten on the Richter scale.'

He frowned at her. 'Only ten?'

She kissed him. 'Probably higher!' She kissed him again. 'I love you so much. I love our new home.'

The sharp female voice rang out again, loudly, right behind them.

'What's to love about it?'

Emily broke free of his arms and sat up with a start. 'What was that?'

Jason, naked, stood and ran to the kitchen. To his amazement, the television was on again, at a loud volume. The same couple arguing.

'What's to love about it? I'll tell you what's to bloody love about it!'

Jason strode over to the command box and pressed the green button. Instantly it turned red.

He grabbed the remote from the glass-fronted cupboard below the television, which housed the Sky box and DVD player, and switched the television off. Then he went back to Emily.

'I think that bloody command thing has a mind of its own. It must have some setting I haven't figured out and put the television back on. I've switched the bloody thing off.'

'It didn't sound like the television,' she said, shakily. 'It sounded like she was right behind us.'

'It did, I know. Maybe it got relayed through that speaker up there.' He pointed at the wall. He lay down beside her again, slipping his arms around her, and kissed her. 'Amazing, we're finally here, in time for Christmas.'

'We need to buy a tree tomorrow, and a load of decorations – all the ones we have are going to look a bit lost here,' she said.

'Yep.'

They had previously lived in a two-bedroom terraced Victorian house in the North Laines district of central Brighton. It was tiny compared to this one and now seemed even tinier.

Jason momentarily disentangled himself from his wife, stood up, filled their glasses on top of the packing case, passed one down to her then rejoined her on the sofa. 'God, so much to think about.'

'Like, what we're going to eat tonight – I'm starving,' Emily said.

'Me too. Ravenous.'

'Mum brought us over a pasta dish and salad, which are in the fridge.'

'I fancy a curry – or a Thai. Why don't we order one in?'

'Nice idea, except we're not in Brighton now – we're in the bundu. I doubt anyone's going to deliver.'

'Good point. Hmm. Let's go out for dins tomorrow – or how about for Sunday lunch? Maybe check out the pub in the village? See what they do? I saw it advertises home-cooked food.'

'We can go there in the morning and see if we can book – if we like the look of it.'

'And ask the shop to deliver papers – the estate agent said they would.'

They lay still. Jason, exhausted, closed his eyes. Even though it was a brand-new sofa he began fretting about bugs. Panic started to set in. Shit, how had he become so carried away?

Suddenly, Emily prodded him in the chest. 'How amazing to do that spontaneously rather than by constantly calculating the right time of every month.'

'Totes!' He nodded and kissed her.

'Right, up – we've work to do. I've got to get my catering area in the garage sorted. I've that twenty-fifth wedding anniversary for eighty people to cater for in two weeks' time, and you have to get your studio set up.'

Getting to his feet, in a hurry to head up to the bathroom to shower, he said, 'Don't you think it was a bit ambitious taking on something like that so soon after moving in?' He shrugged. 'Just saying.'

'We need the money,' she reminded him. 'And he's a big television personality, on that antiques show. It could open all kinds of doors for me in the county. I discussed it with Louise, and she can prep a lot of the stuff at hers.'

Louise Porter was her partner in the catering business.

She prodded him again. 'Go on – up, work! No slacking!'

'I know.'

He had two commissions, both portraits of clients' dogs,

one in oils and one a pencil drawing, to deliver before Christmas. He planned to do both of them over the weekend and Monday, then rush them to his framer. It was going to be tight, but they needed every penny at the moment. And he would have no let-up over the Christmas break – the gallery in London, the Northcote, which had brought him his success that had helped them to buy this house, was putting on a one-man show of his work starting on 8 February. He had promised them twenty-two paintings, the standard number for an exhibition. So far, he only had twelve that were completed and framed. He was going to have to work flat out for the next ten weeks.

'Do that, my love, and I'll get to work on everything else,' Emily said. 'I've got to start unpacking – like sheets, pillows, and our clothes. I'm fine with the catering, but not sure it was such a smart idea to invite my parents for Christmas lunch.'

'I'm not sure it's ever a good idea to invite your parents to anything,' he murmured, under his breath.

Emily looked cross, suddenly. 'What did you say?'

'Nothing, darling.'

'You did, your lips moved!'

'I just said it'll be lovely having your parents here for Christmas Day.'

A female voice shouted out from the kitchen, 'No you didn't!'

9

Emily and Jason both looked around in shock.

He jumped up. 'What the . . . ?'

'Who said that? Who said it?' Emily asked. 'Who is it, who is in here with us?'

'I thought we'd turned the bloody television off!' he ran through into the kitchen.

The television was off.

As he stared at it, Emily's demeanour changed, and she stopped smiling. 'It is off?'

'Yes.'

'Where did that voice come from?'

'I don't know, some glitch with the command box, I would think. Maybe it switched the television back on and then off again?'

'Maybe it didn't. Maybe there's someone playing a game with us? Is there someone in the house?'

'What?'

'I mean it.'

'Of course there's no one here, babes!'

'That voice – that was not the television,' she said.

They pulled on their clothes, then he fetched their glasses, refilled them, and they sat at the kitchen table. He sipped his drink in pensive silence.

41

'What was it?' she pressed.

'Listen, we . . .' He fell silent again, holding his glass in his hand.

'We what? We heard it,' she said. 'We both bloody heard it.'

'There has to be a rational explanation.'

'Good. Tell me, I'm all ears.'

'I think –' he hesitated – 'maybe the command turned on the television and then switched it off again. That *must* be it.' He sipped the remains in his glass. 'Shall I open another bottle?'

'I think we've had enough.'

'I need another drink. Just one glass, OK? We can have the rest tomorrow.'

'Why don't you ask our uninvited guest to open it for us?'

He laughed.

'I'm glad you're finding it funny, because I'm not.'

'There has to be a rational explanation,' he repeated.

'I'm waiting for it.'

He stood up and went over to the fridge, opened the door and removed the bottle of champagne he'd bought to celebrate their moving in, before finding the one the estate agent had left them.

'Telepathy?'

'Telepathy? What do you mean by that?'

He shrugged. 'Maybe we're in a heightened state, you know – moving home. It's a pretty big and traumatic upheaval – probably more than we realize.'

'So, we're picking up each other's thoughts via telepathy? Is that what you're saying?'

'As one explanation.'

'So, let's go with that, for the moment, OK?'

He nodded.

'In which case, what you said about it not being a good idea to invite my parents to anything is not very kind – considering how much they helped us buying our first home, and always willing to help with this. A damned sight more than your parents have ever done.'

He raised his hands. 'You know what I mean.'

'I don't, I don't know what you *mean*. Perhaps you'd like to elaborate?'

He opened the bottle, stood and walked around to refill her glass. 'Darling, I'm sorry, don't let's row on our first day in our new home. We're both tired and I – you know. My parents aren't well off – I'm grateful to your parents, yes, but it just upsets me the way they treat me like I'm a loser. They don't get me.'

'It's not that they don't get you. You know that Dad's a blunt what-you-see-is-what-you-get Northerner. He doesn't get art.'

Jason knew Emily's father had grown up on a council estate with his sick mother – his father had buggered off when he was four. He'd spent his childhood taking care of his mum, worked his way up, from doing a newspaper round to being a building labourer to the success he'd had as a property developer.

'Tell me about it. I'll never forget when I asked him if I could marry you, he looked me in the eye and told me he'd give me his approval the day I stopped pissing about painting pretty pictures and did a proper job, so I could look after his daughter.'

'Well, that's happening, isn't it?' she replied.

'Do you believe it?'

'Totally. I don't just believe it, I *know* it! You are going to be massive, just keep the faith, keep believing in yourself the way I believe in you, my love.'

They stared into each other's eyes.

'Just remember last March eleventh.'

*

It was a date he would never forget for the rest of his life, no matter what happened subsequently. After several years of working in the attic of their tiny house, showing his work in a local gallery in Lewes, and being told that if he wanted to become a serious professional painter, he needed an exhibition, he had found the Northcote in London. The gallery had liked his work and had taken six pieces. They had sold four in the first month and then offered him a one-man show, and set a date of 11 March the following year. But they wanted twenty-two paintings.

For months he had worked furiously, painting landscapes, dogs and his trademark characters drinking in pubs. He financed himself, in between these, with commissions for mostly animal portraits. Four months before the exhibition, he had the twenty-two pieces complete but unframed. But it would need an investment of over four thousand pounds to pay the framer. His only asset was his drum kit – his one recreation away from painting had been as a jazz drummer. Refusing to accept Emily's offer of asking her parents, he had sold it to pay for the frames.

On the night of the show the two of them had travelled to London by train. A bag of nerves, he had dressed smartly in a new velvet jacket, white shirt and chinos, and Emily was in a pretty dark dress. To save money on a taxi, they'd walked to the gallery from Victoria, which had taken far longer than they had thought, through the freezing night air.

Finally, after walking along past closed shop after closed shop, selling furniture, light fittings, and interior décor, they'd seen the brightly illuminated gallery ahead. As they approached, his heart had sunk. There were just about forty people in there, holding glasses of champagne. In all his previous shows in Lewes, the gallery would have been rammed, with a good one hundred guests spilling out into the street. At those they'd invited all their friends, and asked them to bring along their friends, too.

He remembered looking at Emily, flooded with disappointment, and saying, 'Shit. This is embarrassing. This is a fucking disaster. I sold my drum kit for this? Maybe we should turn around and go home.'

'We have to go in,' she had insisted.

Within moments of entering, and being hit by the smell of expensive perfume, a waitress had taken their coats, and another handed them each a glass. As they'd looked around, the gallery owner, Susan Burton, a middle-aged woman who had started the place with her property-developer husband, came over to them. 'Jason, Emily, how wonderful to see you!' she'd given them both air kisses, then announced loudly, 'The artist himself, Jason Danes, is here, with his very charming wife, Emily!'

Almost everyone in the room had turned around.

Jason had wanted to hide.

But Susan had wheeled him, with Emily following in his wake, through the thin crowd to a couple – the handsome man, in his fifties and dressed in a loud chalk-striped suit, with the tan and demeanour of the super-rich, and his wife: a tall, elegant woman with a Chanel bag and classy bling.

'Jason, I'd like you to meet my dear friends, Charles and Clarissa De Montfort-Montefiore. They are dying to meet you and they've just bought one of your paintings – can you tell them about it?'

'Ah,' Jason had said. 'Well – thank you.'

Shit! He'd sold one!

'It is just so *divine*!' the woman had said, in a New York accent. 'Like you see this old man looking at his pint of beer and you just wanna sit down on a bar stool next to him and talk to him. He looks so interesting – like he has really lived life!'

'Well, thank you.'

'How did you ever conjure him up?'

'He's real,' Jason said. 'I was drinking in a pub in Lewes – in Sussex – near where we live, and I thought the same as you. Who are you? What is your story? I actually sneaked a photo of him with my phone.'

'You did? That's awesome.'

He had felt a hand signal from Emily. Shooting a glance at her, not wanting to break eye contact with the one person here who was actually paying money for one of his paintings, he'd turned his attention back to Clarissa De Montfort-Montefiore. 'Well, then I went up to him and just started chatting to him. I've always believed that everyone you ever meet in life has a story. Well, boy, this lovely old guy sure did. He told me he was one of the soldiers who liberated Belsen! He told me there was a senior female SS officer alongside the male Commandant, and just how scared he was of her, even though she was his prisoner. That she was just pure evil personified.'

Emily had given him another hand signal, this one more urgent than the last.

He'd ignored her and continued talking to the couple.

Then Emily had given him yet another signal.

He'd shaken his hand free, but she'd grabbed it again, insistently. She was starting to really piss him off.

'What did he say about Belsen?' Clarissa asked.

'He said that after all this time he could still remember the smell. He said he wakes at least three times a week, in the middle of the night, with the smell in his nostrils.'

At that moment, another couple had come over, friends of Clarissa and her husband, and interrupted them with hugs and greetings.

Emily had seized the opportunity. 'Look!' she'd hissed at Jason and pointed at the walls.

It took him a few seconds to register what she was so excited about. Then his heart had flipped. The red dots. The traditional art gallery marking next to a painting that had been sold.

There were eighteen of them.

Later, back home, Jason and Emily had stayed awake all night, too wired with excitement to sleep. They just kept counting up and then counting up again how much profit they had made.

Almost twenty thousand pounds.

'Shall we have supper about eight?' Emily's voice took him out of his reverie.

'Sure, whenever, are you OK doing it tonight?'

'Yes, it's all prepared, I just have to bung it in the oven.'

Back in the lounge, he picked up his glass before climbing the stairs to the first floor, where he entered the bathroom and washed his hands for several minutes, examining them carefully each time he dried them for anything he might have picked up from the sofa. Then he decided he needed to shower again.

After an unusually short time in the cubicle, he dried and dressed, retrieved his glass and climbed on up and into his studio.

It looked a total mess and he needed to tidy it up, quickly. Against one wall was a battered but comfortable couch, on which were stacked a number of his as-yet-unsold works. Two large packing cases, containing some of his painting materials, stood on the floor. Several tins of white paint from Homebase were lined up on a shelf – the only orderly arrangement so far in the room. In the middle of the floor was his easel – he hadn't yet decided where in the room to place it permanently.

He put his glass down on the trestle table that had long

served him as his work surface, picked up the Stanley knife that was part of his essential toolkit for painting and set to work on the first packing case.

As he did so, he suddenly became aware of a light on in an upstairs room of the house across the road. He looked out and saw a woman in her thirties, with long fair hair, a man of a similar age, with a shaven head and glasses, and two young children – a boy and a girl – all staring across at him.

He gave them a smile and a wave, and mouthed, 'Hi!'

They waved back, all big smiles, just like they had that morning. Nice neighbours!

He turned away and continued to unpack.

10

In the kitchen, Emily shredded a lettuce and dropped it into a glass bowl, diced cucumber and tomatoes and added them, then cut an avocado in half, carefully removed the stone and sliced the flesh into the bowl, adding pine nuts, quinoa and chia seeds, an olive oil dressing, then salt and pepper.

She removed the cover from the pasta bake her mother had made, put it in the preheated oven and called up, loudly, 'Supper will be ready in twenty minutes, darling!'

Next, she pulled a rhubarb crumble out of the fridge, put it in the microwave and closed the door, making a mental note to switch it on a little later, just to reheat it.

To her surprise, the machine suddenly began whirring. She was about to switch it off, when a shadow slid silently across the floor.

'Oh, great, you're down quickly! How hungry are you? I've got some garlic bread in the freezer – I could bung it in the oven if you're—'

She turned around.

There was no one there.

She stared at the doorway to the hall. 'Jason?' Her voice came out small and scared. 'Jason?' Louder. 'Jason?'

She walked over to the hall.

A shadow moved past her.

She spun around.

No one.

She looked at the television. It was off. She turned to the command box. The red off-light was glowing.

She stood still, scared, eyes darting in every direction. Staring out at the darkness beyond the windows. Feeling even more strongly the presence of an unseen person here in the kitchen with her.

Very nervously, looking over her shoulder every few steps, she went over to the cupboard where she'd stored the dinner plates, opened it and lifted out two. Halfway across to the refectory table there was a massive bang, like a gunshot.

Something hot struck her face, hard.

Screaming in shock, she dropped the plates, which shattered on the tiled floor.

Jason came running into the room. 'What—?'

He stopped in his tracks.

His wife was standing in the middle of the kitchen. White stuff in her red hair. Blood pouring down her face. Smoke was belching from the microwave, its door open, swinging, the glass blackened. The walls and ceiling spattered with red splodges.

He ran over to her. 'Em, Em, are you—?'

Then he saw to his relief it wasn't blood, it was rhubarb juice. Her hair was covered in specks of crumble and rhubarb fragments, juice trickling down her cheek. He put his arms around her. 'Jesus, are you OK?'

Sobbing, she said, 'No. NO. I am not OK.'

11

'Maurice, what on earth are you up to, coming in and going out, coming in and going out like this?' Claudette said through a mouthful of Orange Cream, while stroking the cat.

Her husband stood in the doorway in his coat, shaken by the man with the cigar he had just seen outside.

On the television screen, a couple dressed in matching bright-yellow outfits were dancing a tango.

'Are you all right, Maurice?' she said, anxious suddenly. 'You look very pale.'

'I – I – I – I'm fine.'

She shook her head. 'I really think you should go and see Dr Reade. You're behaving very strangely recently, ever since we've moved here. I'm worried you might have had a small stroke, or perhaps you have early-onset dementia.'

'I'm perfectly fine.'

'You need an MRI scan.'

I need a drink, he thought.

'Make an appointment tomorrow morning.'

'I'll do that,' he said and removed his coat, hanging it on a hook in the hall. Then he walked through to the kitchen and headed straight for the drinks cabinet, where he poured himself a large whisky, and knocked it back in one gulp.

As the dancers finished their act, Claudette Penze-Weedell

saw a figure pass by in the hallway again, heading towards the front door.

'Maurice!' she called out sternly. 'Maurice, where are you going now?'

He stood in the kitchen, still very shaken by what he had seen, and heard her voice. He poured himself a second, equally large whisky then walked, ambling at his own pace, back towards the living room.

'Maurice!' she called again.

He entered the room.

'Where did you just go – and why?'

'What do you mean?' he asked.

'I just saw you heading towards the front door.'

'You must have been mistaken, I was in the kitchen.'

She frowned. 'I – I definitely saw you going to the front door.'

'I definitely was not.'

'I saw you!'

'Maybe you're the one who needs to go to the doctor, my love.'

'I'm telling you I saw you! You can't even remember what you did thirty seconds ago. I'm coming with you, you need a check-up.'

He glanced at the screen. 'Who's in the lead?'

'Not the couple I've been rooting for. They've just been eliminated.'

'Ah.'

'*Ah*,' she echoed, with a mimicking tone. 'Is that all you can say?'

'What would you like me to say – or do? Prostrate myself on the floor with grief? Turn up at their funeral carrying the Hanging Gardens of Babylon on my shoulders as a wreath?'

'Don't be so pathetically dramatic.' Turning away from

him, she once again concentrated on the screen. After a short while she glanced back at her husband. 'I'd just like you to show some emotion, some feeling, some interest in what I'm interested in.'

He pointed a finger. 'At all those people prancing around in fancy dress?'

'It's quality dancing – not something you've ever been any good at.'

'No, well, I'm going to a *quality* football match tomorrow. Brighton and Hove Albion against Spurs.'

'What?' she said, crossly. 'Tomorrow is free hot drinks day at Wyevale Garden Centre. With my loyalty card. You know that, you have it in your diary.'

'A free hot drink?'

'Yes!' she said emphatically.

'The petrol to get there probably costs more than the drink's worth.'

'My car is electric, so I don't think so. We need more Christmas decorations, and I've a lot of food still to buy for Christmas dinner – they have a good cheese selection there. We need a Stilton. Stilton and port for your father.'

He did not want to go to any garden centre. Claudette went bonkers in them. Ever since discovering the loyalty cards she seemed to have organized her entire life around their monthly free hot drinks days. But of course, they were never free. On the last one he had attended with her, they had spent over six hundred pounds on plants.

Days before his redundancy.

Now he was conflicted. As a season ticket holder for the Albion – and this might well be the last year for some while that he could afford one – he badly wanted to go. But equally, if Claudette went to claim her free hot drink at the garden centre, God only knew what she might spend. At least if he was with her, he could prevent that. They could perhaps go on Sunday, but that would mean missing his golf.

As he dwelt on the dilemma, a voice inside his head sharply and clearly said, 'Cancel the fat bitch's credit cards and go to the footy! Be a man for once!'

12

In the morning, the kitchen still stank of burned electrics and plastic. Jason, tired after an uneasy night of fitful sleep, sat in silence at the refectory table, reading the microwave instructions while eating his breakfast.

Behind him, Emily, a strip of sticking plaster across the two cuts on her cheek from flying glass, worked on emptying a packing case, thinking. She'd not said anything to Jason about the shadows she'd seen in the room last night, unsure now whether she had really seen them. Sky News was on, the sound low, but neither of them, immersed in their thoughts, looked at the television screen.

'All I did was put the crumble in the oven, in a microwavable glass bowl, with clingfilm – which I'd pierced – covering it,' Emily said.

'The machine's obviously faulty. They'll replace it under warranty, for sure.'

'I'm not sure I want another – at least not from that company. They'll have to do a pretty good job convincing me a replacement won't do the same thing. I'll bring my catering one in from the garage in the meantime.'

'I had a look online,' Jason said. 'I can't find any other instances of something like that happening – other than idiots putting ridiculous things in, deliberately – and that—' He broke off in mid-sentence, distracted. 'Bloody hell!'

'What?'

'I don't believe what I'm seeing!'

'Seeing what?'

Jason pointed out the front window.

Emily looked, not seeing anything. 'What?'

He pointed again. 'Across the road! She looks like she's dressed for a polar expedition!'

Emily peered out and finally saw the woman standing outside her open front door, as a driverless, boxy little purple car reversed out of the double garage and around to the door, stopping in front of her.

'Gosh, that must be one of those self-park cars. How nice, wouldn't mind one of those!' she said.

Moments later a rather meek-looking man in an anorak, carrying a shopping bag, hurried out the front door. He climbed into the passenger seat of the little car as the woman got behind the wheel and they drove off.

'They look fun, our neighbours!' Jason said.

'Fun – not! We must go over later and tell them how much we love their Christmas decorations,' Emily replied, mischievously.

'And perhaps get invited in for a lovely glass of lukewarm Liebfraumilch.'

'You really think they'd be that classy?'

'Now now, don't be a snob, Em. I'm sure they'd be classier than that. Lidl's rosé at least.'

Santa was still rocking away in his grotto, but at least, in the bright morning sunlight, they couldn't see his flashing eyes.

'Oh look!' Emily pulled out a large, embossed album from the packing case. 'Our wedding album! Where shall we put it?'

'Let's see.'

She handed it to him. On the front, against the plain grey background, was a picture of himself and Emily. She was radiant in a cream dress and a sparkly tiara, and he was beaming, in a white shirt, black suit and a buttonhole matching her bouquet of red gerberas. Alongside them were their bridesmaids and his best man.

'Can't believe it was six years ago next July!'

'Me neither!' she kissed him. 'It's not been totally shit, has it?'

Jason screwed up his face. 'Nah, not totally.' He gave her an impish smile. 'There've been some good moments . . .'

'Just a few . . .'

He stood up and embraced her, holding her tight. 'Every second has been amazing. I love you to bits.'

'I love you to bits, too.' She looked into his eyes. 'As soon as we get straight, can we get a puppy?'

He frowned. 'I'd rather a cat, they're cleaner.' He patted her tummy. 'Maybe we'll soon be having some of our own kittens, finally?'

'I'd like three. Ideally, two boys and a girl?'

'Two boys – that's what royalty call *an heir and a spare*.'

'That's horrible!'

'Joke.'

'Not a funny one.' She gently unwound his arms and stepped away. 'So, plan for today?'

'Make love?' he suggested.

'We'll fit that in. First we need to find a garden centre and buy a Christmas tree and then stop by the pub and village store.'

'And then make love?' He put his arms around her.

She shook her head, giving him a quizzical look. 'Why can I never be angry at you for long?'

'Because you fancy me too much.'

She flicked two fingers at him then turned back to the

packing case. As she continued removing stuff, he returned to his breakfast, putting the microwave instructions to one side and flipping through pages of the album as he ate. 'God, it was such an amazing day!'

'It was.'

'Tom and Marianne are coming over some time this afternoon, if that's OK?' he said. 'They're dying to see the place.' Tom Bedford, a fellow painter whose career was really taking off, was his best friend, and Emily got on really well with both him and his wife.

'That's fine. Louise is coming around four to help me get the work kitchen straight, and we have to go through the menu for the anniversary event and make sure we have everything we need for it, this side of Christmas. How's Tom and Marianne's little boy getting on – Kit?'

'Just had his fourth birthday.' Jason finished his porridge and put the bowl in the dishwasher. He went to the window and looked at the little house across the road, where last night he had seen, for the second time, the couple with the young children in the upstairs window. There was no sign of life. And he noticed, for the first time, the blue developers' sign by the front door, with writing so large he could read it from here.

SQUIRREL'S NEST. 34 LAKEVIEW DRIVE.
FOR SALE.

So, who, he wondered, had he seen in the window yesterday? The new potential buyers?

He hoped so. They seemed friendly.

13

Saturday 15 December

Shortly before midday, Maurice Penze-Weedell pushed the fully laden shopping trolley across the busy car park of the garden centre. It had been as costly an experience as he had feared it would be, with Mrs P-W managing to rack up a bill of over three hundred pounds on plants they did not need, cheeses, Christmas tat, new gardening gloves and God knows what else she had bunged in when he hadn't been looking.

Happy wife, happy life, he'd reminded himself.

And at least, he'd consoled himself, they'd had two free hot drinks – a hot chocolate topped with whipped cream for her and a tea for himself. She'd further splurged on a slice of Battenberg cake, which she had enjoyed so much she'd had a second. Now she strode ahead of him, holding out her arm imperiously as they approached her purple car.

'Stop here, Maurice!' she said and pressed the key fob.

As obedient as her husband always was, Claudette's car reversed itself out of the parking space and stopped in front of them. And just at that moment, out of the corner of her eye, Claudette saw a familiar-looking bright pink van approaching. 'Oh my God!' she said.

*

59

'Oh my God!' Emily Danes said, as they drove through the rammed car park of the garden centre, looking for a space. 'Look who's here!'

'It's the Neighbours from Hell!' Jason replied.

She gave his thigh a reproachful slap, hissing, 'Be polite to them!'

'I shall be all sweetness and light,' he answered. 'Here they come, the Addams family, about to meet their neighbours, the Munsters, for the first time. We like neighbours, don't we? We like them fried with a little garlic, and some chilli peppers!'

'Stoppit!'

The older couple were staring at them or, more accurately, gawping.

Emily braked to a halt alongside them and slid down her window. 'Hi!' she said, breezily. 'I think you live across the street from us, in Lakeview Drive?'

The woman gave an awkward smile, and then in a very put-on posh voice said, 'So nice to meet you. Claudette and Maurice Penze-Weedell!' She pointed at her husband, who stood behind her.

'Emily and Jason Danes,' she replied.

'Oh, we know just who you are,' said the woman's husband, stepping forward as if emerging from his own shadow and raising his hat, politely, revealing a shiny head. 'So very nice!'

'You must come and have a drink with us,' Emily said enthusiastically, before her husband could stop her. 'How about this evening?'

'That would be delightful,' said Maurice, his wife nodding and beaming.

'About seven?'

'Perfect!' he replied.

'Doing your Christmas shopping?' Emily continued.

'Oh, you know, a few last-minute additions to the decorations,' Claudette said.

'Such beautiful lights you have outside your house,' Emily said.

'Oh, I am so pleased you like them!' she simpered.

'See you later; seven!' Emily drove into the space their car had vacated, waving gaily.

Jason waved gaily, too. Then, as she slid her window back up, he said, quietly, 'Jesus, what have you lumbered us with tonight?'

'Mr and Mrs *Penze-Weedell*!'

'They look awful.'

Halting the van, Emily turned to him. 'Who was it who said, *Begin each day with a smile and get it over*?'

'W. C. Fields,' he replied.

'You should be on *Mastermind*, my love. You know every damn quote there ever was.'

'"The Bible tells us to love our neighbours and also to love our enemies, because generally they are the same people" – G. K. Chesterton,' he retorted.

'Shut it!'

They got out of the car, smiled at the Penze-Weedells, who were loading the stuff from their trolley into the boot, and walked across to the stack of Christmas trees that flanked the entrance to the main building. They stopped and studied them.

'Anything you see that you fancy?' Emily asked.

'You!'

She kissed him. 'Trees?'

'Something bigger than the – what's their name – Pins-Needles?'

'Penze-Weedell.'

'We need something bigger than theirs.'

'We've been moved in for twenty-four hours and already

we're playing *keeping up with the Joneses*? Come on! We don't even know how big their tree is.'

'Bet you they have one of those fake, shiny ones!'

'Ssshhhh! Keep your voice down, Jason!'

'We could pretend we're Jehovah's Witnesses and don't do Christmas. Or, we could really piss them off and make an even bigger Santa's grotto. How about a ten-foot high, fairy-lit, vibrating dildo for the front garden?'

'You're terrible!'

'They're bound to have a selection in here.'

'Bound to!'

14

Saturday 15 December

'Are you really sure it's going to fit, darling?' Emily asked.

'If it's too tall we'll just have to lop a bit off the top.'

'But the top's pretty – we're so stupid, we should have measured the height of the room.'

There was a howling draught in the van, and the roar of the exhaust and the road, as they drove with the rear doors partially open and held by string, with the end of the Christmas tree poking out. Emily slowed, as the sign to Cold Hill loomed ahead in the bright sunlight.

'I'm starving!' Emily said.

'Me too.'

There was a tantalizing smell of curry from the warm samosas they'd bought in the garden centre for their lunch, along with provisions for the next week, a box of candles and a couple of powerful torches just in case of power cuts. Jason picked up the carrier bag at his feet. 'Want a bite?'

'No, let's wait, we'll be home in five minutes and we've got some nice salads to go with them.'

'I was about to say we could bung the samosas in the microwave!'

'Not funny. Shit, that voice last night,' Emily said. 'I can't get it out of my head. I'm still really freaked by it. Then the microwave exploding.'

'There has to be a rational explanation.'

'Great, I'm still waiting for it. Do you have one?'

'Hopefully the manufacturers will. I've never been totally comfortable with them – microwaves. I googled microwaves last night. They can explode if the wrong things are put in them.'

'Like my rhubarb crumble?' she said. 'What kind of *wrong thing* is that?'

'I don't know – maybe you can't put crumble in a microwave.'

'Don't be ridiculous, of course you can! It's fine to warm it up as I was doing.'

She turned left off the main road onto a winding, narrow lane. They passed a sign saying Cold Hill – Please Drive Slowly Through Our Village, with 30 mph warning roundels, then swooped over a humpback bridge, the tree scraping alarmingly along the van floor.

'Hey, slow down!' Jason said, reaching an arm through the gap between the seats and grabbing the base of the tree.

'Sorry!'

There was a cricket pitch with a small pavilion to their left and a short distance on, a decrepit-looking Norman church on their right. It was set well back and perched high above the road.

They passed through a corridor of terraced Victorian artisan cottages on both sides of the lane, a pretty-looking pub called the Crown, a smithy, a cute cottage with a white picket fence at the end of its immaculate garden and a sign reading Bed & Breakfast – Vacancies, and a shop: Cold Hill Village Store. The lane then went steeply uphill, past detached houses and bungalows of varying sizes on either side.

A tractor came thundering down towards them, a grizzled old man in the cab with a look of grim determination on his face, and making no sign of slowing down. Emily pulled the van hard over to the left, onto the verge, the wing mirror scraping along the hedgerow. 'Thanks a million, mate!' she called out.

'Bloody lunatic!' Jason said.

She carried on a short distance up the hill. A red postbox, partially buried in a hedge, came up on their left, and a high, weathered stone wall on their right. She braked, indicating as they approached the entrance to the new estate, which was marked by two stone pillars topped with savage-looking ornamental wyverns, and open wrought-iron gates. Affixed to the wall to their right was huge blue board, reading:

FOREST MILLS DEVELOPMENTS

COLD HILL PARK, 2, 3, 4 & 5 BEDROOM HOUSES AND APARTMENTS.

SALES AND MARKETING OPEN 7 DAYS, 9 A.M.–5 P.M.

*CONTACT RICHWARDS ESTATE AGENTS.
PHASE 1 COMPLETING SHORTLY.*

They drove in, and ahead was a sapling-lined traffic island with a KEEP LEFT sign, dividing the incoming traffic from the exiting via a short dual carriageway, and which ended fifty yards on in a plethora of road signs: PARKVIEW WAY; COLD HILL CLOSE; THE AVENUE. Lakeview Drive was the first left.

The brand-new road, with brick pavements and Victorian-style street lights, curved to the left past several partially completed detached houses with steel Heras fencing securing them, and no sign of anyone working on them. As the road curved right, the houses were finished, each with sale boards and details fixed close to their front doors.

'Sort of weird being almost the first here,' Emily said.

'I rather like it,' Jason replied. 'Very atmospheric. I'm looking at all these houses, wondering what kind of lives the people who buy them will have.' He changed into a strange, Mitteleuropean accent. 'Zer might be veirdos; swingers; serial killers; it might be so dangerous to go out we vill have to lock all ze doors and stay inside vor effer!'

'Yep, and they'll be pointing at our house and saying, "Zat ist vere zer real veirdos lif!"'

He shook his head. 'Not after they see our neighbours' Christmas decorations, they won't. Then they'll know vere zer true veirdos lif.'

15

'They're coming!' Jason said, standing out of sight, peering through the window. 'And, oh shit, they're bringing us a present – we don't have anything for them.'

'We can get them something, darling – it's still a week to Christmas.'

'Perhaps a nice garden gnome.'

'Lovely. Then we'd have to look at the sodding thing all year round.'

'Yep, bad idea, strike that one.'

In between visitors, they had spent most of the afternoon decorating the tree they'd bought, and getting it to stand straight, as well as putting out their cards – most of which had arrived with postal redirects on the envelopes – and generally making the living room look Christmassy.

The packing cases had gone, and the room looked tidier, the white sofas now with magenta cushions. They had set bowls of olives, nuts, vegetable crisps and mince pies they'd bought in the garden centre on the glass-topped teak coffee table, and placed bowls of Christmas-spiced pot pourri around the room. Flames were dancing in the grate. The room did actually feel really Christmassy, Jason thought.

They stood together at the front door.

'Hello!' said Claudette Penze-Weedell, looking, as before, like she was on the first leg of an expedition to the Arctic.

'Happy Christmas!' her husband said, making it sound like an apology, thrusting a wrapped bottle at Jason, while his wife handed a pot plant in wrapping paper to Emily.

A few minutes later, with their neighbours seated on one sofa and Emily on the other, Jason came in with a bottle of Pol Roger. 'Champagne?' he asked.

'Well, if you have any prosecco that would be lovely,' Claudette said. 'I do find it has so much more flavour than champagne.'

'Champagne would be lovely,' her husband said, giving his wife a stern frown. Then he smiled at his hosts. 'As I don't have to drive, ha ha, that would be very nice.'

'Oh, of course, champagne, how lovely. It does give me indigestion, but very nice, thank you,' his wife said.

Avoiding catching Emily's eye, Jason carefully popped the cork, filled all their glasses, then sat down next to his wife and said, 'Cheers!'

They all clinked glasses.

'Cheers!'

It was followed by an awkward moment of silence, broken only by the sound of Maurice Penze-Weedell munching on a beetroot crisp.

'Such lovely decorations you have outside your house,' Emily said, struggling to start a conversation.

'Why, thank you,' Claudette said in her exaggerated accent. She was wearing a dress sparkling with sequins.

'What a beautiful dress!' Emily said.

'Cost a bloody fortune,' her husband, in a dark suit and tie, grumbled.

'Maurice!' she chided, then looked at the tree. 'How nice to see a *real* tree – it smells so – so—'

'Christmassy,' her husband helped her out.

'Exactly!'

There was another awkward moment of silence.

'You see,' Claudette went on, 'Maurice is an accountant, so we have an artificial tree.'

'Ah, I see,' said Jason, not seeing at all and trying to ignore the nudge under the table from Emily's foot.

'Well, much more practical,' Emily said. 'They don't shed their needles.'

'And it means you don't have to buy a new one each year,' Maurice added, smugly. 'Christmas is quite expensive enough as it is.'

'Oh yes, absolutely.' Emily turned to her husband. 'Maybe something we should consider for the future.'

'Oh, absolutely,' Jason replied. 'Definitely something we should explore.'

'I must say, it's nice to have some neighbours,' Maurice said. 'Been a bit lonely these past weeks.'

Claudette leaned forward and took an olive. After chewing it, she removed the stone from her mouth then held it, expectantly, wondering where to put it.

Emily rushed to the kitchen to find a receptacle. Maurice took another crisp. Jason asked, 'So, are you a Chartered Accountant?'

'I'm a corporate one.'

'Ah, right,' he replied.

Emily dashed back in and placed an empty bowl on the table. Placing her olive stone in it as precisely as if she were moving a chess piece, Claudette said, 'Maurice has been the Chief Operating Officer of a very large insurance company – very large indeed.'

As she spoke, she glimpsed a woman out in the hall walk past the doorway.

'Ah,' Jason said again. 'Insurance.' He wondered how long he could endure these people before he could escape upstairs and get on with painting. Although he hadn't unpacked everything, he had now set up his easel and work materials.

'Do you have children?' Claudette asked.

'No,' Emily said. 'Not yet.'

'Ah. Someone staying here?'

Emily smiled. 'No, just us.'

'You don't have a relative staying – an elderly relative?' Maurice asked.

Emily looked at him oddly. 'No, no we don't, we haven't really had many visitors yet.'

'Today is pretty much the first batch,' Jason said.

Maurice frowned then peered at the coffee table. 'Is that your wedding album?' he asked, leaning forward and peering at it more closely.

'It is, yes.'

Maurice put a handful of crisps into his mouth, picked it up and began thumbing through it. Looking for the woman whose face had been at the window. 'Five years you've been married?'

Annoyed at the idea of these people thumbing through their precious album with greasy fingers, Jason dashed to the kitchen.

'Six in July,' Emily replied.

Jason came back in and placed a paper serviette in front of each of the Penze-Weedells.

'Claudette and I, we've been married for *thirty* years – I'd have got less for murder!' he said, bringing out the old joke again and glancing at his wife. She was not with them. She was staring at something across the room – very rude of her, he thought.

'Thirty years? Wow!' Jason said. 'So, what made you move here?'

'Well, we lived in Brighton for many years,' he replied. 'Very convenient for the kids. But once the last one left home we thought it would be nice to move out to the countryside. I guess that makes us UFBs.'

Jason frowned. 'UFBs?'

'*Up From Brightons!*' Maurice replied.

Claudette shovelled a handful of nuts and crisps into her mouth all at the same time. As she spoke she spattered fragments of each as if her mouth was a shotgun. 'Maurice and I are so happy you've moved in. I told him the moment I saw you, *here come PLOs!*'

'PLOs?' Emily queried, while Jason topped up their glasses, finishing the bottle and hoping not to have to open the second one of the three that he had been keeping for Christmas Day.

'People Like One,' Claudette replied. 'Can you imagine how frightful it would be, on a closed environment like Cold Hill Park, to have difficult neighbours?'

'I can't imagine,' Emily replied.

Jason nodded in agreement.

Maurice nodded, thoughtfully.

There was a stilted silence, relieved only by the sound of crunching from Claudette's mouth.

'So,' Jason said, 'how long have you both been in Sussex?'

'All our lives,' Claudette replied. 'Both of us. Wouldn't live anywhere else.'

'I'm with you on that,' Emily said.

There was another long silence. Mrs Penze-Weedell ate more crisps, nuts and olives. Jason wondered again how long this ordeal was going to last.

'Happy Christmas, everyone!' Emily said, raising her glass.

They all clinked. Then fell back into the same awkward silence.

Emily broke it, addressing Maurice Penze-Weedell. 'So how are you guys spending Christmas?'

His wife answered for him. 'We have our whole family with us this year. Fortunately, our house is very large. We like a family Christmas.'

'Lovely,' Emily said.

'How nice,' Jason added, and noticed, to his dismay, their glasses were already empty again. He opened a second bottle. And half an hour later, having finished the remainder of the bottle from last night as well, found himself having to open a third.

'Have you met anyone else from Cold Hill Park yet?' he asked them.

'No, we haven't. I don't think there's anyone else moved in yet.'

'What about the house next door to you? The one opposite us – number thirty-four?'

'That rather ghastly little house?' Claudette said. 'Mr P-W and I call it the Noddy House.'

'Yes, that one.'

'There's nobody there,' she said. 'I can't imagine who would want to buy it.'

'I've seen a family there,' Jason said.

'Probably viewing,' Maurice said. 'I must say it will be a lot jollier when the estate's fully occupied.'

'Well, all I can say is that whoever has bought it can have absolutely no taste whatsoever,' Claudette declared.

It was nearly two hours later before the Penze-Weedells, having requested and been given a full tour of the house, put on their coats, making all kinds of appreciative comments and issuing invitations for Christmas morning drinks, New Year's Day drinks and an insistence Emily and Jason come to dinner early in the New Year.

As they watched the tipsy couple make their way across the road, Jason turned, quizzically, to his wife.

She closed the front door. 'Jesus! I didn't think they were *ever* going to leave.'

'But, darling, they are *People Like One.*'

'Yeah, right. If I'm ever like either of them, take me out and shoot me.'

'It'll be too late – I'll already have committed hara-kiri.'

'They are just awful. I don't ever want to endure another evening like that!'

'Me neither; at least we can have some peace and quiet for a few hours.'

As he said it, there was a loud bang upstairs.

16

Jason and Emily spun around.

'What was that?' she asked.

He ran out and up the stairs to the first floor and switched on the landing lights. The doors to their bedroom, and all three of the spare rooms, were ajar. He frowned and checked each of the rooms, but could see nothing amiss.

As he went back down, Emily was carrying glasses through to the kitchen. He followed her in and saw to his surprise that the green light was glowing on the command box, and the television was on: an advert showing a car racing up a twisting road.

'I couldn't see anything. Maybe it was a bird striking a window. Or something on the television.'

She looked at the command box. 'I thought we'd left that thing switched off?'

'I'm sure we did.' Testing it, he said, 'Command, dim kitchen lights.'

Instantly, they faded.

Testing it further, he said, 'Command, switch on induction hob ring four.'

He heard a faint whirr from the electric hob.

'Command, switch off induction hob. Brighten lights.'

The whirring sound ceased, and the lights brightened.

'And turn our neighbours across the road into frogs,' he muttered under his breath.

Emily laughed. Then, more seriously, she asked, 'Do we need it? Can't we just throw the bloody thing away?'

'I think it's just a question of getting it sorted, Em. It could be really useful – I'll read through the instructions tomorrow and see what's what.'

She nodded reluctantly, then pointed at the empty bowls. 'That woman is like a sodding hoover. She shouldn't be called Claudette; she should be called *Dyson*. I lost count of the number of times I refilled the olives, nuts and crisps.'

'Three bottles, can you believe it? Our best champagne. Actually, more; almost four.'

'Take the positive, my love,' she said. 'Look on it as an investment.'

'Investment?'

'Uh-huh.'

'In exactly what?'

'Neighbourhood relations. OK – they are awful people. But until more people move into the estate, we need, at least, to get on with them.'

'Why?'

'Come on, darling! How much have you drunk?'

'Not enough. Shall I open another bottle?'

'No!' she said. 'We've a lot to do tomorrow, I've had quite enough. We need some food.'

There was another massive bang above them, like a door slamming in wind.

Emily looked at her husband in alarm.

'The wind?' he suggested.

'There is no wind,' she said in an edgy voice.

He walked to the stairs then hurried up them again.

'Darling,' she called out. 'Be careful!'

He reached the landing at the top of the staircase, checking out their bedroom then each of the three spare rooms again, in turn. All the doors were still open. He climbed the spiral staircase to the loft.

The door there was open, too.

Had it been fireworks somewhere nearby? Had they imagined it?

But they had both heard it. Very distinctly. The sound of a door slamming.

He went back down into the living room. Emily was looking shaken.

What? she mouthed.

He shook his head. 'Couldn't see anything. Maybe we imagined it.'

'We did not imagine it. We both heard it. A door slammed.'

'OK, so – this is a new-build house. They've used a lot of oak. A lot of woods expand and contract as the temperature and humidity change. Maybe they didn't age the oak enough and that noise was made by some of it expanding.'

'And if it wasn't that?'

'Could be our ghost!' he said, jokily.

'That's not funny,' she said. 'We heard a door slam.'

'Hey, darling, come on, lighten up.' He kissed her.

'There's something weird going on,' she said, flatly. 'It's starting to freak me out. I don't know what it is but I'm feeling it.'

'I'm feeling the love of the Penze-Weedells,' he retorted.

'Be serious, Jace. It was the sound of a door slamming. Doors don't slam by themselves, unless there's a wind blowing.' She opened a window. 'Stick your head out – there is no wind.'

'Maybe it was fireworks?'

'Our neighbours said there's no one else living here.'

'They're wrong. There are people across the road. Probably

other people here too that they've not met yet.' He grimaced.
'I mean, who in their right mind would want to meet them?'

'Yep, maybe all the other neighbours here are hiding from
them, and us mugginses got caught.'

'That's because we are PLOs!'

She punched him, playfully, looking brighter.

17

'What cheapskates, not giving us prosecco,' Claudette Penze-Weedell said, back in their house and removing her hat and coat. 'Honestly!' She was slurring her words.

'My love,' Maurice replied, hanging his coat on the hook next to hers. 'That was Pol Roger, a very classy champagne – it was Winston Churchill's favourite, I read somewhere. Personally, I thought it was absolutely the badger.'

'Hmmmph,' she grunted, heading for the kitchen. 'More like the mole's urine if you ask me. I'm ravenous. How rude they didn't give us anything proper to eat – they could have had some decent canapés at least. Nuts, crisps, sausage rolls and mince pies, all shop-bought – and she a professional caterer – you'd have thought they'd have made more of an effort, wouldn't you?'

'Give them a chance, they've only just moved in – I thought they were very kind inviting us at all, on their first full day in their home.'

'That's your problem,' she said, opening up the freezer and searching through the contents. 'You always let people walk over you. That's why they're all lah-di-dah, lording it over the estate in the grand house while we're here in our little serf's cottage – when we could have been there.'

'I think you've had a bit too much to drink, dear,' he said, from the hall. 'This is hardly a serf's cottage – we paid seven hundred and fifty thousand for this house, I'd like to remind you.'

'And now I'm going to have a proper drink,' she said defiantly. She lifted up a frozen Tesco Finest fish pie. 'Would you like that?'

'With peas.'

'You always want peas.'

'I like peas.'

'They are so common.' She pulled out a second item. 'We'll have green beans.'

'Very good, my dear.'

'I can't believe the size of their house. How much bigger than ours is it?'

'Quite a lot bigger.'

Angrily, she removed the packaging, pierced the lid of the fish pie and placed it inside the microwave. 'Command, microwave on, please. Full power, twelve minutes!'

The cooker whirred into life.

She removed a bottle of prosecco from the wine fridge, opened it and poured herself a large glass and carried it through, unsteadily, to join her husband. 'I just do not understand. Why did they not make that house the show house? I thought a show house would surely be the best property on the development?'

'I thought we liked this house very much, my dear,' he said as the television came to life.

'I did,' she said. 'Until tonight.' She swayed a little, then hiccupped. 'But we don't look out onto the lake.'

'I do believe we looked at the property on the plans and it was quite a bit above our budget.'

'Hmmmph.' She sipped her drink. 'Now, this is what I call *nice*. That Winston Churchill always had a cigar in his mouth.

Probably numbed his taste buds – that was why he liked that muck they served us tonight.'

'I thought it was very nice – and extremely generous of them,' Maurice said.

'There's another thing. Didn't they clearly say there was no one else in the house, Maurice?'

'Yes, I think they did.'

'Well, I saw someone – a woman walked across the hall.'

Maurice didn't mention the woman's face he had previously seen at the window.

18

Jason Danes stood in the kitchen, staring down at the command device. He was aware he had drunk far more than normal – was that it? Was he off his face? He had switched the thing off, but it was very definitely back on. This time he pulled the power cable out, placed it on the table and weighted it down with a cook book.

As he walked back out, he bumped into the island unit, then almost knocked over a chair.

Shit. I'm pissed.

He collided with the door frame as he re-entered the living room. Emily was carefully wiping their precious wedding album.

'God, what dreadful people, putting their sticky paws all over this. Did you notice they totally ignored the napkins you gave them?'

'It made me angry – but I couldn't say anything. Did I drink a lot tonight?'

She stared at him. 'Like, yes! You were knocking it back. We all were.'

'I feel a bit smashed.'

'You look it; you're stumbling.'

He glanced at his watch. 'Nine o'clock. We've done over three bottles of champagne and all I've eaten is a couple of peanuts.'

'We've got one of those pies we bought at the garden centre. Fancy that with some baked beans?'

'I fancy you.'

'Ha ha,' she replied, but a little flatly. 'So, what's going on with our wonderfully teched-up home?'

He shrugged. 'Do you want a top-up?'

'No!'

'Probably a good idea. I don't know – I thought I'd switched that command thing off. I know I did. How did it switch itself back on?'

She was looking at him strangely.

'What?'

She shook her head. 'I don't know. Something doesn't feel right.'

'In what way?'

She stared down at the table, looking pensive. 'It doesn't matter.'

'What, darling? In what way?' He went over to her, stood behind her and nuzzled her neck. 'Tell me? What doesn't feel right?'

She shrugged. 'I'm probably just being hypersensitive. They say moving is very stressful – that's probably all it is.'

'I'm sure you're right.' He removed his arms and picked up a glass that still had some champagne in it and drained it.

'Let me ask you something – do you think ghosts exist?' she asked.

'Ghosts?'

'You said something about them, earlier.'

'I was joking.'

'But do you? Do you think they exist?'

'Why are you asking?'

She shrugged. 'I don't know. I just . . .' She fell silent.

'Just what?' he prodded.

'You're an artist, you're a very sensitive person, and you are open-minded.'

'You think we have a ghost here? One that switches back on that box and slams doors?'

'My pissed husband might have thought he'd switched it off and hadn't. But he was downstairs, here with me, when that door slammed.'

'Darling, ghosts inhabit ancient houses. This is a new-build, brand-new. No one's lived here before.'

'It's on an historic site. We don't know what went on before, in the old mansion that was here.'

'Hey, we heard a sound like a door slamming upstairs – but all the doors are open. As I said, it's probably the wood moving, that's all.'

'It's not all.'

He looked hard at her. 'What do you mean?'

She shook her head.

'Tell me – what do you mean, *it's not all*?

She shook her head again. 'Nothing.'

He continued looking at her. Her face was pale, or was he imagining it? 'What do you mean, *nothing*?'

'Forget I said it.'

'Something's bothering you. Come on, share it with me.'

'I'll go and sort the food out,' she said. 'What time did we book the pub for tomorrow in the end?'

'One thirty, and they said they need it back at three, because they're so busy in the run-up to Christmas.'

'That's fine, great.'

She headed through to the kitchen. He followed her, relieved to see the home command box was still unplugged, as he had left it. 'Come on, we always promised each other no secrets. What is it?'

'Honestly, nothing. Forget I ever said it.' She smiled. 'OK?'

'OK,' he said hesitantly.

They kissed.

'I was planning to work tonight but I don't think I can,' he said.

'I was going to get on with unpacking and I don't think I can, either.'

'Let's have supper in front of the telly. There's a couple of Netflix things I really want to see.'

'Good plan,' she said. 'If I can stay awake.'

'Everything's going to be fine. I love this house. I can work here, I know I can.'

She smiled. 'I love it too. It is – it's going to be great for us both.'

'What was it *Penis-Weewee* said tonight? *Happy wife, happy life*?'

Emily laughed. 'Don't you ever dare say that to me!'

He raised his arms. 'Would I ever need to?'

Playfully, she raised her right hand, curled her fingers and gave him the bird.

19

Sunday 16 December

Sleep was one of the few things on which Jason and Emily disagreed strongly. She needed a full eight hours and preferably nine; he resented sleeping more than six. Resented, as he called it, *sleeping his life away*.

Shortly after 7 a.m., having woken once during the night with a headache and taken two paracetamols, he slipped out of bed feeling very hungover. He dressed in his warm winter cycling gear, which he'd unpacked late last night, went down to the kitchen and plugged the command box back in. Then he went through the integral door to the garage, checked the tyres on his road bike, secured his helmet, gave the command for the door to open and wheeled the bike out on to the silent street, commanding the door to shut behind him.

He was delighted to see the Sunday papers, wrapped in plastic, lying on the doorstep. The village store certainly was efficient, he thought. He would bring them inside when he returned; Emily was unlikely to get up before then.

Five days shy of the shortest day, there was very little light. It was a mild morning with a faint drizzle. Although there were no vehicles around, as a precaution he switched on his bike lamps and his head torch, before mounting and heading off, clicking into the pedals.

Shooting a glance at the house opposite, where there were

no signs of life, he passed the infernal Santa's grotto, which had been left on all night, and pedalled along the silent street, passing empty houses with their sale boards on both sides until, after a short distance, the road ended in metal fencing and trespasser warning signs. He turned around, cycled back past the Penze-Weedells, the *Noddy* house next door where he had seen the couple with their children, which looked dark and empty, then around the curves of the long close, passing the as-yet-unfinished and fenced-off shells of houses.

It was rapidly getting lighter. As he reached the end of the estate, he turned right onto the lane, and rode hard up the steep hill, changing down to the lowest gear, standing up for the leverage to keep going, breathing in the heady scents of the wintry country air. After some minutes of hard slog, determined not to give up and walk, he finally crested the hill, and an awesome view of Sussex countryside greeted him, as some kind of reward for his effort. Fields of farmland. Random houses and farm buildings. He could just make out the county town of Lewes in the far distance, in the breaking light. He freewheeled joyfully and at breakneck speed down the far side, passing a field full of alpacas, and nearly lost it on a sharp right-hander.

The exercise and the rush of cold air exhilarated him, and his hangover was going. He felt happier than he could ever remember. A townie all his life until now, he had always hankered to live in the country. Their new home, Lake House, seemed like a fulfilment of his dream. He could paint there for sure. Right now, his mind was like the lake he could see from his studio window – teeming with inspiration. At first the idea of living on an estate had bothered him, but now he realized, and especially after meeting the Penze-Weedells, that on his doorstep would be an endless supply of characters to surreptitiously photograph and use in his work.

He wound on along a country lane, and through a small,

sleepy hamlet, then after another quarter of an hour, he checked his Garmin. Seven miles. Coming up to 8 a.m. Time to head back.

Time to get to work and start painting. A million ideas were jostling for priority inside his head.

Never before, in all his life, had he felt so creative. He would deliver to Susan Burton at the Northcote Gallery, for his one-man exhibition on 8 February, twenty-two paintings that would knock her socks off.

He pedalled like fury, a man on a mission, towards home.

20

There had been a time when Jason would spend an hour and sometimes longer in the shower, washing his hair, soaping himself and scrubbing every inch of his skin, before rinsing off and repeating the procedure over and over. Once, at the height of his OCD, he had spent an entire morning – four hours – in the shower. That was the trigger moment when Emily had insisted on him seeking help.

Their GP had referred him to a clinical psychologist, Dr Dixon, who worked with him on his obsessive rituals, and had connected his behaviour to his very deep fear, as he neared forty, of never succeeding as an artist. The real signs of change in his behaviour had come after his successful one-man show at the Northcote Gallery. Now he was down to an average of only ten minutes in the shower, and on some days even less than that.

While Emily slept on, he set a personal best of just two minutes, dressed and hastily ate a breakfast of porridge, and downed a double espresso while glancing through some of the Sunday papers. When he had finished, he hurried into the hall, pausing to scoop up the *Cold Hill Village Parish Magazine*, which had landed on the doormat, and put it on the hall table before climbing the two flights to his studio, as he now called the loft.

Entering the room, he closed the door behind him. On his left, stacked against the couch, were the paintings and pencil and charcoal drawings he had unpacked from his discarded collection. Much to Emily's dismay, he had a habit of removing from view any pictures he had not sold after six months on display in either the local gallery, the Bluefern, which took his pictures, or the Northcote in London.

As was his ritual before starting to work, he first opened his laptop and scanned down his emails – always looking with an especially keen eye for enquiries about commissions, either from existing clients or from potential new ones. He would follow that by reading through new messages on Facebook and Twitter and checking the number of followers, before lastly checking Instagram on his phone. His most recent post, a painting he was very pleased with, depicting a local landscape looking fiery in a red sunset, had 210 likes when he had last checked – his record so far – and he hoped there had been more likes for it overnight.

But instead of the laptop screen coming to life in its usual way, with a request for his password, it remained dark all over except for a single row of numbers, in white, which appeared in the centre.

Before he could even read them they disappeared and were replaced an instant later by the familiar password request.

He frowned, wondering what on earth the numbers meant. On Friday, both he and Emily had experienced problems connecting their computers to the new router in the house, and their Mac guru, Matt, had talked them through it over the phone. Since then, there had been further glitches with the high-speed fibre on the estate, and it had taken several more calls with their techie before everything was working. 'It's a Mac thing, they don't always like new routers until they get used to them,' the techie had said, as if he was talking about a family pet.

He entered his password and his blue desktop screen, littered with his familiar icons, appeared.

Five minutes later, having checked everything, he walked over to the window and peered out at the Sunday-silent building site, which started just a hundred yards or so away. Phase two, the agent had called it. It was an ocean of mud, trenches, holes, metal fences, wheelbarrows, bendy poles and warning signs. On one side were two Portakabins, and there were several diggers and bulldozers seemingly parked randomly, some yellow, some orange. He saw a pile of rubble, another of bricks under blue sheeting, and a vast stack of steel beams.

He must take some photos for future reference, he thought, so that they could remember what it was like when they first moved in. Also, perhaps tomorrow he'd take some pictures of the workers. He had in his mind some Lowry-inspired images of the men in their hard hats in this vast wasteland. He might make a group of paintings for his exhibition – they would be something different, he thought, inspired.

He turned away and looked towards the lake at the end of the lawn, studying the ducks. There was a group of a dozen or so mallards, and another similar-sized group of Indian runners, each sticking to their own tribe. The two groups were some distance apart, moving around the water, staying close to the island in the centre on which there was a large, bare weeping willow.

When the Bedfords had popped over yesterday afternoon, Tom's wife, Marianne, had said the way to make sure the ducks all stayed was to feed them daily. She recommended buying something like an old milk churn to keep the feed in, to avoid attracting rats.

One mallard suddenly rushed across the water, almost standing up on it, and jumped on the back of another. Doubtless a female, he thought. The female flew off a short distance, landing with a splash. The male hurried after her, caught up and pounced, landing more firmly on her back this time, and pushing her head under water as he shook vigorously.

Jason smiled at the antics; male mallards clearly weren't much into foreplay. And within moments it was over. The female scurried off, shaking herself, and the male, looking like a braggart, returned to his group.

He'd never painted ducks before, but entranced by the view and their behaviour, he decided to go down there later today and do some rough sketches and take some photos. Meanwhile, he had the two urgent last-minute commissions to get on with. One was a portrait of two dogs, a grey labradoodle and a golden one, for a client who wanted it as a surprise Christmas present for his wife, and the other was a pencil sketch of a King Charles spaniel. He had photographs of all of them to work from – the one of the two labradoodles showing them looking cute as hell curled up on a sofa together.

This was just the kind of painting he loved doing. It would be fun, and if he worked hard today and into the night, and all tomorrow, using the quick-drying oils he favoured, with luck he should have it ready to take to the framer tomorrow, and ready for his client, as he had promised, by Thursday.

Some artists who worked in oils used canvas, others painted straight onto hardboard, but a few, like himself, liked to paint on gesso. This was a compound made for him by David Graham, his framer, comprising white glue, calcium carbonate and zinc with white pigment, heated then applied to hardboard; it was a modern version of the moist lime plaster, fresco, that many of the great Italian Renaissance painters, including Michelangelo, used for their murals. Jason liked to work with it because, in addition to brushes, he used a scalpel to get certain effects, one of which was animal hairs, which he achieved by scraping away the paint, very finely, down to the base.

He selected a board from the three different-sized ones stacked against a wall, checked it for imperfections – rare, as David Graham was a total perfectionist, to the point of being a pain in the arse at times – and lovingly placed it on the easel. Beneath it, he pinned the photograph of the dogs and his composition sketches. He worked in three sizes, with prices accordingly. This commission was for a medium-size: 40 x 40 cm.

Walking back over to his laptop, he opened iTunes and went to his playlists, feeling in a London Grammar mood today, and clicked on one of their albums.

As the lead began singing deeply and softly in the background, he tied on his black, paint-spattered apron, pulled a fresh pair of surgical gloves out of the box, and snapped them on.

Next, he went over to his trestle table, on which he had laid out everything he needed – the sheets of paper for mixing his paints, the jar of white spirit in which he kept his brushes, the scalpel and spare blades, the tubes of Winsor & Newton paints, and his pencils and charcoal for sketching.

He selected a pencil then stood in front of the blank gesso board, focusing, getting himself into the zone. Behind him, he heard the sound of the door opening, then felt Emily's presence, coming up behind him. He felt a flash of irritation. She knew how much he needed solitude to work and never interrupted him, unless it was an absolute emergency. And she was well aware how tight he was on time, and just how important this commission was – his client was the CEO of a digital advertising company and had talked about commissioning him to do paintings for the lobby of their London Docklands office. He absolutely had to deliver a good piece, and on time.

For some moments he ignored her, leaning forward and making the first mark on the board, outlining where he felt the sofa should be positioned.

But she was distracting him too much.
He turned around, irritated. 'What, darling?'
It wasn't Emily.

21

Sunday 16 December

It was a woman in her thirties, with short dark hair, smartly dressed in a black suit with a white blouse. She stood there for a fleeting instant with a strange smile on her face.

Then she vanished.

Goosepimples rippled down his skin.

He stared at the door, which he had distinctly heard open. But it was closed.

She had looked so . . . so real. So damned real. He strode over to the door and yanked it open. There was no one outside. 'Emily!' he shouted. 'Emily!'

'Yes, what is it? I'm in the kitchen.'

The image of the woman he had just seen burned strongly in his mind, like a photograph.

So damned clear.

He must have imagined her. But why? From where? From somewhere in his past?

He went down. Emily was at the sink with rubber gloves on, washing the cups and glasses she was unpacking. He stopped and stared at her.

'You OK?' she asked.

He nodded, uncertainly.

'Are you sure? You look very pale.'

He nodded.

'Have you eaten?'

He said nothing, still staring at her.

'What is it?' she asked.

He continued staring at her.

'Hello!' she said. 'Hello!'

He walked over and kissed her. 'Had a good lie-in?'

'I did, I needed it – I'm feeling seriously hungover. Did you go for your bike ride?'

'Fifteen miles,' he said proudly. 'It's just stunning country-side all around here.'

'Wish I'd come with you.'

'Didn't want to disturb you. You were lying, paws up, snoring like a warthog.'

'Thanks!' she said.

He grinned. 'Did you just come into my studio, a few minutes ago?'

'No – I'm trying to get everything unpacked for the catering kitchen. Why?'

'It's OK, don't worry about it.' He turned to go back up.

'What do you mean, did I just come into your studio?'

'Nothing. It's OK. What time shall we leave for the pub?' he said.

'Are we walking or driving? We could walk, then we could have a drink – and it's a glorious day.'

'I'm not going to drink – I've got to work this afternoon – but let's walk anyway. It'll take about twenty minutes.'

'Perfect. Are you really feeling OK? You don't look right.' She peered at him closely. 'Why did you ask if I came into your studio?'

He shook his head. 'Doesn't matter.'

'Are you sure you're OK?'

'Absolutely. Just a bit hungover, too, that's all. Actually, maybe a small hair of the dog in the pub will do me good.'

He made himself another double espresso from the machine and carried the cup upstairs. As he reached the door to his studio he hesitated, feeling a sudden cold draught, and with it a frisson of fear, then pushed it open.

The room was silent. Low winter sunlight streamed in through the windows. He breathed in the smell of white spirit and oil paints, the smells he had always loved. All the same, as he entered, he looked around – for the woman in the smart suit with the curious smile.

The triple-glazed room felt cold, as if the heating had gone off. He went over to the thermostat and checked it. Twenty-two degrees – it should be plenty warm enough in here. He went down to their bedroom, put on an extra sweater and returned to his studio.

The woman was still ingrained vividly in his mind.

Who was she?

Why had he imagined her?

Jan Dixon, his clinical psychologist, warned him that moving home could be a very stressful experience for people, and he might find his emotions seesawing for some while. Perhaps that included hallucinations?

Parking it, now he had a possible explanation, but still unsettled by the woman, he sipped his coffee then focused on his work in progress, and within moments had put her completely out of his mind.

22

Sunday 16 December

The Crown was an attractive Georgian building, let down by a rather shabby modern extension with a corrugated iron roof. The pub was set well back from the road, with a scrubby, uneven lawn in front of it, on which were randomly arranged wooden tables and benches. Two of them were occupied by smokers, nursing pints and well wrapped up.

Although it was still sunny, a biting wind was rising as Jason and Emily walked up the path to the entrance. They both wore woolly hats, and the brand-new waxed Barbours that Emily had excitedly bought, as early Christmas presents to each other, for their new country life. Jason also had on a pair of new hiking boots, which were starting to rub painfully. He was ruing not having worn them in around the house for a few days, first. Although at least, he compensated himself, they did look the part.

In small gold letters above the saloon bar door were the words: LICENSED PROPRIETOR, LESTER BEESON.

As they entered the noisy interior, into the ingrained smell of beer, ancient carpet and wood smoke, Jason peered around, taking it all in with excitement. The wooden tables and chairs looked as if they had been there forever, as did some of the characters. In addition to festive decorations, the nicotine-ochre walls were hung with ancient agricultural artefacts and there was a row of horseshoes nailed to an oak beam above the bar. Below were rows of spirit optics, a photograph of a cricket team and several pewter tankards. A warren of doorways led off to other rooms. He need look no further for the archetypal English country pub for inspiration for his paintings of drinkers, he thought, happily. And there were plenty of candidates here this Sunday lunchtime, hunched on bar stools, standing around or seated in the recessed booths.

Presiding over the L-shaped bar, from behind the counter, was a massively tall and large-framed man in his late fifties; he had a mane of hair, a cream shirt with the top two buttons undone and a large gut bulging his midriff buttons. A younger man and two women worked busily alongside him, pulling pints, pouring wine, jabbing shorts glasses up against the optics.

Instinctively, Jason patted the right pocket of his jeans, checking his phone was there, deciding he would try to take some surreptitious photos.

Then, suddenly, it felt to him as if someone had hit the pause button on a video he was in.

Both he and Emily stopped in their tracks.

Heads were turned towards them. Staring eyes from every direction.

The hubbub of conversation stopped. There was total silence, punctuated only by the *ping-beep-bloop-ping* of a flashing gaming machine on the far side of the room, like a forlorn extraterrestrial left behind on a mission and trying to attract attention.

Jason felt like they were the couple in the film he had seen years ago, *Straw Dogs*, entering a pub full of folk in rural Cornwall. Was he just imagining the atmosphere? He put an arm around Emily and squeezed her, reassuringly.

Almost as quickly as it had happened, the moment passed. The video began playing again. Conversations seemed to resume throughout the room. All except for one old man in a checked lumberjack shirt and grey trousers, seated on a bar stool, who continued to stare at them with open hostility. Jason had a good memory for faces, and he looked like the tractor driver who had thundered recklessly down the lane towards them, passing them without slowing down.

Emily was looking at him strangely again, the same look she'd given him in the kitchen earlier. She waved a hand in front of his face. 'Hello? Darling? Are you OK?'

He nodded.

'I thought you were about to pass out,' she said.

'No – I – I just – had an image – for a painting – flash into my mind. I was trying to capture it.' He smiled. 'I think it's time for that drink.'

Was the shrink right, he wondered, about the trauma of moving? Was his mind in shreds from the pressure of the move plus anxiety over his forthcoming exhibition? Hallucinating?

They waited at the back of the crowd at the bar, until he caught the big guy's eye.

'Yes, sir?'

'We're booked in the restaurant for lunch – name of Jason Danes at one thirty – we're a bit early.'

The barman beamed. 'No problem at all, sir, madam – and welcome to Cold Hill village. If I understand it, you've just moved in?'

'That's right,' Jason said, proudly, happy to be recognized as part of the community.

'Well, we all look forward to seeing more of you both.' He stretched out a hand past the grizzled old man and another old man seated beside him. 'Lester Beeson, I'm the landlord, in charge of this rabble.' He looked pointedly at the man who was still glaring daggers at Jason and Emily.

'Jason Danes,' he replied. 'This is my wife, Emily.'

'All of us in the village are happy to have you both with us; we need a little rejuvenation. Too many grumpy old gits like Albert, here.' He nodded at the grizzled man. 'And old Wilfred over there!' He pointed at an elderly, morose couple seated in a window booth, whom Jason had noticed when they'd entered. They were sharing a pack of crisps, eating without saying a word to each other.

'Wilf!' the landlord boomed across the crowded room. 'Meet some new arrivals in the village! Give them a real Wilf welcome, eh?'

The man, who had lank white hair hanging down either side of his face as if a damp mop had been plonked on his head, picked up his pewter tankard and raised it in the air at Jason and Emily, while his wife just scowled.

'Your table's not quite ready, sir,' Beeson said. 'Can we offer you both – as a tradition to all newcomers to Cold Hill – a drink on the house? A pint of Sussex's finest – Harvey's – for you, Mr Danes, perhaps?'

'Thank you very much. And a dry white wine for my wife.'

'Pinot Grigio?'

'Perfect,' Emily said.

All the seats were taken, so they stood with their drinks a short distance from the bar. 'Cheers, darling!' Jason said.

They clinked glasses. Emily sipped, then wrinkled her face.

'How's the wine?' he asked.

'Lukewarm and horrible.'

'Want me to change it?'

She shook her head.

Behind them, a loud rural Sussex accent said, 'What they doing in here, Lester? You letting standards drop?'

'Shut it, Albert.'

'I'll not shut it. They should never have allowed that development. I told Mary, over my dead body would it go through.'

'Yep, well, you still look pretty much alive to me.'

'Bah! Scandalous. A blooming housing estate, ruined the whole village, that's what it has. He's that painter fellow?'

Jason and Emily, hearing him clearly, exchanged a smile.

'Probably does nudes and all,' he continued.

'I could paint a portrait of you in the nude, if you'd like!' Jason called out.

'Jason!' Emily hissed.

The old farmer stared at him again. Then he broke into a near-toothless smirk. 'Paint me to look like James Bond, eh?'

'Superman, if you'd like – Albert, is it?' Jason said.

'Albert Fears.' The old guy supped his pint, then set it down on the bar top. 'Seen her yet?' he said, suddenly, still staring at him.

'Seen what?' Jason responded, aware of Emily frowning.

The old man smirked again. Two yellowed stumps in a mouth of bare gums. 'They're all around, still. You can't get rid of 'em like that, you know. It's not about bricks and mortar, old or new.' He winked and turned back to his tankard, lifting and supping it again.

'*Who* is around?' Jason asked. 'What do you mean, *they're all around*? Who?'

Albert Fears gave him a piercing look. 'They're around to those what can see them. You know what I'm talking about, don't you?'

'No, I've no idea, I'm sorry.' He turned to Emily, who was looking puzzled.

'Why don't you tell 'em, Harry?' He turned to the equally ancient, wiry man next to him, who had been sitting in silence, pint glass in front of him, holding an unlit briar pipe. A stout, rough-hewn stick was propped against the bar beside him.

Taking his own time, the man pivoted on his stool. He wore a baggy shirt with a red and white spotted cravat, grey trousers and ancient walking boots. His white hair was styled in an old-fashioned, boyish quiff, and he sported a goatee beard. Observing Jason and Emily through sad, rheumy eyes, he said, 'I used to drive the digger.'

'Digger?' Jason echoed.

'Ask anyone, they'll know about the digger.'

Albert grumbled loudly behind him at the landlord. 'Six generations of my family have farmed here, Lester. Cold Hill exists because of the big house. The Lord of the Manor. Now it's a bloody housing estate, we're going to have all these city folk coming along, thinking they're living the bleedin' rural idyll.' He swivelled around and stared hard again at Jason and Emily. 'That's what you believe, isn't it – that you're living in the countryside, eh? But actually you are just living in suburbia. Bah. Good luck to you. You'll never leave. No one ever has.' He swivelled back to his beer.

A pleasant woman in a black polo shirt with the pub's name on it came over, holding a clutch of menus, and told Jason and Emily their table was ready.

'Nice to meet you!' Jason said to both old men, as Emily turned away in disgust.

Neither acknowledged him.

23

Sunday 16 December

They followed the woman through the crowded saloon bar and into an equally rammed restaurant area, with more festive decorations on the walls, and were taken to a small four-seater table in a corner. Jason sat down beside his wife, with his back to the far wall, giving him a view of the room. He was pensive, wondering what the two old men had meant.

'How horrible that man was – and creepy – not sure I want to rush back here again in a hurry,' Emily said.

'I agree – but the landlord seems really friendly,' Jason replied. 'Let's see what the food's like, anyway.'

'Hmm,' she replied, and glanced at the menus the waitress had put on the table – a standard one, a Christmas Fayre three-course special, and the wine list.

There was a roar of laughter from a raucous table of eight beside them.

'Shall we ask for some ice to put in your wine?'

'Good idea.'

They clinked glasses again. 'Cheers, my darling,' Jason said.

'Cheers.' She smiled and took the tiniest sip, screwing up her face. 'Big year next year, eh?'

He nodded, still pensive, and took a gulp of his beer.

'Our new home, your very important exhibition – and I

think someone has a very big birthday.' She gave him a quizzical look.

'Don't remind me!'

'Come on. You once told me if someone hasn't made it by forty, they're never going to. Well, you have made it and you're heading into the big league now.'

'Maybe.'

His birthday was one week after his 8 February exhibition, on 15 February.

'No *maybe* about it. We'll be having a double celebration – your sell-out on the eighth and your birthday. We need to start thinking about it. Perhaps a supper party combined with our housewarming?' With a twinkle in her eyes, she said, 'And I do know quite a good local catering firm.'

'Could I afford them?'

'Oh, they come at a *very* special price!'

'Oh God,' he suddenly said, staring across the room.

'What?'

Lowering his voice, he said, 'Look who's here.'

She turned and saw the Penze-Weedells, wrapped up the way they had been yesterday, following the waitress, who was striding across the room towards them. Mrs Penze-Weedell was striding equally determinedly, her husband trailing behind her, looking sheepish.

'Well!' Claudette greeted them. 'What a lovely coincidence to see you!'

'Very nice to see you too,' Emily replied.

'I don't suppose you'd find it an imposition if we joined you?' she asked. 'You see it is completely full in here and there seems to have been a mix-up over our booking. But this very kind lady –' she pointed a padded-gloved finger at the waitress – 'said you were also from Cold Hill Park and you were at a table for four. We told her you are very dear friends.' She peeled off her peaked hat and put it down in one of the spare places, freeing her mass of hair, which she prodded into position until it was about twelve inches tall, before moments later it collapsed, and long fair hair tumbled around her face. 'You wouldn't mind, would you?'

Jason took a deep breath.

'Otherwise we'd have to walk all the way back and get in the car – but every pub around here is bound to be full, this being the last Sunday before Christmas.'

'Only if you're completely sure,' mumbled Maurice, beginning to unbutton his coat.

Emily looked, helplessly, at Jason. He gave her a wide-eyed signal of desperation back.

'Of course!' Emily said, with a smile like a crack in a fine porcelain vase.

24

Sunday 16 December

The Penze-Weedells went for the full Christmas menus – with extra roast potatoes for Mrs P-W – while Jason and Emily ordered tuna salads and asked the waitress to bring them at the same time as the Penze-Weedells' soup. Claudette pointedly ordered a bottle of prosecco, repeating the word several times in the process to ensure their new neighbours were in no doubt of her good taste. She also asked for four glasses, but Jason – who had now gone off the idea of the hair of the dog – and Emily politely declined, saying they had a working afternoon ahead.

The service was slow, taking almost half an hour for their food to arrive. It was mostly one-sided conversation, in which the Danes had to endure the biographies of all the relatives who would be coming to spend Christmas Day at 36 Lakeview Drive. These were accompanied by detailed family trees, with every relative, according to the boasts of Claudette, being immensely successful. Especially their two sons – one with a firm of City accountants and the other doing *frightfully well* in IT – and their daughter, who had now produced for them three *adorable* grandchildren.

'We'll go and pay at the bar, so we don't disturb the rest of your meal,' Jason said as soon as they had finished.

'Sooooo lovely to see you again,' Claudette said.

'Jolly neighbourly of you to allow us to share your table,' her husband added.

Both Penze-Weedells were in an increasingly exuberant mood, having demolished the bottle of prosecco and now well into a bottle of red wine – which seemed, to Jason and Emily, unlikely to be the only one they would be getting through during their lunch.

'You must come and have drinks with us on Christmas morning!' Claudette said.

'A bit difficult, but thank you,' Jason said. 'We have relatives with us.'

'Bring them too!' her husband slurred.

'We'll catch up soon after,' Jason promised.

'Boxing Day!' she said. 'We insist. Drinks on Boxing Day. Midday, chez nous!'

'That would be lovely,' Emily replied, ignoring the gentle kick under the table from her husband.

'Oh, there is one thing that might be of interest,' Claudette said. 'To you both. A little precaution.'

'Precaution?' Jason queried.

'Yes, yes indeed.' She looked at her husband then went on. 'Maurice and I were under the impression – or should I say, were *led to believe* – that we were the very first residents of Cold Hill Park.' She looked hard at Jason then Emily. 'But we weren't.'

'No?' Emily said.

'No,' she said. For the first time, she looked solemn. 'Apparently, there were three couples who had moved in before us – a few of months earlier. Two just around the corner from us in Copse Walk, and one, with a young family, in 34 Lakeview Drive, that rather ugly little house next to us – right opposite you.'

Jason turned to Emily. 'See, I told you I'd seen people in that house.'

'I don't think so, Jason – you don't mind me calling you Jason?'

'Of course not, Claudette.' He smiled. 'What do you mean *you don't think so*?'

'I don't think you could have seen people in that house,' she went on and looked to her husband for confirmation. He nodded, distantly.

'I've seen them a couple of times; I waved to them, they waved back.'

She shook her head, vigorously. 'It's quite horrible – just one of those terrible coincidences that happen in life some-times. Over the space of two months, all three couples were killed in accidents while on holiday.'

'What?' Emily said.

'We only found out after we moved in. We're not planning any holiday soon, I can tell you.'

25

At the bar, Jason handed his credit card over to the landlord, noticing that the oddball old man with the goatee beard, who had said something about a digger, had gone, leaving just Albert Fears seated there with his tankard.

As he waited for Beeson's hand-held card reader to get a connection, the old farmer turned and peered at him. 'Young man, aren't you?'

'Not that young,' he replied, aware that Emily was looking away, studiously ignoring Fears.

'Oh? Let me take a guess. Thirty-five?'

'Very flattering of you, I'm thirty-nine.'

He noticed the landlord shooting him a glance as he said it.

'Thirty-nine, are you?' Fears went on. 'Birthday anytime soon?'

'Are you going to bring me a present?'

The old man's face broke into a smirk. 'Dunno if I'll need to. No one in the big house ever lived beyond forty.' He raised his tankard. 'Good health, you and your pretty wife. Long life – eh?'

26

Jason and Emily walked in silence through the village, past the store, the smithy, and houses and cottages almost all looking Christmassy. The sky was darkening and it was feeling even colder than earlier. They held gloved hands.

'That was such bullshit, that horrible old farmer,' Jason said. 'About no one living beyond forty. The Penze-Weedells are both well north of the big Four Zero, so screw you, Mr Interbred Local Miserableguts.'

'Three couples from our estate killed in accidents?' Emily said. 'All in the past few months? What's that about?'

'Em, I don't know. Just a freak of statistics?'

'Or a jinx or a curse? Are all of us cursed? What have we moved into?'

'Our beautiful dream home, where we are going to be very happy.'

'Dream on.'

'Hey!' He put his arm around her and hugged her tightly, trying to put out of his mind the people he had seen in the house opposite and the woman who had come into his studio, trying – and almost succeeding – to dismiss them as figments of his overworked, tired brain. 'We are not jinxed, there is no hex, or whatever, OK?'

They walked on in silence.

'Hexes are . . .' he began before falling silent again, trying to frame what he wanted to say.

'What did he mean?' Emily said. 'About no one in the old house ever living beyond forty?'

'He was talking about the past,' Jason replied. 'Life expectancy in the nineteenth century was about forty for a male and I think about forty-two for women. But that took into account infant mortality, death in childbirth, wars. It's very different now. The Penze-Weedells – I rest my case.'

'He gave me the creeps.'

'Just a miserable old git who doesn't like change. Reminds me of that Oscar Wilde line in one of his plays. *Poor daddy's like a pot plant abandoned in a dark corner, wondering where the sunshine has gone.*'

She squeezed his hand, smiling. 'I like that.'

'Wouldn't it be amazing if we had snow,' he said, changing the subject as they approached the pillars with the wyverns on top.

'Amazing,' she echoed but without any enthusiasm. Then she said, 'I just cannot believe the cheek of those people. I was so looking forward to a nice quiet lunch with you, on our own. "Eyyyy don't suppose yew'd find it an imposition if we joined yewwwww?"'

'They're both well past forty – I'd put him mid-fifties.'

'She's no spring chicken, for sure.'

'We need to set some boundaries with them, PDQ.'

'Barbed wire down the middle of the road?'

'Trenches.'

'A moat with a drawbridge? I went to a medium once, in my teens. He said he could see me living in a house with a moat and a drawbridge.'

'Sounds like he might have been prophetic.'

'He also said he could see me with four children.'

They walked on for some moments in painful silence.

'I'm sorry,' she said.

He put an arm around her. 'Did you ever see that cheesy old movie, *Love Story*?'

She shook her head.

'There was a line in it – which became the catchphrase for the movie. "Love means never having to say you're sorry."'

As they walked in through the gates and along the pavement to the left of the short dual carriageway, she said, 'Nice, it's kind of true.'

They stopped and kissed. Then he looked into her eyes. 'I never want to have to say sorry to you, for anything.'

'So I've noticed.'

'Hey!'

There was a tease in her eyes. 'Joking!'

He kissed her again. 'You know, despite that old dickhead in the pub – and the eccentrics across the road – I feel immensely happy here. I've a feeling next year is going to be brilliant. I love my studio – I know I'm going to be able to work well there.'

'And I love my kitchen, and my catering space in the garage. And I agree with you, I'm really happy here too. I love the village, and actually the tuna salad wasn't bad. It would have tasted even better without the P-Ws. Did you hear he called her "High Command" when she was in the loo? Hilarious!'

'But now we have something to really look forward to. Boxing Day prosecco at their house.'

'Can you imagine what it's like inside?' she said.

'It's probably full of those wedding presents we hated and gave to the charity shop! Like that porcelain donkey with the sombrero on its head and the quartz clock in its belly that my aunt gave us.'

'Shame on you for giving away what might one day become a priceless antique.'

'One that'll turn up on the *Antiques Roadshow*?'

'Some years after Hell has frozen over.'

He laughed and hugged her. 'God, I love you so much.'

She looked into his eyes, smiling. 'It's going to happen, a baby will come along. If it doesn't, we'll try IVF and whatever else is going. And if that doesn't happen, we have each other. Right?'

They hugged again. 'Right,' he whispered into her ear.

'Right.'

As they walked on, turning into Lakeview Drive, passing the shells of houses under construction, Emily said, 'What about that other weird old boy, what did he mean when he said, "Ask anyone, they'll know about the digger"?'

'Blind reindeer.'

'What?'

'No eye deer!'

She punched him. 'That is terrible, that's your worst pun ever – and you stole it!'

'Sorry.'

'Didn't you just say something about never having to say *sorry*?' She looked at him quizzically.

27

Sunday 16 December

As soon as they were home, Jason left Emily to the preparations in her work kitchen, made them both a mug of tea and carried his up to the studio. Closing the door behind him, he stood and stared for some moments at his painting of the two labradoodles on the sofa. It glowed in the low winter sunlight streaming in through the window.

He studied each of the dogs, pleased with his progress this morning. It was shaping up well and he could feel their personalities coming alive. He glanced at his watch: 3.45 p.m. With an uninterrupted evening ahead, he should be able to finish it easily.

He sat down at his desk, in front of his laptop, to check his emails and social media, and pressed the return key to wake it up.

But, similar to earlier, instead of the normal request for his password, a row of numbers appeared, fleetingly, on a black screen before vanishing again.

A sharp tap on the window to his left startled him. He jumped, then turned in fear towards it. And saw a man's face.

Shit!

He leapt to his feet in shock.

The man, who looked to be in his forties, smiled cheerily, holding up a cloth and waving with it. Then he squirted something on the glass and began to spread it.

Relief washing through him, Jason smiled and waved back, then returned to the screen. The numbers had disappeared, replaced by the password prompt. He entered it, bemused, scanned his emails and Twitter, then stood up to get back to work.

He put on his apron and gloves, freshened up his paints and went over to his easel. Within minutes he was totally immersed in getting the fringe over the labradoodle's eyes right. He scraped with his scalpel in total concentration to create different shades of grey and some white. This really needed a steady hand, but it was becoming less steady as he continued. The temperature in the room seemed to be dropping. He was cold, freezing cold.

Behind him he heard a sharp click, as if the door had suddenly been closed.

Except, it was already closed.

28

Jason spun around.

Standing in front of him, right in his face, was the woman in the black suit. Shimmering, cold air radiated from her.

Then she vanished.

He stood, shaking uncontrollably. His hands, his legs, his whole body. Goosepimples chased up and down his body.

He had seen her face so clearly. Even more so than before.

With shaking hands, he removed the painting from the easel and set it carefully down on the floor against a wall, then pulled out a fresh gesso board and placed it on the easel. From his desk, he picked up a pencil and began to sketch feverishly on the board.

Totally oblivious to time, he worked away, putting down the image he held in his mind. Somewhere in a distant compartment of his brain he heard Emily calling out and ignored her, working impatiently on. He had to finish this before the image faded.

Had to capture her.

Emily called again, and he still ignored her.

Eventually – it was approaching 8 p.m., he realized, glancing at his watch – he heard footsteps, stomping, angry footsteps, coming up the stairs.

Still he worked on.

Emily stormed into the room. 'Are you deaf?' she said. 'Supper's been ready for—' She stopped in her tracks and stared at the portrait he had almost completed.

'Oh God!' she said. 'Oh my God.'

He turned to her. 'What?'

She stared at the portrait again. Wide-eyed.

In a small, scared voice, she said, 'You've seen her, too.'

29

Ten minutes later, Jason and Emily sat in silence at the kitchen table. On the shelves of their old pine Welsh dresser, which looked oddly out of place against the rest of the modern furnishings, Emily had arranged the 'Good Luck in Your New Home' cards, as well as more of the Christmas ones that had arrived in yesterday's post.

With a shaking hand, he filled their glasses from the bottle of red Rioja he had opened, while the chicken casserole and potato gratin sat uneaten in front of them, along with the salad. On the muted television on the wall, a woman on *Antiques Roadshow* was pointing at an assortment of jewellery laid out on a table.

'Maybe I should heat this up again – I thought we should have something hot after our cold lunch.'

'Thanks. Is this what we bought at the garden centre?'

She nodded, looking at him almost guiltily for using a ready-made meal. 'But I made the salad,' she said, as if by way of reparation.

He dug his fork in and ate a mouthful of the casserole, testing it. It was tepid, but tasty. 'It's OK, doesn't really need heating up, it's good – not as good as yours, though.' He smiled. 'Babes, never feel guilty about having a ready-made supper – I don't, when it's my turn to cook.'

She smiled thinly back. Then said, 'It would be a lot nicer hot.'

He glanced at his watch, anxious to get back to his studio, no chance of a relaxing evening in front of the television. He was going to have to work into the night to get the dogs painting finished, and tomorrow he would have to do the pencil sketch of the King Charles spaniel for his other client. 'I'm fine with it – we could heat it up for a couple of minutes if you'd like?'

'I'm fine with it, too.' She picked up her glass and drank half of it in one gulp. She was still looking shaken.

'So, are we going to talk about it?'

'About?' She put down her glass, picked up her knife and fork and prodded her food. But she did not eat anything.

'About the lady? Tell me what you meant, when you said, *you've seen her too*?'

Emily continued to stare down at her plate, pushing the food around more. 'Yesterday morning, when I was putting my make-up on at my dressing table, I saw a woman in the mirror, standing right behind me. I turned around and she wasn't there. I thought I'd just imagined her. Then last night when we were getting ready for bed, I was looking in the bathroom mirror, cleaning my face, and I saw her again. I knew I was a bit pissed, after the P-Ws had gone, so I figured I'd imagined it again – and I didn't want to say anything in case you thought I was going nuts. But that drawing you've just done – that's her.'

'You absolutely sure?'

'It's her.'

'That's so weird.'

'Is it?' she said, the sharpness of her voice surprising him. 'What's so weird?'

'What do you mean?'

'You're an artist, you draw or paint people, often random strangers you've seen. What's so weird about that?'

He stared at her for some moments, trying to unravel her logic. 'Random strangers, yes, but not random strangers in our house, normally.'

'I'm not sure what normal is at the moment.'

He ate another mouthful, chewing in silence. 'Perhaps . . .' he began, then fell silent again.

'Perhaps what?'

He continued chewing. On the screen behind Emily, one of the presenters was admiring an array of old toy soldiers. 'Perhaps we're both suffering a kind of moving trauma. Dr Dixon warned me that it might take some time to adjust to our new home.'

'Did Dr Dixon also warn you that the ghosts of the previous occupants might still be in residence?'

He smiled. 'No, he forgot that bit.' He reached across the table and took her hand. 'Hey.' He squeezed it, gently. 'Look, you and I are both rational people. Our emotions are bound to be in turmoil; moving home is a big thing. You know what I think?'

'No, what do you think?'

'That maybe we're both picking up on the vibes of a previous occupant.'

'What do you mean, *vibes*?'

'We're all full of energy – maybe the energy of people who've been here before us remains in some way, leaves some kind of vibe that we occasionally pick up.'

'How come we never picked up any before, in our previous homes? And anyhow, there hasn't been a previous occupant, Jason. This is a brand-new house.'

'I meant a previous occupant of the old house. We know this is on part of the footprint of the former mansion here. Perhaps – I don't know – we're picking something up from the past, and we're communicating it to each other telepathically? That's what I think is one possibility.'

'And the other possibility?'

He sipped some of his wine then set his glass down and looked her in the eye. 'It's the one I'm struggling with – because it goes against all my rational thinking.' He looked at her and fell silent.

30

Sunday 16 December

Jason refilled her glass. In the past quarter of an hour, he had not touched any more of the casserole and it was now stone cold.

Emily came from a family of staunch Catholics. While having some faith herself, she rarely went to church. He was much the same, coming from a family of lapsed Anglicans. Although he didn't have any truck with the notion of the biblical God, Jason did believe in a bigger picture – a view they both shared.

Emily finally broke the long silence. 'We imagined it?'

'That's the best explanation I can come up with.'

'Of course,' she said, cynically. 'What else have we imagined? Cold Hill Park? This house? Each other? Do you exist? Do I?'

He squeezed her hand again. 'You exist.'

'Do I? Can you prove it? Can you prove you really exist?'

He stood up, walked around the table and kissed her on each cheek. 'OK? Is that real? Do I exist?'

'I could have imagined that.'

'Want to see my driving licence? Passport?'

'How would I know they're real? Are they any more real than the woman we've both seen and you've just shown me?'

He sat back down and picked up his glass; immediately he put it back down, untouched. 'I can't drink any more; I have to work. Jesus.' He shook his head. 'There's an ancient Mesopotamian saying, that four fingers stand between the truth and a lie. And if you measure that, you'll find it's the average distance between a person's ears and their eyes.'

'Meaning?'

'What you see is what you know to be the truth.'

'So, this woman you drew is the truth? She's what you saw. What I saw? We both saw a ghost.'

'Or . . .'

'Or?'

They both heard a sound above them. Footsteps. Like boots walking across bare floorboards.

Jason froze. Emily looked up, then at him. 'Wh-what? Who – who's that?'

He stood and stared up at the ceiling.

Clump. Clump. Clump.

She was staring at it, too.

Clump. Clump. Clump.

'Which – which room is that?' Her voice was trembling.

He ran out into the hall, sprinted up the stairs, onto the landing and into their bedroom. Stared at the king-size bed with the white cover, the pillows, and the ragged, once-fluffy bear that Emily always placed between the cushions when she made it. *Teddy Boy*: the comforter she'd had since early childhood. He looked around at the mirrored doors of the wardrobe that ran the width of the room. The darkness of the night against the windows; the antique chaise longue they'd bought years ago for a song at an auction, then had re-covered in a light grey fabric. The studded chest at the end of the bed. The white rug on the bare oak floorboards.

'Jason!' Emily called out. 'Jace, are you OK?'

Everything seemed normal. He walked through into the en suite bathroom, looked at the walk-in shower and the large,

Victorian-style bathtub. Stared at his reflection in the mirror above the twin basins.

Silence.

He went back downstairs. Emily was standing at the bottom. 'What – what – was—?'

He shook his head. 'Nothing. Probably as I said before; the oak flooring moving.'

'Moving?'

'You know oak takes a long time to settle in. Remember when we had that oak flooring put down in North Gardens?'

The tiny, Victorian semi-detached cottage in the centre of Brighton they'd lived in previously, where he'd had his cramped studio. That had been a wreck when they'd bought it, and they'd floored the entire living and dining area in oak. They'd had to keep the planks for several months in the house for seasoning, on the advice of their builder, before having it laid. 'Yes,' she said, quietly.

'They probably didn't season it enough here, that's all – just economizing on getting the place built fast. Now the house is occupied, and we have the central heating on, it's probably drying out and shrinking or distorting a bit – that's what's causing that noise.'

'Really? How?'

'I don't know, I'm not a carpenter. Maybe one plank moves, and it causes a chain reaction, or something.'

'Or something else?'

They sat down again at the kitchen table. Emily glanced up, warily. 'So, oak shrinking makes a sound like footsteps? What's going on, Jace? Is someone having a laugh with us? Playing a prank?'

'Like who?'

'I don't know,' she said distantly.

He ate a mouthful of the cold casserole, thinking. Wanting

to calm Emily down, and wanting to calm his own troubled mind. 'Look, let's go for a rational explanation. Maybe she is just someone I saw somewhere but didn't instantly register and she just got logged in my subconscious. One of the many characters I see and bank daily – it's what I do all the time. I see characters and memorize them for future sketches or paintings. In my heightened emotions from moving – according to Dr Dixon – she suddenly popped up. Like I said, couples who are close do sometimes have a kind of telepathic communication. So, you were picking her up, too, from my mind.' He shrugged. 'Maybe?'

'Maybe Dr Dixon gave you the wrong pills,' she replied, coldly. 'What you said sounds total bollocks.'

'Yep, well, I . . .' He fell silent for some moments. 'I don't think ghosts walk across floors in hobnail boots.'

Emily picked up his plate, put it in the new microwave, shut the door a tad too loudly and switched it on.

'Aren't you going to heat yours up too?' he asked.

'I'm not hungry.'

'Come on, you need to eat something.' When the microwave pinged he took out his plate and put hers in.

Five minutes later they sat back down at the table.

'Eat!' he encouraged.

Emily gave him a wan smile. She forked a minuscule amount into her mouth, then took another gulp of her wine. As she put the glass down, she said, '*You'll never leave. No one ever has.* That's what that old git said to you in the pub, didn't you say?'

'Yes. Well, that's fine. We've only just arrived, why would we want to leave?'

'You know what I'm saying and what I'm feeling, Jason. And that other thing he said. *No one in the big house ever lived beyond forty.*'

'So, we should sell up and leave before my fortieth birthday? Is that what you want us to do?'

'I don't know what I want.' She paused. 'Actually, I do. I know what I want. I want to not feel scared in my home, and I'm feeling very scared.'

'I don't want either of us to feel scared, my darling. You think we've both seen a ghost. But this is a new house. Ghosts – if they exist at all – haunt old properties.'

'We're on the site of an old property – you said that yourself.'

He ate some more, thinking. 'Do you want to find a medium to come here and see what they come up with?'

'Maybe we should.' She looked up at the ceiling again.

'So, where do we start trying to find one?'

'Louise is very into all of that. I can ask her.'

'Of course.' He liked Louise, despite being sceptical about the 'gift' she claimed to have. 'Sure, why not?'

'She's coming over again tomorrow to help me finish setting everything up. I'll ask her then.'

'Good plan.'

He finished the rest of his meal and his glass of wine, then made himself a strong coffee and carried it out of the room.

'Say hi to our lodger,' Emily said.

He turned and grinned. 'Any other message for her?'

'Yes, tell her to sod off and go and bother the P-Ws instead.'

The hallway felt as if an icy draught was belting in from an open door. Jason looked at the thermostat on the wall. Twenty-three degrees. He tried to work out how to turn it up higher still, but there was no evident manual override. The draught was even stronger now.

Irritated, he went back into the kitchen and plugged the command box back in.

'Why are you doing that?' Emily asked, turning from stacking the plates in the dishwasher.

'I need to turn the heating in the hall up and I can't see any way of doing it manually. I'm going to call that agent in the morning, and find out how to permanently override this command box.'

'It's got to be in the instruction manual,' Emily said.

'Yep, and I either spend the night reading it or painting. I've got two bloody pictures to deliver by tomorrow night, OK,' he said, walking out, angrily.

The hall felt even colder still. He looked up the stairs and saw the landing light was off. He was sure he had left it on when he came back down just a short while ago. He called out, feeling a bit ridiculous, 'Command, upstairs landing light on!'

Instantly it came on. He glanced at the thermostat, which was now reading twenty-five, and began climbing the stairs. As he reached the first-floor landing and looked up into the darkness above, a cold draught blasted down at him.

Feeling apprehensive, he said, 'Command, top floor light on!'

It came on, instantly. But a split second later, there was a loud pop and the tinkle of breaking glass, and the spiral staircase was plunged back into darkness.

Great.

He looked up the steep steps, his apprehension deepening. Shit. He was feeling scared of going any further. Scared to go up to his studio.

This was their new home! *Come on, man, don't be ridiculous. Pathetic scaredy cat!*

He put a foot on the first tread and felt another cold blast of air coming down from the darkness above. Had he left a window open in his studio?

He walked up a couple of steps, the air even colder still, like entering a walk-in freezer.

Then, as if invisible hands were pushing him, trying to

prevent him from climbing further, he found he couldn't climb any more.

He stood still for a moment. Cold air riffled his hair.

I am not going to be scared in my own home!

He was about to climb on when he stopped again, staring in utter astonishment at what looked at first like a swarm of translucent bees coming down the stairs towards him. Dozens of tiny, bright lights, bending and swirling down the stairs in sync, as one shape.

Like the lights that had remained, fleetingly, as the apparition of the woman had dissolved.

His throat constricted as they moved rapidly down towards him, giving him no time to turn and run.

A split second later, taken by total surprise, he was barged into by a strong, invisible force. He made a desperate grab for the handrail to prevent himself from tumbling backwards as the lights swirled on down, his mug tumbling after them, spattering black coffee over the carpet and wall.

'You might fucking say *excuse me!*' he shouted in both anger and shock.

From below, he heard Emily call out. 'Darling – are you OK?'

Then she screamed.

31

Sunday 16 December

On the television, one of the *Antiques Roadshow* experts, a silver-haired man in a striped blazer, was admiring a porcelain racehorse with a round, analogue clock set into its midriff. The expert was extolling its virtues as a fine, rare, example of Art Deco.

Claudette Penze-Weedell, feeling decidedly sloshed, watched with sudden interest. She held a glass of prosecco in her hand from one of the bottles Maurice had bought for Christmas, which she had insisted he open tonight.

He'd been reluctant at first, telling her she had really drunk quite enough at the pub at lunchtime, and that they needed to watch the pennies, but she had played the card that always worked, telling him to open a bottle if he wanted any hope of action in the bedroom tonight.

She unwrapped and scoffed a Green Triangle, her least favourite of the chocolates, which were all that now remained of the Quality Street collection. She would need to pay a visit to the supermarket tomorrow to buy another tub, or realistically two, to last her through the holidays – so long as she hid them on Christmas Day when all their greedy relatives would be with them, most of them Maurice's. She'd married a man who came from a family of gannets.

'And now to put a value on this,' the expert said. 'Well, if I were to put this to auction, I would place a reserve on it of at least twenty thousand pounds.'

The woman on the screen, in tight close-up, gasped.

Claudette gasped, too. Her eyes shot to the glass cabinet. To the porcelain donkey with the sombrero on its head and the square quartz clock in its belly, which she had picked up in the Martlets charity shop in Brighton for ten pounds.

Twenty thousand pounds!

'Maurice!' she called out, excitedly.

There was no response.

'Maurice!'

She smelled cigar smoke.

'Maurice?'

The smell of cigar smoke became stronger.

'Maurice? What do you think you're doing? You're smoking indoors – you know that I—'

A shadowy figure, with a glowing cigar, passed the open doorway to the hall.

'Maurice, what on earth do you think you are doing?' She jumped up, angrily. Had he taken leave of his senses, smoking indoors? He knew how asthmatic she was. Hurrying to the doorway, with the smell of cigar smoke even stronger there, she yelled, 'Maurice!'

To her right, at the end of the hall, she heard the rattle of a lock. The front door opened and Maurice, returning from his evening constitutional, wrapped up in his coat, hat and gloves, entered.

'Bloody hell, love, it's cold out there tonight!' he said.

32

Jason raced into the kitchen. Emily was standing, looking bewildered and very shaken.

'What is it?' he asked. 'What's happened?'

'I – I –' She grabbed the back of a chair, pulled it out, and lowered herself onto the seat. Then she buried her face in her hands. 'God, oh God.'

'Em, tell me. What?' He laid a hand gently on her shoulder. She was panting, gasping for air. Hyperventilating, he realized. 'Tell me,' he said again, looking around, warily, his own nerves jangling.

Guessing what she was about to say.

'I saw something,' she blurted. 'I saw – I don't know – it was like lights moving across the floor, then they all just vanished into the wall there.' She pointed at the far end of the room, where there was just a work surface and cupboards.

Should he tell her, he wondered? That he'd seen the same thing and it had nearly knocked him down the stairs, backwards? Which might have broken his neck and killed him. His mouth was dry. He did not know what to say. They'd both seen the woman and now they'd both seen this . . . whatever it was. Ball lightning of some kind?

'Let's both speak to Louise – she's coming in the morning?'

'Yes.'

He looked at his watch. Shit, he had to get on with the painting, had to get it finished tonight. Had to. Regardless of what nightmare was happening here that they did not understand.

He went over to the sink and opened a cupboard door beneath it, kneeling down.

'What are you looking for?' she asked.

'I spilt my coffee on the stairs. I tripped on that damned carpet – it's so thick,' he fibbed.

'Go on and get on with your painting, I'll clear it up.'

'Are you sure?'

She nodded.

He retrieved his mug from the bottom of the stairs, made a fresh coffee and, feeling very nervous, went up the two flights to his studio, commanding the lights to switch on inside as he entered the open door.

The window facing the lake was wide open, the cold wind blowing straight through it. Had he left it open? Surely not. He closed and locked it in place, walked over to his desk, put his coffee down, then nervously peered out across the street at number thirty-four.

It was in darkness. No one was in the upstairs room. He sat at his desk and hit the return key to wake up his computer. The password request came up as normal.

He took a sip of his coffee, then in rapid succession checked his emails. There were a couple of virtual cards from friends, announcing they were donating to charities instead of sending Christmas cards out. He'd discussed this with Emily, but they'd decided they still liked sending physical cards – he always designed one each year – and hey, they were good advertising. Then a Jacquie Lawson one. He skipped the video of a dog wandering through snow to the sound of ditzy music and went straight to the details of the sender. It was followed by an email from Susan Burton at the Northcote Gallery, asking how he was getting on with his paintings for the exhibition. He replied that all was going well.

Next, he checked quickly through his social media and when he had finished, he went over to his easel. Removing the portrait of the mystery woman, he placed it face-in against a small stack of his unsold work, then knelt to pick up the portrait of the two dogs from where he had left them, just beneath the window.

As he lifted it up, there was a loud thud on the windowpane.

He dropped the painting. It hit the floor with a jarring bang and fell face down. For some moments, he stared at the window. All he saw was darkness. He ran over and pressed his face against it. Just darkness. The lake somewhere out there and the hill rising beyond. He unlocked and raised the frame. Bitterly cold air blew in. He could see nothing.

Every cell in his body was jangling.

Shit, shit, shit. It must have been a bird – maybe a bat.

He closed the window again, turned away and knelt, dreading what he was going to find. And as he lifted the gesso board up, his worst fears were confirmed. The entire painting was crazed with cracks.

No way could it be fixed. His only option was to start over from scratch. Somehow, he was going to have to find the strength to work all night, if necessary. And he still had the pencil drawing of the spaniel to do tomorrow. Taking several deep breaths, he went over to the window overlooking the street, and looked down at the gaudy lights of the Penze-Weedells' grotto, suddenly finding himself envious of the simplicity of their banal lives.

Five minutes later, with a fresh board on his easel, he downed the cold coffee and started work on the painting all over again, glancing over his shoulder every few moments at the window, waiting for another thud. He was so distracted it took him a long while before he got back into his stride.

Some while later, Emily came into the room and told him she needed an early night and was going to bed. She stopped and looked at the painting.

'I thought you'd nearly finished, you said earlier?'

'I had,' he said. 'Then I stupidly dropped it and it's all cracked – one problem with gesso. I've had to start from scratch – looks like I'm going to have to pull an all-nighter.'

'Poor you.' She put her arms around him. 'Not working out too great so far, is it, my love, our new home?'

33

'What's the matter, dear?' Maurice Penze-Weedell said to his slack-jawed wife. She was staring at him as if he had just landed from another planet.

'Were you just smoking a cigar?'

'No.' He opened his mouth and exhaled minty breath at her. 'No cigar, I don't like cigars, you know that.'

'I – I –'

'You are looking a little squiffy, my dear, if you don't mind my saying so. Perhaps we should go up – you know – to bed?' He tried to put his arms around her, but she brushed them off.

'It's *Antiques Roadshow*! Really!'

He nodded, glumly. She never missed an episode. There were dozens of shows on television where she never missed an episode. Claudette's life was fitted around them.

She turned, walked back into the lounge and settled down on the sofa. Then she reached for the prosecco bottle and topped up her glass. 'You just missed something,' she said.

'I did?'

She pointed at the porcelain donkey on the shelf in the glass cabinet. 'An *objet* just like that was valued at twenty thousand pounds!'

'Blimey O'Reilly!'

'I bought that for ten pounds – and you said I'd been ripped off! Ha! Who's laughing now?' She downed her glass.

Maurice hastily refilled it, thinking, *Keep her in the drinking mood!* He had that feeling he might get lucky tonight. She sometimes turned rampant when she was squiffy – so long as she didn't pass out first.

'Perhaps after the show has finished we should have an early night, my dear?' he ventured.

'I'm not missing the new *Poldark*,' she said. 'It's on at nine. I'm not missing that gorgeous hunk Aidan Turner.'

'We could record it.'

'Why would I want to do that when I could watch it tonight?'

'Well, what if I gave you a better offer?'

She unwrapped the last but one of the Green Triangles. 'There's only one better offer you could give me this evening, dear.'

'Yes?' he said like an eager puppy. 'What would that be?'

'To go out and find me some more Quality Street. You're OK to drive – you only had a couple of glasses at lunchtime.'

He looked dubious. 'I could try – but I think all the supermarkets are closed on a Sunday night.'

'What about petrol stations?' she said. 'Really, I thought you were a man of initiative. Remember what you said that night you proposed to me? You said that if I would marry you, you would always give me what I wanted, no matter what it took? Do you remember?'

'I do, my dearest.'

Maurice hurried from the room, and moments later, above the television, she heard the sound of his car engine starting.

On the screen, an *Antiques Roadshow* expert was examining a collection of commemorative Coronation chocolate tins.

She became aware of the smell of cigar smoke again. Stronger than before. Much stronger.

'Maurice!' she called out.

She heard his car driving off.

A smoke ring drifted past her eyes.

She jumped up and went to the doorway. 'Maurice?'

Behind her, the empty tub fell onto the carpeted floor.

'Maurice!' she yelled.

There was a sharp click and the television turned off.

An instant later the house was plunged into darkness.

Halfway up the stairs, she saw the red glow of a cigar.

'Maurice?'

It moved towards her.

She fled, along the hall and out into the garden, slamming the front door behind her.

All the Christmas lights had gone off.

'Maurice!' she shouted.

34

Sunday 16 December

In his studio, Jason and Emily Danes stood, hugging each other tightly.

'What's happening?' she asked. 'Why is nothing going right for us since we moved here?'

'I don't know, Em. But we'll deal with it.'

'You heard what Claudette said in the pub. About the three families here who have died. What if the whole development is cursed or something?'

'By what?'

She shrugged. 'I don't know. By some malign spirit that doesn't want us here. That thing – woman – we both saw.' She nodded at the gesso board on the floor.

'I don't want to believe in any curse. Coincidences, yes – to me it's just a terrible coincidence those people dying, if Claudette was right. Frankly I think she's bonkers – probably made it up.'

'And if she wasn't making it up?'

'I'll call the estate agent, what was his name – Paul Jordan – in the morning and ask him.' He kissed her. 'Look, that horrible old man in the pub, that farmer, Albert Fears, made it clear he didn't like this development. Maybe he and a bunch of other like-minded locals decided to play silly buggers and try to spook the shit out of everyone moving here?'

'By killing three couples?'

'Let's find out the truth about all of it tomorrow.'

'You really think that old farmer could be capable of playing tricks in our house? Conjuring up a hologram that could speak? Come on, step out of denial-mode and get real,' she said. 'Don't forget what they said in the pub about the history of this place.'

'I am trying to get real, Em. I love this house. You love it, too.'

'I did love it. I don't any more. I wonder if we shouldn't go and stay with my parents until—'

'Until?'

'Until we've cleared out whatever the hell is in here that shouldn't be.'

From out in the hallway a sharp, furious female voice laced with menace rang out.

'Just try.'

35

Sunday 16 December

The BMW's headlights briefly flashed over the shivering figure curled up in the porch, her beehive hair collapsed around her face.

Maurice leapt out of the car, triumphantly clutching a Christmas tub of Quality Street as if it were an Olympic gold medal, and rushed over to his wife.

'What are you doing, my dear?'

She glared up at him. 'An hour and a bloody half. What does it look like I'm doing, you cretin?'

It dawned on him. 'You're locked out!'

'You think I'm here for fun?' Her teeth were chattering. 'Yes, I am. Locked out. Where on earth have you been?'

He held up the Quality Street. 'In search of these! I've been to half the garages in Sussex. How did you get locked out?'

'Just open the bloody door, will you!'

They went inside. It was pitch dark.

'Fuse must have tripped,' he said. Maurice closed the front door and put his arms around his wife and rubbed her back, trying to get her circulation going. She was shivering all over. 'I'm so cold.' She shot a wary glance in the direction of the stairs.

'Stay one second, my love.' He put the chocolates down on the hall table, groped around in a drawer, found a small torch and switched it on. Making his way through into the kitchen, he went into the utility room, opened the fuse box and saw the red master switch was up. He flicked it down and instantly all the lights came on. He hurried back out into the hall and put his arms around Claudette again.

'There was someone in here,' she said.

'Are you sure?'

'There was. A man. Upstairs.'

He started climbing the stairs.

'Be careful!'

She heard him clumping around above her, then he reappeared. 'My love, there's no one. Are you sure it's not all that television you're watching? Are you imagining things?'

'I – I am not *imagining* things.'

He came back down and put his arms around her. She was still shivering. 'That's why you ran out of the house?'

She nodded, bleakly.

He rubbed her, vigorously. 'Better?'

She nodded again.

'I know just how to warm you up,' he said suggestively.

'Good, so get me a glass of fizz before I die from hypothermia.'

'Coming up! I'll get us each a glass and we could have them in a nice hot bath, how about that? That would really warm you up!'

'In your dreams.' Her teeth were chattering – but not enough to prevent her from disentangling from his arms, picking up the tub and carrying it through into the living room and tearing greedily and excitedly at the lid.

Fetching the bottle from the fridge, and a glass for himself, he hurried back into the living room after her. 'My love, what was it you thought you saw?'

'I didn't *see* anything. I heard a sound upstairs and smelled a cigar.'

'A cigar? Don't be daft.'

Sat on the sofa, ignoring him while he opened the bottle, she finally got the lid off and stared at the contents. Feeling warmer and much happier, suddenly.

Strawberry Delight!

She plucked one out, unwrapped it and popped it in her mouth. 'Command! Play *Poldark* on catch-up, please.' As she chewed she stared up at the to-die-for face of Ross Poldark. *Aidan Turner! Sweet Lord! Why can't my husband look like you?*

'Here we are, my sexy beast!'

She took the glass without even looking at Maurice. 'That's what *I* call a sexy beast,' she said, pointing at the screen.

He sat down next to her with his glass and cuddled up to her. 'You used to call me your sexy beast.' He nuzzled her ear and she shook him away, dipping her hand into the tub and pulling out another Strawberry Delight. 'Did I? I don't remember that.'

He looked hurt.

Then froze.

He could smell cigar smoke. Faint at first but getting rapidly stronger.

A shadow moved across the doorway.

'What the . . . ?' he said, but Claudette was engrossed in the television and didn't hear him.

He got to his feet and walked, cautiously, over to the door and looked out into the hall. Nothing there. He sniffed. But the smell had gone – as quickly as it had come.

36

Jason and Emily stood, rooted to the spot, staring around the room. The command module here in the studio was set in the ceiling above his desk. But this voice hadn't come from above – it had come from behind them, through the open door.

'What was that?' she said. 'What was it?'

He strode over and looked down the stairs. 'Yes, hello!' he yelled down. 'Something you want to share with us? Hello? HELLO?'

'Don't,' Emily cautioned.

He turned to her. 'Don't what? Someone speaks to me in my – our – home, I'm sodding well answering them back.' He shouted down the stairs. 'Show yourself – you can say what you want, my wife and I aren't scared of a bloody ghost, OK? Got that?'

Emily followed him and stood beside him. Their eyes met, Emily's wide with fear. Jason put a protective arm around her and held her tight again. He could feel her trembling.

He was trembling, too.

'What was it?' she asked. 'Like, who?'

'Stay here, I'll take a look.'

'No way, I'm coming with you.'

She followed him, one slow step at a time, down the spiral staircase. Into each of the rooms in turn, on the first floor.

Checking the windows. All were locked. Then on down and into the hall. There was nothing in the living room and they went into the kitchen. *Poldark* was on the television, the sound still muted.

'We both heard it, Jason,' Emily said.

'I know.' He went through into the utility room off the kitchen, grabbed the torch from the shelf and went out of the back door, latching it. Emily followed.

He headed past the bin store, to the back garden, and shone the beam all around. 'I'm going to check the front too – make sure there are no speakers anywhere, put there by that bastard Fears, or any other locals trying to scare us,' he said, determinedly.

Finally, having done a complete and thorough circuit, and finding nothing, he went back inside.

'Do you really have to work so late?' Emily asked, following him back up to the studio. 'I don't want to go to bed alone. I'm scared.'

'I've got to get this finished, and the sketch of the spaniel, by tomorrow afternoon, somehow. I've promised David, otherwise he won't get the framing done in time. If I don't deliver these to my clients, I'm not going to get paid – and they're going to be mightily pissed off. I can't let them down.'

'Christmas is still a week away. You give him a lot of business – surely he can still do them if you deliver to him on Tuesday, or even Wednesday?'

'He's going on holiday on Wednesday until after the New Year – he's allocated the time on Tuesday for them both.'

'So, work through tomorrow night. But not tonight, please, Jason.'

He nodded at the couch on the far side of the room. 'How about you crash there while I work on? Actually, it would be quite nice if the two of us were up here – just for now.'

She looked at him. 'Because?'

Because I'm shit scared of working up here alone tonight was the truth. But he didn't say that. He said, 'Because you'll feel safer here.'

To his relief, Emily agreed.

37

Monday 17 December

At eleven the following morning, Emily's business partner sat at the kitchen table with her eyes shut, while Jason and Emily sat facing her, apprehensively. Jason, bleary from tiredness, sipped a strong coffee. Emily was also exhausted from a largely sleepless night, because Jason had worked through most of it, needing the lights on, brightly. Just when she had finally drifted off, it seemed only moments later she was woken by the roar of machinery on the building site.

Louise, a rotund woman with short, dark hair cut into a fringe, was dressed in a baggy, knee-length, cable-knit jumper over leggings and ankle boots. Usually she had an irrepressibly cheerful demeanour with a foghorn of a laugh, but this morning she looked deadly serious and focused.

'Oh-oh-oh-oh,' she said, eyes still shut. 'So much activity. So much. I've got so many spirits all trying to communicate with you, all at once. They're being very naughty, very rude. I'm trying to get some order here, but they're not letting me.'

'What do you mean?' Emily quizzed.

Louise did not respond. Instead, she shouted, nodding her head, 'No, you! Back! Wait your turn!'

Jason looked at her, very sceptical.

Still with her eyes tightly shut, Louise said, 'I'm getting a message for you, Jason. From a woman. She says she's sorry that she damaged your painting last night. She is telling me she was angry that you put her portrait facing the wall – she says she recognizes she has anger issues ever since she passed into spirit.'

How could she know this, he wondered?

Emily looked at her husband. He frowned back at her.

'I'm getting another person now,' Louise said. 'Another woman. She's been in spirit for a long time. She is very angry indeed. She's – she's just full of anger. Now there's a man interrupting. He tells me his name is Harry. He's telling me he used to drive the digger. He's giving me a message for you. He's saying, "Ask anyone, they'll know about the digger." Does that mean anything to you?' She opened her eyes and looked at them.

Jason and Emily stared back at her, as pale as ghosts.

'Digger?' Emily asked. 'Did you say *digger*?'

'There is so much spirit activity. Was there a graveyard here before? That's what it feels like. So much spirit activity. It really needs to be calmed down.'

'When you say *spirit activity*, Louise, what exactly do you mean?' Jason asked. 'What do you mean by a *spirit*?'

'A trapped soul.'

'Soul?'

'What I believe,' Louise said, 'is that all of us have guardian angels – guides – who look after us. If we die of an illness, or just old age, they take our spirits – souls – over to the other side. But sometimes, if a person dies suddenly – they're murdered, or in an accident, for instance – and the guide is not around at that moment, then the spirit doesn't realize the body has gone. It wanders around, lost, trapped here in this plane. It's what we call *earthbound*. An *earthbound* soul.'

'How long are they trapped here for?' he asked.

'Time is different in the spirit world,' she replied. 'We live in *linear* time, we go from A to B to C. You wake up in the morning, say at seven a.m., go for your bike ride, come home at eight a.m., have breakfast, work on a painting, have lunch at one p.m., and so on. It's different in the spirit world; time has no meaning. For spirits it's as if everything that ever was, still is. They go back in time and they go forward in time.'

'Forward?' he quizzed.

'Oh yes, absolutely. That's how they can sometimes show us things.'

'How far forward, Louise?' Emily asked.

'I don't believe there's any limit,' she replied. 'They can go back years, decades, centuries – and forward just as easily, too.'

Jason smiled. 'So, when we die we see the future?'

'I'm sure of it.'

'Could be useful for giving horse racing tips to someone on the earth plane,' he jested.

'Oh, it's been done,' Louise replied. 'But never with a good outcome – that's a misuse the spirit world would frown on.'

'Louise, if we have a spirit here in this house, what do we do about it?'

'It will need rescuing.'

'Rescuing? Who you gonna call? Ghostbusters?' he said, jokily.

'999 and ask for the Spirit Rescue Service?' grinned Emily.

'You phone your local vicar,' Louise replied, firmly.

'Our vicar?' Emily said. 'We don't even know who that is.'

'You could—' Louise was interrupted by a harsh ringing sound.

They all looked around, startled.

It repeated.

The doorbell, they realized.

Signalling to his wife to stay where she was, Jason walked out and over to the front door, and opened it.

A tall, lean man in his late forties stood there, wearing an Aran jumper with a minister's white dog collar just visible, blue jeans and work boots. He had thinning hair and a handsome face with an insouciant, rather world-weary expression that reminded Jason of an actor whose name he could not immediately remember.

He would be a good subject to paint, was his first thought.

'Mr Danes?' he enquired, with a posh public-school voice.

'Yes.'

'I'm the vicar of Cold Hill parish, Roland Fortinbrass. I just thought I would pop round and introduce myself, as you've just moved in. Is this a convenient time? I hope I'm not disturbing you from your work?' He gave a warm smile. 'I understand you are a very celebrated local artist.'

'Struggling, rather than celebrated,' he replied, hesitantly, and smiled. This was such a weird coincidence, his turning up just at this moment, he thought. Should he invite him in now, with Louise here, or ask him to come back later? He made a decision.

'How nice to meet you. Fortinbrass, did you say? Like the character in Hamlet?'

The vicar smiled. 'Well, similar – he had only one "s" in his name – I have two.'

'Ah, right. Please – come in.'

Entering, the vicar said, 'What a simply charming house – it reminds me so much of the original mansion that was here on this site. I hope you and Mrs Danes will be very happy here.'

Closing the door behind them, Jason said, 'Can we offer you some tea or coffee, Reverend?'

'Oh no, thank you, I'm fine, and I don't want to trouble you for longer than is necessary. This is just a very quick visit to welcome you to our little community.'

'My wife and I went to the Crown yesterday, for lunch, and got the feeling some of the locals aren't too happy about this development,' Jason said.

Fortinbrass smiled. 'Well, you have to understand that country folk are very set in their ways. They don't like – or get – change.'

'So it seems.'

'Allow me to speculate that the most vociferous among them was a certain farmer?' Fortinbrass said.

'Albert Fears?'

'Well, I don't like to name names, but I'm afraid yes, Albert is one of those who springs to mind. He somewhat insularly takes the view that to be a local, you have to be born here. Everyone else, in his book, is an interloper.'

'We rather got that impression.'

'Don't let it worry you. It was the same with me, when I came here. Please don't let it put you off. This is a very friendly community and we welcome new blood. Indeed, we badly need it – and especially, if I may say so, someone as famous as you. There is so much talk in the village – everyone is very thrilled to have you and your wife here.'

'We're extremely happy to be here.'

'Without being too personal, Mr Danes, would I be right in saying you've chosen a new-build home because you have an aversion to dirt?'

Jason looked at him, a little miffed at such a personal remark. 'How do you know that?'

Fortinbrass smiled. 'Shall we say, as the vicar it's my job to know about issues with my flock?'

'I'm afraid neither my wife nor I are very religious.'

'But you do believe in *something*, don't you? A bigger picture?'

'Well – yes – who told you that?'

Again, that strange smile. 'As I said, it is my business to know things.'

Jason looked at him for some moments, puzzled by how he could know this. 'Please come through and meet my wife, Emily – we have a friend with us, her business partner.'

'What business is that, may I ask?'

'Catering.'

'Ah. Well, that could be very interesting for me, very interesting.'

They entered the kitchen. To Jason's relief, Louise had her eyes open and was chatting to Emily. He introduced the vicar to both of them.

'How very nice to meet you,' Roland Fortinbrass said, shaking Emily's hand and then Louise's. 'I don't know if any of you are musicians or have good voices, but we are short of members for the church choir, and we are always looking for musicians for our church band.'

'I'm afraid not,' Emily said. 'I've a singing voice that sounds like two cats fighting in a dustbin.'

'And I'm tone deaf,' Jason added.

The vicar turned to Louise. 'How about you?'

'I live in Brighton, I'm afraid,' Louise said. 'I'm just here visiting Emily.'

'What a shame.' Looking at each woman in turn, he said to Emily, 'Your husband tells me you are in the catering business? We must have a chat about catering for one of our church events, sometime. And if there is anything I can ever do for you, please let me know – you can always find me at the Vicarage – the house right next to the church.'

'Actually,' Emily said, shooting a glance at Jason, then Louise. 'There is one thing.'

'Oh?'

'I understand the Church of England has diocesan exorcists in every county.'

Fortinbrass suddenly looked awkward. 'Well, yes, although we prefer the title *Ministers of Deliverance*. Why are you interested, if I may ask?'

'We think we need one to come here,' she replied.

38

As soon as the vicar had left, Jason went up to his studio and rang the number for Richwards Estate Agents. When the receptionist answered, he asked if he could speak to Paul Jordan.

After a short time on hold, he heard the familiar, jovial voice.

'Ah, Mr Famous Artist, sir! Very good to hear from you – how may I be of assistance? And how is everything in beautiful Lakeview Drive?'

'Well,' Jason replied, 'not great, actually.'

'Oh? Oh dear, I'm sorry to hear that.' The estate agent sounded genuinely concerned. 'What's the problem?'

'Well – a few things, really. If I remember rightly, when my wife and I bought the house, you said that we were the second people to be moving into Cold Hill Park – and I think you mentioned there was a family about to complete on the house directly opposite us?'

'Number thirty-four?'

'Yes.'

'Yes indeed, the Lloyds, very charming people.'

'Well, my wife and I went for Sunday lunch at the pub in the village, the Crown.'

'You did?' Jordan sounded a little strange.

'Yes.'

'The Crown?'

153

'Yes.'

'Ah, OK.'

'We happened to bump into our neighbours there – from the house across from ours – number thirty-six.'

'Mr and Mrs Penze-Weedell! What a charming couple. I'm so pleased you've become acquainted with them.'

'Yes, well, the thing is, they told us there had been three families who had also bought homes on the estate before us. We didn't know that.'

Hesitantly, Jordan said, 'Yes. Yes, they did.'

'Is it true all three of them have subsequently died in accidents?'

There was a long moment before the estate agent responded. 'Sadly, yes, I'm afraid. The Bradshaws, Ganeshes and Westermans.'

'Three families from one small estate, all dead in the space of a couple of months? Isn't that more than a bit of a coincidence? It feels pretty bloody weird to my wife and I.'

'Well, yes, I would have to admit that's how it might look.'

'*Might* look?' Jason said. 'To us, it smacks of a hex on this place.'

'Let me put your mind at rest, Mr Danes. Of course, it must seem like a hex or a curse – if you believe in that kind of thing. But the reality, tragic though it certainly might be, is somewhat more prosaic. The Ganeshes, from 7 Copse Walk, were up in Manchester, having a holiday visiting relatives, when the house they were sleeping in caught fire and they were trapped. The Bradshaws, from number thirty-four opposite you, a delightful family with two small children, I understand were poisoned by carbon monoxide from a faulty boiler, in a rented villa in Italy. And the Westermans, from 42 Copse Walk, very unfortunately, were both killed in a boating accident in the Caribbean – they were out snorkelling, and a waterskiing boat apparently didn't see them and went over them.'

Jason absorbed this, reflecting. He had to admit that the geographical distance between Cold Hill and the accidents did reduce the notion of a curse. But . . . 'It's still a very strange coincidence, wouldn't you say? That they all lived here?'

'Coincidences do happen in life, Mr Danes,' Jordan replied. 'Sometimes they are good, happy ones and just occasionally, like these, they are terrible. So sad. But to conclude from these that Cold Hill Park is under some kind of dark cloud – well, I couldn't say that, no. It's a beautiful development, as I think you and Mrs Danes recognized when you made your decision to buy there. Please don't let something like this upset you, so soon after you've moved in.'

'Why didn't you tell us then – or at least before we exchanged contracts?'

'None of these terrible accidents relate to their houses or the development,' Jordan replied. 'I didn't tell you because, firstly, I didn't think it was relevant and secondly, frankly, I didn't want to spoil your enjoyment of your new home in any way.' He paused then went on. 'Look, let me make a suggestion to you and your wife. I've been in this business a long time. Moving house is much less easy than people imagine. I can't tell you the number of times I've seen couples move into their dream home, only to divorce within a few years. It can be a very disruptive period, during which all that you've known and built together is suddenly gone and you have a whole new set of challenges. Please work through it together. You have a truly beautiful new home – for most people it would be a dream. I remember at your first viewing, the expression on your face when you walked into the loft – how you said you knew you could work there. Are you finding it inspirational?'

Hesitantly, Jason said, 'Yes.'

'Well then,' Jordan said. 'There you are! And within a few months, there won't be an empty house on the estate, that I can assure you.'

Jason thanked him, meekly, apologized for taking up his time, and ended the call.

Instantly he wished he had quizzed him more. But at the same time, he knew, he would probably have sounded ridiculous.

He would take the agent's advice, he decided.

Work through it.

He walked over and peered across the street at number thirty-four. There was a people carrier parked in front; a young couple were helping two small children out of the rear seats. They all walked up to the front door, the father thumbing through a set of keys, one of the children skipping along, excitedly. The father unlocked the front door and went in.

Who were they? Jason wondered, feeling a little relieved. It didn't look like an estate-agency viewing – and besides, it would be too soon after the owners had died for probate to have been granted and the property put on the market, surely? Relatives of the deceased seemed the most likely.

Could they be the couple with the two small children he'd seen in the house before?

He liked that as an explanation.

39

Monday 17 December

Jason turned back to the painting of the two labradoodles. But as he tried to focus, he was distracted by the noise from the construction site to the west. His tiredness from his disturbed night seemingly accentuating every sound.

As he worked, he could not shut out the endless roaring and grinding, the jangling clatter of metal chains and tumbling rubble. He hadn't really noticed the noise from the site when they'd originally viewed the house – probably because they were focused on the house and excited. Nor had he really been aware of it on Friday, distracted by the task of moving in.

Was this going to be the reality for months to come, now? At least the workers would be knocking off for Christmas sometime soon – in the next few days – and with luck they'd not be returning until the New Year. That would give him nearly a couple of weeks of peace and quiet, after finishing his two commissions, to concentrate on his portfolio of work for his show in February. Maybe he should get a pair of ear defenders, like many of the workers on the site were wearing, to cut out the din?

An orange crane with a grab-bucket had appeared on the site during the morning, moving slowly across on caterpillar tracks like some giant scaly creature from the Jurassic age. The driver was currently swinging the bucket into a diminishing mountain of rubble – one of a line of them – scooping it up and depositing it into the deep rectangle, a good fifty feet wide and three hundred long, that had been excavated – presumably the foundations for a number of houses.

From time to time, with the light outside changing from bright sunshine to darkly overcast, Jason stepped away from finishing the portrait of the two dogs, opened the window and zoomed in through his camera lens on different workmen. He was collecting dozens of photographs. He loved the starkly contrasting image of the yellow jackets and hats against the dark brown mud of the landscape. Part of his exhibition, he had decided, would definitely be images of these men. It would be different from anything else out there; Lowry-inspired, sure, but very different from that great artist's images.

One worker caught his eye now, spotlighted by the sun in another break in the clouds. An olive-skinned man in a white hard hat, ear defenders and a yellow hi-viz jacket, standing facing the deep rectangle and rummaging in his pocket. The labourer leaned against another mountain of rubble and began rolling a cigarette. The man's body language was such a giveaway; his head was just below the top of the rubble and he was peering around, furtively checking that no one could see him. He'd chosen his position well, invisible to the Portakabin where no doubt the site manager and foreman were working, and to his fellow workers.

Jason snapped away, zooming in even tighter. He already had the name for this painting in his mind. *The Skiver!*

Suddenly, a shadow fell across the pile of rubble, moving steadily, rapidly darkening it.

Jason took his eye away from the viewfinder and looked up, puzzled for a second; the sky was still a brilliant blue.

Then he saw the cause of the shadow. The orange crane had turned away from the stack it had just finished emptying into the pit, to this new one. It was moving steadily towards it. He saw the driver busy in the cab with his controls, unaware of the man lighting his cigarette on the far side of it, craftily out of sight.

The skiver, wearing his ear defenders, wouldn't hear it.

Jason stared, transfixed, wanting to shout out a warning, but he was far too far away. He emitted only a quiet, lame croak.

No!

He watched the two halves of the clamshell bucket of the crane open. Swinging from its cables. Dropping jerkily. Hovering over the top of the stack.

Two huge jaws.

Over the man.

Then, like a bird of prey, it dropped, pouncing, momentarily blocking him from Jason's view.

The two halves closed together, scooping up rubble, then rose sharply again.

With something dangling from them.

Oh Jesus, no.

It was the skiver, being hoisted in the air, his head invisible inside the jaws. All Jason could see of him was from the neck down, body twitching, his legs kicking, work boots flailing.

Abruptly the grab bucket stopped with a jerk in mid-air, and opened.

The skiver's torso plummeted like a rag doll, twenty feet to the ground, toppled sideways and lay still. Blood spewed from his neck.

A second later, something white fell from the bucket, bounced on the ground near the motionless body and rolled. As it did so, something tipped out of it.

Jason stared in utter horror as he realized what it was.

Oh Jesus.

He turned, his stomach heaving, and threw up on the studio floor.

40

Downstairs in the kitchen, Emily glanced at the large round clock on the kitchen wall. It was a replica antique French railway clock, with Roman numerals. 1.15 p.m. Louise had left because she had heard there was a special offer on large prawns at a wholesaler in Worthing, and the saving would be a good boost to the somewhat meagre profit they would be making.

She opened the fridge door and was about to take out a couple of pies for lunch for herself and Jason, when he came in, looking very pale.

'Darling,' she said, alarmed. 'Are you OK? What is it?'

'I – I need a bucket and a mop. Where can I find them?'

'They're in the utility room – why? What do you need them for?'

Hesitating, he said, 'I think I just saw someone die – killed.'

She followed him up to his studio, carrying a bucket of warm soapy water and several cloths.

'Oh God,' he said, entering and ignoring his puke on the floor. 'Oh Jesus, it was horrible.' He stared across at the construction site, his face pale.

'What?' Emily walked over and stood beside him. She saw an orange crane, and a swarm of workers in hard hats all around it.

'I just – just—' He began sobbing. 'Oh God.'

Alarmed, she put an arm around him. 'What's happened?'

'I – I can't believe what I just saw.'

'What? What, darling? What exactly did you just see?'

'It was horrible. Jesus, it was horrible.'

'What, please tell me.'

'An accident – a terrible—' He shook his head. 'Oh God.'

'What's happened?'

'I. Just. Saw. A. Man. Killed. Killed. I saw him killed.'

'Where? There, on the site?'

He continued staring. Shaking. Without answering her.

'Tell me what happened, what did you see?'

All the machines had stopped. There were now twenty, maybe thirty workers standing in a semi-circle. More running over to join them.

In the distance was the wail of a siren, coming ever closer. Followed by another.

A siren screamed by, close to the house. Two paramedics ran onto the site and through a gap that opened up in the semi-circle of workers. They were closely followed by two police officers.

Jason turned away and buried his face in her neck. 'Don't look, Em,' he sobbed. 'Please don't look. Oh God, I could have saved him, I saw – saw . . .'

'Saw what? Please tell me, Jason, tell me. Come away from the window, come on, sit down, can I get you something?'

He shook his head.

She guided him over to the couch and got him to sit down, then joined him. 'Please, tell me what happened, what did you see?'

It took some while before he was calm enough to speak. He told her all he'd seen.

When he had finished, Emily said, 'You need to call the police and tell them – you might be the only witness.'

He nodded. 'Yes, I know. I will do – oh God. I will call them. All he was doing was having a sneaky fag.'

She put her arms around him. 'You poor darling.' She kissed him on the cheek. 'There wasn't anything you could have done.'

'I know.'

Emily cleaned up the vomit, went out of the room and returned a few minutes later, and stood looking at the easel.

'The picture is beautiful – amazing how you've caught their personalities.'

'Thanks.' He gave her a weak smile, his face still sheet white.

'It looks finished.'

'Just about. I'll start on the spaniel soon.'

'Good. Call the police, then try to put it out of your mind and focus.'

'I know.'

They both stood up.

'I was about to make us some lunch. Do you think you could manage anything?'

'Maybe in a while.'

As Emily went back downstairs, he looked again at the painting. After being up all night, he'd planned to crash out for a couple of hours after finishing it, before starting on the spaniel. But he was so wired, that was no longer an option.

More sirens wailed.

He walked over to the window and looked out. It was like a scene from a television crime show. An ambulance, a cluster of police cars, and a dark green van with an emblem on it, crime scene tape . . .

Squinting through the zoom lens of his camera, he closed in on the emblem.

HM CORONER. WEST SUSSEX.

He wondered whether he should dial the Emergency number, 999. But whatever emergency there might have been was over. Instead, removing his gloves and binning them, he dialled the number for non-emergency incidents: 101.

It was several minutes before a call handler answered. Jason told him what he had seen.

The man asked him for his contact details, thanked him and told him someone would be in touch.

He ended the call, turned back and carried on, applying the finishing touches to the painting. Thirty minutes later, removing the portrait of the dogs from the easel, he placed it safely and securely on the floor, face-out, to enable the paint to dry and harden.

It was 2.20 p.m. Feeling utterly shattered, but drawn by compulsion, he walked across to the window and looked out yet again. A square white tent had been placed a short distance in front of the crane. A group of people in blue oversuits and baggy overshoes stood around it, and a police officer with a clipboard stood a short distance in front of them.

Too exhausted to care right now, Jason lay down on the couch and was asleep in seconds.

41

He dreamed he was on a treadmill, pedalling harder and harder, trying to hand a finished gesso board to David, his framer, who was standing at the end of the treadmill, but never able to reach him.

Then a headless torso was dangling from the jaws of a mechanical digger. The legs twitching and kicking as if trying to break free of its grip.

Voices coming at Jason from every direction.

You could have saved him.

Why didn't you try?

He was my husband.

He was my father.

He was my brother.

He was my son.

I loved him so much.

He was a good man.

You could have shouted louder, mister. You could have. You could have saved him, but all you thought about was your art, you selfish bastard.

Jason woke in darkness, in confusion, hot, sweaty, gripped with anxiety. What time was it? How long had he slept? Panicky, he looked at his watch.

Shit!

8.20 p.m.

He'd been asleep six hours! Why hadn't Emily woken him?
8.20 p.m. The sketch of the spaniel had to be with his framer
by 10 a.m. tomorrow. He did a mental calculation. It would take
him a good twenty minutes to get there. Which left him approx-
imately eleven hours to get it done – assuming he worked
through the night – and he had no option but to.

The horror of what he had seen earlier came flooding back.
He rolled over and peered out of the window, feeling the cold
draught through the panes on his face. All looked dark out there,
apart from one patch of bright light. Lit up by it was a solitary
police officer, looking cold and bored, with crime scene tape either
side of him. Beyond, the silhouettes of heavy machinery stood
out against the moonlight, which cast a sinister glow on them.

I could have saved him.

How?

Impossible, he knew, no one would have heard him
however loud he had shouted. But he still felt bad for not trying.
Guilt as dark as the night leached into him, as if via osmosis.

'Shit!' He jumped up, picked his way carefully to the door
and switched on the lights. He blinked as they came on, bright
and harsh – the light he liked to paint by at night. He felt dirty
all over. Filthy. Dirt in every pore of his skin trying, like the guilt,
to worm inside him.

'Get off!' he shouted, shaking his arms, shaking his whole
body.

He hurried down to their bedroom, through into the bathroom and stripped off all his clothes, letting them fall in a heap
on the floor – they'd not yet unpacked the laundry basket,
wherever it might be. Opening the glass door of the shower, he
switched on the rain shower head, which was the size of a
dinner plate, adjusted the temperature until it felt right, then
went in.

For several minutes he stood still, gratefully feeling the powerful, cleansing needles of water on his skin before stepping back. As the water tumbled in front of him, he rubbed shampoo into his hair and soaped, scrupulously, every part of his body. He stepped back under the water, rinsed it all off, then repeated the process.

All the time thinking.

No one from the police had called him back.

I need to phone them again.

It can wait until tomorrow.

Can it?

It had to.

Phoning them now would change nothing. But if he didn't deliver the sketch in time for Christmas, that would be a catastrophe, letting someone down and almost certainly losing himself an important client.

No disrespect, Mr Skiver.

Then he shuddered at the image he could not get out of his mind.

The torso dangling from the jaws of the grab bucket. The man's legs twitching.

The hard hat falling. Bouncing.

The severed head tipping out of it.

Shampoo went into his eyes, stinging them. He closed them tightly and turned his face upwards until it was all washed away. Tentatively, he moved out of the jet and opened his eyes. To his relief, the stinging had lessened. Again, he applied more shower gel and repeated the careful soaping, before going back under the jet.

A second later the water suddenly, without warning, turned glacial. He stepped sharply back, in shock, half opening his eyes, which were hurting like crazy again. He reached forward and pressed the red button on the control panel, holding his hand until he felt the water warming up, then stepped back under the powerful stream of water, raising his face again.

It started getting colder. The temperature plunging. So cold it was hurting.

Shit! He stepped back, rapidly. Opened his eyes.

And saw a woman's face pressed against the steamed-up door.

The woman in the black suit.

42

Startled, Jason stepped back in shock, slipped and fell, bashing the rear of his head against the far wall of the shower.

Numbingly cold water stung his skin as he lay, dazed, for some moments, before crying out in pain and rolling sideways on the slippery shower tray, out of the water jet. He lay there, still very dazed, staring up at the door.

No one was there.

But he'd seen a face.

The woman.

Clambering to his feet, carefully, his head hurting, he pressed the red button for hot water, waiting until the temperature was OK again. As soon as it was, he rinsed the shampoo and soap and quickly switched the shower off, stepped out and grabbed a towel, shaking.

Had he imagined it?

Again?

Five minutes later, he was dressed and downstairs. The integral door to the garage was open – Emily was in there sorting out her catering equipment. Feeling a little shaky, he walked across the kitchen, opened the fridge door and removed a block of Cheddar to make himself a sandwich.

Then he turned back to the fridge and looked around inside

it for a jar of Branston pickle. Behind him, he heard Emily's alarmed voice.

'Darling, what's happened to you?'

He turned. 'What do you mean? I'm fine, just hungry, making a quick sandwich.'

She was staring, alarmed. 'You're bleeding. The back of your head's covered in blood. It's dripping on the floor.'

'What?' He spun round and saw bright red droplets of blood on the tiles.

She ran over to him. 'Turn your head,' she commanded.

He obeyed.

Pressing her hands against the wound and gently probing with her fingers, she said, 'You've gashed it open. God – really deeply. My poor darling, what happened?'

Hesitantly, he said, 'I slipped in the shower. Fell over.'

She grabbed a tea towel, ran it under the cold tap and pressed it against the back of his head. It stung.

'You need to go to hospital to get it stitched!'

'No way.'

'You do!'

'Em, if we go to hospital I'll be there for ten hours waiting to be seen. No way!'

'You've cut it right open.'

'I am not going to hospital. I'm not sitting in A & E with twenty people sneezing and coughing germs all around me. We've both managed to avoid the flu that's everywhere this winter, touch wood. A & E would be a bloody incubator for it.'

'We'll keep a close eye on it. I'll get the first-aid kit. Keep holding the towel, OK?'

He put an arm behind his head and held the wet cloth as she dashed out of the room, returning with the kit.

'This may sting,' she said.

'It's already stinging.'

'I'm not surprised!'

'Owwwwww!' he yelled as she squeezed some antiseptic cream onto the wound.

'I'll try a pad – let's see if that works. Otherwise I'm taking you to A & E whether you like it or not.'

'I have to get the sketch finished tonight, hell or high water.'

'And die from blood poisoning trying?'

'I was in the shower – the wound's clean.'

'How did you fall over?' she asked. 'Old men fall over in showers, not you.'

Reluctantly, she dressed the back of his head. He thanked her and returned to the sandwich he was making.

'You need a hot meal, not a sandwich,' she said.

'I'm fine with a sandwich.'

Shaking her head, she said, 'No client's worth killing yourself over.'

'I'm OK, honestly.'

'You are so not OK.' She peered at him closely. 'You really don't look right.'

'I'm shaken by what I saw and stressed over the sketch, that's all – and tired; I'll take it easy after I've finished it – have a chill day tomorrow.'

'You need to.'

He gobbled down his sandwich and hurried back up to work, carrying a large, strong coffee. He stopped at their bedroom to take two paracetamols from the bathroom cabinet and swallow them, then went on up to his studio and sat briefly at his desk, logging on. A few emails that needed responses. They could wait until tomorrow. He glanced at Instagram, aware it was a week since he had last posted anything there. He quickly *liked* a number of new posts.

Then he walked to his easel, pencil in hand, and studied the photograph of the spaniel rested on the easel's shelf. He liked drawing this breed of dog – with its big, floppy ears and this one's regal pose – and it was his portfolio of spaniel sketches that had led to the Northcote Gallery first taking a serious interest in his work.

A few hours, he figured. That's all it would take him. A £1000 fee. Good money – and for doing what he loved. What was not to like?

He sipped his coffee and set to work, all his concerns parked in another compartment of his mind.

Sometime after 2 a.m. he had finished the sketch. He went downstairs and, after undressing and brushing his teeth as quietly as he could, he took a further two paracetamols for his headache and slipped into bed. Emily stirred, murmuring, 'Did you get it done?'

'Yep.'

'Love you.'

He kissed her and was asleep, exhausted, seconds later.

43

Jason woke shortly after 7 a.m. and went through to the bathroom. As he came back into the bedroom, Emily was sitting up, her bedside lamp on, smiling sleepily. 'You finished the sketch?'

'Yep! I told you when I came to bed.'

'Well done.' She looked across at his pillow and saw it was covered in dried blood. 'Turn around and show me the back of your head, darling.'

He sat on the bed to let her check the wound beneath the bandage.

After removing it, tenderly, she said, 'It's looking clean – and it seems to have closed up a little. Keep it dry in the shower and I'll put a fresh dressing on it. I'd still prefer you to get it looked at.'

Hospitals gave him the heebie-jeebies. 'It's fine.'

Half an hour later they sat at the kitchen table, with the breakfast news on the television, the sound almost muted. Emily sipped one of the protein smoothie shakes she was currently into, and Jason ate a mouthful of porridge.

'What's your plan for today?' he asked.

'I'm meeting Louise in Lewes for a coffee, then we're going off to do a massive shop for the freezers – hopefully get everything we'll need for that twenty-fifth wedding anniversary do.'

'December twenty-eighth, right?'

'Yep. Doesn't give us any time after Christmas. You?'

'First thing, I'm taking the two pictures over to David to get the framing done, then I thought – no one from the police has called me about yesterday – I don't know if I should go to the police station and make a report.'

'You phoned them yesterday?'

'Yes.'

'I'd wait for them to contact you; I'm sure they will. Try not to let what happened distract you – you really need to relax.'

'Yep. I was hoping to, but I'm starting to really panic about the exhibition.'

'How's your head feeling, now?'

'OK.'

She looked at him. 'I just wonder whether you shouldn't get an X-ray done.'

'Why?'

'Why? Because you clearly hit it very hard. You might have some internal damage.'

'It wasn't that hard.'

'No? It looks like it was pretty damned hard to me.'

'I'm fine, honestly.'

He finished his breakfast and went up to his studio. He looked across at the construction site. None of the machinery was operating. There were two police cars and a white forensics van, and several people in hooded protective suits and over-shoes on the far side of the cordon, where the accident had taken place. One was taking a stream of photographs.

Seated at his desk, he logged on to his computer.

And saw white, seemingly random numbers, again, on a black background. He tried to take a screenshot but they vanished before he hit the keys. As before, the login request then appeared.

He called his computer guru and got his voicemail. He left Matt a message asking him to call back, and to do something to stop the glitch causing these irritating numbers from appearing. Then, carefully placing the paintings of the dogs into protective carriers, he kissed Emily goodbye and set off to his framer in Lewes.

David Graham's workshop was, undoubtedly, the most chaotic work environment Jason had ever seen. A huge open-plan loft space, in former industrial premises in the centre of Lewes, there were exposed beams and rafters, shelves crammed with rows of old books and battered old chairs blotched with paint. Each of the several work surfaces was littered with ancient computer terminals, bottles of chemicals, loose papers, strips of wood. In addition, there was a soiled cooker where the mix for his gesso boards was heated up, and propped against a wall was a gigantic roll of bubble wrap.

The framer himself, in grubby overalls with a creased, paint-spattered face and equally spattered grey hair could, if he stood perfectly still, have blended into his environment like a chameleon.

Jason never ceased to wonder at the ability of the man to produce exquisite framing of his work, exactly as they discussed, and always on time. Their relationship, over the past decade, had reached the point where he hardly needed to brief the man at all. He handed him the two carriers and David assured him they would be ready for collection the following morning. He reminded Jason that he was closing up shop at midday on Wednesday until early January, and flying up to the Scottish Highlands.

Feeling relieved and a lot happier than yesterday, Jason went Christmas shopping for Emily. He bought a selection of items, including a gold chain and a cookbook he knew she wanted by the Israeli chef Yotam Ottolenghi, then drove out of Lewes and headed for Cold Hill village, through light, late-morning drizzle.

He turned off the main road and crossed the now-familiar

humpback bridge. He slowed to take a look at the deserted cricket pitch, with its small wooden pavilion, thinking of ideas for cricketing scenes. He would come down and watch a game when the season began.

He drove on the short distance to St Mary's, the decrepit-looking Norman church. It was set well back in a commandingly high position above the road and fronted by an ornate wooden lychgate set in a low, stone wall. Beyond was an uneven grave-yard, filled with rows of weathered headstones, some partially concealed beneath the spreading branches of a massive, ancient yew tree, some almost toppled over. He could see a lot more graves beyond the rear of the church. He pulled up the BMW outside the house adjacent to the graveyard and climbed out.

A faded, barely legible sign he'd passed by the front gate said, VICARAGE.

It was a modest, somewhat square house of fairly modern construction. Peering closer, he could see the window frames and sills were all rotten – what little paint remaining on them was flaking. A number of slates were absent from the roof, several lying broken amid the weeds that covered what was once a front lawn, and the brickwork was in dire need of repointing. With some serious TLC on the house – and garden – it would actually be rather an attractive little property, given the location. He figured the Church must have sold off the original vicarage years before, unable to fund its maintenance. Not that they'd done a good job of looking after the replacement.

He struggled to open the gate, which was sagging badly on its rusted hinges, pushed it aside and walked up the mossy path to the front door. The closer he came, the sadder and more unloved the place looked. The phrase *poor as a church mouse* sprang into his mind, as he pushed the bell in its cracked plastic housing.

He couldn't hear any ring.

He tried again.

Waited.

Nothing.

He rapped the corroded knocker.

Still silence.

He rapped again. The silence that followed was almost oppressive.

Deciding the vicar – and his wife – must be out, he walked back down the path. Just as he reached his car, he saw a figure he recognized from the pub, on Sunday, striding towards him. A wiry-looking elderly man, with white hair and a goatee beard, dressed in a baggy shirt with a spotted cravat, grey trousers and ancient walking boots, and carrying a stout, knobbly stick.

His name was Harry something, Jason recalled. 'Hi!' he said as he drew near. 'We met briefly on Sunday, in the pub.'

The man gave him a strange look. 'Pub?'

Jason smiled, pleasantly. 'You were in the Crown, with Albert Fears, I think it was, at the bar?'

'I was?' The man seemed impatient to walk on, as if he were in a hurry.

There was something definitely odd about him, Jason thought. 'You mentioned something about a digger – that you used to drive a digger?'

'I did?'

Jason wondered if the man might have some form of dementia. 'Do you by any chance know where the vicar might be today?'

'The *vicar*, did yer say?'

'Yes, the Reverend Fortinbrass.'

Observing Jason through rheumy eyes for some moments, he jerked a finger towards the church. 'He's in the back, out in the graveyard at the rear. You'll find him there.' He strode on, deaf to Jason's thanks.

Jason walked down to the lychgate and pushed it open.

Behind him he heard the roar of a tractor thundering down the road. He turned and saw it was Albert Fears, towing a large, rattling trailer full of sheep, with a barking collie at the rear of it, and driving far too fast. Jason waved a greeting at him, but the farmer stared grimly ahead, ignoring him.

He walked in the misty drizzle, up the church path then onto the wet grass and around to the back. Sheep grazed on the hill that rose up steeply beyond the end of the graveyard, which was bounded by a low flint wall. An old man in a cloth cap, he presumed a gardener, was kneeling, tending to a flower bed that ran the width of the wall. Jason could see no sign of Roland Fortinbrass or anyone else as he walked on, passing rows of graves. He stopped by one particularly grand headstone, in marble, standing over what looked like a family mausoleum. A former lord of the manor, he wondered? Curious, he read the names and inscription.

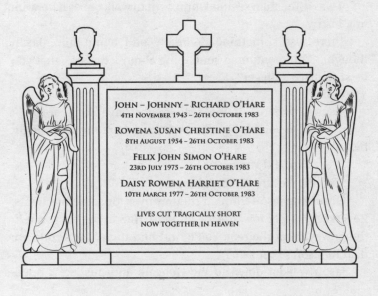

JOHN – JOHNNY – RICHARD O'HARE
4TH NOVEMBER 1943 – 26TH OCTOBER 1983

ROWENA SUSAN CHRISTINE O'HARE
8TH AUGUST 1954 – 26TH OCTOBER 1983

FELIX JOHN SIMON O'HARE
23RD JULY 1975 – 26TH OCTOBER 1983

DAISY ROWENA HARRIET O'HARE
10TH MARCH 1977 – 26TH OCTOBER 1983

LIVES CUT TRAGICALLY SHORT
NOW TOGETHER IN HEAVEN

Jason stared and read each of the inscriptions again. They had all died on the same day. Husband and wife and their children? What had happened? Had they been in a car crash or a plane crash, perhaps? It made him feel sad. Not quite sure of his reason, he pulled out his phone and took a photograph of it, then walked on, glancing around again for the elusive vicar. The strange old boy – Harry – had been very definite that he'd seen him here. He passed another, much simpler and more recent headstone.

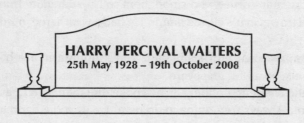

HARRY PERCIVAL WALTERS
25th May 1928 – 19th October 2008

Then a quite fancy one, more recent still, in white marble with black lettering.

OLIVER WILLIAM HARCOURT
27TH SEPTEMBER 1975 – 21ST SEPTEMBER 2015

CAROLINE PATRICIA HARCOURT
17TH APRIL 1979 – 21ST SEPTEMBER 2015

JADE HAYLEY EDWINA HARCOURT
24TH SEPTEMBER 2002 – 21ST SEPTEMBER 2015

Beneath, plainly and poignantly, was the symbol of a cross.

Husband and wife and their daughter? Again, all died on the same day? Another accident? Again, he took a photograph, then strode slowly over towards the gardener, who had a green tool bag lying on the ground beside him. As he approached, he caught a sweet whiff of cigarette smoke.

When he was some distance off, not wanting to creep up and startle the man, he called out.

The man turned and stood, bent roll-up dangling from his lips, a trowel in his gloved hands. He had a weathered, outdoors face.

Approaching him, Jason said, 'You're doing a great job – this is a very beautiful graveyard.'

The cigarette bobbing as he spoke, the man said in a rural accent, 'Always something to do here.' He waved a hand at the graves. 'And none of these lazy buggers are going to give me a hand, are they?'

'I doubt it! That cigarette smells good.'

''Bout the only place I can smoke in peace these days without the missus or someone else yelling at me. At least the dead don't mind; they don't give me any grief about it.'

Jason chuckled. 'I'm looking for the vicar – I was told he was here a short while ago.'

'Vicar?'

'Yes. The Reverend Fortinbrass.'

The man's demeanour changed. He looked bemused. 'The Reverend Fortinbrass, did you say?'

'Yes, I wanted to have a word with him. Have you seen him?'

'Oh yes, I see him most days – he's here all right and he isn't going anywhere.'

'What do you mean?'

The man pointed a gloved finger towards the far wall. 'Over

there, second row, third one in. He's another of the lazy buggers, he is.'

Jason's first thought was that the man was pulling his leg. But there was no trace of humour in his face. Feeling very strange, he turned and headed swiftly, heart in mouth, towards where he had been directed. A row of gravestones.

Second row.

Third one in.

He read the inscription on it with a chill rippling through every cell in his body.

44

Tuesday 18 December

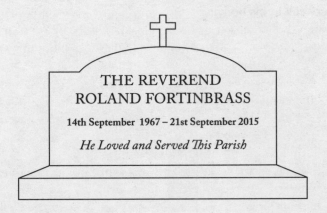

THE REVEREND
ROLAND FORTINBRASS

14th September 1967 – 21st September 2015

He Loved and Served This Parish

Jason stood, stock still, staring at the name. Shaking.

It wasn't possible, there had to be two Roland Fortinbrasses, there had to be.

Dammit, he'd seen the man yesterday, he'd come to their home! Emily had seen him too, and so had Louise.

He walked straight back over to the gardener, who was back on his knees again, working out the roots of a dead plant with his trowel. 'I'm sorry to bother you again. Are there by any chance two Reverend Fortinbrasses?'

'No, sir,' he said, without looking up. 'Not that I've ever heard. Bit of an unusual name for there to be two of them.'

'But I met – my wife and I met – the vicar of this parish yesterday. He came to our house – we've just moved into Cold Hill Park.'

The man shook his head and stood up, taking his time. 'There's no vicar in this parish any more, hasn't been since the Reverend Fortinbrass passed away, back in 2015. Now we have a rector, Reverend Whitely – he covers four local parishes and he's a useless bugger. Not a good situation, if you ask me – he only does two services a month in this church. Mind you, most times he doesn't get more than four people, I'm afraid. It's his teeth, they say, he scares them all. Old Mrs Blackthorne, in the village, told me it's like being preached at by a blooming skeleton with rattling teeth!'

Jason grinned, fleetingly. 'It just doesn't make any sense.'

The gardener squinted at him. 'Sir, I may be old, but I've still got me marbles. That over there is – or was – the only Reverend Fortinbrass.'

'Who lives in the vicarage now?'

'No one, that's been empty these last years. I've heard rumours the Church are planning on selling it.'

Jason thanked him for his time, turned and walked back to the grave of the former vicar, and took a photograph of the headstone.

There had to be an explanation. Was the man who came to see them yesterday a conman? Identity theft? Was that it? Going around posing as a vicar, preying on the vulnerable, the elderly, the bereaved, and the troubled?

But if he was clever enough to carry that off, why on earth do it in the one parish where most people would know the real Reverend Fortinbrass was long dead?

He walked, very puzzled, back to his car, and drove the short distance home.

45

Tuesday 18 December

The Penze-Weedells were faffing around in their front garden when Jason arrived home a few minutes later. Maurice was standing on top of a precarious-looking stepladder, trying to reach one of the Christmas lights that was above him and clearly out of reach, while Claudette hung onto the base of the ladder, shouting instructions to her hapless husband.

If he'd been in a neighbourly mood, Jason would have gone over and offered to help, especially as he was the best part of a foot taller than the older man, but he did not want to get involved. He was just relieved that Emily's van wasn't in the drive, because he badly needed to collect his thoughts. He climbed out of his car and was just unlocking the front door when Matt Johns rang.

'Jason, what's your problem?'

Entering the house and hurrying up to his office, he told his computer guru about the numbers on his screen.

'Can you fire up TeamViewer?' Johns asked.

As soon as he was at his desk and logged in, Jason opened the app and gave Johns the ID numbers and password.

Moments later the cursor began to move across the screen, seemingly on its own, as Johns looked for the problem.

Putting the phone on loudspeaker, and letting him get on with it, Jason thought back to yesterday morning. When he had met Roland Fortinbrass, the vicar had reminded him of someone, but he couldn't think who. A name suddenly sprang to mind.

Alan Rickman!

The actor who had died a while back. That was who the Reverend Roland Fortinbrass reminded him of – a little, anyway.

The tall, thin man in the Aran sweater, his dog collar just visible.

He opened Photos on his phone and scrolled through the pictures he had taken earlier. And in particular, the one of Roland Fortinbrass's grave and headstone.

Next, he looked at the Harcourt family's inscription.

21 September 2015.

The same day.

Coincidence? Sure, it could be. Or had they all been together in an accident?

Had the Harcourts lived in the village? They must have done, or in the area, in order to be buried in the village church-yard, surely – unless they had some other connection to the place.

Who the hell was the man who'd said he was the vicar? Why had he been here?

The media was rife with warnings about identify theft, internet fraudsters. It had to be that, didn't it? The only possible explanation. Some creep, posing as Fortinbrass, intent on in-sinuating himself into their lives before, at the appropriate moment, starting to milk them of cash.

But a very stupid creep. Did he really think he wouldn't get found out in this parish?

He paused in his thoughts.

What if phony Fortinbrass was behind all the strange shit that had been happening in their house? Somehow making it all happen, then lo and behold, he conveniently rocks up claiming to be able to produce a Minister of Deliverance who would clear away the malevolent spirits?

For a large cash sum, doubtless.

'Nope!' Matt Johns' voice suddenly intruded into his thoughts.

Jason picked up the phone. 'Hi.'

'There's nothing there,' Johns said. 'These numbers – I can't see anything.'

'But it's been happening – I haven't imagined it.'

'Beats me. I suggest next time it happens, take a screenshot and send it to me immediately.'

'Sure, OK, I will.'

Johns disconnected. Jason sat down in front of the screen, opened his browser, typed in 'Roland Fortinbrass', and hit return.

The first hit was a Church of England website listing vicars. He scrolled down, through the alphabet, until the Fs. The browser had highlighted the name: Reverend Roland Fortinbrass, MA.

He clicked on it. After some seconds he was taken to an obituary in the *Church Times*.

The Reverend Roland Michael Fortinbrass, of the parish of Cold Hill. Dearly beloved husband of Angela and father of Christopher and Lucinda. Tragically killed in a car accident on 21 September 2015.

Beneath was a photograph.

He double-clicked to enlarge it.

Instantly a familiar image appeared. A tall, lean man, in a jumper, dog collar just visible below a rather weak face. Floppy, thinning hair.

The man who had been in their house yesterday.

But who could not have been.

46

Tuesday 18 December

Jason sat, staring at the dead vicar's face, then saved a copy of the picture to his desktop.

Dead for many years.

Not possible.

Just not possible he had been in their house.

A wild thought crashed, clumsily, through his mind. What if Fortinbrass had a twin brother who was now masquerading as him?

He felt a strong draught, as if the door behind him had opened. Slowly, suddenly very scared, he turned.

The door was closed.

He turned back to the face on his screen. If he showed it to Emily when she came home, she would totally freak out – but he couldn't keep it from her. Whatever was going on here, they had to face it together and deal with it together.

Then he had an idea. Grabbing his phone, he took a photograph of Fortinbrass's face. It triggered another thought. He walked over to his unsold work, stacked against the far wall, turned around the sketch of the woman he'd done yesterday and photographed that too.

Just as he turned it back, face-in against the stack, there was a sound downstairs. Emily was back a lot sooner than he thought – he was sure she'd told him she would be having lunch out with Louise.

He heard footsteps below him, on the first floor.

Clump. Clump. Clump.

Hers?

He went over to the door, opened it and called down, 'Em!'

Silence.

'Em?' he called again, louder.

No response. He crossed to the window and looked down. Emily's van was not in the driveway. Over the road, the Penze-Weedells were still struggling with the stepladder. As he looked at them, he heard the footsteps again.

Clump. Clump. Clump.

He tensed. They were like the ones he and Emily had heard upstairs on Sunday, when they were in the kitchen.

He stood in the doorway, peering down the spiral staircase, waiting for them again, and for whoever was down there.

But nothing happened.

He relaxed. As he'd thought, it was just the oak flooring moving, drying out or expanding, or whatever. He scrawled a note for Emily, in case she came back before he returned, added a couple of kisses, and put it on the kitchen table. He debated whether to take his bike, peering out of the window to check the weather, but it was raining even harder now.

Walking out to his car, he heard Claudette, with her back towards him, calling out to her husband, who was again on the top step of the ladder, looking like an accident waiting to happen. 'Maurice! Maurice, I really don't think—'

He climbed into the car, shut the door and drove off quickly, threading around Lakeview Drive and along towards the estate entrance. As he reached it, a tractor thundered down at reck-less speed. Albert Fears again – busy today, Jason thought. He must lurk here and snap a picture of him; he would make a great subject for a painting. *Angry Man on Tractor.* Perhaps towing the trailer full of sheep, with the barking collie at the tailgate?

Just as he drove between the two stone pillars and pulled out onto the lane, a huge 1960s red and white Cadillac convertible swept up the hill towards him. It slowed, indicating right, making to turn into Cold Hill Park. The driver had a big cigar in his mouth, the woman sitting beside him looking excited, peering through the windscreen. Two kids jumped up and down in the back.

New arrivals, he wondered?

That was pretty much confirmed a few seconds later, when a massive removals lorry trundled up the hill. Great, he thought, another family moving in, another house going to be occupied! The whole estate would have a very different feel once all the properties were being lived in.

Jason drove down into the village, passing the 30 mph sign at this end of the village, then the village store, the pretty cottage on the left with the picket fence and the BED & BREAKFAST – VACANCIES sign and then the smithy. He slowed when he reached the Crown, and turned left down the side of the pub and into its almost empty car park at the rear. Hurrying through the cloying drizzle, he passed a man in an apron standing outside smoking a cigarette, and entered through a side door.

He found himself in a narrow corridor that didn't look like it had been painted in a century, and reeked of the toilets a short distance along. The corridor zig-zagged and as he passed the kitchen the smell improved to one of bacon. He pushed a door at the end and entered the saloon bar.

There was a very different vibe from the bustle of Sunday – everything felt faded and tired and rather cheerless, not helped by it being cold, the fire in the grate as yet unlit. The ingrained smell of beer, old carpet and polish was even more noticeable than when he and Emily had been here on Sunday, because it was now so empty.

Lester Beeson, the massive landlord, towered over the room from behind the bar, wiping a glass and discussing something intently with the man Jason recognized instantly as the miserable farmer, Albert Fears. How had he got here so quickly, he wondered?

The old countryman sat on a bar stool, in his tweed cap and leather-patched jacket, holding a pewter pint tankard. Doubtless his own, Jason thought – it was that kind of a pub.

Ping-beep-bloop-ping. Ping-beep-bloop-ping.

The gaming machine continued its forlorn mating cry, urgently flashing away as if desperate to attract someone's attention. But there were no likely candidates here at the moment. The only other customers were an elderly couple at an alcove table. Both of them wore brightly coloured cagoules, starkly contrasting with their grey countenances.

The man, with wisps of grey hair on his head, sported a hearing aid the size of a golf ball; the woman wore her hair in a bun, atop a face that wasn't made for smiling. They sat opposite each other, the man hunched, the woman primly upright, each eating a ploughman's in silence, as if they had long run out of anything to say to each other. Their mournful faces reminded Jason of two goldfish in a bowl. They'd make subjects, he thought, pulling out his phone and pretending to send a text, but instead discreetly photographing them.

The landlord clocked Jason and gave him a welcoming smile. Fears just stared at him through tiny, aggressive eyes.

'Mr Danes!' Lester Beeson said. 'What can I get you?'

'A Diet Coke, please.'

'Ice and lemon?'

'Thanks. Could I also have a lunch menu?'

'The restaurant's not open today but we have the bar snacks menu available.'

'Perfect.'

Fears was still glaring at him. He gave the farmer a smile but got no reaction.

When Beeson set his drink down on the counter, Jason said to him, 'I've a couple of photographs of people, I wonder if you might know – or have known – them?'

'Let's have a butchers.'

Jason showed him the image of Roland Fortinbrass that he'd taken off the website.

The landlord clearly recognized him instantly. 'That's our late vicar, God bless his soul.'

'Roland Fortinbrass?'

'Yes.'

'He died in 2015?'

Beeson thought for a second.

The expression on Albert Fears' face changed suddenly from hostile to uncomfortable, and the farmer and the landlord exchanged an odd glance.

'That would be right,' Beeson said. '2015.'

'He wasn't very old – how did the Reverend Fortinbrass die?'

'Yes, well.' Again, the farmer and landlord's eyes met. 'A very unfortunate accident.'

'I killed him,' Fears said, suddenly, with no trace of remorse in his voice, just bitterness. 'And the poor sod with him. Bloody fool turned right across me path in me tractor. I didn't have a chance to touch the brake pedal. Hit him side on, crushed him. Yeah. A man of the cloth and all.' He sipped his pint.

There was a brief silence before Fears went on. 'What hope does that give the rest of us, when God can't even look after his own, eh?' His mouth twitched, as if nervously seeking some solidarity, or even sympathy from the two men.

Although shocked by the admission, an irreverent quote popped into Jason's mind. He saw an opportunity to break the ice with the old man. 'Well, wasn't it H. G. Wells who said, *I never drive a motor car in France, because the temptation to run over a priest would be too great.*'

'Don't know no Wells bloke,' Fears said.

Beeson smiled uneasily, and said to Jason, 'The other?'

He flicked to the photograph he had done of his pencil sketch of the woman, and held it up. 'This. Do you have any idea who she might be?'

The landlord took the phone, expanded the image with his huge fingers and studied the face of the woman with short, dark hair. 'Do you have any actual photos of her?' he asked.

'No.'

He frowned. 'Looks familiar but I can't place her. She from this area?'

'I don't know.'

He stuck the camera in front of Fears' face. 'Know this lady, Albert?'

'No, but I'd like to. Heh!' He fleetingly gave a lecherous leer before becoming surly again. 'Hear you've had another accident up your place – yesterday?'

'Another?' Jason queried.

'Someone killed, I heard.' He made a cut-throat sign with his hand. 'Head clean off.'

Beeson nodded, clearly aware of the news.

'I saw it,' Jason said. 'I saw it happen.'

'It's cursed, that place,' Fears went on, ignoring him. 'They shouldn't have called it *Cold Hill Park*, they should name it *Death Park*. Cos that's what happens to everyone who goes there, they die.' He leered again, showing his nasty, stained, predator teeth.

'You saw it?' the landlord asked.

'Yes, I was just looking out of the window.'

'So, tell me what happened; there's all kinds of rumours flying around the village. What did you actually see?' Beeson asked.

Jason told him all the details he could remember, while the old farmer listened, too. When he had finished, Fears said, 'See, I told you, that place is cursed. *Death Park*, that's the right name for it.'

'Why do you say it's cursed?' Jason asked him.

Fears looked at his face for some moments, as if reading something that was written on it. 'You'd have to be stupid not to realize. Everyone dies there. Like I told you, everyone who moves in is dead by forty. So are people who work there. Cursed, I'm telling you. All the couples, in my time, who bought the big house all died, and all before they were forty.'

'How?' Jason asked.

The old man smiled as if he was enjoying himself, enjoying having his moment in the sun. 'There was the O'Hares, back in around 1983 I think it was. They weren't even the first deaths I remember, though.'

'Who owned it before them?'

'That would be Lord and Lady Rothberg. Both bed-ridden by accidents long before they died. They'd had the place since the end of the war. It were taken over in the war by the Defence folk for accommodation for Canadian soldiers and aircrew. A couple of pilots was killed when an upstairs floor collapsed, so my grandad told me. Dry rot – the place was riddled with it. They moved all the Canadians out and boarded the place up as unsafe till the Rothbergs fixed it up. It sat derelict for years after the O'Hares. There were arguments about tearing it down, but it was a listed building – so the arguments went on for ages. They tried to get English Heritage, or the National Trust, one of them to take it over, but they weren't interested.' Fears drained his tankard.

'Can I buy you another?' Jason asked, keen to keep him talking now he had started. But the old farmer gave him a venomous smile. 'Take a drink off you? That'd be like supping with the Devil.' He turned to Beeson. 'Eh, wouldn't it?'

'Another pint, Albert?'

Fears shook his head. 'Got me tractor to drive.' Then he turned back to Jason. 'I don't want no drink bought by you. See, I'm not telling you this stuff because I like you – I don't like you and I never will. I'm telling you because you asked and I'm a polite man. We're all polite folk around here – unlike the riff-raff in your horrible new estate. But we're not worried about you lot, too much. You'll all be dead soon, just like them Molloys, and the Harcourts and the O'Hares before them. The O'Hares all crushed to death in that big fancy Cadillac of theirs.'

Jason frowned, thinking of the coincidence of the car he'd seen turning into the estate earlier. 'Cadillac?'

'Great big thing – from the sixties – beats me what kind of an idiot wants to bring one of them things up a country lane.'

'Did they have an accident, then?'

Fears nodded, almost gleefully. 'Oh yes, they had an accident all right.'

'What happened?'

'I'll tell you. I'll tell you.' Fears looked down, as if studying runes in the bottom of his tankard. 'You'll know when it starts happening to you. Time goes all wrong.' He looked up and gave him a malevolent smile. 'Time *slips*.' He made a chopping motion with his right hand. 'Time-slips. Time goes all peculiar on you. That's what they've all said. It goes out of kilter. They've all said that.'

'Time-slips?' Jason frowned. 'What do you mean?'

'You'll know. You'll know.'

'They've all said? Who is *all*?'

'You'll find out.'

'Is that what caused the accident – with Roland Fortinbrass? Something to do with timing? Did he misjudge it? Get the timing wrong? Did he turn across your path because he thought he had more time?'

Fears peered back into his tankard.

'Are you sure I can't buy you at least a half?'

'I'm very sure, thank you. Like I said, I don't want no drink from a dead man.'

47

Half an hour later, Albert Fears left the pub without saying goodbye. Jason sat at a table and took a bite from his soggy roast chicken and bacon sandwich. It had been served up a while ago, but he hadn't wanted to step away from the old man, who was in full flow. He ate slowly, barely noticing the taste as he mulled over everything Fears had told him.

A rock promoter with a young family had bought Cold Hill House in 1983. He had builders working there for months, discovering more and more what a money pit the place was. Eventually, part of the house had been made sufficiently habitable to move into, but on the morning he and his family arrived, part of the roof, which hadn't yet been touched, collapsed, bringing down an avalanche of masonry on their car; an old, classic Cadillac convertible, crushing them all to death. It was witnessed by the removals men, who had pulled up in their lorry behind them.

It was a weird coincidence, he thought, that he'd seen an old, classic Cadillac barely an hour ago, turning into the estate, and followed by a removals lorry.

The *O'Hare* family.

The name inscribed, four times, on the family mausoleum he had photographed in the graveyard earlier, and which he checked now on his phone. Johnny, Rowena, Felix and Daisy.

Once again, Fears had told him, the partially condemned ruin had remained boarded up and empty for years. Because it was a listed building, and one deemed to be of architectural significance, a steady stream of developers who wanted to demolish it and build an entirely new house on the grounds were refused permission.

Finally, a property man with deep pockets bought it and began extensive renovations. He died in a paragliding accident. Then his company was wiped out in a big property crash. A few years later, in 2015, it was bought by a couple – he'd made some money selling a technology firm, his wife was a lawyer, and they had a young daughter. They'd only been moved in a short while when the mother and daughter were killed in a car crash – and he died of a heart attack on the same day.

The Harcourts.

On his phone, Jason flicked through to the photograph of the Harcourts' headstone and family grave, which he'd also taken earlier. He read their names. Oliver, Caroline, Jade.

Fears told him the final owners of the house were a fund manager and his wife, Sebastian and Nicola Molloy. With a fortune close to a billion, Molloy had the money to do a proper job of the restoration. But he'd had a better idea, Fears had said with a sarcastic laugh. Molloy wanted to tear the old building down and put up a big, modern mansion. The local planning authorities told him he wouldn't have a cat's chance in hell of getting plans through to do that.

One night, soon after permission had been rejected, the house burned down. The fire investigation team believed, but could not prove, it was arson – almost certainly by the owner himself. But no one would ever know the truth, as the whole Molloy family had perished in the blaze. The gossip was that Molloy had planned it but must have miscalculated how fast the fire would spread.

He looked back at the photograph of Roland Fortinbrass. The vicar. Confirmed dead.

But the man had been in their house yesterday, talking breezily to himself, Emily and Louise, and trying to recruit them for the church choir.

He shivered suddenly, involuntarily. *Someone walking over your grave*, his mother used to call it. Was that a time-slip?

A shadow fell across the table, and he looked up to see Lester Beeson towering above him. 'Can I get you anything else?' he asked, warmly.

'I'm good, thanks.'

'Albert's a funny old bugger,' he said. 'This is a pretty friendly village, but you know, you always get the odd one or two in the countryside who don't like change.'

Jason smiled. 'Or don't like anything.'

'Hope he didn't spook you too much. But actually, you should feel privileged he talked to you at all. He never normally speaks to anyone who isn't a local.'

'Someone else said the same. So, how long do you have to live here to become a *local*?'

'For old Fears to regard you as one? You have to be born here.'

'Does dying here make you one?'

Beeson laughed, heartily. 'I'd prefer if you didn't, Mr Danes – we never like losing a customer.'

'Sounds like you've lost quite a few in recent years.'

The landlord sat down opposite him. 'Can I offer you a drink – on the house?'

'Well, thank you – maybe an espresso would be nice, thank you.'

Beeson shouted the order out, loudly, to someone in a back room, then turned to Jason. 'You know, country folk can be very superstitious. They can't look at a coincidence without calling it a curse. All communities get their share of tragedies – they get twenty old folk dead in a coach crash on what should have been a jolly outing, or an entire village church choir wiped out in a minibus. That doesn't make the place cursed, it's just terrible luck and dreadfully sad. You need to maintain perspective. The village of Cold Hill dates back centuries, and the old mansion, Cold Hill House, was a very grand place, owning most of this village, and had a lot of land – over five thousand acres, once. Everyone in the village in former times worked for the estate. I'll bet that if you took all the recent deaths here and up at the old house, plus all the historical ones, and then divided them up evenly over the past centuries, you'd end up close to the national average, maybe even below it.'

Jason stared hard at him. 'Did you say *church choir*?'

'Yes, sadly.'

'Do you mean the church choir from this village was in a minibus accident?'

'Yes. It was terrible. There were twelve of them, all from the village and around here, the youngest was eight. They'd been invited to sing in a festival of church choirs at Canterbury Cathedral. Reverend Fortinbrass was driving them in a rented vehicle and they broke down on the motorway on the way back, in pelting rain. He left them all in the minibus on the hard shoulder of the M25, to stay dry, and went off to find the SOS rescue phone. When he came back, there was nothing left of the bus – it was like matchsticks, I'm told. A lorry driver fell asleep at the wheel and veered off the road, hitting it at 60 mph. Dreadful.'

'How long ago was that?'

'Eight years – be nine, next March.'

'Bizarre in a way,' Jason said, 'that he kind of escaped death by going to phone for help, only to be killed in a road accident some years later.'

'Yes, you could say bizarre. But he was never right after that tragedy. He always blamed himself – and struggled with his faith. He was pleasant outwardly – but –' Beeson fell silent for a moment – 'inwardly, he was broken. From that night it happened, onwards, he was like a dead man walking. That choir had been his passion, he lived for it.'

48

Tuesday 18 December

Jason drank his coffee hastily, making small talk with Beeson. His mind was in turmoil, and he paid his bill and walked swiftly back out to his car. As soon as he was inside, he dialled Emily's mobile, but it went straight to voicemail. He tried Louise's number. She answered after a couple of rings.

'Hi, Louise, it's Jason, is Emily still with you?'

'No, I left her at the wholesalers – she was just heading home with a full van-load of food. She might need some help unloading it all.'

'I – I'm heading home now. I'll – I'll give her a hand.'

'Are you OK, Jason? You sound a bit strange.'

'Yes – well – no, actually. No really. I mean . . .' He tried to collect his thoughts, to make sense of everything. 'Look, the vicar who came to the house yesterday – the Reverend Fortinbrass – who was going to arrange for an exorcist – a Minister of Deliverance or whatever – there's something very strange going on.'

'I'm sorry, Jason did you say *vicar*?'

'Yes. The chap who came yesterday – said his name was Roland Fortinbrass – the Reverend Fortinbrass.'

Louise sounded puzzled. 'Emily didn't mention this – when did he come?'

He frowned. 'Yesterday morning, when you were at the house, you were there, you met him.'

201

'No one came while I was there – it was just you, Emily and myself.'

Was she having a memory lapse or something? 'Louise, he came into the kitchen, we were all chatting with him. He tried to recruit Emily and me into the church choir, then he asked you, too. You told him you lived too far away.'

'I'm sorry,' she said. 'He must have come after I'd left.'

'You *must* remember!' he insisted. 'He asked you if you would like to join the church choir and you told him you lived in Brighton, not in the village. Remember now?'

'Jason, I honestly don't know what you're saying. Are you sure you're OK?'

He suddenly felt hot. He was perspiring. 'Yes – I – I'm . . .' His head felt like it was spinning. 'I – I'm . . .'

'Jason?'

Her voice sounded distant, as if she was calling out to him from the bottom of a well.

He'd felt like this once, he remembered, after eating a duff prawn in a cocktail. Food poisoning. Had the chicken been off? The bacon?

'Jason? Jason?'

Trying to get a grip, he said, 'I'm OK, Louise. Look – are you saying you *really* didn't see him?'

'No,' she said good-humouredly. 'I didn't see anyone apart from you and Emily. Are you sure you didn't imagine him?'

'What?'

'You have a very vivid imagination – you must have, to do all those brilliant paintings.'

'Thanks, Louise, but however vivid my imagination, I didn't conjure up a vicar walking into our kitchen and trying to recruit us all for his church choir.'

'Just saying . . .'

'I don't understand.'

'Where are you, Jason?' she asked.

'I'm in the car – but it's OK, I'm in a car park.'

'Have you been drinking?'

'No way! I've had a Diet Coke and a coffee.'

'Do you want me to call Emily and ask her to come and get you?'

His head was cooling. Clarity was returning. 'It's OK, I think I've realized what's happened. I'm fine, don't worry about it.'

'Are you sure?'

'I'm sure. Are we seeing you before Christmas?'

'Yes, I've got a babysitter. Des and I are coming out with you both – we've booked a table at the Ginger Fox on Christmas Eve.'

'Ah, great, brilliant. OK, see you then, if not before.'

'You really sure you're OK?'

'I'm OK, thanks.'

He ended the call and sat still in the car, staring at the windscreen, which was opaque with drizzle. Remembering. Emily had told him that when Louise went into one of her psychic trances it was like she had gone to another planet, and could never remember anything afterwards. That must be it. It made sense now.

Except it didn't.

She might not have seen the Reverend Fortinbrass in their kitchen, but he sure as hell had, with his own eyes.

49

He started the car, drove out onto the road, headed through the village and back up the hill. There was a simple landmark, a red postbox, directly opposite the entrance to Cold Hill Park. He turned right between the stone pillars and drove in, then along Lakeview Drive.

As he neared their house, he could see from the empty driveway that Emily was not back yet. To his amusement, the Penze-Weedells were still bumbling around outside in their front garden. Maurice was standing, enveloped in a spaghetti tangle of Christmas lights that had evidently fallen from the wall onto him, and he and his wife were gesticulating at each other, clearly having a row. He waved at them as he passed, but neither noticed.

At the end of Lakeview Drive he carried on around the estate, looking for the Cadillac and the removals lorry he'd seen arriving earlier. He drove along silent roads that were not still closed off with barriers, having to make U-turns a couple of times at dead ends, looking at each of the empty houses in turn, some of them finished, some of them just fenced-off shells. He passed a police car parked across the entrance to the still-silent construction site, noticing some police officers beyond, then carried on.

The Cadillac and the lorry had to be here, somewhere. He'd

only been gone an hour and a half – no way could the removals men have unloaded the entire juggernaut in that time, surely?

Unless he'd imagined the Cadillac and the removals lorry. Imagined the vicar.

A Cadillac in which a family of four had died outside Cold Hill House?

The O'Hares.

Oh, sure, a ghost car – and a ghost removals lorry. And a ghost vicar.

After fifteen minutes, when he reckoned he had now covered the entire estate, he headed home, perplexed. Emily's van was now outside, the rear doors open, as was the front door of the house and the double garage's up-and-over door. The Penze-Weedells were nowhere to be seen – presumably gone indoors. The stepladder and tangle of wiring remained on the front lawn.

He pulled on to the driveway just as Emily appeared through the front door. He climbed out and greeted her with a kiss.

'Hi, darling!'

'All OK with David?' she asked. 'Will he get the framing done?'

'In the nick of time – I've got to remember to collect them before midday tomorrow, before he shuts up for Christmas. How did the shopping go?'

She pointed at the packed rear of the van. 'We've got everything we need for the anniversary do. They had an amazing offer on prawns – we have to make prawn cocktail starters for everyone, so we're nicely in profit on that dish!'

'Brilliant!'

'They're still in their shells. It's a pain to remove them, but they're so much yummier than the ready-peeled.'

'Darling, it's your eye for detail that's made you such a success.'

She smiled. 'I just like to give peeps food that I would eat – so long as they're willing to pay for it.'

'I'll give you a hand in with everything.'

For the next fifteen minutes they worked together, removing the bags from the van and stacking the shelves of the upright freezers that lined most of the wall space in the garage.

'How much food do these people eat?' he asked, in wonder.

'It's not just the anniversary event; we've stocked up on basics, too.'

There were fourteen tall freezers in the room, all of them full by the time they had finished.

'Let's hope we don't have a power cut,' he said.

She blanched. 'They don't happen very often, I hope. And when they do, we don't open any of the doors. Everything will stay frozen for several hours.'

'Good.'

They went into the house. The kitchen clock showed it was 2.55 p.m. Emily glanced around at the spotless work surfaces and empty sink. 'Did you have any lunch?'

'Yes. I thought I'd pop down to the pub – do the local thing.'

'Did you indeed? Down the old boozer, eh?' she ribbed.

'I had a Diet Coke. And a soggy sandwich.'

'See anyone? Our lovely neighbours?'

'Just the landlord and that creepy old farmer we saw on Sunday.'

'Lucky you.'

'I actually went to the village to see if I could chivvy up the vicar.'

'Vicar?'

'The guy who came yesterday, Roland Fortinbrass.'

'Yesterday? Roland Fortinbrass? Fortinbrass was a character in *Hamlet*, wasn't he?'

'The *Hamlet* character only had one "s" in his name. The vicar has two, he told me.'

'When did you see him? You didn't mention this.'

'Emily, hello!' He gave her a pointed look. 'The vicar who came when Louise was here, and we discussed getting a Minister of Deliverance, or whatever it's called, to come to the house.'

Her face was blank. 'Came when Louise was here?'

He felt his skin squirming.

'Yes!' he said. 'Yesterday morning.'

'Nobody came, Jason,' she said. 'There was no one else here.'

'Babes, we all chatted with him. He asked if any of us could sing, because he needed recruits for his church choir.'

She was looking at him as if he was mental. 'Yesterday morning?'

'Yes! Just when Louise was doing her trance thing. The door-bell rang, and I went and brought him into the kitchen.'

'How many pints did you have in the pub?'

'None, I promise you! What were you and Louise on?'

'Peppermint tea with ginger.'

'And half a pound of cannabis?'

'Ha ha!'

'You *must* remember him!'

'If you'd brought a vicar in here, into this kitchen, then yes, I would remember him.'

He shook his head. 'I did.'

'Was he very small? Perhaps I didn't notice him?'

He smiled, fleetingly. 'I – I just . . .'

'Just what?'

'I don't know what's going on, unless you and Louise are having a laugh on me. I rang her when I left the pub. She told me she hadn't seen him either.'

Emily was studying his face hard, in a way that worried him.

Was he looking strange? Cracking up? His mind scrambled, clawing and trying to grasp reason. Yesterday morning the Reverend Roland Fortinbrass had rung their doorbell, he'd invited him in, they'd chatted in the kitchen: the vicar, Emily, Louise and himself. He'd asked them if they would join the church choir, and in turn they'd asked him if he could contact the diocesan Minister of Deliverance, which he promised to do.

A promise he would not be able to keep. Because he was dead. Lying in the churchyard at the rear of St Mary's. His name inscribed on his headstone, the epitaph beneath.

HE LOVED AND SERVED THIS PARISH.

50

He'd seen the man's grave; he'd read his obituary only a few hours ago; he had met the man who had been in the accident where Fortinbrass had died. He could hardly have more proof that Fortinbrass was dead.

But the vicar had come to their house yesterday. He'd talked to him. They all had, but now neither Emily nor Louise could accept it. Why were they denying it? He knew the human brain could do strange things, sometimes to protect people from shock or horror. He'd also read about a study of a remote South American tribe, who lived in a rainforest and had never been exposed to the outside world. One experiment that had been done was to fly a helicopter over their village, and then ask members of the tribe to describe what they had just seen. Almost all of them denied they had seen anything. It turned out it wasn't because they were being difficult, or because they were stupid, it was that the helicopter was so far beyond anything they'd ever seen or experienced, they did not know how to process it.

Was this what had happened with Emily and Louise?

'Jace?' Emily's voice was calm but sharp.

He stared at her, his head starting to feel hot again. Swimming.

'Jace, darling, are you ill? Do you need to go to bed? I think

209

you might be suffering from exhaustion – or stress – or maybe a bit of both. You've been working flat out and through the night.'

'I'm OK,' he said, not feeling at all OK. 'Look, there's something . . .' His voice tailed off.

'Something what?'

There had to be a rational explanation, he thought. Had to be. Might Louise, in her trance state, have hypnotized them both? Could that be it? Had she put them into a trance without their realizing and somehow conjured up the spirit of the dead vicar?

He clung to that thought.

Could that be it?

'Something what?' Emily asked again.

'It's fine, nothing.'

'Are you sure?'

'Yep. I'm going to go up and get on. And I've still got stuff to unpack. You?'

She gestured with her arms. 'About two hundred boxes to sort through.'

'Want a hand?'

She shook her head. 'It's more important you get some rest, and that you knuckle down to your work. It's not that long to your show. How many paintings do you have completed?'

'Not many that I'm happy with. But I'm inspired here, brimming with ideas – I just want to get on.' He pulled out his phone and showed her the picture he'd taken earlier of the miserable looking couple in their bright cagoules. 'I've got the title for it! *Romantic Dinner à Deux*.'

She peered at it. 'Oh my God!' She turned to him. 'Promise me – just promise me, solemnly – that we will never get like that!'

'I promise. Orange never was your colour, anyway.'

She punched him playfully.

'Do you like the title?'

'I love it. Go! Go paint it!'

He walked to the door and made his way upstairs to his studio. As he entered, his phone pinged with a text.

A row of letters followed by a number appeared on the screen.

Simultaneously, he saw the same on his computer monitor.

J D E A D 0 9

He took a fast screenshot. An instant later they vanished.

51

Tuesday 18 December

Matt Johns had told him to take a screenshot the next time something appeared. Jason emailed him the one he had just taken, then picked up a new gesso board and placed it on his easel. He donned his apron and gloves, then assembled his painting tools, with difficulty, having to concentrate hard, his thoughts all over the place.

He walked over to the window. Watched a small group of people in white oversuits for a few moments: two of them on their hands and knees, around the area where the worker died. Did they need to be this thorough, he wondered? But at least the site was silent.

Then he picked up a pencil, returned to his easel, opened his photos on his phone and looked for the photographs he had taken in the pub, of the elderly couple in their bright cagoules.

They weren't there.

They had to be! He'd shown one to Emily just ten minutes ago.

He searched again. Again.

His phone rang.

'Jason, hi.'

It was Matt Johns.

'You just sent me a blank email – did you forget the attachment?'

'I'm sorry – it was a screenshot, as you asked for. I had more digits appear, another sequence, this time on my phone and laptop. I'll check and send them again.'

'No problem,' Johns said.

Jason checked the sent folder on his phone email. There was one to Matt. He opened it. It was blank.

He checked his online album. Any screenshot he took should automatically be saved to this. But just like the vanished old couple in their cagoules, there was nothing.

'I can't see them,' he said lamely.

'Do you have the details?' Johns asked. 'I can do my own search.'

'I'm pretty sure it said *JDEAD* and the numbers zero and nine.'

He ended the call, then focused on his blank gesso board. Sod the photographs; he could remember the couple so clearly. It was their stance he needed to get right. The woman prim and upright, the man – her husband most likely – brow-beaten, defeated by life, sitting all hunched in front of her. Worshipping at his own sad temple. The wife with her iron-grey hair who wiped the floor with him.

He set to work, sketching out their positions. The sanctimonious look on the woman's face, doubtless a regular at the parish church. Defeat written all over her husband. Someone miserable as sin, who had left it too late to change anything in his life. Stuck, until death did them part, with a woman he clearly disliked and who clearly disliked him back, every bit as much.

Mr and Mrs Angry.

Yes!

He began to sketch with sudden, furious energy.

52

Wednesday 19 December

Jason was woken with a start by a cold draught on his face. Something clattered down below. He heard the wind gusting. Lying still in the darkness, he was momentarily confused, unsure where he was. He felt anxious; something was wrong. He heard a man's voice, talking, close by. It was a low, coarse, creepy, leering voice.

Jason heard his own heart pounding.

Eyes wide open, he peered at the clock radio beside him. The green digits were flashing '00.00' repeatedly.

There'd been a power cut.

The voice continued. Monotonous. Intoning.

'Oliver, Caro, Jade, Johnny, Rowena, Felix, Daisy, Harry . . '

A voice he didn't recognize. In their house or out on the street?

Shit.

It continued. 'Brangwyn, Matilda, Evelyne . . '

Did they have burglars? What could he use as a weapon?' His brain raced.

Was something moving in the room? A man's shape? There was another blast of cold air.

The voice droned on, repeating, 'Oliver, Caro, Jade, Johnny, Rowena, Felix, Daisy, Harry, Brangwyn, Matilda, Evelyne . . '

Right beside him.

He held his breath, scared.

Then he realized. It was Emily, talking in her sleep. Except it wasn't her voice.

She said the names over again, in a continuous loop.

He reached out his left arm, found the bedside table and, careful not to knock over his glass of water, felt for his watch resting in the charger. He picked it up and looked at it: 2.33 a.m.

'PLEASE TELL ME WHAT YOU WANT!' Emily suddenly shouted out, sounding very frightened.

'Darling!' he said quietly.

'Oliver, Caro, Jade, Johnny, Rowena, Felix, Daisy, Harry, Brangwyn, Matilda, Evelyne . . .' she intoned again.

'Em,' he whispered, not wanting to wake her, but needing to stop her.

She had often talked in her sleep in the past, and never believed him when he told her in the morning. He had an idea. Picking up his phone, he recorded a video of her.

'Oliver, Caro, Jade, Johnny, Rowena, Felix, Daisy, Harry, Brangwyn, Matilda, Evelyne . . .' she intoned yet again.

And again.

Then, in the glow of green light from the clock and from his watch face, he saw a figure moving across the room.

It felt as if electricity was crackling through him. He fumbled for the bedside lamp switch and snapped it on. The room filled with light and he blinked for some moments, with the realization the power was now back on.

'Yrrrr?' Emily said.

There was no one in the room.

'It's OK,' he said, softly.

'Whasser?' she asked.

'It's OK, you were talking in your sleep.'

He heard a rasping snore. She was still asleep.

Jesus, her voice had scared him.

He turned the light off and lay still, his whole body pounding. Outside, apart from the wind, was total silence. Before, in Brighton, where they had lived on a busy street, the night was never completely silent. Traffic noise, the occasional wail of a police siren or of cats fighting, or urban foxes foraging through bins. Nor was it ever completely dark the way it was here.

He lay still for a long time. Emily stopped snoring and began breathing, rhythmically. He closed his eyes, tried to go back to sleep, but his mind was in turmoil. Images came in one after the other. Digits and letters on his screens. Roland Fortinbrass. The face of the woman.

Fretting, suddenly, about oversleeping and not getting to the framer in time, he sat up and reset the clock and the alarm. Then checked his phone alarm, too. David was shutting up shop at lunchtime and flying off to Inverness. If he didn't get there in time that would be it. The two pictures of the dogs would not be delivered for Christmas. He was really pleased with both and was sure his clients would be happy.

He checked the clock and his phone alarm again. Then he closed his eyes, lay back against the pillow and slowly drifted towards sleep. A stern, female voice whispered into his ear.

'You didn't get my eyes right. They're blue, not brown.'

He sat up with a start, wide awake again and in a cold sweat. Snapped on the light.

Nothing.

The room was empty.

Emily stirred in her sleep and rolled over.

He lay back down, turned off the light and closed his eyes.

It seemed only seconds later that Emily was shaking him. Whispering urgently in a terrified voice. 'Darling, darling, there's someone upstairs.'

Above them he heard a loud, steady noise of footsteps.

Stomp. Stomp. Stomp. Stomp.

The sound of someone in heavy shoes pacing angrily across his studio floor.

53

Jason snapped his bedside lamp back on. Emily was staring at the ceiling, bug-eyed with fear. 'That is not floorboards settling,' she said, in a low, shaking whisper.

He got out of bed.

'Don't go up. There's someone there. Call the police.'

They heard it again.

Stomp. Stomp. Stomp. Stomp.

Then a massive crash.

Emily screamed in terror. 'Jason!'

Another crash.

She switched on her lamp, grabbed her phone.

'Don't!' he urged. 'I'll go up.'

'Are you fucking crazy or what?' She stabbed out 999.

He heard a faint voice through the receiver. 'Emergency, which service please?'

'Police,' she whispered.

'Darling! No!'

'There's someone up there, for God's sake!'

'I'll go.'

'No!'

They heard the sound again.

Stomp. Stomp. Stomp. Stomp.

Then a different, female voice through the phone speaker. 'Sussex Police, how can I help you?'

'We have an intruder upstairs, in our house,' Emily said, her voice barely above a whisper.

'Can you give me your name and address please, caller?'

'Emily Danes. Our address is 47 Lakeview Drive, Cold Hill Park, Cold Hill, East Sussex. There's someone upstairs.'

'I'm dispatching a car to you. Stay on the line.'

'Thank you,' she whispered.

The sound was even louder now. *Stomp. Stomp. Stomp. Stomp.*

Emily held the phone up, briefly. 'Can you hear them?' she said.

'That noise?'

'Footsteps.'

'Where are you, Emily?' the call handler asked.

'I'm in our bedroom, with my husband. He wants to go up – the sound is coming from his studio above us.'

'The car will be with you in less than ten minutes, I'm tracking it. Tell your husband not to confront them, wait for the officers to arrive.'

'Thank you,' Emily said, and burst into tears. 'Oh God, please hurry.'

They heard the sound again.

Stomp. Stomp. Stomp. Stomp.

'Oh Jesus,' she said. 'Please ask them to hurry.'

Stomp. Stomp. Stomp. Stomp. The ceiling was shaking.

Jason jumped out of bed, went to the door and pulled on his dressing gown.

Stomp. Stomp. Stomp. Stomp. The ceiling was shaking even more.

'Don't go up there!' she implored.

'Four minutes away,' the call handler said. 'Do you have any dogs in the house that the officers need to know about?'

'No,' she replied.

'I'm going down to let them in,' Jason said.

'Be careful.'

Jason ran out of the room and downstairs to the front door. He flung it open and went out into the front garden into a howling gale. Blue flashing lights were approaching. He went out into the street, holding the front of his dressing gown shut with one hand, waving with the other.

The car pulled up in front of him and almost before its wheels had stopped turning two officers, one male and one female, jumped out and hurried over to him, tugging on their caps, each flashing a torch.

'Is the intruder still on the premises, sir?' the female one, petite and fair-haired and in her twenties, asked. Her colleague was short and burly, and a few years older. Both were bulked-out with stab vests and all their equipment.

'Yes, I think so. Thanks for coming so quickly. Upstairs on the top floor, in my studio.'

Jason led them in, then allowed them to run up the stairs ahead of him, their reflections bouncing off the mirrored walls. 'Next floor up,' he shouted as they reached the landing.

As they hurried on up the spiral staircase to his studio, Emily came out of the bedroom in her dressing gown. 'Thank God,' she said, and followed Jason up.

On the top floor landing, he followed the officers into his studio, putting out a cautioning hand for Emily. The two officers stood in the centre of the room, looking around, puzzled.

There was no one there. Nothing looked disturbed. The easel was in the centre of the floor, as he had left it, with a fresh gesso board in place on it.

'I – I just – just don't believe it,' he said.

'All the windows are securely shut,' the male officer said. 'You say you heard someone up here, walking around?'

'We did,' Emily said. 'We could hear them, loudly.'

'May we take a look around?' the male officer asked.

'Please – anywhere.'

The police went downstairs. Jason and Emily followed them as they checked each of the first floor rooms, and all the cupboards and wardrobes in turn, both officers noting their partially open bedroom window. Then they searched the ground floor rooms, as well as the garage. Finally, they went out into the rear garden, separated and searched down each side of the house.

When they had finished, the four of them sat at the kitchen table, the male officer pulling out his electronic tablet and laying it on the table.

'Would either of you like any tea or coffee?' Emily asked.

'We're fine, thank you.'

'There are no signs of a break-in,' the woman PC said. 'The only window open is in your bedroom.'

'I – I – I'm sure the window was shut when we went to bed,' Jason said. 'I was woken by the sound of the wind and noticed it was open, earlier, so I closed it again.' He shot a glance at Emily. 'I thought I saw someone in the room.'

The male officer went back outside, with his torch, and returned a couple of minutes later. 'There's nothing anyone could have used to climb up to your bedroom, sir,' he said. 'And no footprints in the flower bed beneath the window.'

'There was definitely someone walking around upstairs,' Emily said. 'We both heard it.'

'This is a very new development, isn't it?' the male officer asked. 'How long have you been living here?'

'We only moved in last Friday,' Jason replied.

'We were here on Monday, there was a fatal accident,' he said.

'I witnessed it,' Jason replied. 'I left a message with the police on 101, but I haven't heard anything more, yet.'

'I'm sure someone will be in touch,' the young woman said. Then she smiled. 'I've just realized who you are – Jason Danes, the artist, famous for your dog paintings?'

'Yup.'

'Have you noticed anything missing, either of you?' the male officer asked.

Both shook their heads. 'Not so far, anyway,' Emily replied.

'Do either of you have any enemies? Anyone you might have upset?'

Emily shook her head.

'None that I'm aware of,' Jason said.

'No rivals?' the male officer asked. 'You're a very successful local artist. Could there be someone jealous of you?'

Jason shrugged. 'Possibly.'

'There's no sign of a break-in at all,' his colleague said. 'This is what's strange. Did you have the front door locked, and the safety chain on?' she asked.

'Yes, always.'

The male officer pulled out a card and wrote a number on it. 'I've put on my mobile number – if you think of anything that might be relevant, call me, any time. I'm PC Neil Lang. My colleague, PC Christina Davies, and I will be on until six thirty a.m. If you're worried, call either 999 or my number and we'll get someone straight back here.'

Both Jason and Emily thanked them, and escorted them to the front door.

Neil Lang nodded at the blazing Christmas lights of the Penze-Weedells. 'They've got the Christmas spirit, all right.'

'If they keep those going, you'll end up with coach parties trundling by to see them!' PC Davies said.

'Just what we need,' Jason said. 'Like Christmas, do you?'

'I've drawn the short straw this year – we both have,' she said. 'Lates, four till midnight. The busiest evening of the year for domestic disputes. Relatives who've not seen each other all year, getting pissed and then realizing why they've not seen each other.'

Jason and Emily waited until they had driven off, then secured the front door and went, very shaken, back up to the bedroom. He shut and locked that window, too.

Finally, he reset the alarm for an hour later than he had planned, to 7.30 a.m.

But neither of them slept much for the rest of the night.

54

Wednesday 19 December

Sometime around dawn, Jason lapsed into a fitful doze, only to be woken by the alarm after what seemed like a few seconds. Instantly, his mind went into overdrive. Thinking back over the events of the night.

All of the windows, except for their bedroom, had been securely shut, with locks in place.

Yet, somehow, someone had got in.

In order to walk up and down his studio floor?

Emily was awake beside him. He could hear the soft crushing of her eyelashes as she lay, blinking. He rolled towards her and kissed her. 'You OK?' he asked.

'Not really, no. You?'

'I don't think it was creaking floorboards.'

'What did you see here, in our room?' she asked.

'It looked like someone moving across the floor.'

'In high heels or hobnail boots?'

'I just thought – thought I saw the shape of someone in the darkness.' He shrugged. 'Did you see the glance those coppers exchanged? They clearly thought we were nutters.'

'I don't think so.' She kissed him. 'I think what they thought was, here's a couple just moved into a new place and are spooked out by unfamiliar noises in the night.'

He wasn't sure how to answer her. Was she right?

'We have to do something, Jason. We can't live here like this. We've seen one bloody ghost, you've met a phantom vicar promising to arrange an exorcism and you've seen someone crushed to death out of your window. What have we moved into?'

'Want to move out? We could go and stay in a hotel until we find something else?'

'No. I love this house. There's something very wrong, but are we going to let it drive us out?'

'What does Louise say?'

'That the house needs spiritual cleansing, that's all. We're on a historic site where there've been some tragic deaths. I don't know – she says maybe there's some old souls wandering around, spirits who don't realize their bodies are dead. She's going to talk to someone she knows who specializes in that stuff.'

'Like, in asking ghosts to take their shoes off before they go clumping around in the middle of the night?'

She looked at him levelly and smiled. 'We'll get through this. We'll get it sorted.'

'We will.'

55

'Where are you going, darling?' Emily asked, as, shortly after 9 a.m., Jason hurtled downstairs like a whirlwind, bunged an instant porridge in the microwave, then sat at the kitchen table and began skimming through the *Argus*. His ritual at breakfast was to read the local paper, then the *Guardian*.

He raised a finger to his lips. 'Ssshhhh, I'm on a mission to find us a Ghostbuster and then running some errands for Santa!'

'Oh?'

'Santa says there's a rather lovely lady who has moved into 47 Lakeview Drive, who is going to be in need of a lot of presents on Christmas morning.'

'Really?'

'Uh-huh.'

'And he's appointed you his Little Helper?'

'I think he might have done.'

She gave him a wan smile. 'Don't forget the framer!'

'Dunno if there's going to be enough room for the pictures in my car, with all the presents I'll have for you.'

'So, take the van . . .'

'I'll make room, somehow.'

'Seriously, the framer is number-one priority. And ride your sleigh carefully!'

'David Graham – number-one priority!'

'Then Mr Ghostbuster?'

'He'll be in Santa's sack. Any more footsteps, yell at them to take their shoes off.'

'I'll stick a sign outside the front door. *All ghosts: barefoot only in this house.*'

'Their eyesight might be a bit crap, you know; some of them are probably pretty ancient.'

'Fine, I'll leave a pair of reading glasses out for them.'

'Maybe some garlic and a mirror, too.'

'That's for vampires, isn't it?'

'Might as well take a belt-and-braces approach!'

56

Fifteen minutes after leaving home, Jason steered the BMW up a residential street with substantial houses set well back from the road, all displaying festive lights in their windows or porches. Then he reached the contrasting stark, forbidding Victorian walls of Lewes prison, before entering the narrow high street of the county town of East Sussex.

He parked then made his way along to his framer, where David handed him the two bubble-wrapped and taped packages. After wishing him a happy Christmas and a great holiday, Jason walked back to the car park and placed the pictures in the boot of the car, intending to drop them into the two clients on his way home, then made his way to the library.

It was a while since he'd last been in a public library, but that smell seemed exactly the same in each one he'd ever visited. It was a smell he wished he could capture with paints. The smell of books, of paper seeped in knowledge, learning, information, fun. He glanced at rows of shelves, the spines of countless volumes. So many books, and he'd only read a tiny fraction of the ones he wanted to. And he knew, sadly, he only ever would.

During these past couple of years, apart from a week's holiday in Tuscany when he'd devoured all four novels of the Alexandria Quartet – a treat he'd been promising himself for years – he'd barely read anything, or watched any television

228

either. After painting late into the night, pretty much every night, he would tumble into bed too exhausted to think of picking up a book. But as he stared around now, he felt a twinge of guilt, and determined to work harder at making time to read.

Approaching a middle-aged woman at the front desk, who was looking up at him, he said, 'Hi, I'm after local newspaper archives.'

'Mr Danes, is it?'

He blushed. 'Yes.' He liked being recognized, but at the same time, it always slightly embarrassed him, because he never knew quite how to respond, and whatever he said always sounded a bit lame to him.

She gave him a smile that was much less stern than her glasses. 'I just want to say I'm a big fan of your work.'

'You are? Thank you so much!'

Lame again, he thought.

'We have two of your early pictures in our home. One from your "Pub Bores" series – my husband says he's sure it's a man in the pub he drinks in! And we have one of your spaniels – we have a King Charles who could be its double. They give us so much pleasure.'

'Well – um – thank you.'

'So, local newspaper archives. How far back do you need?'

'How far do you go?' he asked, relieved to get down to the business he was here for. But pleased by her enthusiasm for his work, nonetheless.

'Well, we have the *Sussex Express*, *Argus* and the *Mid-Sussex Times* – but we only keep hard copies for a month. We do have the *Sussex Express* on microfilm, but only as far as 2010. Eastbourne Library will have the *Sussex Express* and the *Argus*, but the same as us, microfilm only going back to 2010. They also have the *Eastbourne Herald*. If you need to go further back you could try the British Library – they have a comprehensive newspaper archive. Pretty much everything, going right back in time.'

'Thanks,' he said. 'Could I take a look at the *Sussex Express* files?'

'Can I help you with anything specific that you're looking for?' she asked.

He hesitated. 'Well, we've just moved into a village near here, Cold Hill. I'm interested in anything I can find about its recent history.'

She looked pensive. 'OK, I'll see if I can find anything while you're looking through the archives.'

Five minutes later, set up at a microfilm reader, Jason began scrolling through the 2015 issues, until he reached September. Then he slowed.

Finally, he reached his goal: 28 September 2015. The report on the deaths of the Harcourt family.

DOUBLE TRAGEDY STRIKES COLD HILL FAMILY

Brighton solicitor, Caroline Harcourt, who was involved in many Sussex charities, was killed alongside her daughter, Jade, a pupil at St Paul's College, Burgess Hill, in a road traffic accident on the B2112 Haywards Heath to Ardingly road last week. In a bizarre twist, an hour later her husband, Oliver Harcourt, was found dead at their family home, Cold Hill House. Inspector Chris Smith from Sussex Police Roads Policing Unit said that despite the extraordinary circumstances, there appeared to be no link between the two, and the events were just a very sad coincidence. This was later confirmed in a statement released by Detective Inspector Sarah Reeves of Sussex Police, who said the post-mortem on Mr Harcourt revealed he had died from a heart attack.

He looked again on his phone at the photograph of their headstone in the graveyard. Then he searched for the family online and clicked on 'images'.

A very posed-looking family photograph, clearly taken by a professional, appeared. He barely glanced at the laid-back looking man in his late thirties, or the rather stroppy girl of about twelve who clearly wanted to be anywhere but in the saccharine, happy families snapshot.

It was the woman who had his complete focus.

The attractive, slightly hard-looking woman in her mid-thirties, with short, dark hair, immaculately dressed. She was staring at the camera, or at whoever was behind the lens, with the same don't-give-me-any-nonsense-and-I-won't-give-you-any-back expression that he recognized. Exactly the way she had looked at him.

It was her, without any shadow of doubt. The woman he had seen in the house. The woman he had sketched, the photograph of whom he'd shown to Lester Beeson and Albert Fears yesterday.

Caroline Patricia Harcourt.

He'd been to her grave and seen her name and dates on the headstone, just as he had seen the vicar's.

17 April 1979–21 September 2015.

And she was just as dead as the vicar.

He closed his eyes and rested his head in his hands, thinking, trying to make sense of any of this.

Emily had seen the woman, too. Seen a ghost.

But not the vicar?

He was feeling scared, really scared. Who could he talk to about this? The logical person would be the rector, Reverend Whitely, the gardener in the graveyard had told him about. But from the gardener's description of him as a useless bugger, *like a blooming skeleton with rattling teeth*, he didn't sound much cop.

He continued thinking, eyes shut, weird images filling his head.

Two ghosts?

He stood up and walked over to his librarian fan. 'Do you know where the Bishop of Lewes lives?'

'No,' she said. 'But it's bound to be on his website. I'll have a look for you.'

She tapped her keyboard, then waited for some moments. 'Sorry,' she said. 'We still have a pretty antiquated connection here.' Finally, after another gap, she said, 'Right, I've got it.'

She read the address out to him, he wrote it down and thanked her. Then he added, 'I'll have to do a new series, "Folk in Public Libraries"!'

'Please do,' she said.

He promised he would seriously consider it.

Another theme for his forthcoming exhibition, he thought!

Then she held up an ancient, dusty, leather-bound volume. 'I found this; it's the only thing that I can see has a mention of Cold Hill in it. It's from the reference section, so I shouldn't really lend it out, but –' she gave him a conspiratorial wink – 'as it's you, I'm sure I can trust you to return it.'

'Wow, thank you. Of course!'

It smelled old. Probably full of germs.

The faded, gold, embossed print read, *Sussex Mysteries – Martin Pemberton*.

'You might even find some inspiration in it for future pictures.'

'I'll guard it with my life!'

'It was down in the stacks. The last time anyone looked at it was twelve years ago, so I don't think it will be missed for a few days!'

Thanking her, he left, and when he reached the car park, he placed the volume safely in the boot of his car. Then he squirted hand sanitizer on each palm and carefully rubbed his hands together.

57

The Bishop's residence was a substantial, 1920s red-brick house at the edge of the town, backing onto fields. It looked more like the home of a successful stockbroker than a man of the cloth. As he drove in through the gates and onto the gravel driveway, Jason was a little surprised to see a Harley-Davidson motorbike propped on its stand near the front door, beside a couple of modest saloon cars.

As he walked towards the porch, he was shaking with nerves. Pressing the imposing doorbell, he stood, trying to compose himself and not sound like a total idiot.

A stern-looking woman opened the door and peered at him suspiciously.

'May I help you?' she asked.

He decided to play the librarian ticket. 'Yes, my name's Jason Danes.'

From her blank expression it clearly didn't register. No fan here.

'I'm a local artist – a painter.'

'I see,' she said. Clearly not seeing.

'I have a problem and wondered if it was possible to have a very quick word with the Bishop.'

'I'm afraid he's an extremely busy man, is he expecting you? I don't have any appointments in his diary for this morning.'

'I have a really urgent situation, could I ask you a favour? I'll wait here – please go into your office and google me and you'll see that I'm not a nutter. And then ask the Bishop if he could just give me five minutes. Please. It's really important, I need his advice very urgently.'

Something in his voice must have touched a nerve in her, because she softened a little.

'Would you like to tell me what exactly you need to see him about?'

'Honestly, I badly need some advice about our house – we've just moved into the area, and my wife and I are very seriously concerned by something that's going on. If I could just see him face to face. Five minutes. That's all. Please.'

To his relief, she invited him in.

He followed her across an imposing, oak-panelled hallway and through a doorway into a reception area that reminded him of a doctor or dentist's waiting room. A row of mismatched chairs were arranged around a table on which copies of the *Church Times*, the *Diocesan News* and an assortment of other ecumenical periodicals were lined up. Bidding him take a seat, she went through into what looked like a tiny office and closed the door.

He had never before met a bishop. Was the Very Reverend Robert Parnassus going to be as stuffy as his name implied? Someone who would look at him contemptuously and dismissively, quote some biblical tracts at him, and send him packing? Or pat him on the head, sympathetically and condescendingly, and tell him to go home and take a couple of paracetamols?

Just as he was contemplating the options, the door opened, and a mellifluous and instantly likeable voice said, 'Good heavens, I don't believe this! My favourite painter in all the world is in my house!'

Jason looked up and saw a handsome man in his early

fifties, with a receding hairline, cool glasses and fashionable stubble, dressed in a dog collar, baggy grey pullover and jeans. He jumped to his feet.

Two minutes later he was seated in the Bishop's modest office which, to his astonishment, had two of his local land-scapes on the wall. 'Wow, you weren't joking!' he said.

'My wife and I are your number one fans!'

Jason shook his head, almost in disbelief.

'Maybe I could do your portrait one day?' he asked.

'I'd love it! Riding my Harley, perhaps?'

'That's yours, outside?'

'My chariot!'

'Nice machine.'

The woman brought them in cups of coffee and a plate of biscuits on a tray. When she left, Robert Parnassus spoke again.

'So, what is this urgent problem you have?'

Jason gave him a brief summary of the events since they had moved into Lakeview Drive. The Bishop listened intently, occasionally jotting down notes on a pad. When he had finished, Parnassus sat silently for a while, his head bowed. Then he looked up.

'OK, you seem a pretty rational fellow, Jason, what's your own take on all this?'

'If you'd asked me this question two weeks ago, I'd have said it was – basically – bollocks. Rubbish. Crap. But I can't dismiss it as that any more.'

He steepled his fingers and leaned forwards. 'So, we have a dead woman, Caroline Harcourt, that you and your wife have both seen. And a deceased vicar, Roland Fortinbrass, that just you have seen? I remember his name well, he died shortly before I was appointed here.'

'Do you believe ghosts exist?' Jason asked him.

'Well, to be honest, that's a bit like asking me if I believe air or water exist. I began life a physicist, long before I became ordained. One of the basic laws of physics is that matter changes but can never be eradicated. Whatever was, always will be. We humans are, among all else, balls of energy. If you were to stab me to death right now – please don't – my energy would dissipate into the surroundings. Just like videotape, the ground beneath us and the walls and ceiling around us are full of carbon and other conductors of electricity. We need to separate, always, the physics – the physical – from the spiritual. This is one of the challenges the modern Church needs to address.'

'And the Harley-Davidson is part of this?' Jason said.

Robert Parnassus looked coy. 'We all have to have our toys, don't we?'

'We do.'

The Bishop became serious. 'So, tell me, how do you feel I can help? Or perhaps I should ask what help you would like from me?'

'What I've learned from talking to locals, in the past few days since moving into our house, is that the site on which the development's been built has a history of tragedy. I've had hints that it is cursed – not something I'd ever normally have believed.'

'And you think this unfortunate fellow killed on the construction site, right in front of your eyes, is part of that – ah – curse?'

'Honestly? I don't know what to think. What I do know is that my wife and I are becoming increasingly scared. I know moving house is meant to be a far more traumatic experience than people realize.' He shrugged.

'That is very true. But what you've told me seems to go beyond that. Most intriguing – but perhaps that's not the right word. I do have an interest in all areas of the paranormal, with my other hat on, as Diocesan Minister of Deliverance.'

'Is that a more socially acceptable term than *exorcist*?' Jason asked.

'Well, to be honest, it's a bit of a faff lugging around a bell, book and candle on a Harley.' The Bishop smiled. 'So, I prefer to look for the logical explanations for what appear to be hauntings, or instances of demonic possession, or disturbances such as apparent poltergeist activity.' He sipped his coffee.

Jason drank some, too. 'What would your initial logical explanation be for our *apparent* situation. A ghost that both my wife and I see – and one only I have seen?'

Absently fiddling with his ring, Parnassus said, 'Well, where I always prefer to start is not by looking at the site where the haunting has occurred, but looking inside the minds of those who have seen it.'

'Is that because Emily and I have both seen ghosts, so we must be crazy?'

Parnassus smiled. 'Not at all, but we always need to remember the complexities of the human mind. Right back in the sixteenth century the Catholic Church was aware of this. The Vatican issued an edict that no exorcism was to be carried out on someone within two years of a bereavement.'

'Really?'

'It was because they felt that the balance of a bereaved person's mind, in the immediate aftermath of their loss, could be disturbed,' the Bishop said. 'Now, please don't take what I'm going to say to you the wrong way. In all of my experience, the overwhelming majority of seemingly paranormal occurrences can be explained by abnormal brain activity in people following a recent trauma in their lives. This is most common from a bereavement, but it can also be from moving house, which as you yourself recognize is far more traumatic than most people realize. Both of these situations can play havoc with mental states. May I ask if you or your wife, Emily, have suffered any such recent bereavement – the loss of a loved one?'

Jason shook his head. 'Touch wood, no.'

'Do either of you dabble in the occult at all – play the Ouija board, for instance?'

'Never,' he replied, emphatically. 'Neither of us have ever been into anything like that. Although Emily's business partner, Louise Porter, is a medium – or claims to be.'

The Bishop's face clouded. 'She is?'

'I don't know if you approve of mediums, or not.'

'Well, there's quite a number of negative passages in the Bible about them, but I don't condemn them out of hand. In the right circumstances some do have a useful role.'

'OK, well, she came to the house on Monday and went into a trance to try to see what might be happening. That was when the Reverend Fortinbrass appeared.'

Parnassus looked at him strangely. 'And only you saw him?'

'Correct.'

'What did your wife's business partner have to say about this lady you both saw – who you think might be Caroline Harcourt?'

'She said something along the lines that she was getting a message for me from a woman. The woman said she was sorry that she damaged my painting, but she was angry that I put her portrait facing the wall.'

He expected a cynical response, but instead the Bishop gave him a sympathetic smile. 'You saw the Reverend Fortinbrass and had a conversation with him, which your wife and this medium, Louise Porter, claim not to remember?'

'Yes, correct.'

'Caroline Harcourt you and your wife have both seen, and the medium has only received messages from?'

'That's right.'

PETER JAMES

Parnassus sat in silence for a while, seemingly immersed in his thoughts. 'Jason, these things that you are telling me are usually, in my experience, triggered by stress, crises, relationship problems. Often it is this stress that seems to produce strange phenomena that brings echoes from the past. I've known couples move into their dream home, only to split up months later. Could any of this have a bearing on what you and your wife are experiencing?'

'I don't know,' Jason replied. 'I'm open to any explanation.'

The Bishop frowned. 'This is not good timing, as we are coming into Christmas week; it's one of the busiest times of my year. Apart from another half hour this morning, I barely have a free moment until after Boxing Day. But there's a priest with considerable pastoral experience who works with me. May I suggest I ask him to come and see you and your wife – perhaps sometime this afternoon?'

'I'd be enormously grateful. Any idea what time?'

'I'll see what commitments he has. Shall we say four o'clock, unless I let you know otherwise?'

Jason glanced at his watch. It was just coming up to 11.30 a.m. 'Perfect.'

'His name is Jim Skeet, he's a good chap. Can you let me have your address?'

Jason gave it to him and he wrote it down. When he finished, he said, 'Shall we pray together?'

The request startled Jason. He could not remember the last time he had prayed. Way back in his childhood. Blushing with embarrassment he mumbled assent, closing his eyes as Bishop Parnassus recited the Lord's Prayer, and finished with a loud, clear, 'Amen.'

'Amen,' Jason echoed.

Parnassus smiled beatifically at him, and for the first time, Jason saw more clergyman than laid-back biker in the bishop.

'If you need me again, Jason, I am always here, or around. Everything will be fine, don't worry. I'll be here to make sure you and your wife have spiritual protection. And you look a pretty healthy chap to me – I think you're going to live a few years beyond forty, whatever that old farmer who doesn't like newbies in his village might tell you!'

Jason thanked him and left. As he headed home, he replayed the strange meeting in his mind. Did Parnassus really believe what he had told him, or was he just humouring him? Either way, the Bishop was sending a clergyman to their house. Jim Skeet. Maybe they could convince him.

Turning into the entrance of Cold Hill Park, he threaded his way along Lakeview Drive. Emily's van wasn't there. He'd give her a call in a minute, to make sure she was back well before Skeet was due to arrive. There was more activity at the Penze-Weedells' house. An electrician's van was parked outside, and there was a man in a parka and jeans halfway up a ladder propped against the wall, with both Mr and Mrs Penze-Weedell standing below, looking up anxiously. None of the lights were on and half of them seemed to have come away from the wall again and were strewn over the front lawn and plants. Jason couldn't help smirking.

As he climbed out of his car, rays of sunshine broke from behind a cloud, and he felt filled with a sudden burst of optimism. Help was coming this afternoon. He liked the aura of calm around the Bishop. Perhaps the visit this afternoon would bring this same calm to the house. Everything was going to be fine, really it would be.

58

Jason let himself into the house, and smiled as he saw the large note Emily had left on the hall table.

Gone to pay Santa a visit to see what he might have brought for my gorgeous husband! XX

He made himself a large coffee then hurried up to his studio and sat at his desk, then he sent a text to Emily.

Babes, please be back by 4. The Bishop sending his top Ghostbuster over. Love you. XX

He took a sip of his coffee – and recoiled in surprise.

It was stone cold.

How? He'd made it less than five minutes ago, a double from the Nespresso machine, with the frothy hot Barista-style oat milk that Emily was sure was healthier than cows' milk.

How could it be completely cold? Was there a problem with the machine, along with everything else? But he'd sipped it on the way up the stairs, and it was so hot then it almost furred the tip of his tongue.

Disturbed, he looked all around. The room felt fine, warm. He heard a grinding roar outside and peered out of the window. The construction site was back in full action, the police now departed.

He opened the contacts on his phone and looked up the estate agent. Then he dialled the direct line number.

Paul Jordan answered instantly and breezily.

'Mr Danes, how good to hear from you, hope you and your lovely wife are enjoying your beautiful home! To what do I owe this pleasure?'

'Well, we still have a few issues, as I mentioned last time we spoke, but yes, we are loving it. I just wondered – I saw a family moving in to the estate yesterday. If you could give me their names, I thought I might pop round and welcome them.'

'Yesterday?' Jordan sounded puzzled. 'I don't think so. No one moved in yesterday – not that I know of – and as we're the sole agents, I would know!'

'They arrived in a great big classic Cadillac convertible, with a removals lorry just behind them.'

'I think you must be mistaken, Mr Danes. I'm afraid it doesn't ring a bell with me. I don't have anyone due to be moving in this week. There's a number of completions scheduled for January, and several viewings booked, but I don't have anyone else moving in before Christmas.'

'I saw them arriving,' Jason said.

'Do you know which house?'

'I don't, no.'

Had he imagined them, Jason wondered, suddenly? The Cadillac and the removals lorry?

Impossible. They had looked too real. Why was the estate agent denying it?

He'd seen the driver with a big cigar in his mouth. A flashy-looking man. A pretty lady seated beside him. Two kids jumping up and down in the rear.

No way had he imagined it.

Had he?

'Ah – OK – I must have been mistaken, they were probably heading somewhere else.'

'Must have been! If we don't speak before, I hope you and Mrs Danes have a very happy Christmas.'

'And you, too.'

Ending the call, he stood up and paced around the room. *Am I going mad?*

New house?

Is my equilibrium disturbed?

He donned his apron and gloves, picked up a pencil and walked over to his empty easel. He began to sketch the next work for his exhibition. *The Skiver.*

For the next hour he was lost in his world of creativity that he loved so much. Working from the photographs on his camera, he had the – now deceased – man exactly. Looking shifty, skulking behind a pyramid of rubble, fingers gripping the roll-up, about to light it.

He hesitated. Should he really be painting a man who was now dead?

But the painting had started before that, when it wasn't a tragic situation. And this wasn't a portrait of the man, it was a distant snapshot of a moment in time. That thought assuaging his guilt, he went over to his work table and began to assemble his paints and brushes.

As he did so a cheeky voice behind him said, 'I thought this whole room would be filled with Christmas prezzies for me!'

He turned to Emily. 'Small is beautiful,' he replied. 'A bag of uncut diamonds really doesn't take up much space.'

She smiled and kissed him. 'So, we have a Ghostbuster? Tell me?'

He told her about his visit to the Bishop of Lewes, and all Parnassus had said.

'Jim Skeet?' she said, when he had finished.

'Uh-huh.'

'I'm curious. Wonder what a Ghostbuster looks like!'

'A tubby, bearded guy, with a sack full of gadgets.'

'In a red suit, with reindeer parked outside?' she questioned.

59

The answer was small, thin, wearing a fawn trenchcoat, beneath which was a clerical shirt and collar and grey trousers, and carrying a large, battered attaché case. He looked about twelve, but must have been north of forty. With the darting eyes of a wary gerbil, and limp, ginger hair brushed forward like a monk's tonsure. The Reverend Jim Skeet was accompanied by a far more confident-looking man, around a decade older and seven stone heavier, with jet-black hair that looked freshly dyed, and a triple chin. He was also wearing a clerical shirt and collar, and jeans, beneath a parka.

'My colleague,' Jim Skeet said, by way of introduction. 'Reverend Gordon Orlebar.'

Jason and Emily led the strange duo through to the kitchen, sat them at the table and produced tea and digestive biscuits. When they were all settled, Skeet, who had a curiously high-pitched voice, said, 'Exactly where did the manifestation – or rather, *manifestations* – happen, Mr and Mrs Danes?'

'Right here in this room,' Emily replied.

'And up in my studio,' Jason added.

'And in our bathroom,' said Emily.

Gordon Orlebar spoke with a far more mature and assured voice. 'We've done our research as best we can, given the short time. Quite interesting really.' Then he fell silent.

They waited patiently for him to continue, but he picked up a digestive and peered intently at it, with a slight frown, as if he had discovered a foreign body present. 'Hmm,' he said. 'Digestives. Can't really beat them, can you?'

'I suppose not,' Emily said, puzzled by his sudden switch of focus.

'Sort of the *comfort food* of biscuits, I always think.'

'So, what did you find that was interesting?' Jason asked, growing impatient.

Orlebar continued studying the biscuit as he spoke. Meanwhile Skeet was rummaging, preoccupied, in his bag.

'Quite a bit of historical activity,' Reverend Orlebar said, calmly, with a relaxed smile, and placed his biscuit on his saucer. 'This whole area, the land on which your house has been built, has something of a history of disturbances.'

'We are aware of some of it,' Jason replied. 'And certainly, if you meet the locals, they are over-eager to talk about it. I think they're resentful of this estate being built. Like they want to scare us off.'

'Locals in the country tend not to like change of any kind,' Skeet said.

'Tell me about it,' Jason said.

'Unrested souls bring negative energy,' Orlebar continued. 'It all needs putting to bed, then hopefully everything will be fine and you will both be able to enjoy your new home.'

'And how do you do that?' Jason asked.

'What the Reverend Skeet and I will do, if you are both agreeable, is hold a service.' He looked at each of them in turn.

'What does that entail?' Jason asked.

'A communion service, in which we will formally lay any restless spirit in this house to rest. First, I'd like you both to tell us anything you can think of, out of the ordinary, that has happened since you moved in – which was very recently, I understand.'

Jason glanced at Emily. 'Gosh, where do we begin?'

'Tell us everything, Mr and Mrs Danes, whatever has been disturbing for you,' Orlebar suggested.

'Well,' Jason said and nodded at the unplugged command box. 'It started with some strange occurrences around that. But it could just have been teething issues.'

'Then footsteps,' Emily said, and pointed up at the ceiling.

They told the two clergymen about the disturbed night, and calling the police. The appearances of the woman, identified as Caroline Harcourt, they had both experienced. And the deceased vicar, Roland Fortinbrass, whom only Jason had seen.

The clergymen listened intently, asking questions as they went along. When Jason and Emily had finished, Orlebar explained the procedures they would carry out, then asked, 'Would you both be happy for us to proceed? Of course, if you would prefer not, then we can just chat. But I understand from your visit to the Bishop this morning, Mr Danes, that you are both very concerned and somewhat distressed by occurrences here?'

'On both counts,' Emily said.

'What would be involved – is there a fee?' Jason asked.

'There is absolutely no charge for our services, we are just here, representing the Church, to help you.'

Jason and Emily looked at each other, then nodded.

'This may sound a bit silly,' Jason said. 'Is there any chance this service, whatever you do, could make things worse here?'

'No,' Orlebar said emphatically, glancing at his colleague.

Skeet nodded equally emphatically. 'Absolutely not.'

'What if our ghost – ghosts – are non-believers?' Emily asked.

If their situation wasn't so serious Jason might have laughed. And he loved his wife for asking the question.

Orlebar was unfazed. 'Ghosts are neither believers nor unbelievers, Mrs Danes. Most Christians would believe that the time to choose whether to be a Christ follower – a believer – or not is while someone is alive on earth. After that we are all in God's hands. He is the one who sorts out the sheep from goats, wheat from tares, and makes the final decisions.'

Skeet chipped in squeakily. 'Also, clergymen like us believe that God has total control over the living and the dead – so it would make no difference if the deceased who are now ghosts had once been believers or not.'

'Exactly,' Orlebar confirmed. 'Prayer is more powerful than any ghost. The Holy Spirit is more powerful than any human spirit. We Christians believe Jesus conquered death and Hell through his death on the cross and resurrection from the dead. He is all-powerful over all principalities and dominions. If you recall the Creed, *He will come again in glory to judge the living and the dead.*' He smiled at them, comfortingly. 'Whether ghosts are believers or not is irrelevant. God has authority over them.'

'Fine,' Emily said. 'Thank you.'

'What if it's a different faith from Christianity?' Jason asked.

Orlebar replied, 'We believe it is the same God for all faiths.'

'Glad we got that one sorted,' Jason said, jokily. Then he fell silent as above them they heard footsteps, clearly and loudly.

Stomp. Stomp. Stomp. Stomp. Stomp.

Skeet looked up, warily, at the ceiling.

'Someone's not happy,' Orlebar said. He gave a benign smile. 'Hey, as your locals told you, no one likes change!'

60

Wednesday 19 December

Over the next ten minutes the two clergymen laid a white linen altar cloth across the kitchen table, on top of which they laid the corporal. Then they donned white albs. From his bag, Orlebar produced a silver chalice, placing it on the corporal, into which he poured red wine while incanting a prayer. Beside the chalice, Skeet solemnly placed a silver paten on the corporal, into which he laid four round white wafers.

Orlebar now produced a silver censer, hung from chains and containing charcoal, which he lit. Grey smoke curled from the thurible, rapidly filling the kitchen with the pungent smell of incense. He lifted the censer up and walked around the room, shaking the smoke in every direction, chanting quietly, as Jason and Emily, still seated, watched in silence.

As he returned to the table, Skeet gestured with his hands for them to stand.

They did as they were bidden. The two clergymen stood on the other side of the table, behind the sacraments, and both closed their eyes, praying silently. Then, in unison, they opened their eyes again and looked at Jason and Emily.

Skeet began the communion. Almost simultaneously, they all heard, loud and clear, the ceiling shaking, and the sounds of footsteps again.

Stomp. Stomp. Stomp. Stomp. Stomp.

Orlebar continued, ignoring the sound.

Stomp. Stomp. Stomp. Stomp. Stomp.

Skeet took over again.

The stomping grew louder, angrier.

Jason and Emily stared rigidly ahead at the two men, not daring to glance at each other.

Like a pair of well-rehearsed musicians, Orlebar took over again.

The stomping above reached fever pitch. It sounded as if, at any minute, the ceiling would come crashing down.

Skeet continued for some moments, then Orlebar again took over, praying loudly and clearly. Finally the stomping stopped.

Orlebar said, pointedly, to Jason and Emily, 'The peace of the Lord be always with you.'

Skeet mouthed the response to the couple.

In staggered unison they replied, uncertainly, 'And also with you.'

The prayers continued for some minutes, culminating in the Lord's Prayer.

Skeet and Orlebar then took communion. When they had finished their dissolving of the wafers in their mouths, and their sips of wine, Skeet nodded at Orlebar, who tried to continue with the service.

The stomping began again, even louder, drowning his voice out.

Skeet gestured for the Daneses to step forward.

Jason and Emily took communion in turn, then stepped back a couple of paces. As they did so, Jason noticed both clergymen were staring past them, transfixed, with very strange expressions. They made Jason deeply uncomfortable.

He and Emily turned.

Caroline Harcourt was standing right behind them.

61

Wednesday 19 December

The woman looked so solid, and so close, Jason could have reached out and touched her. She was as he had seen her before, with short, dark hair, power-dressed in a black suit, white blouse and court shoes, and staring him, levelly, in the eye. Neither friendly nor hostile.

Jason felt the hairs on his neck rising and the same icy wind as before seemed to be radiating from her.

He glanced at Emily. She looked rooted to the spot, her face white with terror.

For an instant it felt like time had stopped. As if the pause button had been hit on a movie. Jason desperately wanted to say something, but he could not open his mouth. Could not move a limb. He was struggling to breathe. It seemed as if all the oxygen had been sucked from the room.

'You may go now,' Orlebar said in his rich, confident voice.

Caroline Harcourt smiled, wryly, in a kind of acknowledgement.

An instant later, as if he was looking at a conjuring trick, Jason saw the woman begin to dissolve in front of his eyes. All the colour bleached out into monochrome. It continued fading, steadily, until there was only a silhouette, formed by a human-shaped cluster of tiny lights.

Then, like grains of sand in an hourglass pouring away, the lights steadily slipped away into the floor.

Within seconds they were gone.

The stomping above them had stopped, Jason realized.

The house felt, suddenly, quite different. Calm. As if some energy that had been there was now dispersed.

He looked at Emily and could see she felt the same thing. The tiniest twitch of a nervous smile on her lips.

Liberated.

They all sat down. Skeet and Orlebar looked shattered.

'You saw her?' Skeet asked.

Both of them nodded.

'She needed to cross over,' Orlebar said. 'I think she was trying to attract attention – that's what all the problems you've been experiencing were about. I don't think you'll have any more disturbances now.'

'That was . . .' Emily began, then shook her head. 'I – did I – what did I see?'

'You will be fine now,' Skeet said.

The two clergymen began packing up.

Jason stood up. 'We're very grateful to you.'

'Let's hope that's the end of it for you both,' Orlebar smiled. 'And now you can enjoy your new home and have a wonderful Christmas.'

She and Jason stood on the doorstep, watching them return to their funny little car that looked like a panel van and drive off.

'I should have taken a photograph of them,' he said. 'They'd make a great painting!'

'Beavis and Butthead?'

He grinned. As they went back inside and shut and bolted the front door he looked, warily, up at the ceiling.

'So?' Emily said. 'What do you think?'

'I think I need a large drink.'

'Me too – a very large one.'

Walking back into the kitchen, Jason said, 'That was weird. *Weird!* Freaky deaky weird.'

Emily opened the fridge and took out a bottle of white wine. 'What was it that Orlebar, said – about historical activity, unrested souls. Negative energy? What were those footsteps about?'

'The power of suggestion?' he ventured.

'Those footsteps weren't *power of suggestion*. They were real. We both heard them.'

'Or imagined we heard them?'

'We heard them,' she said, plainly. 'You know we did.'

He twisted the screw-top cap off the bottle. 'I don't know what the cops thought last night.'

'I do,' she said. 'They thought we were a couple of loons.'

'Shit!' he said, suddenly. 'Shit, shit, shit!'

'What?' she looked at him, concerned.

'My fucking brain is all scrambled. I've got the paintings in my car – I was going to deliver them to my clients on the way home. I got so distracted by the Bishop I forgot.'

'It's Thursday tomorrow; still five days to Christmas. Your clients can wait until tomorrow, can't they? Don't take them tonight. Have a drink and relax.'

He nodded.

'Maybe don't leave them in the car overnight, though.'

'I'll go and get them; I don't want to risk the car being broken into or stolen during the night.'

'By our ghosts?'

He put the bottle down, grabbed his car keys and went outside into the darkness. All the Christmas lights, and it seemed more than before, were blazing again outside the Penze-Weedells' house. He didn't look long enough to see if there were any faces in the windows; he was too concerned about his paintings.

He popped the boot lid of his BMW, raised it and peered inside.

And felt a sudden, terrible, sick feeling of panic.

The boot was empty.

62

Wednesday 19 December

'No. No, oh God, NO.'

Jason stared in abject horror into the empty space. At the tartan rug lying there.

Was this nightmare ever going to end?

Gone.

The painting and the sketch both gone. Stolen. How was he going to tell his clients?

Then he remembered something, and suddenly his hopes rose.

Idiot!

He lifted a corner of the rug and relief instantly flooded through him. The two pictures lay there, sealed and wrapped in brown paper over layers of bubble wrap, as David had presented them to him this morning.

He closed his eyes in relief.

He was really in a state, he realized, lifting the first picture out and propping it against the side of the car. As he lifted up the second one, he saw the book the librarian had lent him, which he had completely forgotten about.

Sussex Mysteries by Martin Pemberton.

He picked it up, closed the boot and locked the car again, carried the book and the pictures back into the house and laid them on the kitchen table.

'What's that book?' Emily asked, looking up from slicing a beetroot.

'Something the librarian lent me – it has a mention of the history of Cold Hill village, apparently.'

'Interesting. Did David do a good job on the framing?'

'Actually, I never checked. He gave them to me like this – he was in a rush, trying to get everything done before he went off.'

'Don't you think you'd better take a look?'

'I wasn't going to – I trust his work completely.'

'It's when people are in a rush that they make mistakes.'

'Not David. We've worked together for too long.'

She gave him a quizzical look. 'These are both important clients, darling, isn't it worth checking? Anyhow, I'd like to see them – you never showed them to me when they were finished.'

He shrugged. 'OK.' Removing a serrated knife from a drawer, he slit open the tape of the first one, very carefully, and slowly slid out the gesso board. 'This is the painting of the labradoodles, and . . .'

His voice tailed off as he pulled the board out further.

Further still.

'What the . . . ?' he said.

Emily stepped over to him. He slid the board completely out of its packaging.

To see there was nothing on it.

Both of them stared in disbelief.

It was blank. A beautifully framed, blank gesso board.

Jason shook his head, bewildered and close to tears. 'What – what's this?' he said. 'What's he done?' He turned it over, as if hoping, miraculously, his painting would appear on the reverse. But there was nothing except the framer's label. 'It's not possible,' he said. 'It's not— What has the idiot done? What's he done? Has he gone fucking mad?'

'Maybe they're both in the other one?' Emily ventured, lamely.

With a sick feeling in the pit of his stomach, he slit the second package open. Then he teased out the single board inside, slowly, fearfully, as Emily watched. With his eyes closed, he pulled the board free of its container and held it up.

There was panic in his voice. 'Em, tell me there's a painting on it. Tell me, for God's sake, tell me.'

Emily said nothing. She stared at it. She didn't know what to say.

The board was just as perfectly framed. And just as blank.

63

Wednesday 19 December

Jason grabbed the glass of wine Emily had poured and downed half of it in one gulp.

'Can you get hold of David?' she said.

'Yeah, right,' he said, sarcastically. 'He's up in the Highlands. I'll just go and ring Charleston Guest House in Gairloch, where he stays every year for Hogmanay. I'm sure he'll be delighted to fly straight back here,' he said. 'He doesn't even have a mobile signal up there.'

'It's not funny, Jason.'

'No? You don't think so? I think it's hysterical.'

'Let's not row.'

'I'm not rowing. I'm – I'm just . . .' He looked at the blank boards again, focusing on them as if it was some kind of optical illusion, and all he had to do was look at them for long enough, the right way, and the images of the dogs would magically appear. 'Tell me you can see the labradoodles and the spaniel. Tell me you can, please tell me you can.'

'Darling, calm down.'

'I. AM. FUCKING. CALM.' His voice rose with every word.

They stared at each other in silence, then Jason sat down and buried his face in his hands.

'How could he have done this? Let me down like this?' he asked.

'Maybe he didn't, what if he put the pictures in, and something happened?'

'Like, the ghosts wiped them, Em?' he said, sarcastically.

'You have a better idea?'

'Yes, he screwed up. His brain was in holiday mode, he was thinking of kayaks, langoustines and a drop of malt, he just screwed up, big time. Leaving me up to my neck in the brown stuff. Two important clients, both expecting me to deliver big Christmas presents for their wives, who are never going to commission another work from me again. Nor will any of their friends. Nor their friends' friends. This is an unbelievable disaster.'

She shook her head. 'No, it's not a disaster. I've had stuff go wrong in catering before. You just have to deal with it.'

'Fine? How do I deal with this?'

'You take a deep breath, go back up to your studio with the two blank boards and you paint the labradoodles on one and sketch the King Charles on the other. So, OK, they're framed, work around it. Get over it. You can do it.'

He stared down at the boards, shaking his head. 'I did such a good job.'

'So, replicate it. You still have a few days – even Christmas Eve, at a pinch,' she said. Then she visibly brightened. 'And here's the silver lining!'

'There's a silver lining?'

'You do the pictures again and deliver them. Then, when David returns you have two pictures waiting for you in his studio, and you can use them in your exhibition – it will be two pictures less you have to do!'

He downed the rest of his glass. 'Yup, that's a possibility. Screw David, I'll bloody do it.'

'Of course you will!' She went over to the fridge, pulled out the bottle and topped him up. 'Relax tonight, we've both had enough stress for one day. I'll make a nice dinner and we can watch something on telly. You can start over in the morning.'

He raised his glass, feeling massively relieved. 'I'll drink to that.'

They clinked glasses.

'I couldn't believe what I saw,' she said. 'That woman behind us, she was so real. She was like a hologram. So real I felt I could reach out and touch her.' Emily shivered.

'When it – *she* – smiled, that was so weird, Em. Do you think she has gone?'

'What do you think?' she asked.

'The house feels – maybe – lighter.'

'It does,' she said.

'They were really strange, those two.'

'Beavis and Butthead?'

He smiled.

'What do you really think?' she said. 'Was it real, or some kind of conjuring trick? Some very clever illusion performed by them?'

'No way. But, honestly? I don't know what to think. I keep going back to that old movie, *The Matrix*. With all that's been going on since we moved here, it feels like we're living in some kind of simulated reality.'

'But the house does feel lighter, doesn't it? They did *something*, didn't they?' Emily insisted.

He tapped his head. 'Something psychological to us?'

'Or they really cleared away something negative?'

'I don't know. I'm not sure what I believe any more.'

She reached forward and picked up *Sussex Mysteries*. 'This has something on Cold Hill village in it?'

'That's what the librarian said. Hey, I didn't tell you, she's a massive fan – she and her husband have two of my pictures!'

'Really?'

'And the Bishop – he had two in his office!'

'You're kidding? You didn't tell me.'

'Nope, I am not kidding.'

'The Bishop had your paintings in his office?'

'He really did.'

'Amazing, I love it. You see, it's happening, darling, your career is really taking off, and you so deserve it!'

'Well, let's see how the next exhibition goes – if I ever get all the paintings done in time.'

'You will.'

Emily began leafing through the book as Jason drank some more wine. 'Shit, what a day. Maybe we've made a huge mistake, moving here. We were happy back in Brighton.' He stood and walked over to the sink.

'We were, but we both had the dream of living in the country, OK?' She continued turning page after page. 'Don't forget that. We *are* going to be happy here.'

He ran the taps, then soaped his hands and began washing them. The act of doing it calmed him. He rinsed the soap off and repeated the process. 'I feel it's my fault; I was the one who originally suggested it, this move.'

'What was it you said, about love meaning you never have to say sorry?'

'Touché.'

She stopped, suddenly, at a page. 'Got it!' she said.

'Got what?'

She raised a hand. 'Gimme a second.'

He rinsed his hands, then soaped them again.

She read, avidly, the brief entry. When she had finished, she looked up at her husband. 'This is really interesting.'

'What?'

'Do you remember the estate agent telling us this house –

this whole part of the development – is built on the footprint of the original mansion, Cold Hill House?'

He nodded, soaping his hands yet again. 'Sort of, vaguely.'

'There's a piece here on the old place!' She began to read aloud.

'*Cold Hill House was built to the order of Sir Brangwyn De Glossope, on the site of monastic ruins, during the 1750s. His first wife, Matilda, daughter and heiress from the rich Sussex landowning family, the Warre-Spences, disappeared, childless, a year after they moved into the property. It was her money that had funded the building of the house – De Glossope being near penniless at the time of their marriage.*'

'Interesting,' he said.

She went on. '*It was rumoured that De Glossope murdered her and disposed of her body, to free him to travel abroad with his mistress, Evelyne Tyler, a former housemaid in their previous home, who bore him three children, each of whom died in infancy. Evelyne subsequently fell to her death from the roof of the house. Did she fall or was she pushed? We'll never know. De Glossope was trampled to death by his own horse only weeks after.*'

'Does it say how old Glossope was?' Jason asked, finally drying off his hands on a kitchen towel.

'How *old*?'

'Yes. Does it give his age, or how old he was when he died?'

She read on, briefly. 'Yes, here! Shit – it says he was killed while out hunting, the day before his fortieth birthday.'

64

'Great,' Jason said, grimly.

Jason walked across, took the book and studied the entry himself, conscious that Emily was watching him closely. As he read, he was thinking back to his conversation on Sunday with horrible Albert Fears.

'Thirty-nine, are you? Birthday anytime soon?'

'Are you going to bring me a present?'

The smirk on the old man's face. *'Dunno if I'll need to. No one in the big house ever lived beyond forty.'* He'd raised his tankard. *'Good health, you and your pretty wife. Long life – eh?'*

But Jason was also thinking back to something much more recent. To the recording he had made during this past night, of Emily talking in her sleep. He pulled out his phone and played it, turning the volume up.

A male voice began to recite names.

'Oliver, Caro, Jade, Johnny, Rowena, Felix, Daisy, Harry, Brangwyn, Matilda, Evelyne.'

She looked at him, bewildered. 'What's this?'

'Recognize any of the names?'

She listened as the playback continued. *'Brangwyn, Matilda, Evelyne.'*

'Who's talking, Jason? Whose voice is that?'

He paused the playback. 'That was two thirty-three this

264

morning. You were talking in your sleep, except it wasn't your voice.'

'That is not me,' she retorted. 'Absolutely no way is that my voice.'

'It was you talking.'

'What do you mean?'

He turned the screen to face her and played it again.

She stared, mesmerized, watching the replay of herself reciting these names. It was dark and fuzzy, but unmistakeably her speaking, she could see her lips moving.

But it was a stranger's voice coming out.

A male.

Watching it creeped her out. She looked back down at the pages of the book. 'Sir Brangwyn de Glossope, Matilda Warre-Spence, Evelyne Tyler? I never heard those names before in my life, until I read them just now. Jason, I didn't know them last night. No way.' She began shaking. 'How?' she blurted. 'I – I – oh God, how? How did they get into my head? I must have been having a dream – a nightmare. How did I say those names? What was going on? Was someone speaking *through* me?'

He grabbed a pen and the kitchen notepad, then started the recording from the top, stopping and starting after each name, in turn, writing them down.

When it had finished, he said, 'Recognize any of the other names?'

Looking shocked, she pointed at the book. 'Some of them are here. Brangwyn; Matilda; Evelyne.' She hesitated. 'Caro – that's short for Caroline. Caroline Harcourt?'

'Could be.'

'What about the others?'

He debated whether to say anything. Should he hold back what he had discovered in the graveyard the day before? It would only freak her out even more. And yet, to say nothing would be dishonest. They'd always promised to tell each other the truth. So that they could deal with problems together.

He shrugged. 'The others are all names on graves in the churchyard, down in the village.' He showed her the photographs he'd taken.

Very deeply shocked, she said, 'I read them all out in my sleep?'

'You did.'

She blanched. 'I'm reciting the names of dead people I don't know, in my sleep? Why? What's that about? Why didn't you tell Beavis and Butthead, while they were here?'

'Because . . .' He was trying to think straight. Why hadn't he told them? He realized the answer. 'Because I hadn't read this book. OK?'

'No, not OK. When I was reciting these names, I hadn't read the book either. So how did I know them? Tell me, how? Who put them into my head?'

'Honestly, Em, I don't know. Look, it's damned weird, really creepy and I have no explanation other than maybe somewhere, sometime, you had read the history of this place and forgotten all about it.'

'That's a bit lame.'

'Are you sure you didn't google it ever?'

'No, but I damned well will now,' she said.

'I've found out a little about the names already – I know how the families died – but I'll have a trawl of the net and see what more I can dig up.' He walked around behind her and rested his hands on her shoulders. 'You and I are positive people, right?'

Hesitantly, she said, 'Yes – meaning?'

'OK, we've had all kinds of weird shit since we moved in. Now we've had the place exorcised – delivered – or whatever they call it. We agree it feels lighter.'

'It did until I read that damned book.'

'Our ghost has gone. We both saw her go. Let's take the positive out of all of this. It does feel better, right?'

Reluctantly, Emily nodded.

'I'll re-do the paintings. We're going to enjoy Christmas in our gorgeous home. We're going to forget about all the shit that's happened; it's in the past, we've dealt with it now, end of.'

'End of,' she echoed, flatly. 'Let's hope so.'

'We've God on our side. He's just a phone call away.' He tapped the business card printed with the name *Reverend Gordon Orlebar* that the Minister of Deliverance had left on the table.

Emily smiled, reached up and entwined her fingers through his. 'It's all pretty ridiculous, isn't it, considering neither of us are believers?'

'It is.' He nuzzled her ear and whispered, 'Just in case it's of interest, I'm suddenly feeling very horny.'

She looked up at him. 'Well, Mr Danes, we may just have to do something about that.'

'Sort of now?' he suggested.

'Now is very good.'

He followed his wife upstairs to the bedroom. They were barely through the door before she started tearing at his clothes. Like a woman possessed, he thought, tearing back at hers. Possessed in a very nice way.

After, as they lay curled up together and drifting into sleep, Jason heard his phone vibrate.

He rolled over and looked at the screen.

J D 1 9 2

E A D 1 9 2

And suddenly he was wide awake, his mind spinning. *JD* Jason Danes. *EAD*. Emily's middle name was Anne. Emily Anne Danes?

The display cleared.

He sat up. Why Emily? Why was her name there? What was 192?

Who are you? What do you want?

He lay in the darkness, fear washing through him.

Why us? Why the hell us?

65

Christmas decorations were strung across the oak beams of the Ginger Fox, and a log fire burned in the grate next to the pub's bar. The interior had a festive aroma of wood smoke and roasting meats.

Earlier that morning, just in time after working through much of the night, Jason had delivered the painting of the two labradoodles and the sketch of the King Charles spaniel that he'd had to painstakingly recreate. Now relieved that he could relax, he and Emily sat at the wooden table facing Louise and her husband, Des, a man who was as thin as his wife was plump. They'd pulled the crackers laid out for them within minutes of arriving, read out the dreadful jokes inside and were now wearing their paper hats.

'Cheers!' Des said. 'Merry Christmas!' He raised his glass of Ridgeview bubbly and the other three raised theirs, clinked glasses, and drank.

'Let's hope ghosts take a day or two off at Christmas, too,' Jason said.

He laughed heartily. The two women looked at each other, a little uncomfortably.

'Never mind Froggie champers,' Des said. 'This knocks the socks off anything!'

'It's – like – yum!' Emily said.

'I like it a lot,' Jason said. 'To me it has all the complexity of a French Grand Marque.'

'Depends which house you're talking about,' Des replied.

Jason knew the man had spent twenty years in the wine industry before being made redundant. He now sold health insurance. Jason couldn't help feeling there was something ironic about that. 'I'm sure you're right.'

'You should try Tattinger 2000.'

'Is that the price or the year?' Jason quizzed.

He smiled. 'Very witty. You'll find the price is a lot less than the year – at present, anyhow.'

'So, how's tricks, Des?' he asked.

'Brilliant, to be honest. I got a birdie at the thirteenth last week!'

'Really?'

He nodded proudly. Really proudly, as if this was his finest achievement of the year.

'Good for you.'

He raised both his index fingers and held them a couple of inches apart. 'And I just missed a hole in one by that much on the eighth!'

'You were robbed.'

'I was.'

Jason had never had the slightest interest in golf, but with so many of his friends passionate about the game, he'd learned the basics, intending one day to paint a golfing series. It was the clothes golfers wore that interested him most, and the more ridiculous, the better.

'What are you doing tomorrow, for Christmas Day, Jason?'

'Got a fairly quiet one – the outlaws coming to us for lunch. We haven't really got the house straight enough for a bigger gathering. You?'

'We've got both sets of outlaws coming, Louise's sister and her four kids. It's going to be anything but quiet.'

Emily and Louise were engrossed in a conversation about Louise's two children, aged five and seven. They were interrupted by a waitress standing over them, reading out the specials, and then asking if they were ready to order. They were.

Seizing his opportunity after they were done with their choices, Jason turned to Louise. 'I need to ask you something.'

'Sure, what?'

'When you were at our house last week, we were talking about time in the spirit world.'

'Yeah . . . ?'

'Is there such a thing as *time-slip*?'

She frowned and sipped her drink. '*Time-slip*?'

'Yes. Sort of where time becomes out of sync?'

'Can you explain a bit more what you mean?'

'Well, for instance, two people in the same room each see something completely different. Like, one person sees someone, but the other person doesn't? Or you do something, have a conversation with someone, say, but then you find out that's impossible because that person isn't around.' He circled his hands around each other, trying to express himself more clearly. 'It's like you've imagined something happen, but you know, you absolutely know you did not imagine it, that it was real.'

She nodded. 'I follow you. As I think I tried to explain last week, time as we know it doesn't exist in the spirit realm. Linear time is a human construct. In spirit everything that ever was, still is, going right back to the beginning of time – and right forward to the end of time, whenever that is.'

'You mean the future?'

'The past and the present and the future are all the same in the spirit realm.'

'So, when we see a spirit – a ghost – it's not necessarily a ghost of the past? It might be a ghost of the future?'

'It's possible.'

He sipped some more of his drink. 'Will a ghost always look the same – always in the clothes they were wearing when they were alive – or at the moment when they died?'

'For a time, yes, before they move on from the earth plane.'

'Move on where?'

'Up through the astral planes. All the time they are unrested souls, they remain on the first levels, in recognizable human form. Gradually, as they move up, they start to lose their earthly trappings.'

'Until what?'

'A few years ago I was in contact with a teenage boy killed on his bicycle, and his family, who held a weekly séance to communicate with him over many years. As his family became more and more comforted, he was able to tell us how he moved on up through the different astral levels.'

He looked at her, finding it hard to believe, yet not able to dismiss her sincerity. 'What was his goal?'

'He told me that his goal was to finally lose all self – all individuality – and become part of the being of light that is at the centre of all existence.'

'A state of nirvana?'

'Exactly. A permanent state of grace, devoid of all earthly concerns and worries.'

'He turns from a human into something like a tree?'

She smiled. 'Not a bad analogy. He was explaining to me how he was going to become part of the energy from which all existence stems.'

Next to him he heard Des telling Emily about his wonderful birdie at the thirteenth hole. Jason tuned him out. 'Does that mean you don't fear death?'

'I don't fear death at all. Death is the beginning of our journey to enlightenment.'

'That sounds very Buddhist, to me.'

'Well, perhaps, except Buddhists believe in reincarnation. I don't subscribe to that. I think we move on from here.'

'And you find that comforting?'

'Very.' She raised her glass.

He raised his and clinked against hers. 'Cheers.' Then he turned to Emily and Des. 'Hey, Happy Christmas, to all of us still on the earth plane!'

They all touched glasses again and drank.

His phone, which he had put on silent, vibrated in his pocket.

He pulled it out and looked at the display.

Despite Matt having assured him, a couple of days ago, that he reckoned he'd fixed the problem, there was another set of numbers on the display. This time just one row of digits.

And it looked like a countdown was in progress.

278137 . . . 278136 . . . 278135 . . . 278134 . . .

A countdown to what, he wondered? The number reduced by a single digit at what seemed to be exactly one-second intervals.

Were they connected to the ones he had seen previously?

Then, just as before, the numbers vanished.

Next time any digits appeared, he was going to try to write them down before they'd gone and then see if he could work out some kind of pattern – although he'd always been rubbish at maths.

'You still with us, Jason?' Des asked.

He looked up with a start. Emily, Louise and Des were all staring at him.

'Sorry,' he said. 'Just a text from a client.'

He slipped his phone back in his pocket. Thinking. Baffled.

66

Wednesday 26 December

'May I offer you a glass of *prosecco*?' Claudette Penze-Weedell said.

'Well,' Jason replied, hesitantly, as he sat beside Emily on a white velour sofa. He would have preferred a large gin and tonic, or a whisky, or just about anything else. But the ghastly woman was already advancing towards them, with two sparkly pink-tinted glasses with gold stems, filled to the brim with a bubbly substance.

'It was an absolute bargain, this fizz,' she said. 'On special offer – not that Maurice and I would ever buy something on price. But this is so delicious.' She gave them a knowing look. 'Simply kicks any champagne into touch, don't you agree?'

Jason sipped. It was particularly dry and tasteless. 'Absolutely,' he said.

Emily sipped and agreed, too. He could almost hear the sound of her gritted teeth.

The detritus of Christmas lay around. Balls of wrapping paper; the fake Christmas tree with just a couple of unclaimed gifts lying beneath it. The mantelpiece above the fake fire lined with cards, with more cards on shelves and on a string across the end wall.

'Fill your boots!' Maurice encouraged. 'You don't have far to drive home, do you, ha ha!'

'So, did you have a nice day yesterday?' Emily asked.

'Oh we did, yes,' Claudette replied. 'Sixteen for Christmas lunch. Although I suppose you, with your catering business, Emily, would take that in your stride.' She hurried out of the room.

Maurice leaned over towards them, conspiratorially. 'High Command managed to burn the turkey. Left it in the oven too long. Burned to a crisp, the skin was. Bit of a disaster, actually. You had a good day, did you?'

'We had the outlaws,' Jason said.

'Outlaws, ha ha! Had mine, too. They left a few minutes before we murdered them, ha ha.' He looked at Emily. 'I'll bet you're a wonderful cook.'

'She is,' Jason said.

'I'll bet she is!'

Emily was staring at something across the room and didn't appear to hear either of them.

'I'll bet you another thing – that your turkey was perfect, eh?' Maurice said. 'Not cremated?'

Jason answered for her. 'It was, thanks. But now she's fretting because she's got a wedding anniversary to cater for in a couple of days: eighty people. They want prawn cocktails for starters. Can you imagine making eighty prawn cocktails? The amazing thing is she never gets flustered!'

'I could eat the lot!' Maurice Penze-Weedell said. 'Love prawn cocktails, I do. Know what they say about the perfect wife?' he said to Jason.

'I do. If I'm thinking what you're about to say, don't even go there.'

'Maurice, don't you dare!' Claudette silenced him in his tracks, returning with a tray of plates stacked with sausage rolls, mince pies, cheese and pineapple sticks, and crisps. She set it down on the table.

Maurice reached out and stuffed a sausage roll in his mouth.

'You'll have to forgive my husband,' she said, shoving an entire mince pie into her own mouth. Spraying flakes of pastry, she added, 'He's such a gannet.'

'I wanted to ask you something,' Maurice said, looking at their guests. 'You've been here just on a fortnight, and we've been a few weeks longer. Have you noticed anything strange, at all? You know, anything out of the ordinary?'

'Maurice!' his wife said, sharply, again.

'Strange?' Jason queried.

'A chap wandering down the street, outside, at night, smoking a cigar?'

'This is utter rubbish!' Claudette said, sitting down on the opposite, matching sofa, alongside her husband, and grabbing another mince pie, as if scared they would be gone. 'This is a complete invention by my husband to explain why he comes home every night after his *constitutional* – which is meant to be his evening walk on his doctor's orders – reeking of tobacco smoke.'

'Utter *rubbish*, my love? Aren't you forgetting something? Only a week ago you ran out of the house after thinking you saw someone upstairs – smoking a cigar!' He looked at Jason and Emily. 'She was out in the cold, freezing.'

'I don't want to talk about it,' Claudette said. 'Let's talk about something more cheerful. What are you both doing on New Year's Eve? Perhaps we could celebrate together?'

Jason shot a warning glance at Emily. 'I'm afraid we are already committed.'

'My love, I don't think we should ignore the issue of something strange going on,' Maurice said. He looked, quizzically, at Jason, then Emily.

'The only thing I've noticed is some people, from time to

time, in the house next door to you. Number thirty-four,' Jason replied.

'Oh, we've seen them too,' Claudette said. 'The sister and brother-in-law of the couple who were so tragically killed. Maurice and I have chatted with them, such a lovely family. They're executors of the estate, sorting everything out.'

'Ah, right,' Jason said, feeling mightily relieved. 'I'm afraid I've not seen Mr Cigar Man close up.'

'Of course you haven't.' She turned and glared at her husband. 'I'm afraid, my love, your little lie's been caught out.'

'He's there every evening,' her husband said, defensively.

'Of *course* he is. How convenient, he's there just so you can smoke your cigarette, and don't tell me you don't have any; I've checked your coat pocket every day, and every day there is one cigarette less in the packet.'

She turned, sweetly, to the Daneses. 'Oh dear, your glasses look almost empty. Some more bubbles?'

Jason looked down and saw, to his surprise, that both his and Emily's glasses were drained. Emily was still staring, distracted, at something on the far side of the room. Before they had a chance to refuse, they were topped up to the brim, and Claudette bustled out of the room to fetch another bottle.

'He is there,' Maurice said. 'Every time I go out, I see him across the road, standing beneath a street light. But when I try to chat to him, he buggers off. Are you sure you haven't seen him?'

Jason shook his head.

'Claudette is convinced I'm making him up, but I'm not.' He shrugged. 'Damned queer fellow, that's all I can say. Downright rude; I instantly thought he must be from one of those *affordable houses* somewhere else on the estate, but of course they haven't been built yet.'

Jason raised his glass, awkwardly. 'Well, cheers, Happy Christmas!'

'Happy Christmas to our famous neighbours!' Claudette said, coming back in with a freshly opened bottle. 'I think we're going to be really good friends. Maurice and I were only just saying how lucky we are to have such wonderful neighbours.'

'I'll drink to that,' Jason said, politely, raising his glass, and realizing it was empty. As was Emily's.

Once again, they were topped up.

Emily pointed across the room. 'Such a lovely piece, that!'

Jason followed the direction of her hand, as did both their neighbours. She was pointing at a walnut display cabinet. Behind its glass windows were several Capodimonte figurines: a pair of dancers in Regency costumes, a cobbler in a vest mending a pair of shoes and a tramp in a floppy hat seated on a bench with a bottle in his hand. On a separate shelf, as if in pride of place, was a porcelain donkey wearing a straw sombrero, and with a quartz clock set in its belly.

'Capodimonte!' Claudette exclaimed. 'Maurice and I collect it, you know,' she said proudly.

'So very tasteful,' Emily said, with sarcasm so thinly veiled Jason wanted to kick her. She'd clearly drunk too much.

'So glad you like them!'

'I particularly love the donkey,' she went on.

'Do you know, Maurice and I were watching *Antiques Roadshow* recently, and there was one, almost identical to that, which was valued at twenty thousand pounds. Can you believe it?'

'My love,' her husband corrected her. 'It was a Victorian *racehorse*, not a donkey, that was valued so highly.'

'So? Your point is?' she rounded on him.

'They are somewhat different pieces.'

'*My* point is, my love, that our donkey is in the same style, exactly.'

'Perhaps,' Maurice said, dubiously. 'But I think if you consult any antiques guide, you will find that quartz clocks had not been invented in the Victorian era.'

'Where did you get such a lovely piece?' Emily asked.

'You won't believe it!' Claudette said, proudly. 'We bought it in a charity shop in Brighton. Quite a find, wouldn't you say!'

'Oh yes,' Emily replied. 'Quite a find. Clever you!'

'Tell Maurice! I paid ten pounds for it and he chided me for wasting money. Can you believe it? It was one of my fiftieth birthday presents to myself.'

'No,' Emily said. 'I can't believe it.'

'Your *fiftieth* birthday?' Jason said, disguising his cynicism well. The woman looked closer to sixty. 'No way are you fifty!'

'Hard to believe, isn't it?' Claudette said. 'Maurice tells me I don't look a day over thirty-five.'

'You don't!' Jason said.

'I'll be fifty-five next birthday,' Maurice boasted.

He looked closer to seventy, Jason thought. 'I'd never have believed it!'

'Everything in moderation!' Maurice said. 'That's the secret!'

Two more refills later, Jason and Emily finally made their escape, walking tipsily across the road.

They said nothing to each other until they were back in their house and safely out of earshot.

67

'I don't believe it – do you?' Emily said, and giggled.

'Believe what? The shit wine?'

'It was shit.'

She shook her head, heading into the kitchen. 'God, I need a drink of something decent.' She opened the fridge door and took out a bottle that was still a quarter full from last night. She poured the contents into two glasses, handed one to Jason and sat down.

Then she broke into a broad smirk.

'What?' Jason asked.

'The donkey!'

'The donkey – what about it?'

'You didn't recognize it?'

'Should I have done?'

'Hello! That wedding present your Aunt Minette gave us that you hated so much?'

It was coming back to him now. 'Yes.'

'You agreed we should give it away, along with a bunch of other gifts we didn't like, so I took the stuff to the charity shop. That was it, in her cabinet – the one she thought was worth twenty thousand pounds because she'd seen *Antiques Roadshow*!'

'Probably something similar,' he suggested.

She shook her head. 'No, I went over and looked at it

carefully. Claudette opened the cabinet and let me pick it up. There's an L-shaped chip out of the base, about a centimetre long, which happened when I dropped it. I remember – I thought the whole thing was going to shatter.'

'That is so bizarre!' he said.

'Feeling bad now about us giving it away?'

'Not any more. I'm so happy it went to people who get so much pleasure from it.'

'And you'll still be happy when you see it on *Antiques Roadshow* being valued at twenty grand?' she asked.

'Along with a flying pig?'

She laughed. 'Can you believe the coincidence, though?'

'Nope, very strange. Also, there's something very interesting – she's fifty and he's nearly fifty-five. So much for the bollocks about no one living beyond forty here!'

'Maybe they're ghosts.'

'Ghosts?'

'Uh-huh!' Her eyes twinkled. 'Maybe they're dead and we just didn't realize.'

'Could any ghosts be as horrible as them?'

'True. We have a better class of ghost on this side of the street.'

'I'll drink to that!'

As they clinked glasses, a loud report, like a gunshot, startled them.

'What was that?' she asked, nervously.

Jason hurried out into the hall. He looked around, then fixed his gaze on the mirror lining the stairs, on the right. There was a crack in it. Like a high-voltage warning sign. A single line, with two jagged spikes.

Emily joined him and saw it too.

'How – how did – how?'

There was another report and an identical crack appeared in the mirror on the left.

Emily grabbed him in fear. 'Jason?' she whispered. 'Jason, how did—?' She fell silent as there was another crack right behind them.

An identical split had appeared in the window beside the front door.

She screamed.

There was another crack.

Followed by another.

Then another.

'Jason!' she yelled.

Another.

Another.

'Jason!'

Another.

She gripped his arm, hard.

Another. Above them.

Another.

Crack.

Crack.

'Call the police,' she whispered.

Crack.

'Call them!'

Crack.

Then a long silence.

'Call the police, darling, call the police!'

'You saw their reaction when they came last week. They're not going to turn out for a few cracked panes of glass.'

'Who's doing it? Maybe it's kids, with a catapult or airgun?' Emily said, clearly having little faith in her own suggestion.

Jason, closely followed by his wife, hurried up to his studio. He went in ahead of her, turning on the lights and looking around.

'Jesus.'

All the windows had an identical crack to the ones downstairs, right across the middle.

'What is it, Jason?' Emily said. Her voice was barely a whisper. 'What is it? What's happening?'

Without answering, he went back down to the first floor and checked each of the spare rooms in turn, then the master bedroom, before heading on down in numb silence, and checking out the kitchen.

Every mirror and every window in the house had an identical crack. A single line, broken with two jagged spikes, before carrying on again.

'What is it, what's done that?' Emily asked, shaking.

There was another, much louder, splintering crack right above them.

They both looked up, in terror.

Another identical crack had appeared above them, right across the kitchen ceiling. Tiny fragments of plaster, like dust motes, fluttered down.

68

They ran out into the hall and through into the living room, looking up at the ceiling again. 'Subsidence,' he mouthed, almost silently.

'What?'

'Subsidence, there's something wrong with the foundations. The builders have fucked up with the foundations. Something's seriously not right.'

'It's not subsidence, Jason, is it? You know it isn't. It is *not* subsidence.'

He continued staring at the ceiling. His voice trembling, he said, 'I don't think ghosts break windows or make cracks in ceilings.'

'Or smoke cigars out in the street? Or turn up disguised as vicars?'

A sharp, malevolent, female voice rang out from the kitchen.

'Nor speak from a command box that's been unplugged!'

They froze.

Emily looked at him, her face the colour of ice. 'Wh-what was that?'

Cautioning her with his hand to stay where she was, he walked back to the kitchen. As he entered, he heard a man say, in a northern accent, 'It's not unplugged, Lulu, you daft bitch!'

To his surprise the television was on. A young couple, in a

284

modern kitchen, were both staring at an identical command box to their own.

'I unplugged the bloody thing, I'm certain I did, Ray, to stop the alarm waking us every morning.'

'At what time would you like an alarm call?' the device spoke in a commanding female voice.

'I don't want a bloody alarm call.'

'I'm sorry, I don't understand your request.'

The man on the screen looked, exasperated, at the woman.

There was a close-up of the device, clearly plugged in.

'I don't understand,' she said. 'I unplugged it!'

'Yeah, right, so it just plugged itself back in?'

Jason felt Emily's arms around him. 'At least we have one rational explanation,' she said.

'Except I didn't turn the television on, and nor did you.'

'Maybe one of us touched the remote?'

'I'll take that, for now.' Jason looked at the very-definitely unplugged device on the table.

'So will I.' Emily shot a glance at the ceiling again.

He picked up the remote and turned off the television. 'I'll call Paul Jordan first thing – we need to get a surveyor, urgently.'

'Where are we going to find one in Christmas week? The agency's probably shut until after the holidays.'

'I have his mobile number.'

'You do? Call him now? I don't think we should risk staying here tonight.'

'Em, this place was built by one of the UK's best-known developers. They must know what they're doing. There's a bit of subsidence, but it's not falling down.'

'Absolutely, they know what they're doing – like killing one of their site workers?'

'That was a tragic accident.'

'I don't want to be another tragic accident, OK? Call him now.'

Reluctantly, Jason scrolled through his contacts list, then hit the estate agent's name.

Jordan answered on the fourth ring. He sounded totally pissed. 'Jason, my friend! Happy Boxing Day! You know – to you and your lovely wife. I trust Santa Claus did you both proud – even though he might have had difficulties finding you on the new estate, unless he has a very up-to-date satnav!'

A baby was screaming in the background.

'I hope you had a good Christmas, too,' Jason said politely.

'Oh, we did, still going on! You have no idea how – how . . .' His voice tailed off.

'Hello?' Jason said, wondering if he had lost the connection.

'Have you seen it? Bloody brilliant, just brilliant.'

'I'm sorry?'

'*Die Hard*. Bruce Willis. Incredible film!'

'Paul, we have a problem – a very serious problem.'

'Bruce Willis has one too – terrorists, but really they are robbers – it's just brilliant.'

'Maybe he can sort out our problem, Paul, if he's that brilliant?'

'I'll send him over, pal! Anything else I can do for you?'

'Actually, yes. I think our house is falling down.'

'Can it wait until tomorrow?'

Jason covered the mic on his phone and looked, helplessly, at Emily. 'He's completely shitfaced.'

'He has to do something.'

'He's going to send Bruce Willis over.'

'That's not funny.'

Jason looked up again at the ceiling. 'Paul, we have a very serious problem, we need urgent help.'

There was no reply.

'Paul!' he said, loudly. 'Paul!'

A faint voice said, 'I've dropped my phone. Anyone see it?'

Angry and frustrated, Jason ended the call. 'We're not going to get any sense out of him.'

'Maybe we should bail out and spend the night in a hotel?' Emily suggested.

'We've both drunk too much to drive.'

'We could call a taxi.'

'It's Boxing Day night, Em – there won't be an empty hotel room in the county.'

'We could go and stay with my parents.'

'Thank God this didn't happen yesterday when your parents were here. I can imagine what your dad would have said.'

'Dad wouldn't have let us spend another night here until it was all sorted. He'd have insisted we go and stay with them.'

'And he'd have twisted it all around, so it was somehow my fault for not having the place properly checked out or something. You know how he grabs any chance to get a dig in.'

'Jason, that is so not fair. We had a very happy day with them.'

He didn't respond.

'Come on, we did!'

'Were you and I in the same house yesterday? Your father criticized the champagne, saying it was too young, and that I should know to keep it at least two years before opening it. Then he had a go at me for not leaving the foil on the neck of the white burgundy because it makes the bottle look more elegant. And then he told me I'd served quite the wrong red with the turkey and I shouldn't have decanted the bottle because it wasn't of a quality or an age that needed it. Oh, and when I cut him a piece of Cheddar he yelled at me, "*ne coupez pas le bec*", because I apparently cut it from the pointed end, which must have ruined everyone's Christmas.'

'He's very fussy about his wines, you know that.'

'I did my bloody best. Next time I'm sodding serving him some of Mrs P-W's bargain prosecco. Can I actually do anything right for him?'

'He means well; as I've said before, it's just his blunt way.'

He took a deep breath, trying to calm down. 'Look, babes, I'm sorry, we're both rattled; let's cool it. This house is *not* falling down. We have a problem with subsidence and there's been a tiny bit of movement, that's all. There're some hairline cracks in the ceilings and some cracked windows.'

'*Some?* Every ceiling, window and mirror in the house. Why are you in denial about it?'

'I don't think it's dangerous,' he said, flatly. 'And I don't think a ghost did it. Ghosts might be damned spooky, but I doubt they have the power to cause subsidence!'

'So everything is fine, is it?'

'I'm not saying that, I know it's creepy, but there has to be an explanation – this is an architect-designed house and the build quality is very high.'

'Oh, really, that's why it's falling down, is it?'

'It's not falling down. New buildings often move from subsidence – or settlement – which has put everything out of alignment, causing the walls to twist a fraction. That's all it would need to do to create the cracks; just the tiniest movement. They all twisted a little and that caused the windows – and the fixed mirrors – to crack. That doesn't mean the place is falling down.'

'Is that what you're going to tell me when we wake up, crushed and trapped inside fallen masonry? *If* we wake up?'

69

Despite her anxiety, within minutes of going to bed Emily fell into a deep sleep. Jason lay awake for a long time, reading a Linwood Barclay thriller she had given him for Christmas, but unable to concentrate. He kept staring up at the thin, jagged crack all the way across the ceiling, watching to see if it worsened.

Finally, shortly after 1 a.m., he put the book down and switched off the light. He woke with a start a while later. The clock showed 2.24 a.m. Emily was still sound asleep, breathing deeply. Not wanting to wake her, he reached across, lifted his phone off his bedside table, switched on the torch app and shone it upwards. So far as he could judge, the crack was still no larger – if anything it actually looked less bad, but that was probably because of the weak beam of light.

He slipped out of bed, went up to his studio and checked the ceiling there. It was definitely no worse than earlier, either. He went on to check all the rest of the rooms in the house. Finally, satisfied there had been no further movement, and no cause for alarm, he went back to bed, relieved, closed his eyes and fell asleep a short while later.

When he woke again, his clock showed 7.42 a.m.

The bedroom was bathed in a weak glow. Emily was still asleep. He switched on his bedside lamp and looked at the ceiling.

And frowned.

The jagged crack had gone.

The ceiling looked fine.

He again climbed out of bed, slowly, pulled on his dressing gown and walked out of the room onto the landing. The mirrored walls either side of the staircase below were also no longer cracked.

Hurrying up the spiral stairs, he went into his studio. There was no longer a crack in the ceiling, nor in any of the windows.

Am I dreaming, he wondered? He went down and checked each of the spare rooms on the first floor and found that the cracks had gone from their ceilings and windows, also. It was the same downstairs.

Nothing.

He stood in the kitchen, staring up at the ceiling and then at the windows. Nothing. Nothing. He looked at the refectory table where, last night, flakes of plaster had fallen. There were none there now.

How could that be?

He switched on the Nespresso machine, waited for the green lights to stop blinking, then popped a capsule into it.

Am I going mad? he wondered, looking up at the ceiling again, and then at the windows. Everything looked completely normal. As the coffee machine rattled away, he walked over to the window, where there had been a massive, jagged crack last night. There was no trace of it.

'Hi, darling!'

He turned, as Emily walked in sleepily, barefoot, swathed in a white towelling dressing gown.

He went over and kissed her. 'How did you sleep?'

'Like a lamb! Wow, I was just out for the count. Just as well, I've got a lot to do today. How did you sleep?'

He pointed at the window. 'Notice anything odd?'

She walked to the sink and peered out. 'There's a whole

bunch of ducks on the lake – have you seen? They must have flown in! We must buy a milk churn or some other container for feed. There's Wishing Wells Farm at Hickstead, which sells all that stuff. We should go there when we're not too busy.'

'Sure. But what I mean is, the window.'

'The window?'

He pointed upwards. 'And the ceiling.'

She gave him a strange look. 'I'm not with you.'

'The cracks!' he said. 'They've gone!'

'Cracks?' She looked genuinely puzzled.

He waved a hand in front of her face. 'The subsidence – we were discussing evacuating the house last night because of all the cracks. They – they've gone.'

Emily stared at him. 'Darling, I'm sorry, I've no idea what you are talking about.'

'Last night . . .' He fell silent for a moment. She was looking at him extremely strangely. 'Last night, the house was cracked all over, right?'

'What do you mean?'

'The mirrors up the stairs. All the windows, ceilings?'

Again, the strange look. 'Did you have a bad dream?'

He glanced up again at the ceiling. At the white paint and the down-lighters. There was absolutely no sign there had ever been a crack. Like the glass in the windows.

'We – we discussed moving out and going to stay with your parents,' he said.

'You must have had a weird dream.'

'You don't remember any of that?'

'I have a slight headache. All I remember is that horrid stuff the P-Ws kept pouring down our throats. I'm not surprised it gave you nightmares!'

Puzzled, he walked over to the coffee machine and poured the hot froth into his cup. 'Want a coffee?'

'I'm going to have one of my teas.'

'I'll boil the kettle for you.'

He emptied the kettle, refilled it and switched it on. 'I . . .' He began, then fell silent.

'You what?'

He sat down at the table with his coffee. 'Last night we came back here after tunnelling out of the Penze-Weedells, and we heard a loud crack, right?'

She shook her head. 'No.'

'How pissed were you?'

'About the same as you!'

'First the mirrors either side of the staircase, then the windows, then each ceiling. You wanted us to go to your parents because you thought the house was falling down, and we had a bit of a row. You *must* remember.'

'Darling,' she said, 'we came back here from the Peenies and you were totally pissed, and zonked. That's what I remember.'

He stared at her, feeling very strange. Was that the explanation? He sipped some coffee, trying to reflect back, to think clearly.

Had he dreamed it all?

Everything in the house was as pristine as the day they'd moved in.

That had to be the explanation. There wasn't any other that made any sense.

'You don't have a hangover?' she asked.

'I don't.'

'You sure deserve one!'

Relief was flooding through every vein in his body. He must have dreamed it . . . and yet. He was certain he hadn't. Was there something wrong with Emily? he suddenly wondered, very concerned. She had no recollection of the Reverend

Fortinbrass turning up last week. Now she had no recollection of all the cracks last night.

He tried to think it all through. Emily's partner, Louise, had no recollection of Fortinbrass, either.

Emily put her arms around him. 'You're under a lot of stress with your exhibition looming, my love. Maybe you should go and see Dr Dixon again and get him to help you calm down?'

'Maybe,' he agreed, hesitantly. Perhaps she was right. Something was not making sense at the moment. He looked up at the ceiling again. Not any sign of a crack.

He kissed her, feeling troubled. 'What's your plan for today?'

'Full on, prepping for the anniversary dinner tomorrow, and I've just had a call from Louise; she's down with flu. She's going to stay in bed today and try to shake it off, so she can be with me tomorrow, come hell or high water. Great, eh?'

'Can I help you?'

'You need to get on with some more paintings for your exhibition. I'll manage. Got the glorious task of peeling seven hundred prawns, to make eighty prawn cocktails. I took them out of the freezer and put them in the fridges overnight.'

'I don't remember you doing that.'

With a teasing grin, she said, 'I don't think you remember very much at all after leaving our sweet neighbours. Do you remember the porcelain donkey?'

'Twenty thousand quid, on *Antiques Roadshow*.'

'I'm impressed. So, you weren't totally smashed.'

'I'll be working in my studio. Shout if you need anything.'

'I'll be OK.'

'Adore you.'

She kissed him.

70

Thursday 27 December

Jason finished his coffee, then went for an hour-long bike ride, in bright, frosty sunshine. When he returned, he chopped up some fruit and mixed it into a bowl of cereal, fetched the papers from the hall mat, and thumbed through the *Argus* and the *Guardian* while he ate his breakfast.

Afterwards he had a thirty-minute shower. It was the longest he'd had for many days, and it surprised him, with all the stress of recent events, that he hadn't had a relapse. He soaped and rinsed himself repeatedly, before getting dressed in jeans and a sweater and going up to his studio, looking all around for any sign of the woman before closing the door behind him.

He was finding it hard to dismiss all that had happened last night as a dream. And yet, what other possible explanation was there?

He sat at his desk and logged on, in turn, to his email and social media. All seemed normal. He replied to a few posts and then logged off again, aware that he had to knuckle down.

He placed a fresh gesso board on the easel, put on his apron and gloves and began to mix his paints. But he was too distracted, his mind somewhere else.

I did not imagine last night. I did not dream it.

He looked out of the window at the building site and scene of the accident, and realized the police hadn't called him back yet. Wondering whether to call the PC directly rather than go through the tedium of the long wait on the 101 number, he peered closely at the box on the desk, which was where he put the business cards of everyone he had ever met, and started working through it. Looking for a name. PC Neil Lang. The officer had written his direct phone number on the card he'd left.

He couldn't find it.

Had he left it in the kitchen somewhere?

He hurried downstairs. The integral door to the garage – commandeered by Emily and Louise as their catering kitchen – was open. He checked the refectory table and a couple of kitchen drawers, but the card wasn't there. He hurried across and leaned through the open door to the garage.

Emily, dressed in an apron and protective gloves, her hair up inside a sterile hair-net, stood at a long trestle table covered in a white cloth, laying out rows and rows of glass bowls.

'Em,' he said, 'where did you put the business card from that police officer, Neil Lang?'

'Police officer?'

'One of the two who came here last week – Wednesday night.'

She replied without looking up, 'I don't remember any police officers coming here last Wednesday night. What police officers?'

He stepped back, feeling giddy, suddenly. Had he imagined them, too?

Humorously, she added, 'Were they the ones that came with the vicar I couldn't see?'

He looked at her, feeling very strange, as if he was in some kind of altered reality. 'You don't remember?'

'I think I would have remembered police officers coming here.' She continued with her work.

'We had a conversation about them.'

'We did?' She gave him a strange, blank look and shook her head.

He hurried back up to his study, sat at his desk, and dialled the non-emergency number for Sussex Police, 101.

To his amazement, it was answered after a couple of rings. 'Sussex Police, how can I help you?'

'I'd like to speak to PC Neil Lang, please.'

'One moment, please.'

Out of the window to his right he saw the Penze-Weedells coming out their front door. Claudette held up something in her hand, and stabbed it with a gloved finger. The key fob. Seconds later, as he still waited on the line, he saw the garage door open and their little, box-shaped, purple electric car reverse out and stop, obediently, in front of them. They got in, Claudette in the driver's seat, and a few seconds later they shot off and out of sight.

'Hello, caller, we don't have any record of a PC Neil Lang, I'm afraid.'

'You don't?' He spelled out the name.

The operator sounded friendly. 'Not in Sussex Police. I've checked the records.'

'But he came to our house – last Wednesday, December nineteenth. He was with a colleague, PC Christina Davies.'

'I'll check her for you, if you can hold? May I take your name, please?

'Sure, it's Jason Danes.'

'Danes.'

He spelled it out for her, phonetically. 'Juliet Alpha Sierra Oscar November, then Delta Alpha November Echo Sierra.'

'Mr Jason Danes?' she replied, with no hint of recognition of his name.

'Yes.'

'One moment, please.'

A car coming along Lakeview Drive, going slowly as if looking for an address, caught his attention. He blinked. It was the huge red and white 1960s Cadillac he had seen before. The driver, sitting on the left, had a large cigar in his mouth; a woman sat beside him, and there were two excited-looking children in the back.

Just as he had seen before.

As they disappeared from view the operator came back. 'I'm really sorry, we don't have any record of a PC Christina Davies. Are you sure they are with Sussex Police, sir?'

'I thought they were.'

Suspicious, she asked, 'Do you want to report this as possible fraud, sir? There have been instances of fraudsters, locally, posing as bogus police officers.'

'No - er - no, I don't think they were after any money. Look - could you help me with something else, please? We live in the Cold Hill Park estate. Last Monday, December seventeenth, I witnessed a fatal accident on the construction site. I phoned this number and spoke to the gentleman who answered, saying I had seen the whole thing happen.'

'What exactly was that, sir?'

'It was the construction worker who was killed by a bull-dozer. I said I'd seen the whole accident happen, but I'm a little surprised no one's been in touch to take a statement from me.'

'Well, yes, that does sound a bit odd, sir. A construction site worker killed. You don't remember the name of the call handler by any chance?'

'No, I'm afraid not. But I gave him my name and phone number.'

'Your number is showing here, sir. Let me check this out - are you all right to keep holding.'

'Fine.'

This time it was several minutes before she came back to him, sounding apologetic but a tad less patient than before. 'Mr Danes, you say you reported a fatal construction site accident you witnessed, on Monday, December seventeenth?'

'Correct, yes.'

'Look, I'm very sorry, sir, but I've checked very carefully; there is no record of any accident at Cold Hill Park on that date.'

Jason could not believe what he was hearing. 'I saw it! I saw the whole thing happen from my studio window. The poor guy was beheaded by the bulldozer jaws. There were police officers at the scene for several days after, for God's sake!'

The tone of her voice changed, as if she was now talking to an infant. 'Mr Danes, I am very sorry to tell you this, but there was no reported death at Cold Hill Park. I've had a colleague check the local newspapers and there is no mention of it, either. You've just asked me to put you through to two police officers who do not exist, and you are now claiming to have witnessed an accident that did not happen. I'm very sorry, Mr Danes, but I really cannot help you any further, unless you would like to report possible fraud?'

'No, well – thank you,' he said, lamely.

As he ended the call, his mind in turmoil, he heard Emily screaming.

'Jason! JASON! Help me! OH MY GOD, HELP ME!'

71

He sprinted down the two flights, into the kitchen and through the door to the garage. And stopped, horrified, in his tracks.

It was the sour reek of the creatures that struck him first, before the full horror of what he was seeing.

Cockroaches.

Everywhere.

Two tall, commercial fridge doors were open, filled with the crawling brown creatures. The air in the garage was thick with them flying around. The floor was a sea of them.

Emily stood, utterly petrified, in their midst, crying hysterically. They were crawling over her hair and one was on her cheek. He flapped one away from his face, took a step forward and heard a crunch underfoot. He batted another away from his face, then another, turned back and slammed the door shut to stop them going into the house.

'Help me, for God's sake, Jason, help me!' she screamed.

The creatures were everywhere he looked. On the walls. The floor. The ceiling. In the air.

He lunged towards her, his shoes crunch, crunch, crunching on the moving carpet. Two landed on her face and she smote them away.

'Help me!'

One struck his right cheek and he slapped it hard. Another flew into his left eye.

'Get the fuck off!'

He grabbed her hand and physically pulled her across the floor, crunching on dozens of the vile creatures. He opened the door and pushed her through, followed and slammed the door behind them. Even so, several of them had entered the house, some scuttling along the floor, others flying clumsily around.

Emily was sobbing.

'Em, what the hell's happened?'

There was one crawling through her hair. He flicked it away with his fingers.

'Oh God,' she said, shaking, close to collapse. 'Oh God, oh God, oh God.'

'Where did they come from?' he asked, gently.

'Oh God, oh God, oh God,' she said again.

'Em,' he raised his voice. 'WHERE DID THEY COME FROM?'

Her reply came out in a high-pitched squeak. 'The bloody freezer. The bargain prawns, I told you, Louise found this incredible deal.'

A cockroach landed on his chest. He brushed it off.

'This can't be happening,' she said. 'Tell me it's not happening.'

'Where did she get this *incredible deal* from? We'll get rid of them.'

'Oh God, oh God, oh God.'

'Calm down, calm down, Em, we'll get rid of them.'

'I've got to make eighty prawn cocktails and a main course and deliver it all by six o'clock tomorrow. Don't tell me to calm down!'

'Being hysterical won't help. We'll deal with it, we'll sort it out.'

'Louise is in bed with flu and I've got a kitchen full of roaches. This is my worst nightmare.'

'We're going to deal with it. Where did these come from? Just what scumbag fraudster sold you seven hundred cockroaches?'

'It was Louise; I told you she had an incredible bargain on them from the wholesaler.'

'Your normal wholesaler?'

'No, a different one.'

'Now you know why they were so cheap; you've been conned.'

'You think we bought cockroaches?'

'Obviously you did.'

'No way. They were prawns,' she said adamantly. 'Do you think I can't tell the difference between a prawn and a cockroach? It was prawns that went into the freezer, frozen *prawns*.'

'And someone performed a conjuring trick and turned them into roaches? Is that what you're saying?'

'Do you have a better explanation, Jason?'

'Yes – frozen in bags packed in ice, couldn't they look similar? How carefully did you check?'

'I'm a chef,' she said. 'I know the difference, OK? It was prawns that went into those fridges to defrost, not cockroaches.'

'I read somewhere that cockroaches have the same protein as prawns.'

'Oh, great, we're going to serve up eighty cockroach cocktails? That will do very nicely for my reputation.'

'Stick a bit of cocktail sauce on and no one will know the difference,' Jason said breezily, trying to lighten her up.

'You're right, they won't. Until the hostess sues me for fraud, and seventy-nine other separate people sue me for food poisoning. This is not a time to make jokes, Jason.'

A cockroach scurried along the floor right beside her. She crushed it with her plimsoll. 'Yech.'

'Another interesting fact about cockroaches,' Jason said. 'They stopped evolving several thousand years ago. They're one of the few creatures that would survive a nuclear attack.'

She looked at him. 'Do I really need to know this, right at this minute?'

'Just saying.'

'And here's what I'm *just* saying.' She fell silent.

'What?' he probed.

'I need seven hundred prawns, now.' She fell into his arms, sobbing. 'You've got blank paintings; I've got roaches not prawns. What have we done, moving here? This house hates us.'

'Babes, don't be ridiculous, of course it doesn't.'

'No? Well, it sure has a strange way of showing us its love.'

'You think our ghost turned the prawns into cockroaches?' he asked, incredulously.

Before she could reply, his phone rang. The display showed *Paul Jordan*. He answered.

'Mr Danes, I have to apologize, I believe you rang last night when I was a bit – how should I put it – out of it?'

'You could say that.'

'Was it something urgent?'

'Well, it was. But –' he batted another roach away and looked at Emily – 'look, that emergency has passed. I have another, different one. I need two things, right away, immediately. You have a lot of contacts – I don't know if you can help us?'

'What do you need?'

'We've an infestation of cockroaches, and my wife is trying to prepare for a big dinner tomorrow – like for eighty people.

We need an exterminator here, urgently, to get rid of the roaches, and a cleaner. And we need to find seven hundred large prawns, today – this morning. Do you by chance have any contacts for seafood suppliers?'

'Cockroaches and prawns? Better make sure you don't get those mixed up, ha ha!'

'I'm serious, we need help. Dealing with the roaches and sourcing the prawns.'

'Seven hundred large prawns?' he whistled. 'Well, actually, it so happens I can help you on both counts. Springs in Edburton is the biggest wholesaler of frozen fish and seafood in the county, and they are very near you. I know the owner and can give him a call. I know another place down by Shoreham Harbour if Springs can't help. And I know the chap from a company called Go Pest. I can give him a call, too.'

'We'd be immensely grateful.'

'Leave it with me.'

They went back into the garage, opened the door and, armed with broomsticks, began attacking the creatures. Ten minutes later, Jordan rang back.

'All sorted! Go Pest is on his way to you, and Springs have over eight hundred large prawns in their freezers. They are closed for the Christmas break, but the owner's said he can meet you there in an hour.'

'You're a bloody star!' Jason said.

'We're a full-service agency at Richwards!' he said. 'Anything else I can help you with today?'

Jason hesitated. 'Well, yes, there is something. At the risk of sounding a bit odd, have any of the other residents of Cold Hill Park mentioned any strange – like uncanny – occurrences? By that I mean, something out of the ordinary?'

'Such as?' Jordan asked.

'Ghosts?'

Jordan was silent for just a moment too long. His voice, when he finally answered, was just an octave or two higher. 'Ghosts? No, absolutely nothing of that kind, I can assure you, Mr Danes. These are all beautiful new homes – I think ghosts prefer creaky old houses, ha ha!'

'There used to be a creaky old house on this site.'

'Well, yes, indeed. But if you're asking me, I can tell you that if I was a ghost, I wouldn't want to hang around a noisy construction site for very long.'

'So,' Jason asked. 'If you were a ghost in an old house that was being knocked down, what would you do?'

There was another short silence. 'Well, I don't think I'd go and haunt a new-build, that's for sure!'

There was something strained and unnatural about the estate agent's voice. But at this moment, Jason did not rise to it. He thanked him, took down the name and address of where to collect the prawns and ended the call.

A short while later the Go Pest man arrived, in full protective clothing, to fumigate the garage and clear the roaches from there, and any that had entered the house.

Jason helped Emily move all the glass bowls into the kitchen in the house, then shut the garage door and left the exterminator to it.

'What a nightmare,' she said, gloomily.

'I'll come with you to get the prawns,' he said.

'No, it's OK, you need to get on with your work,' she said.

'I'm coming with you. Just give me five minutes to seal up all the paints I've left open, OK?'

'OK.'

He hurried back up to his studio. But as he entered the room, he felt hazy, distracted, his mind all over the place. His eyes were blurry. Everything was in soft focus. His head felt hot, as if it was burning. Instead of sealing his paints, he looked around again for the card from PC Neil Lang.

Down below he heard the sound of an engine starting. He peered out of the window and to his surprise saw Emily reversing her van out of the driveway.

'Em!' he banged on the window, shouting. 'Wait! Wait!'

She drove off, far faster than normal. Recklessly fast. She was, ordinarily, a steady, cautious driver. Why hadn't she waited?

He stood watching until she was out of sight, then turned back to his easel. But all he could think of was PC Lang. Who did not exist, according to the Sussex Police operator. Feeling very confused, and a little giddy, he sat at his desk and looked around, instead, for the business card from the Reverend Orlebar. He was certain he'd left it in a prominent place.

He riffled through a stack of cards and still could not find it. Where was it? Turning to his computer, he googled the Bishop of Lewes, found the phone number and dialled it.

It was answered by the briskly efficient woman's voice he remembered from last week.

'Hello,' he said. 'It's Jason Danes.'

He expected recognition, but instead was greeted impersonally.

'I'm sorry, did you say Jason Names?'

'Jason *Danes*.'

'May I help you, Mr Danes?'

'Yes – I came to see the Bishop last Wednesday.'

'Last Wednesday?' Her voice sounded dubious.

'Yes. December the – er – the nineteenth.'

'You came to see him on December nineteenth? Here in Lewes?'

'Yes – I'm the painter.'

'I don't believe we had any painting done last week.'

'No,' he said, clumsily. 'I mean I'm the artist – Jason Danes.'

'And you say you came to see the Bishop?'

'Robert Parnassus, yes.'

'Last Wednesday? Here at his house?'

'That's right.'

'I think you must be mistaken.'

'No, I'm not, I met him around mid-morning on Wednesday.'

'I'm sorry, Mr Danes, but that's simply not possible.'

'I think *you* must be mistaken,' he said. 'I came to see him.'

'No, I think it's *you* who must be mistaken, Mr Danes. The Bishop wasn't in the country last Wednesday.'

72

Thursday 27 December

Jason opened the calendar on his laptop to double check; 19 December was the date, definitely, that he had gone to see the Bishop.

'I don't understand,' he said. 'We *are* both talking about the same person, the Very Reverend Robert Parnassus, Bishop of Lewes?'

'We are.' The Bishop's private secretary was sounding frostier by the second.

There was a brief silence while Jason checked the calendar yet again. 'Well, I came to his house last Wednesday morning and I had a conversation with him. I was delighted to see he had two of my paintings in his office.'

'Two of your paintings in his office?'

'Yes.'

'The Bishop has no paintings in his office. None at all. He has a few personal photographs of his family, but I can categorically assure you he has no paintings or art of any kind in his office. I don't wish to be impolite, but I think you must be confusing the Bishop with someone else.'

Jason was now seriously wondering if she was right. 'I just don't understand, I really did meet with him.'

'I would know,' she said. 'I have nothing in my diary.'

'Ah,' he said, his hopes rising. 'You see, I didn't have an

appointment. Are you not the lady I saw? Does he have another assistant?'

'No, he does not,' she said, very firmly. 'What exactly was the nature of the conversation you claim to have had, Mr Danes?'

'Well, we've just moved into a new house, and we've been having some very strange things happening – some odd phenomena – which have been deeply disturbing to my wife and myself. I asked the Bishop if he could help us in any way.'

'Mr Danes, that's really not possible,' she replied, her politeness starting to fray around the edges. 'I have his diary in front of me. Last Wednesday, December nineteenth, the Bishop was away on a retreat in the township of Soweto, in South Africa. He only returned to England on December twenty-second, to be here in time to carry out his Christmas duties.'

Jason heard this, feeling deeply puzzled. 'I'm sorry, you must think me mad, but I definitely met with him on December nineteenth. He arranged for the Reverend Gordon Orlebar and the Reverend Jim Skeet to come to my house – and they did come, that afternoon.'

'Can you repeat those names?' she asked, distinctly testily now.

'The Reverend Orlebar and the Reverend Skeet.'

'You are saying they came to your house? On Wednesday December nineteenth?'

'Yes. They carried out a communion service, to help a spirit pass over to the other side, if I'm understanding correctly.'

'Mr Danes, I'm finding what you are telling me very difficult to comprehend. Please don't think I'm being unhelpful, but what you are saying is simply not possible.'

'Why do you say that?'

'Well – both Gordon Orlebar and Jim Skeet did work for the

Church in exactly the capacity you mention. Very tragically they drowned in a boating accident off the coast of Senegal, while on a break during a mission for the Bishop's charity there, five years ago – in fact, almost exactly five years ago this week.'

73

Jason ended the call in total shock.

He sat at his desk, staring into space.

How much, since they had moved here, was real?

Maybe Emily was right, and he should go to see Dr Dixon again.

Caroline Patricia Harcourt. The woman he had sketched. Had he sketched a ghost?

Reverend Fortinbrass?

Orlebar and Skeet, who had come to their house just over a week ago – but who had been dead for five years?

I am very definitely insane.

I am very definitely not *insane.*

He returned to a new blank gesso board, and studied the photographs of the now-dead construction worker, *The Skiver*, on the easel at the base of the board, trying to focus, to return to some semblance of normality. Often, he could think most clearly when he was immersed in a piece of work.

He started to work on the sketch of the man leaning against a pile of rubble, who had been nonchalantly rolling a cigarette.

All the time his thoughts kept returning to his bizarre conversation with the Bishop's secretary. It wasn't possible. It *couldn't* be possible.

And yet.

And yet.

After an hour he took a break, went downstairs and made himself a mug of coffee. Not having any appetite, he grabbed an energy bar for his lunch and carried both back up to his studio. He sat, briefly, at his desk, eating the bar and sipping the froth from his coffee. Through the window he saw the Penze-Weedells' purple car returning from whatever expedition they had been on, pull up outside their front door.

The ridiculous couple began unloading package after package from the rear of the car. Sale bargains, no doubt. They were both looking mightily pleased with themselves. Maurice unlocked the front door and lugged some packages in, while his wife unloaded even more – impossibly more – boxes and carrier bags from the little car which seemed, at this moment, to have a Tardis-like capacity.

Claudette ducked back in and pulled out another two large boxes.

How much more, Jason wondered?

The answer was a lot more. Heavy-looking boxes, these. Bargain prosecco? he wondered, mischievously.

Finally, she had finished. Several towers of boxes were lined up, with Maurice trotting in and out, carrying them in. Claudette stood imperiously outside the front door, holding up what looked like the key fob. The up-and-over garage door began to rise. Moments later the purple car, driverless, started moving in an arc towards the garage.

Maurice picked up another box and staggered back inside.

His wife turned and appeared to bark some instruction to him. With her peaked cap and padded clothes, she looked, to Jason, like a pantomime penguin. He grinned at the mental image of her in a zoo.

Then froze.

The car suddenly stopped, in mid arc, and began reversing, gathering speed alarmingly.

Oblivious to it, Claudette was gesticulating to her husband, who was somewhere inside the house.

The car was heading straight back towards her.

Jason tried to shout a warning through his triple-glazed window.

The car was closing on her.

Frantically he hammered on the glass, tugging at the window lock.

Then, utterly helpless, he watched the car strike her in the midriff, slamming her into the wall beside the front porch and pinning her against it. Her cap flew off. Bright-red blood spattered the brickwork either side of her.

Somehow, miraculously, she was still alive, her head turning from side to side, her mouth opening and shutting. Maurice came running out of the house, looking utterly panic-stricken as he saw his wife. He ran to the car then jumped into the driver's seat to release her.

Jason finally got the window open, in time to hear Claudette's screams of agony.

But instead of the car moving just a couple of feet, it raced forward, into the road, out of control, with Maurice in shock behind the wheel, looking more a passenger than driver, his open door swinging backwards and forwards. The car accelerated fast, zig-zagging across the road.

At that exact moment, Jason saw to his utter horror Emily's pink van coming along Lakeview Drive in the opposite direction.

'No!' he screamed.

Impotently.

He saw there were two people in Emily's van. He stared, frozen in horror and disbelief, as the Penze-Weedells' car headed straight for the van at high speed.

Emily was at the wheel. He, himself, was sitting beside her in the passenger seat.

Not possible. No. Not possible.

Oh God.

The purple car struck the van head-on in an explosion of metal splinters, steam, flying shards of glass as thick as a cloud. The van catapulted backwards and sideways, rolling over and over. He heard the sickening metallic boom. The Penze-Weedells' car carried on, the bonnet crumpled, careering across the road and head-on into a tractor with a bulldozer bucket that was thundering down the street from the same direction as Emily.

The shovel sheared the roof of the car almost clean off. A few yards on, pushing the crumpled wreck of car in its path, the huge vehicle stopped. Jason saw the driver in the cab, smiling with grim satisfaction. He looked like Albert Fears.

It was Albert Fears.

Jesus, no. No.

Maurice Penze-Weedell's torso sat behind the wheel of the roofless little car. The headless stump of his spine stuck up through his blood-soaked anorak and woolly scarf.

The car's horn blared, steadily and unremittingly.

Jason, as if in a trance, stabbed out 999 on his phone, blurted out what had happened, then hurtled downstairs and out into the street, his eyes streaming tears.

74

As he stood, momentarily looking around, trying to take it all in, Jason could see no sign of Emily's van. It simply wasn't there.

He ran up to the mangled wreckage of the purple car and stared, beyond, along Lakeview Drive. No van.

Had he imagined it?

He must have. There was no van. Very definitely no van.

He turned and sprinted back towards Claudette Penze-Weedell, who lay, misshapen and motionless, in front of her house. There was a ghastly, bloody imprint of her body, like a shadow, on the brick wall above her. Her midriff was split open, her intestines spilled out onto the paved driveway either side of her, and blood was pooling all around her. A fancy crocodile handbag lay on the ground close by.

The car horn continued blaring.

He stared down at her, numb with shock. Her eyes were open, glazed, her mouth agape, as if she had stopped saying something mid-sentence. Was there anything he could do for her, he wondered, racking his brains, trying to think back to a first-aid course he'd once attended with Emily as part of her qualifications in catering. From the state of her he didn't think Claudette was still alive. Even so, he knelt and clumsily felt for a pulse, curling his finger and thumb around her wrist, pushing the band of her Rolex watch up her arm a little.

He could feel nothing. A mobile phone began ringing. It was coming from inside her handbag, he realized.

A shadow fell over him. He turned to see Albert Fears standing behind him.

'He came straight at me,' Fears said, almost proudly.

'He did, I saw it,' Jason responded, numbly, as if he was dreaming this.

Very faintly, in the distance, was the wail of a siren. It was growing closer by the second.

'Straight at me,' Fears said.

He did not appear to have noticed the body of Claudette Penze-Weedell.

'I couldn't do nothing,' Fears continued. 'Stupid bastard. You saw it? You know then, right?'

'Right,' Jason said, reluctant to concede anything to the man. And suddenly, unable to help himself, he turned away and vomited.

The siren was growing closer still, approaching fast. It was followed by another, more distant. Then another.

'Got a weak stomach have you, young man?' Fears said, snidely.

Jason had to restrain himself from standing up and punching the farmer's smug face.

Over the next hour, Lakeview Drive, cordoned off with blue and white tape, became totally clogged with emergency service vehicles. Three police cars, a Collision Investigation Unit van, two ambulances, a fire engine, as well as police officers and support staff, several in white protective clothing.

Jason was led away to his house by a female police officer. She asked him to give a witness statement, which she typed into a tablet. When he had finished, he asked the officer if she had attended after the death of the construction site worker the previous week. The officer told him she hadn't and wasn't aware of it. 'Three deaths in a week?' she queried. 'A very unfortunate coincidence.'

'Indeed.'

'I find that things happen in clusters,' she said. 'People often say things happen in threes, don't they?'

'They do,' he agreed bleakly.

'Well, however sad and tragic it has been, let's hope that's it, sir, and you and your wife can enjoy your new home now.'

'Thank you,' he replied dully.

The officer blushed slightly. 'I'd just like to say that I'm a very big fan of your work.'

'You are? Thank you!'

'My husband and I have a King Charles spaniel. I didn't realize who you were until just now, so I do apologize.'

'No need, at all.'

'I'd actually been thinking about – if I could afford it – commissioning you to do a portrait of our Sally, as a birthday present to my husband.'

'Well, I'd be delighted to do it, and I'm sure I could give a discount to a police officer!'

'I couldn't accept that, sir. But that is immensely kind of you.'

Through the window he saw two people wheeling a trolley with a black bag lying on it. The shape inside the bag was human.

His stomach churned, like a cement mixer. Cold water coursed through his veins. His mind went back to just a short while ago. The Penze-Weedells, happily unloading their Christmas sale bargains.

Minutes later both dead.

Was it just a freaky cluster, as the officer had said?

Or something much darker. Had he and Emily moved into some kind of a portal to Hell?

He'd seen her and himself in the van, struck, rolling over.

He was snapped out of his thoughts by his phone ringing. It was Emily.

'What's happening?' she asked, anxiously. 'The police have sealed off the road and won't let me through. I've got all the prawns and I need to get them into the house and put them out to defrost, urgently.'

'Thank God you're OK, you're safe.'

'I'm safe, yes, are you OK?'

'I'll come and find you.'

75

Thursday 27 December

Jason hurried away, walking quickly past the carnage of the purple car, avoiding looking in. His view was blocked, in any case, by police and fire and rescue officers. He picked his way through all the emergency vehicles, had a quick word with the police officer on guard at the cordon of blue and white tape, then ran up to Emily's van, which was parked outside the shell of a partly built house. She was standing beside the vehicle, looking ashen.

'What's happened?' she asked. 'Are you OK?'

'I'm fine.'

'The police wouldn't say anything. They just told me there'd been an incident. I was so worried something had happened to you.'

'Our neighbours,' he said, shakily. 'Claudette and Maurice. Horrible. Their car malfunctioned – something went horribly wrong. They're both dead.'

'What?'

'They're dead.'

'No.'

Another wailing siren was approaching.

He held her in his arms. She felt limp, like a rag doll. 'It was horrible.'

'Tell me it's not true. Tell me you are joking?'

'I saw it, from my studio window.'

'What did you see?'

'Let's get your prawns. They said they'd allow us through. Just don't look at the car when we walk past it.'

'Why not?'

'Honestly Em, don't.'

Five minutes later they lugged the plastic bags filled with prawns into their house, and Jason slammed shut the front door, against the horror and the horn that was still blaring. Inside there was a stink of chemicals from the fumigation. To his surprise, the Go Pest man had gone, but had left instructions.

'I looked,' Emily said. 'I couldn't help it.' She fell, sobbing, against him. 'Dead? They can't be dead.'

'I'm afraid so. He was OK, not a bad old stick. I can't believe we were having drinks with them only yesterday.'

'I can't believe it either,' she said. 'Tell me it's not true.'

'It is true. But it's OK.'

'No, it is not OK. Nothing is OK. We are living in a fucking nightmare.'

The horn suddenly stopped.

'Just tell me we are imagining all of this, Jason. Tell me it's not happening.'

For some moments he had no answer. He didn't know any more what was real and what wasn't. 'It's just a terrible accident. Something went wrong with their car – I don't know what. I – this may sound odd – but I thought . . .' He fell silent.

'Thought what?'

'I thought I saw you coming. That Maurice was driving straight at you. I thought . . .' He fell silent again.

He didn't know what else to say.

Mechanically, on autopilot, he helped her put all the bags of prawns into the twin sinks, and began to run cold water over them, before laying them out on defrosting trays.

'I'll help you peel them when they're done,' he said.

Tears were running down her face. 'Where's it going to stop?'

'It has stopped.'

'Has it? Or has it just started?'

'What do you mean by that?'

'It's not going to stop until we're all dead, is it?'

'What do you mean?'

'You know what I mean. Until everyone here is dead.'

'Come on, Em, we've always dealt with any problems in the past by being strong. Let's be strong now. Get on with your preparations for tomorrow and shout if you need me to help. Meanwhile, I'll go back up to my studio. Try to ignore – forget – what's going on outside, OK?'

She nodded. 'Wait a sec.' She tore off a sheet of kitchen towel from a roll, wetted it under the tap, then stepped forward and wiped away remnants of vomit from around his mouth. 'I love you,' she said, her voice barely a whisper.

'I love you too.'

He climbed the stairs back up to his studio, trying to put out of his mind the horror of what had happened, and for the next five hours he worked hard, blanking out the police activity down below. Finally, he stood back from his easel and studied the painting of *The Skiver*. He was pleased with it. He felt he had captured the essence of the furtive, lazy man, against the backdrop of the hub of activity going on.

Just one final tweak, he felt, stepping forward and picking up his thinnest brush, and dipping the tip into white paint.

76

With her catering facilities in the garage out of action, Emily had transferred all the items she needed for tomorrow's party into the house. In the kitchen, she was busy putting all the lettuce she had washed, along with the prepared tomatoes and cucumber, into separate plastic tubs, ready to assemble the prawn cocktails the following day. She paused occasionally to take a sip from the very large glass of white wine she had poured herself.

When she had finished, she mixed up the cocktail sauce, adding her own spin on it: paprika, tabasco and horseradish. She already had several trays of prawns that were almost ready to peel now. Her plan was to finish all the prawns tonight and store them in the fridge, ready to transport tomorrow.

Next, she would put the first of the bowls of lamb tagine, which she had previously prepared, into the double oven, on low heat, to slow cook overnight. Tomorrow, when – hopefully – Louise would be well enough to help her, they would prepare and pre-cook the vegetables, as well as the six salmon en croûtes that had been ordered for pescatarians, and two vegan dishes. The canapés, chosen by their client, were already prepared and at Louise's.

They were back on schedule, she thought, with relief.

As she closed the oven doors, she suddenly sensed someone standing behind her.

She turned.

There was no one.

The whole kitchen was feeling like a fridge.

Her breath came out as vapour.

She shivered. The temperature seemed to have dropped, dramatically. She closed the door to the hall, but the room felt even colder still.

And again, she sensed someone standing behind her.

Then she heard a click, and felt a sudden jolt of static electricity on her shoulder.

She spun round.

And stared straight into an angry, shrivelled face.

77

Finally, completely satisfied now, Jason removed *The Skiver* from his easel and laid it carefully against the wall. He put a new gesso board on the easel, and removed the photograph of the construction worker. His mind turned to the miserable old couple in the pub – he could see them sitting there, but could he recall their faces enough to paint the detail he wanted? It was a bugger that the photograph had gone.

In his mind the old man had been saying, *I should have divorced you twenty years ago but now I'm stuck with you until death truly do us part.* And the woman was saying, *I don't like you but you're better than nothing.*

More in hope than anything else, he clicked on his photo album on his phone and, to his amazement and joy, the photograph was back. Had it really ever gone, or had he mistakenly filed it elsewhere?

All had been quiet downstairs for a long while. Outside, in the street below, some bright floodlights had been set up. He glanced out and saw a team of people, in white oversuits, on their hands and knees inside the cordon doing a fingertip search, while another group, identically dressed, was filming or photographing with a large camera.

He was hungry. Maybe he'd grab a bite to eat before he started, make a strong coffee, and work on into the night. He realized he was almost living on coffee and would have to try and cut his caffeine intake after the exhibition, when things quietened down.

The door burst open behind him.

78

Thursday 27 December

Emily stood there, looking terrible and breathless, close to hysterics, her chef's cap about to fall off.

'Jason!' Her voice was close to a scream.

'What?'

'There was someone standing behind me in the kitchen.'

'What do you mean?'

'A woman.' She nodded at him, as if he should know who it was.

'A woman? What do you mean? Who?'

She started shaking. So much so that for some seconds she struggled to speak, then finally she blurted, 'Angry. She looked so angry. Hideous. Oh God, so horrible.'

'What woman do you mean?'

'In the kitchen.'

'How? Did you open the door to the garage or something? Paul from Go Pest told us under no circumstances should it be opened until he advised us. Don't you remember?'

'I. Did. Not. Open. The door,' she said adamantly.

Her tone was enough to snap him out of denial for a moment.

'She was standing behind me. She was there and then she wasn't. I saw her. Then she vanished.'

'Can you describe her?'

'She was horrible. So horrible. She had on a sort of long, blue dress, like really old-fashioned, with yellow shoes and a really wrinkled – wizened – old-lady face. She spoke to me.'

'What did she say?'

'God, her voice was kind of croaky, and vile – really nasty. Evil.'

'What did she say Em?'

'She said, *No one ever leaves here.* Then something like, *You'll be joining me, soon. You and your husband. Everyone here always does. Don't bother buying him any birthday presents. He won't need them here.*'

He wrapped his arms around her, aware of the surgical gloves on his hands. She was shaking uncontrollably.

'Babes, we're going to sort this out.'

'I saw her. I *saw* her. She touched me. I heard her speak. And, oh yes, she said something else. She said to tell you her name is *Matilda.*'

'Matilda? Why does that ring a bell?'

'Why? I'll tell you why it rings a bell. That history book you brought home from the library, remember?'

It was on his desk. 'Yes. The one we googled.'

'I read the bit out to you last week.' She marched over, picked the book up and thumbed through it. Then read aloud.

'*Cold Hill House was built to the order of Sir Brangwyn De Glossope, on the site of monastic ruins, during the 1750s. His first wife, Matilda, daughter and heiress from the rich Sussex landowning family, the Warre-Spences, disappeared, childless, a year after they moved into the property. It was her money that had funded the building of the house – De Glossope being near penniless at the time of their marriage. It was rumoured that De Glossope murdered her and disposed of her body, to free him to travel abroad with his mistress, Evelyne Tyler.*'

'Matilda De Glossope is the woman you saw in the kitchen?'

'You tell me.'

There was a loud bang above them.

The room was plunged into darkness.

79

With the torch beam from his phone, Jason made his way downstairs, closely followed by Emily, through the kitchen and into the utility room. He found the fuse box, opened the lid and immediately saw the red master switch that had tripped. He flipped it back up and the lights came back on. He closed the lid.

'It didn't just trip by itself,' Emily said.

'These things are very sensitive. A bulb blowing can trip them.'

'Or a ghost?'

Just as he smiled, it tripped again with a loud report.

As loud as a pistol shot.

The lights went out.

Right behind them they heard a hideous cackle of laughter.

Jason froze. Then he turned, shining the beam of his torch into the darkness. It lit up the washing machine, the tumble dryer and a stack of laundry awaiting ironing; then the stark terror on Emily's face.

The laughter cackled again.

He turned the torch back on the fuse box, and again reset the tripped switch.

This time the lights stayed on. For a few seconds.

They clicked off.

Darkness.

Another cackle.

'We can't stay here,' Emily said. 'We have to get out, now.'

The same malevolent voice rang out. 'No one ever leaves.'

Emily clutched Jason as a strong gust of wind blew through the room. The door slammed shut behind them.

A scream rang out.

A baby cried.

Another gust of wind, even stronger.

Jason pointed his torch beam at the fuse box and pushed the switch back up.

It clicked straight back down.

A child screamed, followed by another child. Screams of terror.

Then a roaring, crashing, rumbling that sounded like falling masonry.

'Jason!' Emily shouted in terror, clutching him.

'It's OK, Em.'

'IT. IS. NOT. FUCKING. OK.' Emily gripped him even tighter.

They stood still for some moments.

Then everything went quiet. There was a click, and the lights came back on.

Jason looked at the fuse box. The switch that had tripped and had been down was now back up.

Their eyes met. Frightened eyes, trying to make sense of what had just happened. Both trying to find something in each other's expression. Some explanation. Some comfort.

Jason had a thought. 'Come with me.'

He raced through to the kitchen and over to the command box. It was plugged back in. On the wall, the television was on. A loud cackle came from it. The camera cut to a petrified young couple, as an old woman, in a blue dress and yellow shoes, with a hideously wrinkled face, glided, like an apparition, towards them.

A child screamed, followed by another child.

From the TV, there was the sound of falling masonry.

The couple onscreen turned and fled.

The old woman following them cackled, 'No one ever leaves!'

On the screen, the couple reached the front door. It would not open.

The sound of falling masonry grew louder. Louder. The petrified couple looked up and around them.

An instant later they were buried in an avalanche of rubble.

Emily looked at Jason. 'That was the woman.'

'The one you saw?'

Looking numb, she nodded. 'Did she switch the command box back on? Put the plug in?'

Jason had no answer. 'Maybe one of us did – without realizing it?'

'Oh sure, I do things without realizing it all the time, don't you? Come on, get real. Neither of us plugged it back in.'

'So, the lady on the screen did?'

'She was standing behind me. Maybe she did.'

Jason looked at his wife. She claimed she hadn't seen the Reverend Fortinbrass. She had no memory of the police officers turning up. Nor of so much else. Was there something seriously wrong with her? Could it be a brain tumour? Making her act oddly, imagining things – and forgetting so much?

Or was it him? Was he going mad? Was he the one who was imagining things? The accident on the building site? The meeting with the Bishop?

No question, they had both seen the ghost of Caroline Harcourt. But what about everything else Emily said she had no recollection of?

Had she been messing about with the fuse box switch in the darkness? Had she plugged the command box back in?

Instantly, he dismissed that as clutching at straws. And yet, could he dismiss the idea, totally, that Emily was, somehow, very disturbed? Disturbed enough not to have noticed she was filling the freezers with cockroaches?

He really did not want to go there, but what other explanation could he come up with?

Other than the one he did not want to face.

'Jason,' she said quietly, calmly. 'We can't stay tonight.'

'Em, look, there's something wonky with the electrics – a power surge or something – I don't understand electricity that well. I've got to get on with my painting, and you've tomorrow to prepare for.'

'You really think you're going to concentrate on painting tonight? And that I'm quietly going to beaver away in the kitchen with a harridan standing behind me? There's nothing wonky with the electrics. It's not the electrics. The electrics are fine. It's this house, that's what's wonky. We have to get out. You know we do, you're just in denial.'

'Fine, and go where?'

'Anywhere but here. My parents?'

'I'm not going to your parents.'

'Why on earth not?'

Because I'd rather deal with a lady in a blue dress with a shrivelled face than have to endure your father's scorn, he wanted to say.

'We can come back in the morning, first thing, and get on,' she said, pleading. 'I'm scared. I'm really scared. We've made a terrible mistake moving here, you know it, too.'

'Babes, listen. I'm with the Bishop on this one. All the stress we are going through is bringing up echoes from the past – that seems to make sense to me.' He didn't dare tell her that, according to the Bishop's secretary, their meeting never happened.

She stared at him. 'You are determined to find *rational* explanations at any cost, aren't you?'

'What do you mean by that?'

'You are, accept it. We've moved into a seriously haunted and dangerous house. One that does not want us here. You're in denial.'

'I'm not in denial. I've always had an open mind. We know there's a dark history to this whole site. I accept that ghosts exist – we've both bloody seen at least one. But what I don't accept is that they can do any harm.'

'You didn't see that old woman standing behind me.'

'You didn't see the vicar.'

She looked at him and shook her head. 'Are we going to play some game of tit-for-tat? Come on, we're grown-ups, this isn't about who saw what.'

'I'm not playing games, that's the last thing I want to do, OK?'

'Fine. The last thing I want to do is spend tonight here. You can if you want. I'm going, I'm out of here. I'm going to my parents.'

Jason looked at his wife. Saw her resolute expression.

And realized he, too, was more than uncomfortable about the idea of staying here alone.

80

Thursday 27 December

Ten minutes later, with overnight bags hastily packed, and their coats on, they went outside. To Jason's surprise, the street was deserted. All the emergency vehicles had gone, and the tractor, along with the wrecked purple car and all the police and emergency service workers. Emily's van was back on the driveway.

It was as if nothing had happened.

'What the hell?' Jason said. 'They've cleared this all up PDQ. Who drove your van?'

'The police asked me to leave the key in it, in case they needed to move it,' she replied.

'Well, that was decent of them.'

Across the road, the Penze-Weedells' house was in darkness. They walked over to Jason's BMW, and just as they reached it, they heard the swoosh of a car, travelling at speed along Lakeview Drive.

It was a huge Cadillac convertible. At the wheel was a man smoking a cigar, the tip glowing red in the darkness. In the glare of a street light he saw a woman in the passenger seat and the shape of two children in the rear.

Moments later, its tail lights vanished around the corner. But the smell of cigar smoke lingered.

'I've seen that car several times,' Jason said. 'The estate agent said it doesn't ring a bell, but I saw it arriving last week, followed by a removals lorry. I'm sure they're living on the estate somewhere.'

'It's a bit vulgar, don't you think?'

'I love those big old Yank tanks!' Jason said. 'That's a Cadillac Eldorado. It would make a great painting, the whole family in it, excited to be arriving at their new home – don't you think?'

'Mr and Mrs Flash-Vulgar,' she said.

'Too bad about the Penze-Weedells – I'm sure they would have ended up besties with these people.' He pressed his key fob to unlock the BMW's doors. To his surprise, nothing happened.

He pressed again.

Nothing.

'Shit, the battery must have gone.' He put the key in the lock, instead, and twisted it. There was a brief moment of reluctance, then the door locks released.

They climbed in. Jason was a little puzzled that the interior lights had not come on. He pushed the start button.

Nothing happened.

He tried again. A weak click from under the bonnet, then nothing. And again.

'Shit, a flat battery. What's caused that?'

'Shall we try mine?' Emily hurried out of the BMW and over to her van. She tried opening the door, but it was locked. 'Don't say they've taken the key? Bloody idiots.'

'Your spare's in the hall drawer.'

She opened her handbag and removed the house keys – and frowned.

'The key's here, on my key ring.'

'I thought you left it in the van.'

'So did I. I must have . . .' She frowned again. 'I'm certain I left it in the ignition.'

'Maybe you took it out by mistake.'

'And they pushed the van here? Wouldn't the steering lock have been on?'

'Yup, well, the police have tools for getting into cars, I imagine.'

She pressed the key fob to unlock the doors. Just like with the BMW, nothing happened. She unlocked it manually, got in and tried to start the engine.

The battery in this vehicle was dead, too.

'What's going on?' she said.

Jason, standing in the street, was looking around warily.

'Both cars can't have flat batteries, Jason.' Her voice was on a knife edge. 'How can that happen?'

'Maybe there was some kind of electrical surge that's knocked them both out?' he reasoned.

'And this surge somehow plugged back in our command box? And fried your brain in the process?'

He pulled his mobile phone out of his pocket. 'I'll find a taxi company.'

But as he brought the screen alive and tapped on the Google app, he frowned. The screen went black.

'Em, can you try yours, I'm out of power.'

She took her phone out of her bag and tapped the screen. Then tapped it again. 'Dead,' she said. 'It's dead. How's that possible? Bloody battery life on this thing – I charged it this afternoon.'

'Let's try the landline.'

They went back inside and through to the kitchen, where the cordless phone sat in its base station.

It was dead, too.

81

Thursday 27 December

Jason plugged his phone into the mains charger. After a short while, a red line appeared on the screen. Seconds later it vanished, to be replaced by two digits.

60

They were static.

'What the fuck?' he said.

'Who are you talking to?' she asked, jumpily.

He stared at the screen. *60.*

Sixty what?

He felt clammy, a sick feeling of dread in the pit of his stomach. The sense that someone – or some*thing* – intensely malign was watching him. The hairs on the back of his neck rose.

There was a distinct click. The sound of the front door opening. Someone walking in.

'Hello? Who's that?' Emily called.

Jason followed her out of the kitchen. The front door was wide open and a bitterly cold wind tore through the hall. He hurried over and slammed the door shut. 'Must have not closed it properly when we came . . .'

He stopped, realizing the wind wasn't coming from outside. It was inside. A howling gale, as if every door and window in the house was wide open. It rippled their clothes, tore at the roots of their hair. Panic-stricken, Emily's eyes darted in every direction.

Then, just as suddenly as it had begun, the wind died, completely.

They stood still, staring at each other in bewilderment.

'What was that?' she asked.

He shook his head. He didn't know, he really did not know. He went through into the living room to check the windows, but they were all shut. They were shut in all the other rooms he looked in. How much more, he wondered, silently, could either of them take?

'I'll try online, see if I can get a taxi that way,' he said, and headed up to his studio. Emily followed close behind, her hands gripping his waist all the way up.

He sat at his desk and tried to log on. But the computer wouldn't connect to the Wi-Fi. The curves of the black fan symbol chased up and down repeatedly, hunting for a connection. Suddenly the room was plunged into darkness.

Emily shrieked.

It had gone dark out in the street, too. Pitch dark.

Jason looked out of the window. 'The street lights have gone off. There must be a power cut.'

'Shit!' Emily said. 'No, it can't be – what about all the food in the fridge? All my prawns will be ruined.'

'They'll stay cold for several hours, won't they?'

'For a few hours, so long as I keep the door shut. Oh shit, shit, shit.'

'The power will be on quickly.'

'Oh yes? We've not had a power cut here before. What if it's not back on in a few hours? Do you have any idea what that would mean? We can't even phone the electricity company to find out what's happening. If I could start my van, I could switch the refrigeration on in that and put them there for the night, they'd be fine. But I can't do that. We should have bought a generator – I did think about it.'

'A bit late for that.'

'Yes. And now we're totally trapped.'

'We're not trapped. We can walk down to the village. We'll phone for a taxi from the pub – or the RAC, get them to start your van, then we can put the prawns in.'

'What if the power's out there, too?'

'I'm sure they'll have a landline, and the landlord's a helpful guy.'

'Anything's better than staying here in the dark, with a fucking ghost wandering around.'

Holding hands and using his torch, they carefully descended the spiral staircase, carried on down into the hall and out of the front door.

'Got the key?' he asked.

'Yes.'

Jason closed the door behind them. A strong, cold wind had suddenly got up, and a gust, as ferocious as the one in the house, blasted them, as if it had followed them out. A tarpaulin in the front garden of the half-built house next door was flapping noisily. As they walked along the pavement, still guided by Jason's torch beam, they both smelled the strong aroma of cigar smoke. A short distance along, on the other side of the road, there was a red glow.

Jason pointed the beam across and saw the silhouette of a man, standing beneath an unlit street light, smoking a cigar.

'Hi!' he called out.

There was no response.

He tried to step out into the road, but Emily held him back. 'Jason, careful, who is he?'

In a lowered voice Jason answered, 'Must be the chap

Maurice Penze-Weedell was talking about, who he always sees on his evening constitutional. Hi!' he repeated.

Again, there was no response.

'Any idea how long this power cut is going to last?' Jason called out, louder, to the stranger.

No response again.

He freed himself from Emily's hand and began crossing towards the figure.

'Jason!' she cautioned. Then louder, 'Jason!'

As he reached the far side, a shiver ripped through him.

There was no one there.

He looked up and down the street. No one.

No smell of a cigar.

'Jason!' Emily cried out.

He turned, confused and alarmed, and hurried back over to her. 'He – he's vanished.'

'Please can we go? Please?' She began striding off at a fast pace and he had to step up his own to keep up with her.

'We have to get out of here,' she said.

'He just – vanished,' he said, finally catching her up.

'If he was ever there.'

'We both saw him.'

She said nothing, just kept walking, staring doggedly ahead. After a few minutes they reached the entrance to the estate, and turned left, down the hill towards the village.

The lights in all the houses down the hill were also off.

'The joys of country living,' Jason said. 'Eh?'

'I'm not finding too many joys.'

The wind was blowing even stronger now, a full-scale gale, and they were having to lean into it, struggling to walk against it. Almost, Jason thought – knowing how irrational it was – as if the wind was trying to push them back to the house. His hair was being torn painfully from the roots and he wished he'd thought to wear a hat or baseball cap. Emily reached in her pocket and tied a scarf around her head. A tin can rolled along, clattering loudly, blown across the lane in front of them. Leaves scudded, twigs and small branches skittered across their path.

'Listen, Em, it's going to be OK, I promise. We'll be looking back at all this one day, soon, and laughing about it.'

'We will? It's never going to stop, is it? The house hates us, it wants us to leave.'

'No, it doesn't. Trust me, Em, it wants us to stay.'

'Trust you?'

He stopped and turned her, gently, to face him. Staring into her eyes in the darkness, with the faint glow of his torch, he said, 'We love each other and that's all that matters. We're strong together. Remember our wedding vows? *To have and to hold, for better, for worse . . . ?*'

She just stared at him.

'Em, we'll get through this.'

They carried on down the hill in silence, passing the large words of the sign – COLD HILL – PLEASE DRIVE SLOWLY THROUGH OUR VILLAGE – and suddenly Jason exclaimed, joyfully, 'Yayyyyyy!'

They could see lights ahead. Street lights. House lights.

'Does that mean our power might be back on?' Emily asked.

'Hopefully.'

'This might be on a separate circuit or something.'

'True.'

He turned. Lights were now back on in the houses further up the hill, behind them. 'Look!' he said.

'Thank God.'

'Want to go back?'

'No. Let's get to the pub, call a taxi, then we can pick up our bags and go to my parents.'

'Sure.'

A few minutes later they reached the first of the village street lights, right across the road from the village store.

But it was no longer a village store.

There was a whole new plate-glass shopfront. The name had changed. The sign above now read, in smart, modern lettering, COLD HILL GALLERY.

Lights were blazing inside, and it was rammed. A party was in progress. Smartly dressed people, holding champagne flutes, nodding, chatting, some smiling, mostly serious, intense.

Jason and Emily looked at each other in astonishment.

'What the hell?' he said. 'When did that happen?'

'The village store.' Emily shook her head in disbelief. 'The village store's gone.'

'But –' he was trying to think clearly – 'we had our newspapers delivered this morning.'

'They must have moved.'

'Must have. But where? How could they? I only drove past a few days ago.'

They crossed over. As they drew nearer, Jason could see paintings hung around the walls, some with a red dot on them.

His paintings.

Then the small, discreet sign on the door.

PRIVATE VIEWING. 6.30 p.m. – 9 p.m.
BY INVITATION ONLY

He looked again at Emily. The door opened and a couple emerged. Jason and Emily slipped through and entered the mêlée. There was a heady smell of dense perfume and cologne, mingled with a fainter tinge of paints and a quiet, subdued murmur of voices. People stood, admiring the paintings, some deep in discussion, pointing out details approvingly. A waitress with a tray laden with glasses filled to the brim moved through the room. As she headed in their direction, Jason reached out for two glasses, but she glided past, as if he and Emily were invisible and the tray in her hands was just an illusion.

Someone will recognize me in a minute, he thought.

An elegantly dressed woman, with a sweep of finely coiffured fair hair, clearly the gallery owner, or director, who reminded him of the owner of the Northcote Gallery, was addressing a small group of men and women.

'We are so lucky to have secured these quite exceptional pieces from the estate – his last works and, in my view, his very best.'

She pointed at his painting of *The Skiver*. Then at the one – he was certain he had not yet even done – of the miserable old couple in the pub. Next to it was another painting he had planned but not yet started, of a mechanical digger operator on the construction site.

'Jason Danes,' she proclaimed, 'was the natural successor to Lowry. Had he lived, I think he would have become one of our truly great artists. There's no question that all twenty-two of his works here will rise in value over the coming years. I see these as a *must* for anyone interested in twenty-first-century British art. It is so tragic he was taken from us at such a relatively early stage in his career.'

Jason stepped forward towards her. 'Actually, I'm Jason Danes and I'm very much still here.'

Seemingly not hearing him, she went on. '*The Skiver* has such a sense of character. Danes caught this fellow quite exquisitely. Just by his very posture, you can sense the man's lazy personality.'

'Hello!' Jason said.

No one took any notice of him as they all turned to look at the painting.

'Jason, I want to go,' Emily said.

'This is my private view!' he said. 'We need to be here.'

'They don't want us. We're irrelevant.'

'Em! Babes! I'm – this – these are my pictures! We have to be—'

But she was already out in the street.

He followed her. 'Em! We can't just leave!'

'They didn't invite us,' she replied.

Now he knew for sure he was dreaming. Had to be. 'We don't need an invite for my own private view, Em!'

'We do for this one.'

They walked on a short distance, then he stopped again, staring, puzzled, at the cottage which, last time he had passed, had a sign outside saying, BED & BREAKFAST – VACANCIES.

The sign was gone.

The white-picket fence at the end of its cute front garden had gone, too, and so had the garden. It had all been paved over, and parked on it were two cars, squeezed together: a Porsche and a Mini Countryman.

'What's happened there?' she asked.

'We're going to wake up.'

'I am awake.'

'No, this is all too weird,' he said. 'Two big changes to the high street in the past week.' He pointed. 'That was a B&B when we arrived here. How could it have changed so quickly? There was a garden out front. How can they have paved over the entire front garden so quickly – and over Christmas?'

As they walked on, he felt increasingly disoriented and light-headed. As if he was drunk or stoned. 'Maybe whoever's bought it is a builder,' he suggested, 'and perhaps they did do it during the Christmas break, Em? Perhaps the owners of the village store owned the B&B too, and sold both of them together?'

'I've no idea – I just don't think anything around here can

surprise me any more,' Emily replied. Then, an instant later, she stopped in her tracks and exclaimed, loudly, 'Oh shit!'

'What?'

'That does.'

She pointed ahead, on the other side of the road. 'Look! Look!'

He looked. At the pub. The Crown.

But it wasn't the Crown now.

A large, chic, grey sign with black lettering said, prominently, BISTROT TARQUIN.

Several flash cars were parked outside.

Jason looked at Emily, bewildered.

'We were here a week and a half ago,' she said, dumbfounded. 'We had Sunday lunch here. And then you had a sandwich here a couple of days later.'

'Maybe the landlord—? Maybe he decided to spruce it up?'

'Also in the past week? Is the whole of Cold Hill having a makeover?'

They went in through the front door. And stopped.

Stared.

The whole place had completely changed. The old wooden bar had been replaced with a steel and glass one, behind which was a wide, open hatch through to the busy kitchen. The manky old carpet was gone, and the floor was now limed wooden planks. The walls were freshly painted a soft grey, lit with modern, stainless steel fittings. The interior was filled with round glass tables and grey suede-covered chairs, with a candle burning on each table. Smart-looking diners were dotted around, eating designer food, drinking from fine crystal, while tall, impossibly chic waiting staff, all dressed in black, moved around as if they had been choreographed. Just inside the entrance, an elegant woman with sculpted hair stood behind a Perspex lectern with a built-in lamp, ready to greet diners.

She did not look up as they approached her.

'Wow!' Jason said. 'This is some change!'

She still did not look up.

Jason felt the door open. A couple walked in behind them. Two very classy-looking women, one with long dark hair, the other blonde, razor-cut.

'We're a bit late,' the dark-haired one said. 'We reserved in the name of Saltmarsh.'

'Demetra?' the greeter looked up at her, full of smiles.

'Yes.'

'Follow me, please.'

Jason and Emily watched the two women being seated. Within moments, a waiter glided to their table with menus.

The greeter returned to her lectern and made a mark on her tablet; presumably, Jason thought, ticking off the reservation.

'Is – er – is Lester Beeson around?' Jason asked her.

She did not look up.

He turned to Emily.

She wasn't there.

82

Thursday 27 December

Jason looked behind him, then across the restaurant. There was no sign of Emily. Had she gone to the loo?

Where was that now? Everything had changed in here. The door he remembered from before, which used to lead to the toilets, was now an alcove with a curved banquette.

'Excuse me,' he said to the greeter. 'Which way are the loos?'

Busy checking what looked like a seating plan of the room, she did not react.

'Erm – the loos?' he repeated. 'Could you tell me where they are?'

This time she did look up, but not in response to his question. It was to smile at another couple who had just entered. An instant later they were in front of him, blocking his view of her.

How rude of them barging past him – and of her to ignore him, he thought, indignantly.

'Name of Nick Godfrey,' the man said.

'Party of four?'

'Correct.'

'Your guests are already here, Mr Godfrey.'

She took their coats and led them off.

Jason turned around, utterly bewildered. He went back outside into what seemed to be turning into a hurricane. There was no sign of Emily. He returned to the restaurant. 'My wife – she came in with me,' he said to the greeter. 'Is it possible you could check the Ladies for me? I think she must be unwell.'

Yet again the woman did not appear to notice him. She tapped busily on her tablet, then looked up and right through him, with a blank expression.

'My wife,' he said. 'I think she might be unwell – is it possible that—'

Now four people suddenly stood in front of him, blocking his view of her again. He heard her check the reservation name, then gather their coats and lead them to a table. Jason followed them in, feeling very weird, as if both conspicuous and inconspicuous at the same time. He was walking strangely, his feet unable to feel the ground, almost as if he was floating. None of the diners took any notice of him.

I'm freaking out. Having a panic attack. Need to get home and wash my hands. Get in the shower.

He saw a sign for the toilets, in a completely different location from before, and went through into a unisex cloakroom. A woman came out of a door with a female gender symbol on it. 'Is there another lady in there, by chance?' he asked her.

She walked straight past, without answering.

Was everyone in here this rude? he wondered.

He went over to the door, not daring to go in. 'Emily?' he called out. Then, louder, 'Em? Are you in there? Are you OK?'

No response.

Sod it. He decided to go in and see for himself. 'Em?' he called out, cautiously. 'I'm coming in!'

The toilet was empty.

83

Thursday 27 December

Stepping back out into the restaurant, Jason was finding it hard to focus. All the faces of the diners were blurry, as if he was looking at them through misted-up glass, and the room seemed to have become two-dimensional, so he could not tell how far he was from any of it.

He felt panic rising.

Where was she?

His phone pinged, suddenly.

15

Fifteen what?

He crashed into a table, but the four occupants did not appear to notice, and miraculously no glasses fell over. They ignored his profuse apology. He weaved towards the door, as if he was completely drunk, still unable to feel his feet on the ground. Was there another room where Emily could be? Had she gone outside?

'She's vanished,' he said to the greeter.

No reaction.

'You didn't see a lady – my wife – go outside?' He was aware of the desperation in his voice.

His phoned pinged a second time. Was it a text from Emily? He looked down.

14

The countdown again? It seemed to be going more slowly now. Why?

He went out into the street, into the howling gale. There were white flecks, like sleet, in the air.

'EMILY!' he shouted, looking around, frantically. 'EMILY? EM!'

Had she panicked and gone back home to check on the fridges? She must have done – but why on earth had she just gone off without saying anything? And on her own, back to the place that was scaring her so much?

13

In the distance, a figure was moving away. Hurrying. As it passed beneath a street light, he could see it was Emily. Her coat, her headscarf.

'EM!' he raced after her, still unable to feel his feet.

His phone pinged again.

12

He increased his pace, but Emily was increasing hers, too. As he passed under another street light it went out, as did the one ahead, and she disappeared from view in the darkness. He carried on, flat out, but didn't feel any sense of exertion. She appeared beneath another street light, then that went out, too. The rest of the hill ahead was pitch black.

'EMILY!' he yelled.

11

He carried on in the darkness, impervious to the wind and the sleet. Darkness that was getting heavier and denser with every step.

Ping.

10

The beam of his phone torch was weakening; as if the dark was absorbing it like blotting paper.

9

'Em, wait, wait for me, I'm coming with you, I'll help you with the fridges, the van – we'll get the van started, somehow.'

8

He arrived at the entrance to Cold Hill Park, rushed in and turned left into Lakeview Drive. Ahead he saw a blaze of lights, far brighter than the street lights, which were now all back on.

7

Text her?

6

He tried to find their message thread.

5

His fingers wouldn't move properly. He couldn't make the keys work.

4

Rounding the curve, he heard the rattle of a generator. A female police officer with a clipboard stood in front of police tape stretched across the street. Beyond it, resting on its roof, was Emily's van, just visible through a team of fire and rescue workers in their bulky outfits. A battery of floodlights on stands shone down on the scene. The tractor was a short distance further on. Jason saw the same cluster of emergency vehicles that had been there earlier. To the right was an ambulance, its interior lights on. Another ambulance was parked just in front of it, as well as a paramedic's car.

A young man in a sharp suit was standing by the officer, with a notepad.

Ping.

3

Jason's throat tightened. He broke into a run and reached the police officer. 'My wife, you have to let me through. That's my wife's van!'

There was no reaction from her.

'Joel Barber from the *Argus*,' the man in the sharp suit said to the officer. 'I just need a quick statement on what's happened here.'

'We have a multiple fatality accident,' she answered, matter-of-factly. 'Two confirmed dead – one male and one female. Another male is trapped, and a female is in that ambulance and critical.' She nodded at the vehicle. 'I don't have any further information.'

'Can you give me any names?' the reporter persisted.

'I'm afraid not, sir, no, not until next of kin have been informed. Now I must ask you to leave.'

'Can you just confirm that one of the victims is the Sussex artist, Jason Danes?'

'I cannot confirm any identities at this stage.'

Jason ducked under the tape, the officer making no attempt to stop him, and ran to the badly mangled van, its front crumpled almost to the windscreen. Hundreds of prawns lay scattered around on the road.

Fire and rescue officers, using hydraulic cutting gear, were sawing through a door frame, while two paramedics were working on a trapped, motionless male figure in the passenger seat. The top of his scalp had been sheared off, exposing his brain. His torso was split open, his intestines uncoiled and hanging grotesquely down.

Ping.

2

Jason stared, numbly, in disbelief. He was that trapped figure in the van.

'We're losing him,' one of the paramedics said to his colleague. 'No pulse.'

Jason continued staring. No. It could not be. No.

Ping.

1

That was it, Jason thought, his brain racing frantically. It's an alarm. It was going to wake him. It was going to ring any second.

A message appeared on the screen.

J D E A D 0 0

And now, in that fleeting moment, he understood the significance.

The message disappeared and was replaced with just a single number:

0

Silence.

The display went dark and his torch went out.

84

'Excuse me, what are you doing in our house?' Jason Danes asked, as the well-dressed couple, the man in a suit, the woman in jeans and a leather jacket, followed Paul Jordan up the spiral staircase and walked straight past him and Emily, into his studio.

All the furniture and his easel were gone. The room was bare.

'This is a fabulous room, Mr and Mrs Middle – I'm sure you'll agree,' the estate agent said.

'Fabulous!' the man echoed, looking around.

'It is!' his wife said, enthusiastically. 'Stunning!' She went over to each of the windows in turn, looking out. 'It has a real *wow* factor!'

'I'm sorry, what are you doing here?' Jason asked.

No one heard him.

'The *wow* factor indeed, Mrs Middle!' Jordan said. 'It could be an office or an amazing bedroom! This is such a wonderful house. It's the best house on the entire development, I can assure you of that, no question. To be honest, the build quality of a Forest Mills home is second to none. They don't scrimp on anything; all the fittings are the best that money can buy. It is a rare opportunity to find this house back on the market so soon after the completion of the development, I can tell you.'

353

'The kitchen is stunning, too,' she said.

'Quite stunning!' Paul Jordan echoed. His eyes darted to the doorway, to the figure of a man and a woman standing, watching them, then back to his clients.

'Oh, look!' she exclaimed, peering down. 'Primroses are out on the front lawn! I hadn't even noticed them! See them, Kevin?'

'Well, it is Primrose Day today,' Jordan said. 'April nineteenth. Such a wonderful time of year this, everything coming up in the gardens and in the countryside. The perfect time to be moving into a new home, I always think.'

'The lake is awesome – what a beautiful view.' Her husband was peering out. 'Ducks, coots, moorhens. Mallards, and what are those with the long necks?'

'Indian-runner ducks,' Jordan replied, again glancing at the doorway. The figures were still there.

'So,' Kevin Middle said, checking the compass app on his phone. 'This way is facing north, right?'

'Yes, indeed, Mr Middle, and the hill beyond the lake forms part of the South Downs National Park, so it can never be built on.'

'Unlike the other directions?'

The views through the other windows were across rows of modern houses.

'The estate is complete,' Paul Jordan said, 'So there won't be any more building. I can genuinely say this is the best-designed modern development I've ever had the privilege of working on. I don't think there's a single house here that is unsympathetic to the location. The architect, in my humble opinion, is little short of a genius. This particular house is inspired, of course, on a smaller scale, by the original mansion that stood here. Cold Hill House. You'll find an interesting history if you look online.'

The couple looked at each other, smiling. 'What do you think, Sarah?' her husband said.

'Darling, you know what this room feels like to me?' Sarah Middle said. 'An artist's studio! This would be such a wonderful room to paint in. The light in here is just amazing.'

'You're an artist, Mrs Middle?' Paul Jordan asked.

'My wife is very talented,' her husband said, proudly.

'Cold Hill village has a new gallery that specializes in showing the work of local Sussex artists,' the estate agent said. 'I'm sure they would be most interested in your work.'

Blushing, Sarah Middle replied, 'I don't know if I'd be good enough to have an exhibition. I'm a rank amateur, self-taught. I'm what professional artists call a *Sunday painter*. I do water-colours – I specialize in flowers. I love it but I'm not sure I'm really any good.'

Her husband put his arm around her. 'Sarah, darling, don't put yourself down, you're very talented.'

She blushed. 'I don't think so.'

'Well, Mrs Middle, it's very odd you should say that, about this room being a studio.' Jordan hesitated. The figures were back in the doorway, watching him. 'No, sorry, forget I said it.'

'Odd?' Kevin Middle quizzed. 'What do you mean by that?' He suddenly sounded like the lawyer he was.

The agent looked flustered. 'Well really, I shouldn't have – er – said anything.'

Even more the lawyer now, Kevin said, sternly, 'Mr Jordan, you are trying to sell us this property – I don't think you should be concealing anything from my wife and me.'

'No – honestly – it's not any nasty secret or anything of that nature. It's just a little bit of history.'

'History?' his wife asked.

'Yes – you see, the extraordinary thing is that this room actually was an artist's studio! Quite a famous artist, in fact. He and his wife actually lived here, albeit briefly. What attracted them most of all was this room, which he made into his studio.'

'Why did they move?' she asked.

'Well – they didn't actually *move*.' Suddenly, Jordan began stepping from foot to foot and didn't seem to know what to do with his hands. 'It was the freakiest of coincidences – one you simply could not make up – and frankly wouldn't want to. Shortly after they moved into this property, there was a terrible tragedy. A completely freak accident with the people who lived across the road.' He pointed through the window, his discomfort becoming more and more intense and urgent. His face looked hot and clammy. 'Shortly after the couple moved in here –' he hesitated – 'do you really want to hear this?'

'Yes,' Kevin Middle said, and his wife nodded in agreement. 'We do.'

Jordan continued. 'The Penze-Weedells, across the way, had one of these new electric cars, with all the automatic features such as self-park and autonomous driving. It went wrong one afternoon, shot out of the drive and hit a van owned by the couple who had only recently bought this house, head on. The husband was killed outright. His wife remained in what I think they call a *persistent vegetative state* for some time, before passing away, too.'

'I think I read about this,' Sarah Middle said. 'It rings a bell.'

'Of course!' her husband said. 'Jason Danes, right?'

Jordan nodded, glancing again, uneasily, at the figures in the doorway. 'Yes. I imagine one day there will be a blue plaque outside.'

'They lived here?' Kevin Middle said. 'What an amazing coincidence!'

'It is,' Jordan agreed. 'Truly horrendous. Less than a couple of weeks after moving in.'

'Oh no,' Middle said. 'I didn't mean about the accident.' He smiled. 'You see, my wife and I are big Jason Danes fans. In fact, we were among his earliest patrons, we like to think.'

'We went to his very first private viewing,' Sarah Middle chipped in.

'We did!' her husband confirmed. 'There was something about his work that reminded us of an artist whose prices were way beyond us – Lowry.'

'We have over a dozen of Jason Danes's works,' his wife said, proudly. 'He lived here? I can't believe it.'

'It would be so very fitting to hang them here,' her husband said.

'Of course,' Jordan said. 'Oh yes, of course, absolutely. What a tribute!'

'Such a tragedy that Danes will never know our passion for his work,' Sarah Middle said.

'If he'd lived, he'd be up there, one day, among the greats, no question,' her husband added.

Paul Jordan glanced again at the doorway. At the two figures who were still standing there. Watching them.

He smiled back at his clients, who were both in their late thirties. 'Indeed. For sure. Oh, absolutely.'

And he knew for sure, absolutely, that one day soon they would both be meeting Jason Danes.

ACKNOWLEDGEMENTS

Writing novels may seem to outsiders to be a solitary task, and much of it really is. But my books would never happen without the hard work of many great people I'm blessed to have around me, and those I turn to for research help, who are invariably immensely generous with their time and in sharing their knowledge, in my quest to make my novels, although fiction, feel as authentic as possible.

Thank you in particular for research help on this book to Tom Homewood; Chief Superintendent Lisa Bell, Divisional Commander of Brighton and Hove Police; Michelle Brooker and all the staff at Lewes Library; David Graham; Canon Simon Holland; Jan van Niekerk; The Reverends Ish and Irene Smale; and Bishop Dominic Walker, OGS.

A massive thank you to Susan Ansell, Graham Bartlett, Dani Brown, Martin and Jane Diplock, Chris Diplock, Anna-Lisa Hancock, James Hodge, Sarah Middle, Helen Shenston, Mark Tuckwell and Chris Webb. To my agent, Isobel Dixon, and all at Blake Friedmann and to everyone at my UK publishers, Pan Macmillan – including Sarah Arratoon, Jonathan Atkins, Anna Bond, Wayne Brookes, Stuart Dwyer, Claire Evans, Daniel Jenkins, Neil Lang, Sara Lloyd, Louise Patel, Alex Saunders, Jade Tolley, Jeremy Trevathan, Charlotte Williams, Natalie Young, my copy-editor Susan Opie and my wonderful publicists at Riot, Preena Gadher, Caitlin Allen and Emily Souders. And an extremely special mention to Geoff Duffield, who believed in me from the very beginning.

I need to single out a few people above all others – my good friend, David Gaylor, my tireless assistant, Linda Buckley, my wife Lara, who has brilliant insights into characters and is my total rock. And of course lastly (although I'm sure they know, really, they come first!) our dogs, Oscar, Spooky and Wally and all the other furry and feathered creatures in our ever-expanding menagerie.

As ever, thank you, my wonderful readers! I always love to hear from you – your letters, emails, blog posts, tweets, facebook, Instagram and YouTube comments give me such constant encouragement.

contact@peterjames.com
www.peterjames.com
www.youtube.com/peterjames Peter James TV
www.facebook.com/peterjames.roygrace
www.twitter.com/peterjamesuk
www.instagram.com/peterjamesuk
www.instagram.com/peterjamesukpets

COMING SOON

FIND THEM DEAD

Turn the page for an extract from the latest
Detective Superintendent Roy Grace novel . . .

1

Mickey Starr gazed into the night, feeling restless and apprehensive. And afraid. It wasn't fear of the darkness but of what lay beyond it.

Going to be fine, he tried to reassure himself. He'd done these Channel crossings before without a hitch, so why should this one be any different?

But it was. No escaping the fact. This *was* different.

Fear was something that had never troubled him before, but throughout this trip he had been feeling a growing anxiety, and now as the shore grew closer, he was truly frightened. Terrified, if it all went pear-shaped, what would happen to the one person in his life who had ever really meant anything to him and who loved him unconditionally. Whatever bad things he may have done.

Wrapped up against the elements in a heavy coat and a beanie, roll-up smouldering in his cupped hand, the muscular, grizzled, forty-three-year-old stood on the heaving deck of the car ferry, braced against a stanchion to keep his balance.

In prison, some eighteen years back, his cellmate, an Irishman with a wry sense of humour, had given him the nickname *Lucky Starr*. Mickey should feel lucky, he'd told him, because he had a spare testicle after losing one to cancer in his teens, a spare eye, after a detached retina in one had put an end to his boxing career, and a spare arm for the one he'd subsequently lost in a motorbike accident.

It was 4 a.m. and he was fighting off seasickness. He wasn't feeling particularly *lucky* at this moment, out here in the middle of the English Channel, in this storm. He had a bad feeling that maybe he'd used up all his luck. Perhaps he should have found someone else to come with him after his colleague had pulled out at the last minute due to sickness. He always felt less vulnerable and conspicuous when he had a female companion with him. Maybe the Range Rover he was driving was too shouty?

Put it out of your mind, Mickey, get on with the job.

The sea was as dark as extinction. The salty spray stung as he squinted through the bitter wind and driving rain. His confidence in tatters, he was wondering if he was making the most stupid mistake of his life.

Calm down. Pull yourself together. Look confident. Be lucky!

Be lucky, and soon he would be home, back with his younger brother, Stuie, who totally depended on him. Stuie had Down's Syndrome and Mickey affectionately referred to him as his 'homie with an extra chromie'. Many years ago, Mickey made a promise to their dying mum that he would always take care of him, and he always had. His 'differently-abled' brother had taught Mickey how to see life in other ways, more simply. Better.

He wouldn't be doing any more runs for the boss after this. He'd talked with Stuie about setting up a business with the cash he'd stashed away – nice money from the small quantities of drugs he'd pilfered from his boss on each run, too small for him to ever notice. Although this time he'd added substantially to the cargo, and a very nice private deal awaited him. Big proceeds – the biggest ever!

But now he was riddled with doubt. All it needed was one sharp-eyed Customs officer. He tried to shake that thought away. Everything was going to be fine, just as it always had been on each of these trips.

Wasn't it?

Stuie liked cooking and constantly, proudly, wore his 'special' chef's toque Mickey had bought him for his birthday last year. Mickey had planned to buy a chippy as close to Brighton seafront as he could afford – or in nearby Eastbourne or Worthing, where prices were lower. But with the money he stood to make now, he'd be able to afford something actually *on* Brighton seafront, where the best earnings were to be made, and he had his eye on a business in a prime location near to the Palace Pier that had just come up for sale. Stuie would work in the kitchen preparing the food and he would be doing the frying and front-of-house. All being well, in a few days he'd have the cash to buy it. He just had to get his load safely through Customs and onto the open road. And then – happy days!

He swallowed, his nerves rattling him again, breathing in the noxious smells of fresh paint and diesel fumes. The boss had patted him on the back a few days ago, before he'd headed to Newhaven, and told him not to worry, all would be fine. 'If shit happens, just act normal, be yourself. Be calm, take a deep breath, smile. Yep? You're *lucky*, so be lucky!'

The 18,000-ton, yellow-and-white ship ploughed on through the stormy, angry swell of the English Channel, nearing the end of its sixty-five-nautical-mile crossing from Dieppe. Ahead, finally, he could now start to make out the port and starboard leading lights of the deep-water channel between the Newhaven Harbour moles, and beyond – spread out along the shore even more faintly – the lights of the town.

A short while later a tannoy announcement requested, 'Will all drivers please return to your vehicles.'

Starr took a final drag on his cigarette, his fifth or sixth of the voyage, tossed it overboard in a spray of sparks and hurried through a heavy steel door back inside, into the relative warmth, where he made his way down the companionway stairs, following the signs to Car Deck A.

No need to be nervous, he told himself yet again. He had all the correct papers and everything had been planned with the military precision he had come to expect of the boss's organization, after nearly sixteen years of working loyally for him. Well, pretty loyally.

The boss had long ago told him this was always the best time of day to pass through Customs, when the officers would be tired, at their lowest ebb. He glanced at his watch. All being well, he'd be home in two hours. Stuie would still be asleep, but when he woke, boy, would they celebrate!

Oh yes.

He smiled. It was all going to be fine. Please, God.

2

At 4.30 a.m., Clive Johnson sat in his uniform dark shirt, with epaulettes and black tie, in the snug, glass-fronted office over-looking the cavernous, draughty Customs shed at Sussex's New-haven Port. The Border Force officer was sipping horrible coffee and thinking about the beer festival at the Horsham Drill Hall next Saturday – the one light at the end of the tunnel of a long, dull week of almost fruitless night shifts and big disappointment among his team, so far.

An average height, stout man of fifty-three, with a friendly face topped by thinning hair, Johnson wore large glasses which helped mask the lenses he needed for his poor eyesight, steadily deteriorating from macular degeneration. Coincidentally and helpfully, his wife owned a Specsavers franchise in Burgess Hill. So far he'd kept his condition from his colleagues, but he knew to his dismay that it would be only a year or two, as the ophthal-mologist – who worked for his wife – had informed him, before he would have to give up this job he had come to love, despite its frequent unsociable hours.

Rain lashed down outside, and a Force 7, gusting 8/9, was blowing. One of the sniffer dogs barked incessantly in the handler's van at the far end of the building, as if it sensed the team's antici-pation that maybe, after a week of waiting on high alert, acting on a tip-off from a trusted intel source, this might be their night. Although 'trusted' was a questionable term. Intelligence reports were notoriously unreliable and often vague. It had indicated that a substantial importation of Class-A drugs was expected through this port imminently, concealed in a vehicle, possibly a high-value one, and coming in on a night ferry this week. Which was why tonight, as for the past six days, they had a much larger contingent of officers than usual present here at Newhaven, backed up by Sussex Police detectives and an Armed Response Unit waiting on standby. All of them growing bored but hopeful.

The roll-on, roll-off *Côte D'Albâtre* had just docked after its four-hour voyage and was now disgorging its cargo of lorries, vans and cars. And there was one particular vehicle on its manifest emailed earlier from the Dieppe port authority that especially interested Clive.

Apart from real ale, his other passion was classic cars, and he was a regular attendee at as many gatherings of these around the country as he could get to. He never missed the Goodwood events, in particular the Festival of Speed and the Revival, and he had an encyclopaedic knowledge of pretty much every car built between 1930 and 1990, from its engine capacity to performance figures and kerb weight. There was a serious beaut arriving off this ferry, one he could not wait to see. Bust or no bust, it would at least be the highlight of his week.

One problem for the officers was in the definition of 'high value' vehicle. The source of the report was unable to be any more specific. Dozens of cars came under that category. They'd been pulling over and searching many vehicles that might match the description, including a rare Corvette, to date without any success. All they'd found so far was a tiny amount of recreational cannabis and a Volvo estate with a cheeky number of cigarettes on board – several thousand – all for his personal consumption, the driver had said. On further questioning he'd turned out to be a pub landlord, making his weekly run, turning a nice profit and depriving HMRC and thus the British Exchequer of relatively small but worthwhile amounts of cash. They'd impounded the Volvo and its cargo, but it was small fry, not what they were really interested in. Not what they were all waiting for.

As the week had worn on, faith in the intel was fading along with their morale. If tonight came up goose egg too, Clive would be losing most of his back-up.

The first vehicle off the ferry to enter the Customs shed was a camper van with an elderly, tired-looking couple up front. Clive spoke into his radio, giving instructions to the two officers down on the floor. 'Stop the camper, ask them where they've been, then let them on their way.'

Body language was one of Clive Johnson's skills. He could always spot a nervous driver. These people were just plain tired, they weren't concealing anything. Nor was the equally weary-looking businessman in an Audi A6 with German plates who followed. All the same, to deliberately make his target nervous if he was behind in the queue of cars, he ordered two officers to pull the Audi driver over and question him, too. The same applied to another elderly couple in a small Nissan, and a young couple in an MX5. The lorries would follow later. Some of these would be picked out at random and taken through the X-ray gantry, to see if there were any illegal immigrants hidden among their cargo.

Clive had heard the period between 3 a.m. and 5 a.m. called the *dead hours*. The time before dawn when many terminally ill people passed away. The time when most folk were at their lowest point. Most, maybe, but not him, oh no. Just like an owl, he hunted best at night. Clive had never set out to be a front-facing Customs officer because he had never been particularly confident with other people in that way, too much small talk and pretence. He used to prefer back-room solitude and anonymity, the company of tables, facts and figures and statistics. When he'd originally joined Customs and Excise, before it was renamed Border Force, it had been because of his fascination – and expertise – with weights and measures. He had an excellent memory which had served him well as an analyst in the department before he had, rather reluctantly, accepted a move a few years ago to become a frontline officer, after his superiors had seen in him a talent for spotting anything suspicious.

Over these past seven years he had proved their judgement right. None of his colleagues understood how he did it, but his ability to detect a smuggler was almost instinctive.

And all his instincts told him that the driver of the approaching Range Rover towing an enclosed car trailer unit looked wrong. Nervous.

Nervous as hell.

He radioed his two officers on the floor.

3

When anyone asked Meg Magellan what she did for a living, she told them straight up that she was a drug dealer. Which she really was, but the good sort, she would add hastily, breaking into a grin. In her role as a key account manager for one of the UK's largest pharmaceutical companies, Kempsons, she sold and merchandized their range of over-the-counter products into the Tesco store group.

She also tried, mostly unsuccessfully, to augment her income by betting on horses. Never big stakes, just the occasional small flutter – a love of which she'd got from her late husband, Nick, whose dream had been to own a racehorse. The closest he'd got was to own one leg of a steeplechaser called Colin's Brother. She'd kept the share after Nick's death, as a link to him, and followed the horse in the papers, always putting a small bet on and quite often being pleasantly surprised by the nag getting a place – with even the occasional win. Whenever the horse ran at a reasonably local meeting, she would do her best to go along and place a bet and cheer him on, along with the two mates, Daniel Crown and Peter Dean, who owned the other three legs between them. She'd become so much closer to them both since Nick died. In a small way they kept Nick alive to her and she could see his humour in them.

At 4.30 a.m., Meg's alarm woke her with a piercing *beep-beep-beep*, shrieking away a dream in which Colin's Brother was heading to the finishing post but being strongly challenged, as she shouted encouragement at the top of her voice.

Avoiding the temptation to hit the snooze button and grab a few more precious minutes of sleep beneath the snug warmth of her duvet – and continue the dream – she swung her legs out of the bed and downed the glass of water beside her.

She had to get up now. No option. At 9 a.m., in less than five hours, she was presenting her company's latest cough-and-cold remedy to the Tesco buying team, seventy miles of stressful traffic to the north of here. Normally, she'd have stayed at a Premier Inn close to the company's headquarters. A ten-minute drive instead of the three hours facing her now, if she was lucky with the traffic. But this wasn't a *normal* day.

Today, her daughter – and only surviving child – Laura, was heading off to Thailand and then on to Ecuador as part of her gap year. She and Laura had rarely been apart for more than a few days. They had always been close, but even closer since five years ago, when they'd been driving back to Brighton from a camping holiday in the Scottish Highlands.

Always car-sick, Laura sat in the front. After Nick had done a long spell at the wheel of their VW camper van, Bessie, Meg had taken over from her husband, who then sat in the back with their fifteen-year-old son Will, and had slept. As she'd slowed for road-works on the M1, an uninsured plumber, busily texting his girlfriend, had ploughed his van into the back of their vehicle, killing Nick and Will instantly. She and Laura had survived, and their injuries had healed, but their lives would never be the same again – there was no going back to normal family life. Meg would have given anything to have even the most mundane day with her family one more time. Of course, friends and relatives had rallied around her and Laura in the days and months after the accident, when it felt as if they were living in a surreal bubble, but eventually and inevitably life went on, grief had to be dealt with, and as the years passed people stopped talking about Nick and Will.

Not one day went by when she didn't think of them and what might have been.

Meg had stayed home to be with her daughter on what was to be their last night together for several months. This summer, Laura had saved up for this gap-year backpacking trip, with her best friend, before she went off to study Veterinary Science at the University of Edinburgh.

Nick, who had worked for the same company as Meg, had often jokily discussed with her what life would be like one day as empty-nesters when Will and Laura eventually left home. A positive man, they'd made all kinds of plans – perhaps to take a gap year themselves, which neither of them had done in their teens – and head off to travel Europe, and maybe beyond, in their beloved Bessie.

Laura was a good kid – no, correct that, she thought – a *great* kid. One of the many things she loved about her bright, sparky daughter was the way she cared about animals. Meg was charged now with looking after Laura's precious pet guinea pig, Horace, and her two gerbils, as well as her imperious Burmese cat, Daphne.

When she came back home tonight to their small, pretty, mock-Tudor semi close to Hove seafront, Meg was painfully aware she would be truly alone. Home to a new reality. A real lengthy period alone. And when Laura returned from her gap year, she'd then be getting ready to move to university. No more music blasting from Laura's bedroom. No more questions on homework to help her daughter with. No more running commentaries on who was going out with who, or the geeky boy who had been trying to chat her up. A big, lonely, empty nest.

God, she loved her daughter so much. Laura was smart, fun and incredibly streetwise. Above all, Meg always knew she could trust her to take care of herself when she went out into town with her friends. Every night, apart from when she had to spend time away from home, travelling on business, they would sit down and have supper together and share their days.

But not any more. Tonight, she'd be alone with her memories. With Laura's beloved pets – hoping and praying none would die while she was away – and with the photographs around the house of Nick and Will with her and Laura when they were a family of four. *You have children?* people would ask. Meg would reply, 'I have two.' It wasn't true, but she did, back then.

'I am a mother of two children, and I am a wife. But my son and my husband are dead.' She never found those conversations any easier.

And to add to her concerns, her employer for the past twenty-odd years, ever since she had left uni, would be moving next year from nearby Horsham just forty minutes' drive from here, up to Bedfordshire – a two-and-a-half-hour grind. No date had been fixed yet but, when the time came, she would have to make the choice either to stay on or take the redundancy package on offer.

Meg showered, got herself ready then went down into the kitchen to make some breakfast and a strong coffee. Daphne meowed, whingeing for her breakfast. She opened a tin and the cat jumped up onto the work surface, barged her arm and began eating, though she had barely started scooping the fishy contents out. 'Greedy guts!' Meg chided, setting the bowl on the floor. The cat jumped down and began to scoff the food as if she hadn't been fed for a month.

Moments after Meg sat at the table, beneath a large framed photograph on the wall of Colin's Brother passing the finishing post at Plumpton Racecourse half a length ahead of the next horse, she heard soft footsteps behind her and felt Laura's arms around her. Laura's face close against hers, wet with tears. Hugging her. She ignored the five earrings cutting into her cheek.

'I'm going to miss you so much, Mum.'

'Not as much as I'm going to miss you.' Meg turned and gripped both of her daughter's hands. Laura's dark hair was styled in a chic but strange way that made her think of garden topiary. She had a scrunchie on one wrist and a Fitbit on the other and was dressed in striped paper-bag trousers and a white T-shirt printed with the words, in an old-fashioned typeface, YOU MAKE ME WONDER.

Meg smiled through her own tears and pointed at it. 'That's for sure!'

Her daughter had changed so much in these past few years. And recently seemed to be changing week on week with new piercings appearing. From nothing a year ago, she now had, in addition to her ears, a nose ring and a tongue stud, and, horror of horrors, she'd had her first tattoo just this past weekend – a small hieroglyphic on her shoulder which Laura said was an ancient Tibetan symbol for protecting travellers. Meg could hardly argue with that.

Laura's expression suddenly darkened as her eyes darted to the right. Freeing her hands, she pointed at a pile of plastic carrier bags. 'Mum, what are those?' she chided.

Meg shrugged. 'I'm afraid I'm not Superwoman, I forget things sometimes, OK?'

Laura shook her head at her. 'OK, right, we're meant to be saving the planet. What if everyone forgot to take their own bags to the supermarket every time they went shopping?'

'I'll do my best to remember in future.'

Laura wagged a finger at her then leaned forward and kissed her. 'I know you will, you're a good person.'

'What time are you leaving?' Meg choked on the words.

'Cassie's mum is picking us up at 6 a.m. to take us to the airport.'

Cassie and Laura had been inseparable for years. She'd been the first to get a piercing and of course Laura had to follow. Now Cassie had three tattoos – God knows what Laura was going to come back with after their long trip.

'You'll keep in touch and let me know when you've landed?'

'I'll WhatsApp you every day!'

'You're all I have in the world, you know that, don't you, my angel?'

'And you're all I have, too, Mum!'

'Until you meet the *right person*.'

'Yech! Don't think there's much danger of that. Although maybe when we get to the Galapagos next year, I might kidnap a sea lion and bring it back.'

Meg smiled, knowing she was only half jesting. Over the years, Laura had brought all kinds of wounded creatures into their house, including a fox cub, a robin and a hedgehog. 'Be careful in the water, won't you – don't forget about those dangerous rip tides and currents?'

'Hello, Mum! Didn't we grow up on the seaside? I'll be careful! You'll look after all the animals – don't forget the gerbils?'

'I've got all your instructions.'

Laura had written a detailed list of their food and the times they liked to be fed.

'And special hugs and treats for Master Horace?' She was

struggling to speak now, her voice choked. 'Don't be sad, Mum. I love you so much and I'll still love you just as much when I'm over there.'

Meg turned her head and looked at her daughter. 'Sure, I know you will,' she said.

And the moment you get on that plane, you will have forgotten all about me.

That's how it works.

4

Shit, Mickey thought, his nerves shorting out as he obeyed the two Border Force officers' unsmiling signals to pull over into the inspection lane. This wasn't supposed to happen. *Shit shit shit.*

Be calm. Deep breath. Smile.

That was all he needed to do. But at this moment there was a total disconnect between his mind and his body. His ears were popping and his armpits were moist. A nerve tugged at the base of his right eye; a twitch he'd not had for years suddenly returned at the worst possible moment imaginable.

Stepping out of the office, Clive Johnson continued to observe the driver's body language as the vehicle and trailer came to a halt. The man, who was wearing a black beanie, lowered his window, and Johnson strode up and leaned in. He smelled the strong reek of cigarette smoke on the man, noticing his badly stained teeth; the tattoo rising up above his open-neck shirt. He was wearing leather gloves. His skin had the dry, creased look of a heavy smoker, making him appear older than he actually was – probably around forty, he thought.

'Good morning, sir, I am with the UK Border Force,' Johnson said with consummate politeness.

'Morning, officer!' Mickey said in his Brummy accent. 'Bit of a ride that was. Good to be on terra firma!'

The man had almost comically thick lenses, which made his eyes look huge, Mickey thought.

'I'll bet it is, sir. I'm not much of a seafarer myself. Just a few questions.'

'Yeah, of course, no problem.'

The man's voice seemed to have risen several octaves, Clive

Johnson noticed. 'I will need to see the documentation for your load. Have you come from anywhere nice?'

'Dusseldorf, in Germany.'

'And where's your destination?'

'Near Chichester. I'm delivering a vehicle for LH Classics.' He jerked a finger over his shoulder. 'They've purchased this vehicle on behalf of a client and they're going to prep it for a race in the Goodwood Members' Meeting.'

'And what is the vehicle you are transporting?'

'A 1962 Ferrari – 250 Short Wheelbase.'

'Pretty rare. Didn't one of these sell at auction recently for nearly £10 million, if I'm correct?' Clive Johnson said.

'You are correct. But that had better racing history than this one.' Johnson nodded approvingly. 'Quite some car.'

'It is, believe me – I wouldn't want to be the guy responsible for driving it in a race!'

'Let's start with your personal ID. Can I see it, please?'

Starr handed him his passport.

'Are you aware, sir, of the prohibitions and restrictions of certain goods such as drugs, firearms and illegal immigrants for example?'

'It's only the car and me!' Starr said cockily, pointing his thumb towards the trailer.

Johnson then asked him a number of questions regarding the placing of the vehicle in the unit and its security on the journey, which Starr answered.

'Can I now see the paperwork for the vehicle?' Johnson said.

Mickey lifted a folder off the passenger seat and handed it to him. Johnson made a show of studying it for some while. Then he said, 'I'd like to see the vehicle, please, sir.'

Immediately he noticed the man's fleeting hesitation. And the isolated beads of perspiration rolling down his forehead.

'Yeah, sure, no problem.'

Mickey got out of his car, butterflies in his stomach, telling himself to keep calm. Keep calm and all would be fine. In a few minutes he'd be on the road and heading home to Stuie. He went to the rear of the trailer unit, unlocked it and pulled open the doors to reveal the gleaming – almost showroom condition – red Ferrari.

Clive Johnson ogled the car. Unable to help himself, he murmured, 'Ah, but a man's reach should exceed his grasp, or what's a heaven for?'

'You what?' Mickey said.

'Robert Browning. That's who wrote it.'

'Oh,' Mickey said, blankly. 'I think you're mistaken. David Brown – he was the man who created Aston Martins. DB – that stood for David Brown.'

'I know my cars, sir,' Johnson said, still inscrutably polite. 'I was talking about Robert Brown*ing*.'

'Dunno him, was he a car designer, too?'

'No, he was a poet.'

'Ah.'

Clive Johnson stepped back and spoke quietly into his radio. Moments later a dog handler appeared, with an eager white-and-brown spaniel on a leash with a fluorescent yellow harness.

'Just a routine check, sir,' Johnson said. And instantly noticed a nervous twitch below the man's right eye.

'Yeah, of course.'

The handler lifted the dog into the trailer, then clambered up to join it. Immediately, the dog started moving around the Ferrari, occasionally jumping up.

'Make sure it don't scratch the paintwork, I'll get killed if there's any marks on it,' Mickey said.

'Don't worry, sir,' Clive Johnson said. 'Her claws are clipped regularly, her paws are softer than a chamois leather.'

The handler opened the passenger door and let the dog inside. It clambered over the driver's seat then, tail wagging, jumped down into the footwell and sniffed hard.

Its demeanour and reaction were a sign to its handler that the dog had found something.

Mickey watched it, warily. His boss had told him not to worry, they'd used new wrappers, devised by a Colombian chemist, that would stop sniffer dogs from finding anything. He hoped his boss was right. Certainly, the dog seemed happy enough – it was wagging its tail.

5

As the dog handler led the spaniel back down from the rear of the trailer, he exchanged a knowing glance with Clive Johnson, who climbed up and peered into the car. Looking at the spoked wood-rim steering wheel. The dials. The gear lever with its traditional Ferrari notched gate. He opened the door and leaned in, sniffing, and that was when his suspicions increased. Authentic classic cars had an ingrained smell of worn leather, old metal and engine oil.

This car did not smell right.

He removed a wallet stuffed with £50 notes from the door pocket. Sniffer dogs were trained to smell not only drugs but also cash. Was it going to turn out to be just an innocent wad of cash in a wallet, after all this? Hopefully not.

He jumped back down onto the shed floor, turning to Starr. 'I'm seizing the wallet and its contents pending further investigation as the cash could be evidence of criminal activity.' He sealed the wallet into an evidence bag in front of him.

Mickey could feel his anger and anxiety growing. 'What are you doing, is that really necessary?'

Johnson ignored the question. 'Is the car driveable?'

'Yes,' Mickey said, pointedly.

'Good. What I'd like you to do, please, is reverse the car onto the floor. I need to weigh it.'

'Weigh it?'

'Yes, please.'

The butterflies now raised a shitstorm inside Mickey's belly. He tried not to let that show. 'No problem.' He began removing the wheel blocks.

The sound of a classic Ferrari's engine starting was more beautiful than any music to Clive's ears. It was a sound that touched his heart and soul. Poetry in motion. But the engine noise resonating around the steel walls of this shed had little of that music. Just like the smell of the Ferrari's interior, the engine noise was also not quite right. He stood behind, waving the car down the ramp, watching the wheels, the tyres. The way the car sank on its haunches as the rear wheels reached the concrete floor.

He walked around the car, having to force himself to focus on his task and not simply be blown away by its sheer animal beauty. Yet the more he looked at it, the more something else did not seem right. He guided the driver, smiling pleasantly all the way, along the shed and over to the left onto the weighing platform built into the floor. He made the driver back up, move over further to the left, go forward, reverse again then stop and get out of the car.

Clive looked at the readout. And his excitement began to rise. He had checked earlier, when he'd received the manifest, the kerb weight of a proper 1962 Ferrari 250 SWB. It should be 950 kilograms.

This car weighed 1,110 kilograms.

Why?

Many classic cars were rebuilt, or even faked from new, some using chassis numbers from written-off wrecks while other rogues brazenly copied existing numbers. And not always with the original expensive metals. Some were rebuilt for an altogether very different purpose. Was he looking at one now?

In a few minutes he would find out.

He walked over to the driver's side of the Ferrari, smiling, giving the impression that everything was OK. Instantly, he could see the change in the driver's demeanour.

Mickey smiled back, relief surging through him. *Got away with it! Got away with it! Yesssss!*

He was so gleeful that he wanted to text Stuie. He would be with him in a little over an hour, on the empty roads at this time of morning. But he decided to wait until he was well clear, to get out of here as fast as he could in case the officer had a change of mind.

Then the Border Force officer stepped up. 'Just before you go on your way, sir, I'm going to have my colleague drive it through the X-ray gantry.'

Mickey felt a cold flush in his stomach. *Be calm, deep breath, smile.*

Clive Johnson stood in front of the X-ray's monitor, watching as the vehicle was driven through the scanner, until he had the completed black-and-white image. Almost immediately, he could see an anomaly: the tyres should have been hollow, filled with air as all tyres normally were. Instead, the scanner showed they were solid.

Johnson was excited, but still mindful of the value of this car if it was genuine, despite his suspicions. The least intrusive place to start, from his past experience, would be with the spare wheel.

He opened the boot and, joined by two colleagues, removed it. They lifted it uneasily out of the vehicle, alarm bells ringing at the weight of it. One of the officers rolled and bounced it. He then spoke to his colleague, who produced a Stanley knife.

Mickey watched in horror as the man ripped through it.

'For God's sake, that's an original that came with the car!' Mickey shouted, desperation in his voice. 'Do you have any idea what you might be doing to the value of this Ferrari?'

'I'm very sorry, Mr Starr, the car's owners will of course be compensated for any damage done during the examination if the car proves to be in order,' Clive Johnson said.

'Can I have a smoke?'

'I'm afraid this is a no-smoking area.'

'Well, can I go outside then?'

'I'm sorry, sir, not at this moment,' Johnson said. 'We need you to be in attendance to observe what we are doing.'

There was no *hiss* of escaping air as the officer sliced the blade deep into the tyre wall. For some while he worked the blade around in an arc, until finally he pulled away a large flap of rubber.

In the gap it left, a plastic bag filled with a white powder was clearly visible. The officer reached in to pull it out and held it up, showing those present what he had found.

'Most people fill their tyres with air, sir.' Johnson moved forward towards Mickey. 'I believe this package contains controlled drugs and I'm arresting you.'

Mickey stared at him for a fraction of a second in complete blind panic. Trying to think clearly. A voice inside his head screamed, *RUN!*

Mickey shoved the officer harshly sideways, sending him stumbling into the wall, and sprinted forward, racing through the shed. He heard shouts, a voice yelling at him to stop. If he could just get out of here, out into the dark streets, he could disappear. Hole up somewhere or steal a car and get back to Stuie.

His foot hit something painfully hard, a fucking wheel brace, and he sprawled forward. As he scrambled desperately back to his feet, someone grabbed his right arm, his prosthetic arm.

He twisted, kicked out backwards with his foot, felt it connect and heard a grunt of pain.

His arm was still being held.

He spun. Two men, one with the big glasses. He lashed out with his left arm, punching Four-Eyes in the face, straight in the glasses, sending him reeling backwards, then he lashed out at the other, much younger man who was still holding his arm. Aimed a kick at his groin, but the officer dodged it and Mickey lost his footing, tripping backwards, falling, his entire weight supported now by the man holding his arm.

As he staggered back, trying desperately to keep on his feet, he picked up the wheel brace and registered the momentary shock on the officer's face. Then he rushed him, headbutting him with all his strength, and heard a *crunch* as he did so.

The officer, blood spurting from his shattered nose, fell to the ground. Mickey sprinted again, past a parked van with amber roof lights, and out through the far end of the shed into chilly early morning air and falling rain, into darkness and towards the lights of the town beyond.

Safety.

A voice yelled from the darkness, 'Stop, Police!' Flashlight beams struck him, and an instant later two police officers, one a man-mountain, hurtled from seemingly nowhere towards him. Mickey swung the wheel brace at the big one's head but too late;

before it could connect, he felt like he'd been hit by a fridge. A crashing impact, the momentum hurling him face-first to the ground. An instant later there was a dead weight on top of him. A hand gripped the back of his neck, pushing his face down hard onto the wet road surface.

Instantly, using all his survival instincts and martial arts training, Mickey kicked out backwards, catching his assailant by surprise, and in the same split-second reached up, curled his left arm round the man's thick neck and gave a sharp pull. With a startled croak, the man rolled sideways as if he was as light as a sack of feathers.

Freeing himself, Mickey rose to his feet and, before the startled officer could react, slammed his powerhouse of a southpaw fist into the man's jaw. As the officer staggered backwards in agony, Mickey sprinted again towards the lights of the town. He overtook several foot passengers and reached the junction with the deserted main road.

Thinking hard and fast.

Glancing over his shoulder.

In the distance, he saw bobbing flashlights. People running, but a good few hundred yards behind him.

He was about to cross the road when headlights appeared. Hesitating in case it was a police car, and ready to melt back into the darkness, he saw it was an Audi with German plates. The driver clocked him and slowed to a halt, putting down his window.

Mickey stared in at a serious-looking man in his thirties in a business suit. In broken English, the man said, 'Hello, excuse me, I've come from the ferry but think I have taken a wrong turning. Would you know the direction towards London?'

Mickey slammed his fist into the side of the man's neck, aiming it directly at the one place that would knock him unconscious instantly. He opened the door, unclipped his belt and shoved him, with some difficulty, across into the passenger seat. Then he jumped in, familiarizing himself in an instant with the left-hand driving position, and accelerated hard away, ignoring the insistent pinging of the alarm telling him to fasten his belt.

Something more insistent was pinging inside his head.

Get home to Stuie before the police get there.

In his red mist of panic, he figured so long as he got home, everything would be all right. He and Stuie, they were good. They were a team.

'I'm coming,' he muttered. 'Stuie, I'm coming. Going to scoop you up and we'll head north up to Scotland, lie low for a bit. I got friends there on a remote farm. We'll be safe there.'

And maybe safe in this car. Had anyone been close enough to see him taking it? He'd have to chance not. He'd call Stuie, who always slept the sleep of the dead, and tell him to get up, pack a bag and be ready to leave the moment he arrived. The way to get him to move fast would be tell him it was a game and that he could bring his chef's hat!

He put his hand down to the front pocket of his jeans to tug out his phone.

It wasn't there.

6

Shit, Mickey thought, trying to concentrate on driving, panic rising again. *Shit. What numbers did the phone have on it?* It was a burner he'd bought a couple of weeks before the start of the trip.

There was a groan from the passenger seat, which he ignored as he concentrated on navigating through the outskirts of the town, away from the harbour and towards the A26.

A couple of minutes later, driving like the wind, he shot out of the industrial area and onto the long, twisty, rural part of the road, checking his mirrors constantly. There was nothing so far. Just more of that darkness.

A bus-stop lay-by loomed up ahead. He braked hard and swung into it. Then he ran round to the passenger door, bashed the German unconscious again and dragged him, out of sight, into dense undergrowth. Not great but the best he could do, short of killing him. Returning to the car, he drove on at high speed. Thinking.

What a mess.

All his great plans down the toilet.

Jesus.

The boss was going to be furious – but that was the least of his problems right now.

He carried on, flat out up the winding country road that he knew well, 70 . . . 80 . . . until he reached the roundabout at the top. Right would take him towards Eastbourne. Left towards Brighton on a wide dual carriageway taking him directly to Stuie in Chichester. They would head north towards London and the circular M25 around it. And then towards Scotland. Find a service station and steal or hijack another car there.

He turned left, checking his mirrors again. Nothing. Only street-lit darkness. Wide, fast, empty road ahead now for many miles. He floored the accelerator and the car pushed forwards – 80 . . . 90 . . . 100 . . . 120. He slowed, approaching a bend, aware of the roundabout ahead. Right would take him through the Cuilfail tunnel into the county town of Lewes, straight on along the fast road, past the University of Sussex. He carried straight on over the roundabout, accelerating hard, still nothing but darkness behind him. Thinking.

Suddenly a sliver of blue appeared in his mirrors. Like the glint of a shard of broken glass. Had he imagined it?

Then it appeared again. More insistently.

What?

He drove on as fast as he dared, crossed another roundabout, then accelerated along a fast, straight stretch, the needle passing 130 then 140 kph. He only slowed a fraction as he took a long right-hand curve and powered up a hill.

The slivers of blue in his mirror were getting brighter. Gaining. Strobing in all his mirrors.

Shit, fuck, shit!

Cresting the top, he raced down the far side. In two miles or so was another roundabout, off a slip road to the left. That would give him three options – towards Brighton, towards the Devil's Dyke or towards London.

Which would they be expecting him to take?

He held the accelerator to the floor.

The lights behind him were gaining. Closing.

Then, to his horror, just ahead of him, blocking off two of his options – to go straight on or take the slip road – there was an entire barrage of blue lights.

Taking his chances, he powered straight on.

As he shot through, between all the flashing lights, he heard a series of muffled pops and the car suddenly began to judder, snaking right, then left, then right again. Out of control. He'd driven over a fucking *stinger*, he realized.

The car was shaking violently. Swerving right towards the central reservation, then left, towards the verge. Somehow, he got it straightened out and carried on, with a loud *flap-flap-flap* sound.

The blue lights were right up his rear now and the interior of his car was flooded with blazing headlights.

He ploughed on, wrestling with the steering wheel in sheer panic, the car slowing despite keeping the pedal to the metal.

More headlights in his mirror now. A marked police estate car suddenly pulled level with him on his right, then darted in front of him, replaced seconds later by another identical car on his right.

The one in front braked sharply.

He stamped on his brakes, too, swerving left, right, left, the Audi totally unstable again. As he pulled away from the verge on his left, he banged doors with a loud, metallic *boom* with the car to his right.

Headlights in his mirror dazzled him. Flashing. Flashing.

Right up his jacksie.

He was totally boxed in, he realized. Fucking T-packed.

Trying to think.

Running on what felt like four flat tyres. Maybe even just rims now.

The car in front was slowing. He rear-ended it, then slewed to the right, banging doors once more with the police BMW alongside him.

Slowing more.

He looked desperately right, then left, for a gap. Something he could swing through.

His brain raced.

Had to get away. Take them by surprise?

He wrenched the steering wheel hard right. Banged, with a loud clang, into the BMW again, and an instant later, with no time to brake, slammed into the rear of the police car which had halted in front of him.

Before he could even unclip his seat belt, his door was flung open and a police officer in a stab vest loaded with gear was standing there, joined a second later by a colleague. He was yanked, unceremoniously, from his seat and pushed, face-down, onto the road surface.

'Michael Starr?' a male voice said.

He twisted his head to look at the man, and retorted in what he knew was a futile act of defiance, 'Who are you?'

PC Trundle of Sussex Road Policing Unit introduced himself, then arrested and cautioned him.

'Save your breath, I know the law,' Starr retorted.

'Do you?' said Trundle's colleague, PC Pip Edwards. 'Then you should know better than to be driving with four flat tyres. Tut, tut, tut! You could get a big fine for that.'

'I'm guessing that's not why you've stopped me.'

'Really?' Edwards retorted. 'That's pretty smart thinking. Ever thought about going on *Mastermind*?'

'Very funny.'

'There's someone at Newhaven Port wants a word with you, matey boy. Because we're kind, obliging people, we're going to give you a lift back there – so long as it's not inconveniencing you?'

7

As dawn was breaking outside, Clive Johnson sat in his office with the bag of white powder he'd removed from the spare tyre, listening on his borrowed police radio to the update from the Road Policing Unit. He was wearing forensic gloves, video recording what he was doing and ensuring that he was protecting possible traces of DNA, fibres and fingerprints. He slit the bag open and performed a brief chemical analysis on a sample of the contents. It tested positive for cocaine – and a very high grade.

He knew that the current street value of this drug in the UK was around £37,000 per kilogram. Which meant, if he was right in his calculation, judging from the weight of the Ferrari, there could be close to six million pounds' worth of drugs inside that beautiful vehicle, maybe even more.

And the car wouldn't be looking quite so beautiful by the time every panel had been removed and its bare entrails exposed.

Twenty minutes later, cuffed to an officer, Mickey was frog-marched back into the shed and up to the Ferrari where the Border Force officer who had first questioned him was now, once again, standing. He had a piece of sticking plaster on his bent glasses, one lens of which was cracked, and was not looking as friendly as before. 'Decided to come back, did you? Very obliging of you.'

'Haha,' Mickey said, sourly.

'I won't keep you too long, Mr Starr,' Johnson said. 'But as a formality I do need you to witness our continued examination of this vehicle.'

Much too late, Mickey knew, he tried reasoning with the man.

'Look, see – I just got hired to transport the car – I didn't know there was nuffin' in it.'

'Is that so?' Johnson said. 'Did you not have the slightest inkling?'

'Honest to God, no. I'm just a driver, right, hired to transport the car. I don't know about any drugs. I'm totally innocent.'

'Which is why you assaulted me and ran away, is it?'

'I – just got scared, like.'

'I suppose I do look a bit scary, don't I?' There was a hint of humour in the Border Force officer's voice. But not much.

Clive Johnson stared hard at Mickey. 'Mr Starr, I believe these packages contain controlled drugs. I am also arresting you on suspicion of being knowingly concerned with the illegal importation of a Class-A drug.' He cautioned him. 'Is that clear?'

'Clear as mud. I need a fag. Can we go outside so I can have one?'

'I'm afraid not, and I'm not one to preach,' Clive Johnson said, 'but you really ought to think about quitting. Smoking's not good for your health.'

'Nor is being arrested. You should try prison food.'

'Well, if it's not to your taste, have you ever thought about making better career choices?'